Alan Parks worked in the music industry for over twenty years before turning to crime writing. His debut novel *Bloody January* was shortlisted for the Grand Prix de Littérature Policière, *February's Son* was nominated for an Edgar Award, *Bobby March Will Live Forever* was picked as a *Times* Best Book of the Year, won a Prix Mystère de la Critique Award and won an Edgar Award. *The April Dead* was shortlisted for the McIlvanney Prize for Scottish Crime Book of the Year and *May God Forgive* won the McIlvanney Prize for Scottish Crime Book of the Year 2022. He lives and works in Glasgow.

@AlanJParks

***

Praise for the Harry McCoy series:

'This is Scottish noir at its gritty darkest . . . a cracking read'
Irish Independent

'Bloody and brilliant'
Louise Welsh

'Brilliant . . . should grace the bookshelves of every crime fan'
Sunday Times Crime Club

'Parks has clearly studied the masters of tartan noir but has
his own
The T

'Gripping and
Quintin Jardine

'Parks knows the city intimately, and this comes across
effortlessly on the page'
Scotland on Sunday

MAY GOD FORGIVE

ALAN PARKS

CANONGATE

This paperback edition published in Great Britain and Canada in 2023 by
Canongate Books

First published in Great Britain and Canada in 2022
by Canongate Books Ltd, 14 High Street, Edinburgh EH1 1TE

Distributed in Canada by Publishers Group Cânada

canongate.co.uk

1

British Library Cataloguing-in-Publication Data
A catalogue record for this book is available on
request from the British Library

ISBN 978 1 83885 679 3

Typeset in Bembo by Palimpsest Book Production Ltd,
Falkirk, Stirlingshire

Printed and bound in Great Britain by Clays Ltd, Elcograf S.p.A.

In memory of Peter Gildea

'There is always some madness in love. But there is also always some reason in madness.'

– Friedrich Nietzsche

'Hotel rooms inhabit a separate moral universe.'

– Tom Stoppard

20th May 1974

ONE

McCoy was almost at Wilson Street when he started to hear it. People shouting. The clatter of police horses' hooves on the road. Car horns blaring. Then a chant, quiet at first. He couldn't quite make it out to start with but it got louder and louder the closer he got to the court. And then he could hear exactly what the crowd were chanting.

HANG THEM! HANG THEM HANG THEM!

He turned onto Brunswick Street and stopped dead. The entrance to the Sheriff Court was surrounded by at least a couple of hundred people. So many that they'd started spilling off the pavement. The traffic was backed up both ways, taxi drivers half out their cabs to see what was going on, buses overheating, their engines steaming in the wet.

He couldn't see Murray anywhere. The crowd had totally blocked the street. He was going to have to try and make his way through, see if Murray was on the other side.

McCoy decided discretion was the better part of valour, started mouthing *HANG THEM! HANG THEM!* along with everyone else and pushed his way through. The crowd was made up of all sorts. Had to squeeze his way past men, women, even little kids. Some of them were holding home-made signs on wooden poles, umbrellas or raincoats over their heads, all of them had the same face contorted with fury.

The chanting was building momentum and the crowd surged towards the court entrance. McCoy felt himself being pulled along, wasn't anything that he could do. He was squashed between a man in a denim jacket with a Zapata moustache and a middle-aged woman, the type you normally saw in the front row when you watched the wrestling on the telly, well used to screaming for blood.

The only thing keeping the crowd back from the court entrance was a line of twenty or so uniforms with interlocked arms and two mounted policemen using their horses to block the way. He caught the eye of one of the uniforms who recognised him.

'This way, Mr McCoy!' he shouted. 'Over here!'

McCoy struggled forward, managed to get to the front of the crowd, and ducked under the uniform's arm.

'Thanks, Barr,' he said, patting the man's back. 'Saved my life.'

Barr nodded, grimaced as a sign saying AN EYE FOR AN EYE knocked his cap off.

'Fuck sake,' said McCoy. 'You need more bodies here, do you not?'

'You're telling me,' said Barr. 'They're supposed to be coming down from Central. No sign yet.'

'You seen Murray?' McCoy had to shout, the chanting had having started up again.

'Goldbergs!' Barr managed to get out before the crowd surged against the line again.

McCoy looked down the street, could see Murray, sheepskin car coat and trilby, sheltering in the back entrance of the department store. He was looking directly at McCoy, shaking his head. McCoy couldn't hear him but the chances were Murray was muttering 'bloody clown'.

McCoy hurried down the back of the police line, dodged between the cars stopped on Wilson Street and joined him in the doorway.

'I thought you should see this,' said Murray. 'Get you back in the swing. Didn't expect you to get caught up in the bloody thing.'

'Couldn't think how else to get through. I didn't realise how mental it was. Thought I was going to get trampled. You need some back-up.'

'That right? I just got Faulds to call in the cavalry,' said Murray. 'But thanks for the advice.'

'You ever seen anything like this before?' asked McCoy, watching the crowd working itself up for another go at the police line.

'Once,' said Murray, searching his coat pockets for his pipe. 'Peter Manuel. Back in fifty-eight. I'd only started a week. I was trying to hold the line like those poor buggers are now. A woman spat right in my face. Don't know what she thought I'd done. I hadn't murdered anyone.' Murray found his pipe, shoved it in his mouth, and looked at McCoy. Didn't seem happy. 'You look bloody awful.'

'Should have seen me three weeks ago,' said McCoy.

'At last,' said Murray, pointing over McCoy's head.

McCoy turned to see a blue police van pulling up at the edge of the crowd. Boos and jeers went up when a dozen uniforms got out and tried to make their way through the crowd towards the entrance. They weren't having much luck. Crowd was refusing to let them through, waving their signs in front of them. Angry red and black letters painted onto wood.

REMEMBER THE SALON GIRLS. NO MERCY FOR KILLERS!

A line of women were standing on the pavement off to the side, heads bent in prayer, front pages of newspapers stuck on to bits of board.

FOUR DIE IN ARSON FIRE HORROR

A man in a paint-splattered boiler suit climbed up onto a letterbox and started shouting, hands raised in the air like an orchestra conductor.

HANG THEM! HANG THEM!

Kept saying it over and over until the crowd took it up, shouting along with him.

HANG THEM! HANG THEM!

The police back-up finally managed to push their way through the crowd and set up another line behind the first one. A double row of grim-faced police, arms interlocked, half their caps already gone in the struggle. As the chant got louder and louder, a bottle flew through the air, smashed at the policemen's feet. There was a moment of quiet, an intake of breath from the crowd, and then the cheering started. Another bottle sailed through the air, then another. A woman by the police line fell, hands on the back of her head, blood already seeping through her fingers.

'Jesus Christ,' said McCoy. 'This is getting out of control.'

He turned to tell Murray they had to do something and realised he'd moved off, was standing by the open door of a panda parked down the street. He was leaning in, giving instructions to Hughie Faulds sitting in the driver's seat, radio in hand. McCoy saw Faulds nod, start speaking into the radio. He turned back to the crowd and saw the injured woman sitting on the kerb, blood all down her pale blue coat. A girl aged six or seven next to her bawling her eyes out, her sign lying in the gutter.

'For fuck sake,' said Murray, back at his side. 'Have these people got no bloody sense?'

'I don't get it,' said McCoy, watching a man in the crowd lift his wee girl up on his shoulders so she could see better. 'Why did they do it? Why would you want to kill three women and two kids?'

Murray was chewing the stem of his unlit pipe, no hope of firing it up in rain. 'One of them's got previous. Set fire to a garage and his primary school. Pyromaniac.'

'What about the other two?' asked McCoy. 'They like that as well?'

Murray shook his head. 'Just two lads apparently, small-time stuff.'

'So, what?' said McCoy. 'The other two were just along for the ride and killed four people?'

BRING BACK HANGING! BRING BACK HANGING!

Murray pointed to the crowd with his pipe stem, had to raise his voice. 'Don't think it matters much to these clowns. All they want is blood.'

'I heard Tobago Street got a tip-off. That right?'

Murray nodded. 'Case like this one – wee lassies dead, women – even the villains want it solved and quick. Honour amongst thieves goes straight out the window. Anonymous phone call into Tobago Street Station. Told them there were three lads in a flat in Roystonhill. They brought them in, one of them still had the receipt for the petrol in his trouser pocket.' He glanced over at the court. 'Not wasting any time, they're charging them today.'

'If they can get them through the crowd that is,' said McCoy as the uniforms tried to hold back another surge. A line of photographers he recognised from the evening papers were standing under the awning across the road, chewing gum, looking bored, waiting.

'Tobago Street were bloody lucky,' said McCoy. 'Faulds is the only good cop they've got. The rest of them are useless. A tip-off's the only way they were ever going to get something like this.'

Murray put his pipe back in his pocket. 'Aye, well, it might be up to me to change that.'

McCoy looked at him. 'What do you mean?'

'Pitt Street's great new idea. They want me to run both stations.'

'And what did you say to that?'

'What do you think I said? Tobago Street's a fucking disgrace, has been for years. It needs someone to . . .' He stopped. Pointed. 'Oh, Christ, here we go.'

A navy-blue prison service van had turned in from Ingram Street. For a second or two everything went quiet and then someone shouted, 'It's them!' and that was it. All hell broke loose.

The crowd pushed through the police barriers and swarmed the van. Hammering on the sides with their fists, kicking at it, using the poles of their signs to try to smash the windows. The photographers got as close as they could without being trampled in the mêlée. The van driver kept going, slow and steady, knew if he stopped, they were done for. A man fell to the ground as the wing mirror of the van hit his head. A glass bottle exploded on the windscreen.

GET THEM! GET THEM!

The police separated for a few seconds and the van turned, accelerated down the ramp to the court entrance. The police line quickly joined up again, uniforms pulling people out the way as the iron shutter of the vehicle entrance rolled down and the van disappeared from sight.

And just as fast as it had started, the chaos was over. The chants died down and the crowd dispersed, people picking up broken signs, muttering that the police had been too rough, sitting on the pavement to inspect their cuts and bruises. Photographers took the film out their cameras and gave the spools to the boys who ran back to the papers. A wee kid in a cowboy outfit was crying, wandering round looking for his mum.

McCoy and Murray stood in the rain, watching the scene in front of them.

'Crowds can be ugly things,' said Murray. 'Dangerous. Saw it in my National Service. Palestine. Not something I'd like to see again.' He stuck his hand out the shelter. Grimaced and pulled it back in. 'You would think this bloody rain would put the buggers off.'

'Don't think anything's going to put them off,' said McCoy. 'It's a big day out.'

'Aye, well, they won't have long to wait. It's a special sitting – murder charge, no chance of bail. Quick appearance before the sheriff to read the charges and that's it. They'll be back out in fifteen minutes.'

A taxi rounded Wilson Street and Murray stuck out his hand. 'I'm going back to Pitt Street. You going to wait for the van coming out?'

McCoy shook his head. 'I've seen enough. Going to head back to Stewart Street.'

Murray started to walk towards the waiting taxi. Stopped. 'You sure you're well enough to be back?'

McCoy nodded. 'Fit as a fiddle. Olympic standard.'

TWO

McCoy watched Murray's taxi turn in the direction of Pitt Street, leant back into the doorway and managed to light up. Fit as a fiddle was what he would keep saying, even if it was a lie. At least another month of bed rest they had told him when he left the hospital a couple of days ago. No work, no stress, no smoking and no drinking. And here he was back at work, lit fag in hand.

The four weeks in hospital had driven him almost mad with boredom. The thought of another four staring at his bedroom ceiling and eating boiled cod and mashed potatoes was more than he could stand. Bleeding ulcer or no bleeding ulcer, he'd take his chances.

His stomach must have heard him. Started grumbling. McCoy felt in his pocket for his bottle of Pepto-Bismol, then remembered he'd left it on the bathroom shelf in the house. Time to buy yet another bottle. He headed for the chemist in Bell Street. Rain was teeming down now, pavements swimming. Could feel damp in his left sock. He needed new shoes. Needed a lot of things. New shoes, a new suit, a couple of shirts. A haircut as well. Was over his collar at the back, surprised Murray hadn't made a comment. Maybe that's what he'd do this weekend. Go and buy the stuff he needed, go to Green's in King Street and get a haircut. Changed days indeed. He must be getting old. That's what weekends were for now. Not for going out and getting out your head, for doing chores.

He sheltered under the chemist's awning, looking at the gift sets of talcum and bath cubes while he finished his cigarette. Had to confess he was glad the fire had happened in Tobago Street's patch, no matter how useless they were. He was well enough for day-to-day work, not sure his stomach would put up with the stress of a big case like that. He dropped his cigarette into a puddle and stepped inside.

Two minutes later he came out, bag in hand. He screwed the top off the Pepto-Bismol and took a slug. Felt like some kind of alky drinking out a bottle in a brown paper bag. The chalky fluid slid down his throat and he grimaced. He was starting to really fucking hate the taste of the stuff.

He was screwing the top back on when the chants started up again. Fainter now, but he could still hear them, same old stuff.

HANG THEM! HANG THEM!

The prison van must be leaving the court, had riled the crowd again. Murray was right, the whole thing couldn't have taken more than fifteen minutes. McCoy started along Bell Street, heading for the High Street and the taxi rank.

The chants got louder and louder and he looked back towards the court. He was just in time to see the van turn onto Bell Street, a few stragglers running behind it, battering on the sides. It was heading for the High Street too, quickest way to Barlinnie. As it drove past McCoy noticed a big crack in the windscreen, had a fleeting glimpse of the stony-faced driver. It moved on, stopped at the lights at the end of the road.

The lights changed to green and McCoy watched the van

ease out. It had only gone a couple of yards when a speeding lorry appeared out of nowhere and rammed into the side of it. There was an almighty bang, a mist of shattered glass, and suddenly the van was up in the air. Seemed to sit there for a minute then crashed back down onto the road and skidded along the street, sparks flying up from beneath it, until it hit a lamppost and ground to a halt in a cloud of dust and exhaust fumes. Lay there on its side, wheels turning.

McCoy realised he was holding his breath. Let it go and started running. Up ahead, three men jumped down from the cab of the lorry, ran to the van and scrambled over it. They were dressed in dark boiler suits and balaclavas, two of them with crowbars and one with a bolt cutter. In a couple of seconds they had levered the back door open, pulled it wide and disappeared inside.

McCoy kept on running, needed to find a phonebox or hope that some of the cops from outside the court had heard the bang and were on their way. A black estate car screeched up to the side of the van and the driver got out, ran round the car opening all the doors. Shouted at the men in the van to hurry up. A second later one of the boiler-suited guys emerged from the back, dragging a stunned prisoner, hands still cuffed, then pushing him into the back seat of the car.

McCoy could hear sirens in the distance, didn't know if they were coming here or if there was more trouble back at the court. He was out of breath, struggling to keep running, but he was still fifty yards away. The other two prisoners stumbled from the van, made their way to the estate car and got in.

The driver hit the accelerator hard and the back of the car fishtailed as the tyres tried to get a grip on the wet tarmac. McCoy was close enough now to see the driver's eyes through the holes of his balaclava, caught a glimpse of a prisoner behind him, red hair and a huge grin on his face as the tyres finally caught, the car powered forward and McCoy jumped out the way just in time. He went over on his ankle, fell onto the road, and sat up just in time to see the car speeding off towards the Saltmarket. His hands were wet and gritty, looked down to see petrol from the van pouring out the ruptured tank, running down the hill. He got to his feet as a pale blue Viva with no number plates pulled up. The men from the lorry got in and the car sped off after the estate car.

McCoy tried to shake the petrol off his hands, shouted at a man standing watching to go and call the police and limped over to the van. The wheels were still spinning, horn going. He helped the driver out through the smashed windscreen, blood everywhere, his arms and face covered in cuts and bits of broken glass.

He sat the man down on the kerb and tried to calm him down. He was moaning, trying to pull bits of glass out his arm. McCoy could see an ambulance and two police cars coming down the High Street towards them. He sat down beside the driver and told him he was going to be okay, to leave the glass alone. Tried not to look at his ruined face.

An ambulance pulled up beside them and the medics got out, started to attend to the van driver. McCoy left them to it and walked towards the police cars. He stopped, turned to the gathering crowd and shouted, 'Any witnesses to what just happened please make yourself known and go to the police cars.'

A couple of people stepped out the crowd, a couple scuttled away, not wanting to get involved.

McCoy put his hand on the roof of the police car and stood for a minute. The pain in his stomach was taking his breath away. Hoped what he thought was about to happen wouldn't. Didn't work. He tried to get behind the wall so no one would see. Didn't make it. Leant over and threw up half a bottle of pink gunge into the gutter. Stood up and wiped his mouth, realised the uniforms from the cars were staring at him.

'Who's going to take my statement?' he said.

THREE

'So, how you feeling now?'

McCoy was sitting opposite Murray in his office. Familiar smell of Ralgex and pipe tobacco, framed newspaper back page on the wall – HAWICK TAKE TITLE – that had travelled to every office he had ever had. A younger Murray holding his arms up in triumph.

McCoy shifted in his seat, knew there wasn't much point lying. Murray knew him too well. Tried anyway. 'My ankle's a bit sore, twisted it when I jumped out the way. Quite a first day back. Not often you—'

'That's not what I'm talking about,' said Murray. 'As you know fine well.'

McCoy could hear the rain battering against the window behind Murray's desk, a phone ringing out in the office, someone shouting about car keys. Swallowed over, got his fags out his pocket. All he could do was come clean. No way out of it.

'In that case, terrible,' he said. 'It feels like my stomach is full of broken glass all the time. Hurts if I eat, hurts if I don't.'

'Looks like you haven't been. You're swimming in that suit. How much weight have you lost?'

McCoy shrugged. 'Not sure.' He wasn't going to tell Murray it was nearly two stone.

'You tell them everything? Over at Tobago Street?'

'Yep,' said McCoy. 'Not much to tell to be honest, was over and done with in about two minutes. A lorry, estate car and a Viva. Well planned. Went like clockwork. Viva and estate car are God knows where, probably burnt out by now. They're towing the lorry to the police garage to go over it. Stolen no doubt. Faulds is waiting until the van driver's been stitched up so he can interview him.'

Murray sat back in his chair, started digging in his pipe bowl with a penknife, ash falling into the bin by his side. 'So, what are we going to do?'

'Wait for the results of the search, I suppose. See if anyone left any fingerprints in the lorry. See if the witness statements turn anything up.'

Murray sighed. 'Stop playing funny buggers. What are we going to do with you?'

'I'm fine,' said McCoy. 'I just had a bit of a setback, I—'

Murray was shaking his head. 'A setback? You were puking in the street on your first day back. You should be back in the hospital.'

McCoy could feel his heart sinking. Had the feeling that if Murray got rid of him now he'd never get back, be spending the rest of his life in and out of hospitals. Maybe a desk job at best. 'My stomach's bad, but it's not that bad. Today was a one-off. It won't happen again, I promise.'

Murray rubbed at the sandy-coloured bristle on his face. Noise like sandpaper. 'That's not something you can promise.'

McCoy nodded his head, waited for the axe to drop.

'Look, son, it's for your own good,' said Murray. 'You're not well. I don't want you getting any worse. People die of ulcers, you know. My Uncle Bernie for one.'

'I just need a bit of time. I'll be better in a couple of days. Don't do this to me, Murray. Please.'

Murray sighed again. 'This bloody rescue or hijack or whatever it was, I'm going to run it out of Tobago Street with Faulds.'

McCoy went to protest then saw the look on Murray's face.

'You're not up to it so don't start. What have you got on?'

'Not much. Haven't been assigned anything yet. Not sure what Wattie's got going on.'

Murray shook his head. 'Don't make me bloody regret this, you hear?'

'Yep.'

'You were right, what you said at the court. The lads they got for the arson at the hairdresser's never felt right. It was all too quick, too easy. Everyone just glad they had someone to parade in front of the newspapers – including me. But with this bloody rescue we can't pretend any more. There's more going on here than a maniac and two neds setting something on fire for kicks. What happened this afternoon takes planning, intelligence and money, lots of it. And a commitment to getting those boys free. Need to know why someone cares that much. Maybe then we'll find out why they set the bloody salon on fire.' He lit up his pipe, disappeared for a few seconds in the cloud of blue smoke. 'So, what I want you to do,' he said, waving it away, 'is two things. One, help young Watson out with whatever bloody case he's working on. Christ knows he'll probably need it, and two, try and find out more about what really happened at that bloody hairdresser's. For once you have my permission to go and have a chat with all the low-level chancers you call your pals. The town was already buzzing with rumours about the fire. Fuck knows what it'll be like after this afternoon. Any of the three lads important enough for someone to want to rescue them from getting knifed in the back at Barlinnie? That sort of stuff. Okay?'

McCoy nodded. Would have said yes to cleaning the cells at this point, anything to avoid going back to the hospital.

Murray leant across the desk, looked him right in the eye. 'And believe me, son, if I hear from anyone that you've been sick again, then all bets are off and I'm signing you off sick indefinitely. Got me?'

McCoy nodded again.

Murray sat back, shook his head. 'Why is nothing ever simple with you, McCoy?'

McCoy shrugged. Stood up. 'Your guess is as good as mine. And, Murray? Thank you.'

FOUR

A trail of blood ran across the backyard. Red-soaked concrete stretching from where the man had hit the ground to his broken body a few yards away. Must have crawled for a bit after he landed. McCoy inched towards the body and had a look. Not much to see but an old man, face down, head cracked open, left leg bent in a way a leg was never supposed to be. His right hand was lying in a puddle of oily rainbows and watery blood, long nails stained yellow by tobacco, one finger twisted right across the others. His journey had taken him a bit further from the dirty black building he'd jumped from and a bit closer to three overflowing industrial bins in the corner of the yard. McCoy wasn't sure why he'd bothered.

He stepped back, sighed and wondered what he'd done to deserve this mess. He hadn't even made it to his desk after leaving Murray's office. Billy from the front desk had handed him the chit.

'Everyone else is busy on the fire so Murray said you could cover this.'

'Hello to you too, Billy,' said McCoy, looking at the chit. 'Miss me, did you?'

Billy looked McCoy up and down. 'Didn't even notice you were gone. Mind you, now that you mention it, things have been a bit cheerier round here past month or so.'

McCoy read the chit again. Just to make sure. 'A suicide? You're joking, aren't you?'

'Nope,' said Billy, already halfway back to the front desk.

'Wattie in?'

'Nope,' said Billy again. 'No seen the big bastard all day. Better get going.'

So here he was, trying to avoid looking at a dead body or stepping in its blood. He leant out the bin shelter by the yard wall and looked up at the tall brick building behind him. If the guy had jumped from the top that was a good fifty, sixty feet, enough to kill anyone, you would think. Not this guy though. Somehow he'd survived, dragged himself through the soaking newspapers and empty Eldorado bottles before he died.

McCoy eased back in against the wall, wasn't doing much good, he was getting soaked. The back yard of the Great Northern was a dump at the best of times, never mind in this rain. The bins stank, smashed bottles the guests had chucked out the back windows dotted all over the concrete and a giant roll of sodden carpet with a ripped carrier bag full of clothes on it by the wall. There was even a copy of *The War Cry* dissolving in the puddle by his feet. A Salvation Army man smiling up at him, big cardboard cheque in his hand.

There were Models all over Glasgow. Model Housing as they were properly called. Places for single men with nowhere else to go. His dad had spent time in them and McCoy was never out of them when he was on the beat. Drunken fights, stolen money, men dead in their beds when the morning alarm went, hands still clutching a half-empty bottle, plastic bag of belongings under the bed.

'Who phoned it in?' he asked. He was going to say the uniform's name, but he'd forgotten it already. Some new guy he'd never seen before. Smith? Something like that.

'The manager,' the uniform said. 'About half nine this morning.'

'Smith, can you—'

'Smythe,' he said. 'PC Smythe.'

'Sorry,' said McCoy. 'Can we get an ambulance?' He paused for a minute as the pain from his stomach flared up. Leant against the wall waiting for it to pass. Hoped he wasn't going to have to sit down on the wet concrete. Realised Smythe was watching him, gritted his teeth and tried to stand up straight. 'We need to get the body to the morgue after the doctor okays it. And for fuck sake can we get a tarp over it? That should have been done by now. Then get Andy the photographer, all the usual crew. Know what you're doing?'

Smythe nodded and hurried off along the lane leading down the side of the building.

Satisfied he was as far away from the body as he could get, McCoy stood close into the wall and lit a damp cigarette on the third attempt. He looked at his watch. He'd only been there ten minutes and he was already soaking. Almost wished he was back in his warm hospital bed. His stomach started to ache as he drew the smoke into his lungs. No smoking and certainly no drinking as they kept telling him. Penance for surviving a perforated ulcer. Penance that had lasted until he'd got home from the hospital and found a packet of Regal in an old jacket he never wore.

He looked up at the building again. A row of pale and whiskered old faces were lined up behind the windows, staring down into the backyard. One man with a long white beard crossed himself and turned away, disappeared into the gloom.

McCoy wondered how much it had hurt to hit the ground like that. Still, he could hardly blame the poor bugger. If he ended up in a place like this, he'd jump out the window too.

He looked at the pool of blood again, looked up at the windows. Seemed to have landed quite a way out. Did he run and crash through a window? Couldn't have, there was no glass anywhere. Must have run and jumped from the roof. Wouldn't have thought an old guy like him would get up that much speed. He realised his cigarette had gone out, too wet. Dropped it in a puddle. At least the doctor would be happy.

He turned the collar of his raincoat up and tried not to feel too sorry for himself. He would have to go in and try to find out what happened by asking a bunch of blokes who'd lost touch with reality a long time ago. 'Wet brain' they called it. Years of drinking taking its toll. Fuzzy memories and shaky hands. Just hoped his dad wasn't in there.

McCoy decided to make a run for it. He sprinted round the side of the building onto Royston Road, grabbed the double door and yanked it open. He stood for a minute in the hallway shaking the rainwater off. Smell of the place hit him immediately. Unwashed clothes, boiled food and the same floor cleaner they used in every children's home he'd ever been in.

'You must be the detective?'

He turned.

A middle-aged man wearing a suit with a brown cardigan and tartan slippers was standing there. 'PC Smythe said you'd be in soon,' he said.

McCoy held out his hand to shake. 'Harry McCoy.'

The man took his hand and shook it. 'Gerry Swan. Come on and I'll make you a cup of tea. You're soaked through.'

Five minutes later McCoy was sitting in Swan's office, mug of tea in hand, rain battering at the windows. The walls were the same pea green as the corridors, a painting of ships on the Clyde and a framed safety certificate hanging on them. Swan was sitting opposite. He was a wee man, could only have been five foot, looked like a kid sitting in his dad's chair.

He pulled a form from a brown file on his desk. 'Alistair Drummond,' he said. 'Hadn't been with us long, three nights just.'

'What was his story?'

'I wish I could tell you,' said Swan. 'Think I only met him once. We average sixty or so men a night in here and they come and go. Some stay for one night, some have been here for years. I know the regulars but there's just too many to keep track of.'

'Who found him?'

'Me. I started at nine, made a cup of tea, did some paperwork, got up to put the radio on for the half nine news and saw him out the window. Falling . . .' He settled himself. Started again. 'I thought someone had thrown a rug or something out the window. It was only when he hit the ground I realised. Wasn't the sound of a rug . . .'

McCoy took a sip of his tea. Rotten. Smell of the place was starting to get to him. What was it they said? That was the sense that brought back memories. That floor cleaner was the smell of his childhood. All this place needed was a waft of church incense and he wouldn't be able to stop himself running out into the street. He tried to concentrate.

'That happen a lot here?' he said. 'Suicide?'

Swan sighed. 'Sadly, yes. A lot of our men have problems. Alcohol mainly. Some have psychiatric conditions. Some have been thrown out by their wives or families. Some of them are just at the end of their tether. We try to offer a place of sanctuary but sometimes that's not enough. We can only do what we can do.'

'He have any pals, this Drummond?' asked McCoy, trying to ignore the smell and the stink of sanctity coming off Swan.

Swan looked at his file. 'His cubicle is next to Bert Cross. He might be your best bet.'

McCoy nodded. Got up. Swan made to get up too.

'Probably best you stay here,' said McCoy. 'Smythe will probably need your help setting things up.'

Last thing McCoy wanted was the boss of the place standing over his shoulder, making sure the men said the place was a joy to live in. Sanctuary, my arse. Models were where men waited to die, the end of the line. Most nights his dad would rather sleep on the street than in a place like this. Was only when the weather got really bad he tried to get a bed. Even being in for one night gave him the heebie-jeebies. Like living in hell's waiting room, he said. Looked like Alistair Drummond had decided to jump the queue.

FIVE

McCoy walked up the steps, shoes echoing on the stone, heading for the day room on the second floor. Realised he hadn't thought about his dad for a long while. Didn't even know if he was still alive. Last time he'd seen him was a few years ago. Standing outside the Squirrel on a Saturday night. No shoes on, bottle in his hand shouting about God knows what. Telling everyone they could go fuck themselves.

He was so lost in thinking about his dad that he almost stepped on a man lying across the stairs. The man smiled up at him, no teeth, his brown suit and bright red shirt covered in stains.

'Just needed a wee rest,' he said. 'These stairs are a bugger.'

McCoy held his hand out. The man looked surprised, but he took it and McCoy hauled him up, tried to ignore the smell and put his arm round him. 'Come on,' he said. 'I'll help you up and you can do me a favour.'

'Sure thing, son,' said the man. 'Sounds like a deal.'

McCoy pushed the door of the day room open with his foot and they went in. Place reeked of misery and despair. Scuffed wooden floor, sagging old armchairs pushed against the half-tiled walls. A couple of long wooden tables with chairs around them in the middle. No TV, no radio, just a series of embroidered Bible quotes in frames along the walls. Was like stepping back into Victorian times. Those of the men who were alert enough turned to look at McCoy. Most of them just kept staring at the floor.

McCoy lowered the old boy into one of the armchairs and brushed himself off.

'Now, how can I help you?' said the man. He gave him another toothless grin. 'Hope it's no money you're after 'cause I've got hee-haw.'

McCoy shook his head. 'Just need you to point out Bert Cross.'

The man screwed up his eyes, surveyed the room. Pointed to a man wearing a raincoat three sizes too big for him in an armchair by the window. 'That's him.'

McCoy thanked him and walked across the room. Cross was reading a tattered copy of *The People's Friend*, yellow finger tracing the words. He realised McCoy was standing in front of him. Looked up. He had bright blue eyes, shockingly alive in his lined and battered face.

'Bert Cross?'

The man looked wary.

'Harry McCoy. Detective. Can I ask you a few questions about what happened today?'

Cross nodded. Smiled. 'You can. But you know what? A wee drink might help me remember.'

'It's ten o'clock on a Monday morning,' said McCoy. 'There's nowhere to buy a drink at this time.'

Cross looked at him as if he was mad. 'Son, there's always somewhere open if you know where to go.'

*

Ten minutes later they were coming out the lift on the tenth floor of the Charles Street high flats on the other side of

Royston Road. A hallway painted dark red, lino on the floor, six doors. Cross knocked on a yellow door, pot plant on a wrought-iron stand beside it. The decorative effect was somewhat spoiled by the twenty or so cigarette butts stubbed out in the soil. The door opened a crack and a woman with her hair in curlers, scarf tied round her head and dressed in a nylon housecoat, looked them up and down.

'Hold out your money,' said Cross.

McCoy got his wallet out and held up a couple of pound notes. The woman smiled and the door swung open.

Inside the flat wasn't that different from the Model. Same collection of old men sitting around on chairs and a sagging couch. Only real difference was that here they were drinking. Drinking the way professional drinkers did. No chatting, no watching TV. Just drinking. Bottles held firm in their hands, eyes fixed on the walls.

Cross took the money from McCoy and handed it to the woman. 'Two bottles, Sadie, and need to have a wee chat in the kitchen,' he said.

Sadie nodded and they followed her through. McCoy caught a glimpse of a bedroom. An elderly man sitting up in bed, striped pyjamas, a teddy bear in his hands, radio playing softly, blank look on his face.

The kitchen was small, warm and remarkably dirty. Orange geometric wallpaper peeling off to reveal brown damp patches on the plasterboard. The floor was just hardboard, covered in splashes and stains. Flies were buzzing around a pile of unwashed dishes by the sink. The woman reached into a cupboard above the grease-coated cooker and brought down two Irn-Bru bottles full of a brownish liquid and put them on the table. Left them to it.

McCoy walked over to the window and had a look out. Couldn't resist. People moaned about high flats all the time but McCoy quite fancied living in one, liked the idea of having a view. Even with the driving rain, he could see out over Royston Road below and the spire of Royston Church in the distance. The paths up to the flats were laid out beneath him, woman pushing a pram, Rainmate on, toddler following behind. From here he could even see the burnt-out hairdresser's next to the off-licence. It was still roped off, uniform standing outside it.

'Want some?'

'What is it?' McCoy nodded at the bottles.

'Best not to ask,' said Cross, pouring a good measure into a dirty mug that said *World's Best Dad*. He held the bottle out. McCoy shook his head. Even without the ulcer, ten o'clock was a bit early for him.

'Please yourself,' said Cross, who poured some more in the mug and threw half of it back. Face lit up as it hit. 'Just to let you know, son, my memory isn't what it was, and once this stuff kicks in, what little of it that's left will disappear pretty quick, so I'd get a move on. What was it you wanted to ask me?'

'Alistair Drummond,' said McCoy.

'Poor bugger,' said Cross, taking another swig. Raised his mug in salute. 'To the faithful departed.'

'Was he a pal of yours?' asked McCoy, sitting down and trying to avoid putting his hands on the sticky tabletop.

'More of an acquaintance. He only came in the other day,' said Cross. 'He was sitting on his bed looking lost, and we got talking. I told him about this place, and he said, fuck that, I'm no drinking that gut rot. So, he says, let's go to the pub. I tell him I've no money and he says that doesn't matter. We ended up in the Big Glen. He had money all right, loads of it. I saw it in his wallet. We had a few drinks and I asked him why he was staying here when he had all that money. He didn't say at first, then a few drinks in he tells me he's got a flat but it's been broken into and he's scared. Didn't want to go back there.'

'Scared of what?' asked McCoy.

Cross shrugged. 'Don't know. He just seemed jumpy, kept looking about all the time. Said he just wanted to disappear for a while, lie low. Had even shut down his business.'

'What was that then? Stockbroker, was he?'

'Very funny. He sold stuff at Paddy's Market. When I asked him what, he just tapped the side of his nose.'

McCoy sat back in his chair. Couldn't be. 'You sure? Paddy's?'

Cross nodded, took another slug and wiped his mouth with the sleeve of his raincoat.

'Did he call himself Ally?' asked McCoy. 'Not Alistair?'

'Aye, said my name's Ally when I met him.'

'Fuck,' said McCoy. 'I know him! Swan in the office told me he was called Alistair, I never even thought. Did he have yellow teeth? Bit sleazy-looking?'

'Well, you said it, not me. I'm no speaking evil of the dead. I don't want to be haunted by his bloody ghost.'

The kitchen door opened and a man in a worn suit and busted black leather slip-ons came in. 'Bert, just wondered if you had a drop you could spare. I—'

'Fuck off,' growled Cross. 'You're getting nothing.'

The man looked like he'd expected that answer, shut the door again.

'Minging bastard. He still owes me a bottle of bloody tonic wine. Needs to pay that back before he's getting anything else off me.'

'Dirty Ally,' said McCoy, still trying to take it in. 'I can't believe it. You wouldn't have thought Dirty Ally would kill himself. He's not the type. Too bloody wily.'

'Well, he did.'

'Maybe he got shoved off the roof by somebody.'

Cross reached for the bottle. 'Nope.'

'How come you're so sure?'

'Because I saw him do it. I was in the backyard this morning going through the rubbish trying to find ginger bottles to take back. Couldnae find any and was about to go back in when I saw Ally on the roof. I looked up and waved, but he didn't wave back, and before I could do anything, he jumped.'

'Why'd you not tell Swan you saw it?' asked McCoy.

'Because he's a cunt and I wouldn't give him the steam off my pish.'

★

McCoy left him opening the second bottle and made his way back towards the Great Northern. They were setting up the crime scene when he got there. Smythe and a couple of other uniforms trying to put a tent up over the body in the pissing rain. Last thing he wanted to do was look closely at the man's broken face but he knew he had to. He ducked under the tent. Could hear Smythe telling the photographer to wait a minute, the boss was having a look.

The body was face down on the concrete, half the skull missing. McCoy felt his stomach lurch as he realised he could see brain through the long wet hair. Just had to get it over with. He held the body by the shoulder and rolled it. The head started to turn and, sure enough, McCoy found himself looking into the lifeless, destroyed face of Dirty Ally. He let go and stepped back, letting his stomach churn, hoping he wasn't going to be sick. The wave of nausea passed and he pushed the tarpaulin aside and went back out to the rainy yard.

'All yours,' he said to Smythe and the photographer.

He walked round to the front of the building, stood inside the entrance out the rain. Lit up. Couldn't believe it was Dirty Ally. He'd known him for years. Sold second-hand scud mags at Paddy's, developed photos for people who couldn't take their film to Boots. What could have scared him enough to hide in the Model? Scared him enough to jump off a roof rather than face whatever it was?

Ally knew how to take care of himself. He had to, he mixed with a bad crowd. Pimps, backstreet pornographers printing up illegal stuff, men who liked taking pictures of wee boys with no clothes on. He'd been at it for years, wasn't the type to be easily shocked or rattled. Why would someone break into his flat? And why was that enough to make him run?

He realised Smythe was hovering. 'Sir? Think we're about done here.'

McCoy nodded. 'Let's get back to the station then. Get out this bloody rain.'

SIX

'Murray said you were in,' said Wattie as McCoy walked into the office at Stewart Street.

'I was,' said McCoy, 'for about two minutes.'

Nothing seemed to have changed much in the month he'd been away. Same rows of cheap wooden desks, electric typewriters that didn't work half the time, cloud of cigarette smoke over everything, constant ringing of telephones.

'How you feeling?'

'Same as always,' said McCoy, taking off his raincoat. 'Fit as a fiddle. Olympic standard.'

Wattie shook his head. 'You must be better, you're back to your usual sarcastic bastard of a self. Where have you been anyway?'

McCoy sat down at his desk. He had to admit he was glad to be back. It was much better than staring at the hospital walls.

'Where was I? I was working. The real question, Mr Watson, is, where were you?'

Wattie looked a bit guilty. 'I had to drop the wee man off at his gran's. Mary's been called in to the *Record*. All hands on deck after this morning.'

'No surprise.'

'She's away speaking to the relatives,' said Wattie, trying to put a sheet of paper into his typewriter.

'Lucky her,' said McCoy, sitting back in his chair. 'How did those clowns at Tobago Street manage to get them in the first place?'

Wattie shrugged. 'Fuck knows. Normally they can't tell their arse from their elbow. Seems they raided a flat in Roystonhill. Had a tip-off, I think.' He managed to crumple the paper between the holding bars of the typewriter, took it out and tried again. 'Tell you something, I wouldn't want to be one of those lads. The whole of Barlinnie would have been waiting for them, and I don't blame them. It's a pure shame what happened at the salon. Breaks your heart.' He shook his head, looked close to tears.

It wasn't just Wattie who was taking what had happened hard. It seemed as though the whole of Glasgow was in mourning. News of the fire had broken when McCoy was still in the hospital. The morning it was reported, he'd seen a couple of the nurses crying, newspaper spread out in front of them. That night, the doctors and patients all gathered round the TV for the six o'clock news. The image of the hairdresser's and the crying women surrounding it was the first story featured. More than a few sobs as they showed the pictures of the wee girls in their communion dresses. Even McCoy had found it difficult to watch.

'Did they find out why they did it?' he asked.

'Don't know,' said Wattie. 'Christ knows why anyone would do something like that.' He finally gave up, rolled the paper into a ball and dropped it into his bin. 'Soon as I heard about it I had to go and get the wee man out his cot, give him a hug. There but for the grace of God . . .'

'How is my godson anyway?'

'Wee Duggie? He's gnawing at everything, crying his eyes out. Teething. It's like blue bloody murder.'

'Nasty. I'll come and see him when he's over it.'

'Don't blame you. I'd keep well away just now, he's being a right wee bastard.'

'By the way, guess who's gone and topped themselves?' said McCoy.

'What?' asked Wattie, mind seemingly still on the horrors of a teething baby.

'That's where I've been. The Great Northern, and, if I ever end up in there, you've got my permission to shoot me.'

'Was your dad there?'

McCoy shook his head. 'Didn't see him. Mind you I wasn't looking that hard.'

'Who was it?' asked Wattie.

'Who what?'

Wattie rolled his eyes. 'Who bloody killed themselves?'

'Ah! Dirty Ally.'

Just as he said it McCoy's stomach tightened in pain. He held onto the edge of his desk and waited for it to pass.

'Christ, I thought that old bugger would go on forever,' said Wattie. 'Why did he do that then?'

'God knows,' said McCoy. 'Seems he was scared of someone, or something. Was hiding out in the Great Northern of all places. Makes you think what—'

'No,' said Wattie. 'No, it doesn't. He killed himself. That's the end of it. Why he did it isn't our problem. I know what you're like and I'm not spending the next two weeks wandering all over Glasgow with you trying to find out why the clatty old bastard offed himself.'

'Well, that's me told,' said McCoy.

SEVEN

At six p.m., McCoy stepped out the station and back into the rain. He'd spent the rest of the afternoon looking over the paperwork that had accumulated on his desk since he'd been gone. Had found it hard to concentrate, mind kept going back to the fire. He hadn't eaten anything all day, was too scared to, wasn't sure his stomach would hold up. A yellow light shone through the rain and he crossed the road. Stuck his hand out.

'Royston Road,' he said, getting in. 'At Provanhill Street.'

The driver nodded, put his flag down.

Figured he may as well start at the scene of the crime. Have a look at Dolly's Salon. Wasn't sure he was going to learn anything he didn't already know, but he wanted to see it for himself. He'd been in the hospital too long, felt disconnected. Didn't know what was going on in the city, who was saying what, who was making moves, who was on the rise, who was falling. Needed to find out what people were saying, what the rumours were. Background stuff but important stuff. Just him and a night in the big bad city.

The taxi passed the cathedral then stopped at the traffic lights next to the Royal. He looked up at the big hospital building, lights on in every window. A wee girl from the fire was in there now. She was the last one left, the only survivor. Her sister and mum both gone in the fire. Ghosts already.

McCoy lit up, looked at the burning match. Why would anyone want to set a hairdresser's on fire with people inside? He lit his cigarette off the match and waved it out. It wasn't like Glasgow was unfamiliar with arson. Happened quite a lot, empty buildings in the way of developments mysteriously going up in flames, tit-for-tat gangland wars ending up in pubs being torched. But a hairdresser's in Royston? Didn't seem worth the bother.

He was never quite sure where Royston began and Garngad ended, or if they were just two names for the same place. Had given up trying to find out, could never get two people to agree about it. Whatever it was, it was a rough part of town. Used to be a big Irish area, now it just seemed full of people who couldn't afford to move away. Place had been decimated by the new motorway, heart torn out of it, and all that was left were some shops struggling to stay open, a couple of pubs with no windows and whoever was unlucky enough to be staying at the Great Northern.

The taxi arrived at Royston Road. McCoy paid the driver, turned the collar of his raincoat up and stepped out.

Dolly's Salon wasn't much more than a blackened hole now. Police tape was still up, fluttering in the wind. Could still smell scorched wood in the air, even with all the rain. Wasn't much to see. Just an ordinary hairdresser sandwiched between a butcher and a TV repair shop, same as every other high street. People had left things on the pavement outside. Bunches of flowers, Mass cards and sympathy cards that had almost dissolved now. Even a handmade sign, names of the dead painted on a wooden board with *Rest in Peace* written below.

He realised someone had come to stand beside him. He turned to see a young woman, silently reciting, rosary beads in hand. She'd a long coat on and a scarf tied around her head, but they weren't doing much good. She was soaking wet. She wiped at her eyes and McCoy wasn't sure if she was wiping away rain or tears.

She turned to him, shook her head. 'Still can't believe it.'

'Did you know them?'

'A wee bit. I work in the Galbraith's along the road. Dolly used to come in to buy the tea and biscuits for the customers. We said hello, talked about the weather, that was all, but she was a nice woman. People liked her.'

'You're soaking,' said McCoy. 'Come on and I'll buy you a drink.'

She looked at him.

'Sorry,' he said, realising what that sounded like. He dug out his police card. 'Detective McCoy. Like to get a bit of background if I could.'

She looked uncertain, then pointed up the road. 'The Big Glen. There'll be some of the other girls from the shops in there, always are. Might know more than me.'

There were. McCoy ended up at a round table in the lounge surrounded by five women and a cloud of tobacco smoke, hairspray and perfume. As far as he could see he was the only man in there. Men in the bar, women in the lounge, as was the universal rule. As a concession to its female clientele the lounge had been done up. Had a proper Wilton carpet, mirrors on the maroon and gold walls, wee lights in glass globes above the tables.

He'd been introduced to them all as 'the man from the polis' and had forgotten their names already. The only one he remembered was Una, the woman he'd met outside the shop. They were of a kind, the women round the table: shop assistants, dinner ladies, juggling useless men and weans and second jobs as cleaners. Royston women.

'Joanne was there,' said Una, 'when it happened. Weren't you?'

A woman in her fifties, permed hair, big glasses and a blouse with roses printed on it nodded. 'I'd come out Daly's—'

'Daly's?' interrupted McCoy.

'The butcher's. Where I work. Had come out for a fag before the deliveries arrived. I was standing in the bus shelter, was pouring as bloody usual. So I'm standing there and these three boys run past, towards the school. Going pelters they were.'

'Wee bastards,' said one of the women. A chorus of agreement.

'So I looked back, wondering what they were running from, and just as I did . . .' She stopped, took a drink of her gin and lemonade. Had told this story before. Knew her timings. Continued. 'And just as I did, it was like something off the telly, an explosion kind of, and the whole front of Dolly's went up in flames. Real flames, I mean, then the big front window must have broken and there was a bang and there was glass all over the pavement and then it was like a bloody fireball. You couldn't even see the shop any more, all you could see was flames and smoke, could feel the heat on your face. Then people started screaming and running, and I went back into Daly's and told them to phone 999 quick.'

She sat back in her chair, silent tears running down her cheeks. The woman beside her put an arm round her, told her to let it out and she started crying, really crying, pushing her face into the woman's shoulder and weeping.

'Why would someone do that?' asked Una. 'Wee girls and women. Who would do something that evil?'

McCoy realised all the women were looking at him, looking for answers. Answers he didn't have. 'That's what we're trying to find out,' he said.

He stood up. Put a fiver on the table, thanked them and told them to get some drinks on him. He headed for the door, was almost there, when he felt a tug on his arm. It was one of the women, a younger girl who hadn't spoken.

'I didn't tell them,' she said. 'About the boys getting away. Got a late edition of the *Evening Times* on the way here. Only thing they're hanging onto is the fact the people who did it are in jail. I can't face telling them they're not. It'll break their hearts all over again. You're going to catch them, aren't you?'

McCoy nodded, was all he could do.

'Make sure you do. Do it for them, for them lost in the fire. They were just ordinary women, but they deserve it.'

EIGHT

McCoy started making his way back towards the city centre. Plan was to stop at a few more pubs on the way. Despite the rain, he was enjoying being out in the fresh air. The hospital was always too warm, stuffy. The streetlights were just coming on, bus and car headlights shining through the drizzle. Wasn't quite sure what he was going to do when he got to the first pub. Had the feeling he'd have a look at the pint and his stomach would turn over. Time to find out.

The Lamppost at Duke Street wasn't a pub he was familiar with, and it turned out to be half full of jakeys from the Great Eastern across the road and ordinary people from the high flats behind. He got a drink, didn't drink it, stood at the bar, lit up. Couple of old guys at the tables were reading the evening paper, heads shaking every so often.

He stayed long enough to listen to the two men next to him discuss how the three lads should have been handed over to the relatives of the dead girls and that they should have been allowed to do what they wanted with them. It was only right. After what they had done, they were too good to hang.

When they moved on to telling each other they should bring back National Service he decided he'd had enough. He left the pub and started walking down the High Street. Only other case he could remember where people were as angry as this was the Moors Murders. Just like Hindley and Brady, the three boys seemed to have crossed a line, done something so bad they had become something other than human, something unforgivable.

He was just about to go into the College Bar when he heard someone shouting his name, turned to look round and Charlie the Pram was crossing the street towards him. McCoy waved, hoped he was in one of his less manic moods.

'Charlie!' he said. 'How's it going?'

Charlie shrugged. 'Not too bad.'

He'd the handle of his pram tied to his wrist with a rope. It had been stolen before, was making sure it didn't happen again. The pram itself was full of everything Charlie held dear. Mostly notebooks and paper bags covered in tiny indecipherable writing.

'I heard you weren't well,' he said, scratching at the back of his neck as usual, crescents of dried blood under his fingernails.

'Who told you that?' asked McCoy, genuinely surprised.

Charlie thought for a minute. 'I don't know. You better now?'

'Getting there,' said McCoy. 'You hear about the fire at the hairdresser's?'

'Poor wee lassies.'

McCoy dug in his pocket looking for loose change. Found a quid or so, put it in Charlie's pram.

'You always were a good man, Harry McCoy.'

McCoy smiled. 'I'm not so sure about that.'

'I am,' he said. 'And I know these things. The fire?'

McCoy nodded.

'Remember what it burned.'

Charlie scratched at the back of his neck again and set off up the hill towards the cathedral. McCoy watched him go. Had no idea what he was talking about. Not sure Charlie did either.

He pushed the pub door open and was greeted by Andy behind the bar. Andy's dad had been a polis, down at Temple. McCoy had met Andy a few times when he was still a teen-ager, had taken over the pub with his dad when he retired. The pub was pretty empty, weather keeping people at home. Andy told the young barmaid with a pair of granny glasses on that he was taking his break and told McCoy to sit down, he'd be over in a minute.

McCoy picked a table near the back, sat down and took off his coat, laid it on the radiator in an attempt to dry it out.

'Got you a pint,' said Andy, sitting down. 'That okay?'

'Fine.' McCoy took a small sip.

'Heard you were at that stramash down the road,' said Andy. 'We heard the crash from all the way up here. Bloody lorry must have been going at some whack.'

'It was. I was just walking along from the court and saw it. Lucky timing. You hear anything about what's going on?'

Andy nodded, leant forward as if it was a secret. 'My dad said that he spoke to one of the guards that took them to the cells before they saw the sheriff. One of the boys was acting the big man apparently, saying not to worry, his dad would get them off.'

'Which one?'

'Don't know,' said Andy. 'The guard thought he meant his dad was going to get them some hotshot lawyer, not ram the bloody van with a lorry. That's mental. This is Glasgow, not bloody Chicago.'

'He say anything else?' asked McCoy, trying another sip.

'No, but it's all anyone in the pub's been talking about all night.'

'Anything worth knowing?'

'Don't think so. Just a lot of very angry people. Hate to say it but you lot are getting it in the neck. Seem to think it's your fault they managed to get away.'

'Not sure anyone could have known that was going to happen,' said McCoy.

'Probably not, but people are riled up, and with they boys gone they need someone to blame.'

Andy went back to work, and McCoy sat there for a bit ignoring the pint in front of him. Didn't want to risk another sip. Far as he could see, Andy was right. People had a right to be angry and it was only going to get worse. Trouble was, if people were angry at the polis they were less likely to help, be too busy calling them for everything. He put his hand on his raincoat, almost dry. Time to go.

Rain was still on outside, getting heavier. He started walking, feet destroying the reflections of the streetlights in the puddles. He was wet, tired, and his stomach was really starting to hurt. He dived in under the awning of the Colonial, got his Pepto-Bismol out and had a swig. He'd probably learnt as much as he was going to about the salon fire. The pubs were full of angry folk blowing smoke up each other's arses.

It was probably worth finding out which one of the boys had been mouthing off. If he was stupid enough to get caught, he might well have been stupid enough to let something slip. Needed to remember where the rumour came from though. Andy's dad was a nice enough guy, but he was a retired cop and retired cops were all the same. Couldn't let go, always trying to put themselves back in the picture, let people know that they weren't just ordinary blokes, that they knew what was really going on.

McCoy got to Glasgow Cross and stopped at the taxi rank. Time to go home. Time to concentrate on the salon case. Time to leave other things well alone. But he couldn't. He walked past the taxis and kept going down the Saltmarket. Some itches needed to be scratched.

NINE

The Empire Bar was tucked under a railway bridge. It was long and low-ceilinged, a kind of bunker with alcohol. Apart from the fact the drink was cheap, there wasn't an awful lot to recommend it, but its proximity to Paddy's Market meant a lot of the stallholders drank there, including Dirty Ally. McCoy had seen him in there a few times, sitting up the back, usual carrier bags full of God knows what on the floor beside him. More often than not he was with his pal and that's why McCoy was here.

He stepped inside, shook the water off his coat and headed for the bar. Person he was looking for was there already, propped up. Half and a half in front of him.

'Pint and another round,' McCoy said to the barman, nodding at the half and a half.

Lachy Orr looked round, held up his glass in salute. Said, 'Cheers, son,' in a voice that still had traces of his Island origins.

'You remember me?' asked McCoy.

Lachy shook his head.

'Friend of Ally's,' he said.

Lachy looked at him. 'Hang on, you're the polis boy, aren't you?'

McCoy nodded. 'Wanted to ask you about Ally.'

Lachy sighed. 'Come on then. We'll sit down. Thought someone might be coming round.'

An elderly woman with a tiny dog in a bag and wearing a silk headscarf with pictures of Blackpool on it was just leaving a table. She stood up. 'All yours boys,' she said, revealing bright white false teeth. 'Off to brave the storm. Wish me bon voyage!'

McCoy did, and put the drinks down on the table as Lachy took his time to ease himself onto a chair.

'This bloody weather,' he said. 'Plays havoc with the arthritis.'

McCoy wasn't surprised he was suffering. Lachy must have been getting on for eighty. He must have been tall in his day and there was still a trace of red in his grey beard but now he was stooped, looked his age. After a toast to 'absent friends' McCoy got straight into it.

'What happened?' he asked. 'I still can't believe it.'

Lachy shook his head. 'I didn't think it was bad enough to make him do that.'

'What wasn't?' asked McCoy.

'You don't know?'

McCoy shook his head. 'I heard he was scared of something, that's it.'

Lachy took a drink of whisky, rearranged his weight on the chair. Started. 'Couple of weeks ago I'm standing at my stall, rearranging the merchandise, I hear a noise and I look up. Some guy is pulling all the stuff off Ally's stall, all the magazines and the boxes of photosets, everything. It's happened a couple of times before, but it's always Holy Rollers, Pastor Jack Glass types. But those guys make a noise, shout and scream about pornography and sinfulness and the like. Not this guy though. He's saying nothing, just looking straight at Ally, wrecking the stall. And the funny thing is, Ally's not doing anything to stop him. No shouting, no trying to drag him away. He's just watching him do it. Face white.'

'Who was he, this guy?' asked McCoy.

Lachy shook his head. 'Just looked like any other bloke, young guy. When he was gone I asked Ally who he was and he just shook his head, started picking his stuff up off the floor.'

'Was that it?'

'Nope. Couple of weeks later it happened again. This time the guy poured petrol over the stall, stood there with a box of matches. Told Ally that was his final warning. He shut up the stall after that.'

'Christ,' said McCoy. 'And he never said what it was about?'

'Tried to ask him but he wouldn't talk about it. Just told me to leave it be. Next day, he's not at the stall, or the next after that. All shut up. Then I meet him in here one night about a week later, and he tells me his flat's been broken into. He was in some state, kept watching the door, jumpy, like. Tells me he's going to lie low for a while and will I look after his lock-up? I said yes and that was the last I saw of him. Then I heard today. Poor bugger.'

Lachy seemed to be looking through McCoy, mind elsewhere. 'You sure he killed himself? Sure it wasn't an accident or something?'

McCoy shook his head. 'It definitely wasn't an accident. Spoke to someone who saw him do it. His lock-up still there?'

Lachy nodded, dug in the pocket of his trousers and handed McCoy a key. 'You take it, son. Be nice if you could find out why he did it.' He smiled, half the teeth in his mouth gone. 'And get the fucker who drove him to it.'

★

McCoy stood under the bridge by the Empire, staying out the rain and hoping for a taxi to come along. Jingled the key in his pocket. Ally had killed himself: there was no crime to investigate, no reason to try and find out why. What was done was done. He needed to concentrate on the fire at Dolly's Salon, give something to Murray. Last thing he needed was to go look at a locker full of second-hand scud mags. A taxi turned in from London Road, and McCoy stepped out and waved. It really was time to go home.

21st May 1974

TEN

McCoy walked up the stairs of the close and knocked on Wattie's door. Hadn't slept much, woken up at five with stomach pains as usual. Watched the sun come up over the cranes at the bottom of the hill. Waited until six to call Murray and tell him what he'd heard. Not much if he was being honest, wanted to check something before he told him about the lad saying his dad was going to get him off, see if it was just boasting or not.

He could hear people moving about in the flat, a muttered 'who the fuck is that at this time?' from behind the door. He was just about to knock again when the door was pulled open to reveal Wattie standing there. Looked like he hadn't been up long, suit trousers, socks and vest, hair all over the place and a smiling Wee Duggie in his arms.

'McCoy? What are you doing here?' he asked.

McCoy smiled at the baby. 'I've come to see the organ grinder, not the monkey. Mary in?'

'What?' asked Wattie, looking confused. 'Why do you want to see her?'

'Need to talk to her. That all right with you, is it?'

Mary appeared over Wattie's shoulder. Afghan coat on, bag

over her shoulder. Hair held back with two cherry clasps, usual make-up featuring most of the colours of the rainbow.

'Is what all right with you?' she asked, getting an umbrella out of the stand by the door.

'How about I give you a lift to work?' asked McCoy. 'We can talk in the car.'

Mary nodded. 'Sounds good to me. It's pishing down out there and I'm late for the bus already.' She turned to Wattie. 'You'll remember to take his monkey with him to my mum's?'

At the word 'monkey' Wee Duggie held up the small stuffed monkey he was holding for everyone to see.

'I'll make sure he's got it.' Looked like he'd no idea what was going on.

'Don't forget, or he'll scream for it all day.' She leant in and kissed Wattie then kissed Wee Duggie.

'I'll see you at the station later,' said McCoy, rubbing what little hair Wee Duggie had on his head. 'You and I need to have a chat.'

Wattie's face fell.

'Nothing bad. Murray just wants me to help you out with your case.'

They left Wattie standing in the doorway, still looking a bit nonplussed, Wee Duggie starting to whimper, monkey dropped on the floor.

'To what do I owe this honour?' asked Mary as she opened the car door and got in.

McCoy started the engine, pulled out into Maryhill Road. 'Need to know about the three guys that got arrested for the salon fire. I heard you went to see the relatives yesterday?'

'Who told you that?'

'Your other half, was his excuse for coming in late. Had to drop my godson off at your maw's. And his beloved monkey no doubt.'

'You mean the relatives of the three guys you let get away?' asked Mary, flipping the sun visor down and looking at her hair in the mirror. Didn't look too pleased with it. 'Those guys? What do you want to know about them for?'

'I need a bit of background, need to get up to speed quick. Might help us find them.'

'And what do I get for this valuable information?' asked Mary.

McCoy stopped at the lights at Bilsland Drive, rummaged around in the glove compartment, found a Pale Ale bar towel and wiped the condensation off the windscreen. 'The joy of knowing you have helped the constabulary bring justice to the people of Glasgow,' he said.

Mary's head was down, digging in her bag, finally found what she was looking for and pulled out a hairbrush. 'Fuck off, McCoy. I help the constabulary every bloody day by picking up after the daft bastard and making his tea. Now, unless you've suddenly become the good Samaritan, which I very much doubt, you wouldn't be driving me to work unless you really, really needed to know what I know.' She started brushing the back of her hair. 'So make me an offer.'

'Okay. I'll be nice to Wattie for two weeks and I'll help solve whatever case he's struggling with. How's that?'

More brushing. 'And as I said, fuck off.'

The lights changed, and McCoy started the car, continued down the road. Knew he'd have to come up with something.

'How's about an eye-witness report on the daring rescue of the three lads? I was there, you know, saw the whole thing happen, got all the juicy details.'

Mary stopped brushing, suddenly looked interested. 'Were you?'

'Yep. Anonymous bystander you can call me.'

Mary pointed out the car window. 'Pull over at Jaconelli's. You can buy me a coffee.'

★

'They're a weird bunch, to be honest,' said Mary, blowing on her coffee. They were in the back booth at Jaconelli's, wood-panelled walls dampening the noise of what looked like half the taxi-drivers in Glasgow ordering their breakfasts in between shouting insults at each other.

'What do you mean?'

'Just that they're not three lads you would think would be pals or do something like that. Colin Turnbull's the only obvious one.'

'That the pyromaniac boy?' asked McCoy.

Mary nodded. 'Been in and out of care and foster homes since he was wee.' She looked at McCoy. 'Sorry.'

He shrugged.

'I spoke to his last foster parents. Nice people, wee bungalow in Baillieston. Apparently, he set fire to his primary school when he was eleven and the Scout hut at Hogganfield Street when he was thirteen. Told me he was a nice lad but there was always something not quite right with him, completely obsessed with fires.'

'These kids brought up in care, always something wrong with them,' said McCoy, smiling. 'Cannae trust them.'

'You said it, not me. Anyway, the poor wee bugger's been going to psychiatrists on and off all his life. Seems like he was always going to do something like this and there wasn't much anyone could do about it. Makes some sort of sense. It's the other two that are harder to understand.'

McCoy took an experimental sip of his coffee, waited to see how his stomach would react. 'How come?'

'Danny Walsh's dad is in prison. Saughton, I think. I spoke to his mum. She's got four other kids, lives in a dump of a flat in Anderston, half the street's been knocked down for the motorway. Should have kept going and done the lot. When I say dump, I mean dump. I didn't want to sit down in case I caught something. According to her, Danny's a good boy—'

'Course he is.'

'But he fell in with the wrong crowd at school. Been done for shoplifting, breach of the peace, the usual stuff. Poor cow didn't seem to have that much of a grip on real life, never mind how Danny ended up setting fire to something. Think she was full of Valium or whatever else doctors give women that can't cope. Started telling me she thinks people shouldn't have landed on the moon, God didn't like it. As you can imagine, I got out of there as soon as I could, went back to the *Record* and called someone I know at the Cruelty. The family are "known", as they say. Seems Danny's been pretty much fending for himself since he was twelve or thirteen. The mum showed me a picture of him. Good-looking boy despite it all.'

'And the other one?'

'Didn't get very far with him. Malcolm McCauley. Bloody family refused to see me. Great big house out Uddingston way. A Rover and a Jag in the drive. I should know, I got chased all the way down it.'

'Really?' McCoy pushed his coffee away. Stomach had said no chance.

'Yep. So I did a bit of digging. Turns out the father, Tom McCauley, owns a big building company.'

'What? McCauley McCauley's?' asked McCoy. Hadn't made the connection immediately. Let out a low whistle. Someone like that may well have enough money and clout to organise what had happened to the boys.

'He's loaded. Malcolm and his brother went to St Aloysius. The brother went on to Glasgow Uni to do law while Malcolm got expelled for selling hash. Dad made the police investigation go away but it seems that was the end of Malcolm's brilliant career. According to the extremely accommodating and, thankfully, extremely eager to spill the beans neighbour next door, he's been living in communes and squats round Garnethill way. Occasionally turns up at the house asking for money.'

McCoy sat back in the booth, watched a taxi-driver, cash box in hand, feed money into the jukebox. Tried to think. Frank Sinatra started to sing 'My Way'. Not what you needed at half seven in the morning.

'So how did those three get together?' he asked. 'I don't get it. Were they pals?'

'Me neither,' said Mary. 'And why set fire to a bloody hairdresser in Royston, then be stupid enough to start talking about it in a pub a couple of hours later?' She pushed her empty coffee cup away. Smiled. 'But that, Harry, is your problem.' She dug in her bag and got her notebook and pen out. 'Now,' she said, 'start talking – and I want details.'

ELEVEN

McCoy stopped, turned up his collar, tried to light up. Collar wasn't much use, ended up having to pull the raincoat over his head. Managed to get his cigarette lit and then reappeared. They were standing on the road as a group of black-clad mourners in the back of a taxi rolled past them. McCoy just managed to resist the automatic urge to cross himself.

Sighthill Cemetery stood on a hill in the north of the city, sandwiched between Springburn and the Pinkston works. Must have been a couple of acres at least, rows of graves stretching out into the distance. Normally you would get a good view from up here, but between the constant drizzle and the huge Pinkston cooling tower right in front of them blocking their view, there wasn't much to see. They waited until the taxi had passed and started walking again.

'You think you're up to this?' asked Wattie. 'Being back at work?'

'Yep,' said McCoy. 'Murray's not too sure though. Some fucker snitched on me, told him I was throwing up on duty.'

'So I heard, along with everyone else.'

'Murray doesn't think I'm up to front-line stuff, still thinks I'm too sick.'

'Probably are. You look bloody awful,' said Wattie, grinning.

'Yes, thank you for your diagnosis, Doctor Watson. Very helpful.'

'So what does Murray want you to do?'

'Not me. Me and you. That's why I'm wandering about in this graveyard getting bloody soaking. Wants me to have a look at your case, see if I can help and have a wee nosey about in the background of the salon fire.'

'What does that mean?' asked Wattie.

'God knows,' said McCoy 'Speaking to your wife this morning was my big idea. Bit lost as to what to do now.'

'I thought Tobago Street were doing the fire?'

'They are. That's why Murray's going over there. We're just going to stay out the way, see if we can turn anything up.'

Wattie sucked air through his teeth. 'Tobago Street aren't going to be happy about that.'

'Nope. But they don't know, and if they do find out, that's Murray's problem. You know what he's like, thinks they're idiots. He only trusts Hughie Faulds so he's down on numbers. Got a feeling he might have to move us from the background to the main investigation once he finds out how bad they really are. So,' he turned to Wattie, 'if he asks you about me, I'm fit as a fiddle, right?'

Wattie nodded. 'This way.'

They stepped off the path onto the grass and squelched up the hill, shoes and trouser hems soaking after a few steps, McCoy's ankle playing up a bit when he put weight on it. They passed a fresh grave, long pile of earth with decaying flowers on it, note attached to one bunch, half faded.

To the best wee Mammy there ever was, love from Sharon and George

'There's deer up here apparently,' said Wattie. 'They eat the flowers on the graves. One of the uniforms saw one, timid wee thing.'

'So would you be if you were a deer that lived in Sighthill. You'd be permanently shitting yourself. Is it much further? I'm soaked already.'

Wattie stopped, got his bearings, pointed to a mausoleum in the distance, a square grey stone building about the size of a garden hut, all carved crosses overgrown with moss and faded inscriptions. 'Just up there, behind that thing. Can still see some of the tape.'

McCoy squinted at the long stretch of yellow tape dancing in the wind. Started walking again. 'How did they find the body? This is the back arse of nowhere.'

'A guy was walking his dog and—'

'It's always a bloody dog walker. Sometimes I think all they do is lurk about looking for dead bloody bodies.'

'Finished?'

'It's true though.'

They were almost at the mausoleum now, kept trudging through the long, wet grass. McCoy could see the flattened patch where the scene of crime team had been stamping about. 'That where she was?'

Wattie said yes.

McCoy stood by the patch, looked at it. One good thing about being in the hospital, he hadn't had to look at places like this. Sad, lonely places where someone's last breath had been squeezed out their body. Imagined lying on the grass too weak to fight back, knowing this was the end. He crossed himself, looked up at the clouds scudding across the sky.

'You all right?' asked Wattie.

McCoy nodded. Wasn't.

'The man was walking his dog Saturday morning, sixish,' Wattie continued. 'Only found her because his dog kept barking until he came over. Girl was lying there. She'd been strangled. Approx. age fifteen to seventeen.'

'Sexual assault?' asked McCoy.

'Not according to Phyllis, no.'

'That's strange. Usually is in cases like these.' They moved into the lee of the mausoleum, wind and rain settling down a bit. 'So who was she?'

'That's the problem,' said Wattie. 'We don't know.'

'What?'

'She had a wee bag with her but no ID. Just a couple of quid, a lipstick, the pill, hair stuff, bits and bobs. Nothing special about her clothes, high street stuff. Bus Stop, Chelsea Girl, that sort of thing. No identifying marks, no scars. Nothing to single her out.'

'You check all the missing persons?' asked McCoy.

'Nobody matching her description's gone missing in the past three months. A few girls as you would expect but none that match. And no one has come forward to report her missing. That's three days now.'

'What else did Phyllis say?'

'Not much. Thought she was fifteen, sixteen, sexually active, strangled by a thin rope or cord. Some evidence of barbiturates in her system.'

'So she wasn't fighting back?'

'No sign of it. Mind you, she was a slip of a thing. Not sure it would have made any difference if she had.'

McCoy looked around. They were in an isolated bit of the graveyard: no real paths, no real reason to be here. At night it must have been pitch-black, no light from the streetlights on Springburn Road. 'The dog walker check out?'

Wattie nodded. 'Tucked up in bed on Friday night with his girlfriend. Both of them doctors at the Western.'

'Cosy,' said McCoy. He stuck his cigarette in the corner of his mouth, held out his hands. 'Let's see the file.'

Wattie handed it over and McCoy opened it, tried to keep it out the rain. Hated looking at crime scene photos, people reduced to what they were when they died. Splayed out, limbs twisted every which way, bits of grass in their hair, clothes pulled off. The indignity of death laid out for everyone to see. And always that same look in their eyes. A sort of resignation at their fate. This one wasn't any different.

The girl was wearing a light raincoat, a sparkly dress, platform shoes, one on, one lying beside her. Her hair was short, bit like Mia Farrow in *Rosemary's Baby*. Still possible to see she was pretty if you looked beyond the livor mortis and the raw red mark around her neck.

'So she'd been out somewhere by the looks of it?' asked McCoy.

'Looks like it. According to Phyllis, she was killed between twelve and two the night before Fido found her.'

McCoy flicked through some more photos, variations on the same ugly scene. He closed the file. 'If no one's reported her missing, might mean she lived by herself?'

'Or with the person who murdered her,' said Wattie.

'Good point,' said McCoy. 'You sure she wasn't sexually assaulted?'

'Yes,' said Wattie. 'Phyllis was sure.'

'Okay, if it was domestic, then the nearest houses are a good ten-minute walk away. I can't see her boyfriend or whoever it was carrying the body up here. Too much chance of being seen. So let's imagine she was already here. What would she be doing here late on a Friday night?'

'If she was a working girl, maybe she went with a punter in a car?' said Wattie. 'He picked her up somewhere in town, drove out here for a bit of peace and quiet?'

McCoy looked at him. Shook his head.

'What?' asked Wattie. 'What's up?'

'Minute you assume that's what she was, everything goes to shit. You stop thinking properly. Start thinking she was killed by a punter and that's the end of that. You close your mind.'

Wattie looked apologetic. 'Not punter. Boyfriend.'

McCoy lit up again, looked down at his trousers, wet up past his knees now. 'So he has a car. But why would he dump her here? Too much chance of being seen. I don't get it. You'd drive out to the country, somewhere isolated.' He looked around, just graves and more graves stretching out over the hill. 'What else have you been doing?'

'Been showing her picture round the Green and Blythswood, seeing if any of the working girls recognise her.'

McCoy muttered, 'Give me strength,' under his breath.

'No luck. Couple of them said something interesting though. Said she was too young and well-dressed to be working the streets.'

McCoy was beginning to get annoyed now. 'They told you that and you're still thinking she was killed by a punter?'

'Not any more. Sorry.'

'What else? May as well get it all out.'

'I even asked that nutty woman with the van who goes to Blythswood at night. Hands out cups of tea and Bible tracts?'

'Moira? The Holy Roller? Christ, is she still going?'

'She is, and she said the same thing. Girl didn't look like she worked the streets. Dressed too fashionably is what she said. Whatever that means.'

'So two different sources told you she was unlikely to be a working girl and yet you—'

'Come on, Harry, I'm not—'

'Not bloody thinking is what you're doing. Sexually active girl who's been murdered. Must be on the game then. This is the kind of shite I had to put up with ten years ago. I'm no doing it now. There's really nothing on her to identify her?'

Wattie shook his head. 'Next thing I was going to do was give her photo to the press, see if they would run it.'

McCoy shook his head. 'They're not going to run a photo of a dead fifteen-year-old girl. Even for them that's too much.'

'I know,' said Wattie, nodding down at the file. 'Brown envelope.'

McCoy flicked through the file again. Fingerprint sheet. More photos. Copy of Phyllis's autopsy report and a brown envelope. He opened it and took out a strip of photos, the kind you got taken for your passport in railway stations. Looked at it. The first three photos were of the girl: one smiling, one sucking her cheeks in to look like a model, one with her tongue sticking out. The fourth one was different.

In that one, there were two boys in the photo with her, looked like they'd barged into the booth for the last photo. Both looked about the same age as the girl. One facing the camera, thick blond hair cut short, one turned away, long brown hair. All three of them laughing, caught out by the flash.

'Who are they?' asked McCoy.

'Don't know,' said Wattie. 'Pals by the look of it.'

'Okay, let's get the nicest photo of her copied and printed up. Ask the press office in Pitt Street if they can get it in tomorrow's paper.'

They started walking back to the car, rain teeming down. McCoy trying not to think of a fifteen-year-old girl out here at night. Must have been terrified before anything even happened to her. Life had hardly started and now it was over. At least this girl had a chance of getting her case solved. She was young and pretty. The papers would be interested, people would be interested. MYSTERY GIRL FOUND DEAD. If she had been ten years older, worn out with a life on the streets, they wouldn't even bother taking her picture to the papers. Case would just move down the ranks until nobody cared any more.

A couple of seagulls flew down, landed on the cemetery wall. McCoy pushed his wet hair out his eyes, got the car keys out his pocket. Thought back to the patch of flattened grass and what had happened there. The fear she must have felt in the darkness. Decided that, no matter what, he'd find the fucker who left her there.

TWELVE

McCoy was too wet to care what he looked like. Back in the office, he took off his trousers and socks and hung them over the radiator. Couple of wolf whistles from Temple and Mitchell, which he greeted with a bow and two fingers stuck up at them. Wattie was doing better. He had his football kit with him, had changed into a pair of shorts and long red football socks.

McCoy sat down at his desk, was just about to pick up the phone when he heard muffled shouting coming from Murray's office.

'Thought he was in Tobago Street?' said Wattie.

'Must have come back,' said McCoy. 'Better tell him what Mary said.' He stood up.

'I don't even want to say this,' said Wattie.

'But?'

'But could she have been a different kind of working girl? Not working the streets. More of an escort? That would explain why she was all dressed up. Out for a meal or a drink before the dirty deed.'

McCoy thought for a minute. 'Could be. Get her photo round the Albany, Central Hotel, those kinds of places. Get the concierges to have a look. They normally keep track of the girls on their patch. Not the worst idea you've ever had, Watson. Now, wish me luck.'

'You going in with no trousers on?' asked Wattie, nodding to McCoy's bare legs.

'Shite.'

Wattie dug in his bag, pulled out a pair of muddy tracksuit trousers, held them up. 'Better than nothing.'

'Not sure about that,' said McCoy, pulling them on. 'Look like I've just gone ninety minutes against Clyde Juniors.'

Murray was on the phone when McCoy went in, and he pointed at the chair in front of his desk. Whoever was on the other end of the line was getting it in the ear. McCoy listened for a bit – *incompetent, useless, a waste of space* – then tuned out. Tried to think what they could do next about the girl in Sighthill Cemetery. Maybe she wasn't from Glasgow. If she was from Aberdeen or Edinburgh, that might be a reason no one had reported her missing. Needed to tell Wattie to get the picture in the *Press and Journal* or the *Scotsman*. Glasgow papers wouldn't be enough.

'What the fuck are you wearing?'

McCoy looked up and Murray was shaking his head. 'Got soaking at Wattie's crime scene.'

'Getting anywhere?'

'Just started. Need to find out who she is, that's the number one priority. Not going to get very far without knowing that. Going to get her picture in the paper, see if that shakes anything out. How's Tobago Street?'

Murray harrumphed. Got his pipe out his pocket. 'The sooner they shut that place down, the better. I couldn't work over there. Whole place was driving me mad. I've left Faulds supervising the van driver and the court officer interviews.'

'An inside job?' asked McCoy.

'Could be,' said Murray. 'It would explain a lot, would have made the whole thing a lot easier. Things people will do for a cash bung.'

'All the more reason to look at McCauley the builder. He's the only one with any money.'

'Right. You go and see him. Faulds is busy with his interviews.'

'Will do. What are Pitt Street saying about the missing boys?'

'What do you think? Find them. No matter how. You spoken to any contacts yet?'

'A couple, more tonight.'

'Let's hope, then. Pay for it if you need to. Somebody must know something. At least four blokes in that raid. One of them might have a big mouth.'

McCoy stood up. Saluted. Went to go.

'Oh, and McCoy? Put some bloody trousers on.'

McCoy did what he was told, and put his trousers on, only slightly damp now. He sat down at his desk, picked up the file and started flicking through it again. Autopsy notes didn't tell him anything he didn't already know. Wondered how a fifteen-year-old girl could get murdered and nobody seemed to notice or care. Wasn't like Wattie hadn't been trying, he'd done what he was supposed to do. In a case like this, they needed a break, some luck, a tearful confession. Had the feeling they weren't going to get it. They were in for the long haul.

THIRTEEN

Mary had been right enough. It was a big house. A long ranch-style bungalow, immaculate garden, looked like it belonged in an American suburb rather than five miles outside Glasgow. McCoy drove up the drive and parked behind the Jag. Turned the ignition off. Listened to Wattie snoring for a minute. Shook him.

'Wakey, wakey.'

Wattie opened his eyes, sat up in his seat. 'Must have fallen asleep,' he said, wiping his mouth. 'Sorry. I'm only getting a couple of hours' sleep a night with the wee man teething.' He yawned. 'Feel like I'm wandering about in a fog most of the time.'

McCoy knew the feeling. He was just about to open the car door when the front door of the house swung open and a middle-aged man ran out, waving his arms. Face red already.

'No!' he shouted. 'No bloody press! I've had enough of it! Get out my bloody driveway – that's private property!'

McCoy stepped out the car, held up his police badge. 'Mr McCauley? Detective McCoy, Glasgow Police. Can we have a word?'

The inside of the house was as flash as the outside. All geometric wallpaper and long low couches, a broken-stone fireplace stretching across one wall. A sleek Bang & Olufsen stereo and a big picture window looking out at the fields beyond. McCoy refused the offer of the couch, pulled a chair out from around the glass dining table and sat on that. Watched Wattie sink into an orange leather sofa and knew he'd made the right choice.

McCauley stood in front of the fireplace, didn't look happy. Even with the cashmere golf sweater and the crocodile-skin loafers, he still looked like a builder. Weather-beaten face and a bulky frame, thick calloused fingers wrapped around his china mug.

'Sorry about that,' he said, not sounding sorry at all. 'Thought you were one of they reporter bastards. You people should be keeping them away.'

'Been bothered a lot, have you?' asked McCoy.

McCauley nodded at the pile of newspapers on the coffee table. Each front page showed a variation of the rescue story.

'Have to say, it must have been a shock hearing what your son has been involved in,' said McCoy. 'Four people dead.'

'My son isn't involved in any bloody thing,' said McCauley. 'He's been railroaded into something he didn't do. You lot should be ashamed of yourselves.'

'Don't think there was much railroading going on,' said McCoy. 'From what I hear, he confessed straight away.'

McCauley shook his head. 'I don't believe that for one minute. Won't be the first or last time you've tried to frame an innocent man.'

'It's not up to us, Mr McCauley. We don't have that power. It's up to the courts to decide whether he's innocent or not. That's how it works.' McCoy looked at McCauley, at the framed Rotary Club membership on the wall, at the line of Lladro figures on the mantelpiece, the Modigliani print over the fireplace. Had just about had enough of him and his opinions already. He smiled. 'But that's not going to happen, is it? Not now.'

'What do you mean?' asked McCauley, eyes narrowing.

'Well, him and his pals have gone, haven't they?' said McCoy. 'Whisked away into the night.' He shrugged. 'And without them, no trial.'

'I don't care about that. Trial or no trial, my son is innocent. What I want to know is who's taken them. Why are you not working on that instead of harassing me?'

'You invited us in for a chat,' said McCoy. 'Not sure how we're harassing you, Mr McCauley. Quite the opposite in fact. I thought we were being very polite.'

McCauley grunted. Muttered, 'Cheeky wee shite.'

Now McCoy had really had enough. 'Okay. Since you're so convinced we're harassing you, we may as well do it, eh?' He could see Wattie wincing out the corner of his eye. 'You could've just employed a good lawyer, you know? Would've been easier.'

'What?' McCauley looked wary. 'What're you talking about?'

'You're so sure your son is innocent. If he is, a good lawyer would've got him off no bother. Might've been easier than your wee escape plan.'

'What are you on about?' asked McCauley, knuckles white round his mug.

'Doesn't matter if you think your son is innocent. That's not what most people think – quite the opposite in fact. There were crowds of them outside the court dying to get a hold of him and give him the doing of his life. Makes me think the boys in Barlinnie must feel the same way. Can't see them holding back, not after they saw the pictures of those wee girls caught in the fire. Chances are your son wouldn't have made it out there alive, never mind got to a trial.' He gestured round the living room. 'You've done well. A smart man, rich, powerful. Maybe you just decided to make sure he never got to Barlinnie.'

There was silence. Just the starburst clock on the wall ticking, a dog barking in the garden outside.

McCauley took a breath. 'Let me tell you something, you ignorant fucking prick—'

'Mr McCauley, there's no need for—' said Wattie.

McCauley turned to him. 'And you can shut it too. Right?'

Wattie held his hands up.

'The last time I saw my son was two months ago. Right here in this living room. He was standing where you are. Told me to fuck off, told me I was a bourgeois cunt and that he never wanted to come back here again. And he hasn't, despite his mother trying and trying.' He moved towards McCoy, finger jabbing in the air. 'I know my son enough to know that he wouldn't do what he's accused of. But you know what? Other than that? That boy is a mystery to me. Has been ever since he was about twelve. His mother and I have tried everything, done everything, and it's all been thrown back in our faces. So, at this point I'm not sure I'd cross the road to piss on him if he was on fire, never mind organise some fucking mental stunt to get him out of jail.' McCauley's face was red now, spitting as he spoke. 'Now, if you've finished, you and your pal can get the fuck out of my house before I do something I shouldn't.'

★

'I'm surprised he didn't lamp you,' said Wattie, getting in the car. 'Most men would have. What's up with you anyway? You let him have it with both barrels.'

'Not my fault. He started it,' said McCoy.

'That right? What age are you anyway? Nine? You're supposed to be a bloody detective, not picking fights in the playground.'

McCoy sat down in the front seat. 'Maybe I think he's a bourgeois cunt too.'

Wattie shook his head and started the car. 'I don't understand you sometimes.'

'What else was he going to say? He's the only one with the resources to have done it. Course he's going to say he didn't and give us a reason why. He's not daft.'

'You really think he did it?' asked Wattie. 'He's a builder, not a bloody criminal mastermind.'

McCoy shrugged.

Wattie shook his head, started the car.

Ten minutes later they were stuck in a traffic jam near Baillieston. McCoy was sick and tired of being in the car. Not sure he'd achieved much pissing off McCauley so quickly. Now his guard would be up twice as much as before. Maybe he was out of practice. And Murray wasn't going to be happy. He yawned, half listened to Wattie trying to answer the questions on the quiz show on the radio and failing.

Was so bored he opened Wattie's file again. The photo strip fell out onto his lap, he picked it up, looked at it. She was a good-looking girl all right, hard to believe no one had noticed she was missing yet. McCoy was just about to put it back in the file when the last picture caught his eye.

'Fuck,' he said. 'Fuck.'

FOURTEEN

'It's not a social visit,' said McCoy. 'You coming? Or you want to sit in here like a big wean?'

Wattie shook his head, got out the car. They crossed and started walking up Memen Road. McCoy was so used to taxis refusing to drive up here, he'd made Wattie do the same thing. Memen Road was a place you avoided unless you really, really couldn't. It wasn't just the fact that Stevie Cooper lived here that put people off, the whole street was full of tenants nowhere else would take.

The gardens in front of the tenements were a wasteland of rubbish, broken toys and blackened and scorched patches where fires had been lit. Cooper had colonised the last two closes. He had a flat there, and didn't want anyone else around him, so the other tenants had been persuaded to move out – mostly with the help of iron bars and razors.

'Mr McCoy!'

McCoy looked up to see Jumbo walking towards them. He still had no idea what Jumbo ate every day, but he kept getting bigger and broader. Six foot three of a brick shithouse bodyguard.

'All right, Jumbo? How's things?' asked McCoy, shaking his giant paw.

'Good,' said Jumbo, not even managing to convince himself. 'What's up? Is it Cooper?'

Jumbo looked round, checking no one could hear him. 'Mr Cooper's been a bit' – he stumbled trying to find the word – 'unsettled . . . since Billy went. . . since Billy.'

'That's natural,' said McCoy. 'Used to rely on him. He been drinking and drugging again?'

Jumbo looked guilty.

'I'll have a word. He in?'

Jumbo nodded. Stepped aside.

Unlike any others in Memen Road the stairs up to Cooper's flat were clean, smelled of bleach. Iris must still be making her daily visits. McCoy just hoped she had been and gone already, couldn't face another barrage of insults about 'useless polis'. They got to the top of the stairs and knocked on the shiny black door. More Iris at work.

A couple of seconds later the door was opened by a girl in a dressing gown. Reeking of booze. Late teens, dyed blonde hair, figure that would stop a clock.

'Tell him McCoy's here.'

Door was shut over.

'You still haven't told me why we're here,' said Wattie.

'All will be revealed. If I'm right, we could be up and running with your case.'

Door opened again. 'Says he'll be twenty minutes,' said the girl. 'You can wait in the kitchen.'

A shout from in the flat. Cooper's unmistakable bellow. 'Lynn! Get your arse in here.'

McCoy was looking at his watch when Cooper eventually appeared. Usual walk, like he was on a ship in heavy seas. Usual jeans, blue short-sleeved shirt and blond quiff. Only thing that had changed was that he seemed to have got broader since McCoy had last seen him. Must have been using the facilities when he went to see his boxers at the gym. Knuckles on both hands were bruised and cut. Right one swollen up. Cooper must have been teaching someone what happened when he didn't get his way.

'That's forty minutes,' said McCoy.

'Fuck you,' said Cooper, filling a pint glass with water from the tap. 'Where would you rather be? In bed with her or sitting here with you two?'

'Fair point,' said Wattie.

'Didn't know you had a new flame,' said McCoy.

'I don't,' said Cooper. 'I only met her last night. Just told Jumbo to give her money for a taxi home.'

'What a gent,' said McCoy. 'Glad to see chivalry's not dead.'

'So how was it?' asked Cooper, leaning against the sink. 'The hospital.'

McCoy shrugged. 'What you'd expect. Boring. I slept most of the time.'

'I came to see you, you know,' said Cooper, rooting around in the bread bin. He found a dry roll, started eating it.

'Did you?' McCoy was genuinely surprised. 'I don't remember.'

'You wouldn't,' said Cooper through a mouthful. 'Was just after you went in. You were out for the count. Tubes going in and out. Doctor said you were in a bad way.'

'You know what doctors are like,' said McCoy. 'Always exaggerate.'

'You looked bloody awful. Thought I was going to have to track down your old man. Wasn't looking forward to that.'

'You'd be lucky. Fuck knows where the old bugger is.'

Cooper sat down at the table. 'You just come here for a wee sit down and a cup of tea? Knew you polis were lazy bastards.'

'Sort of official, actually,' said McCoy. 'Need you to look at something.' He dug out the brown envelope from his pocket and handed over the strip of photos.

Cooper looked at it. 'Nice-looking girl.'

'The bottom one,' said McCoy. 'Look at the bottom one.'

Cooper looked again. Brought the strip up to his face and peered at it. Looked at McCoy.

'It's Paul, isn't it?' said McCoy.

Cooper nodded. 'Where'd you get this?'

'You recognise the girl?'

Cooper shook his head, handed the strip back.

'You know where he is?' asked McCoy.

Cooper shook his head. 'Wish I did. Haven't seen him for over a year. Foster parents phoned me, said he'd run away again, that they were done with him. Looked for a couple of weeks but the wee fucker had disappeared off the face of the earth. Thought he might have gone to Ireland, stay with the relatives, but they haven't heard from him either.'

Suddenly struck him, colour drained from his face. 'Why have you got his photo? Is he dead?'

McCoy shook his head. 'Not him. The girl is though. We need to speak to him.'

FIFTEEN

The Bells was the nearest pub, and Cooper said he needed a 'bloody drink' after McCoy scaring him so there they were. Sitting round a table at the back, weak light from the windows cutting through the smoke and the dust, illuminating how truly miserable the place was.

'You've got to be able to drink something,' said Cooper.

McCoy shook his head. 'I'm not supposed to drink anything.'

'Well, fuck that. You've been in that bloody hospital for a month. What do you want?'

McCoy sighed. At least he'd tried. Knew it wasn't going to work but he'd tried. 'A Guinness,' he said. 'Get me a Guinness.'

Cooper looked at Wattie. 'You?'

'Pint, please.'

Cooper walked up to the bar.

Wattie waited until he was out of earshot. 'That's the first time he's ever looked at me.'

'Wouldn't take it personal, he's just not that fond of polis,' said McCoy. 'If he's not told you to fuck off already, you're doing well.'

'Great,' said Wattie. 'I'm honoured. So who's Paul?'

'His son,' said McCoy.

Wattie looked surprised. 'His son? I didn't know he had a son.'

'Neither did he until a couple of years ago. The mum died and the social got in touch with him. The mum had left a note saying that if anything happened to her, Stevie Cooper was the father of her son. One-night-stand thing, I think. She never told him she was pregnant.'

'Christ.'

'Wasn't that sure until he saw the boy – no denying it then, he's his double. He tried to become his guardian, but the court wouldn't let him, not with his criminal record. So Paul's been in foster care, well, running away from foster care. Must be fifteen or sixteen now. Don't think the social will spend much time looking for him, getting too old.'

Cooper arrived back with the drinks and sat down. 'So, what's the story?'

'The girl was found dead on Saturday morning, body left in Sighthill Cemetery. Nothing in her bag but some make-up and these photos. We still don't know who she is. Hopefully Paul will be able to tell us.'

'If you can find him,' said Cooper. 'He's no talking to me, by the way.'

'Why not?'

Cooper looked a bit guilty. 'Last time I found out he'd run away, we had words.'

'Words?' asked McCoy, eyebrows raised.

'All right. I leathered him. He deserved it.'

'Any idea where he is now?'

Cooper shook his head. 'Somebody told me they saw him in that posers' pub in town. The one with that mad car coming out the walls.'

'The Muscular Arms?'

'That's it.'

'Thought he was only fifteen,' said Wattie.

'He is,' said Cooper. 'Always been big for his age, runs in the family. Look, I know you're McCoy's pal and all that, but can you fuck off for ten minutes? Need to speak to him. Private, like.'

Wattie looked at McCoy. McCoy nodded and Wattie shook his head, stood up and headed for the door.

Cooper waited until the pub door closed behind him. 'Same person that told me he was in that pub also told me he was with Dessie Caine's young team.'

'He's not running with Caine's mob, is he?'

'Don't know,' said Cooper. 'Might be though. He's a big lad, can take care of himself. Found that out when I leathered him. But the last thing I need is him mixed up with Dessie Caine.'

'I thought Caine was all holy now, hanging about with priests. Making donations to build chapels and all that stuff.'

Cooper took a drink of his pint. 'He may well be, doesn't stop him being a right bastard. From what I hear, things are starting to get ugly between him and Johnny Smart. Turf wars.'

'Really? Who'd think Royston would be worth fighting over?'

'Dessie's no just Royston any more. He's Dennistoun as well and he wants Haghill. Been expanding his empire big time.'

'Ah,' said McCoy. 'So you don't want Paul getting caught in the crossfire.'

'To be honest, I don't care if the wee fucker gets his face opened, but if he does, I'll have to do something about it, and way things are at the moment I'm in no shape to take on Dessie or Johnny Smart.'

'You not found anyone to replace Billy yet?'

Cooper held up his bruised hands. 'What do you think? I'm back on the bloody front line. Half of me thinks fuck it, cash it all in and go legit.' He grinned. 'And the other half thinks fuck that for a game of soldiers, no ready for the quiet life yet.'

'You shouldn't be doing that stuff any more,' said McCoy. 'You've got too much to lose.'

'You telling me how to run my business now, are you?'

'No, I just think you should be careful.'

Cooper's face changed in an instant. Leant into McCoy. Hissed at him. 'And I'm telling you to fuck off and mind your own business. Got it?'

McCoy nodded.

'Didnae hear you.'

'I've got it. Mind my own business.'

And just like that, the anger had gone and the old Cooper was back. Grinned at McCoy. Everything right with the world again.

'What about Paul? He could be a good number two. He's young, fit. Keep it in the family.'

'And he thinks I'm a fucking dick,' said Cooper.

'That's 'cause you're his dad. All teenagers think their dads are dicks. But he's getting older, things are different now, he's growing up. If he's running with Dessie's mob, he must be capable.'

Cooper sat blowing smoke rings into the sunbeams, watching them dissolve. 'Not the worst idea,' he said eventually.

'Good. And as a thanks you can come with me to the Muscular Arms tonight. Better wear your best gear.'

SIXTEEN

'Someone here for you.'

Billy the desk sergeant looked over at the bench in the corner of the front office. McCoy looked over to see a woman in her sixties sitting on the iron bench beneath the poster warning of Colorado beetle. She was dressed smartly, hat, gloves, shiny handbag held on her lap.

She looked up, smiled. 'Mr McCoy?'

McCoy nodded, reminded Wattie to get onto the national papers with the photo of the girl and walked over.

She stood up, held her hand out to shake. 'Alison Drummond. I believe you found my brother Alistair. I wondered if I could have a word?'

McCoy couldn't bring himself to take her to the stinking interview room, so he led her down the street to the City Bakeries on Milton Street that had a Lite Bite cafe attached. Found a table in the window and ordered two teas. Miss Drummond took her gloves off, folded them over the top of her handbag and looked at him.

'Did it seem like he suffered?' she asked.

McCoy shook his head. No way was he telling her about

Ally's dying crawl across the yard. 'He died as soon as he hit the ground,' he said. 'Broke his neck.'

She sighed. The tea arrived and McCoy poured, wondering if there was anyone less likely to be Dirty Ally's sister.

Miss Drummond took a sip. 'Did you know my brother?' she asked. 'Before yesterday I mean?'

'Not well,' said McCoy 'But we ran into each other every now and again.' Wondered if she knew what Ally did for a living.

'At Paddy's Market?' she asked. Then smiled. 'No need to be discreet, Mr McCoy. I was well aware of what Ally got up to.' She stirred her tea. 'I wish you had known him when he was younger. He was different then, vibrant, full of life.'

'What happened?' asked McCoy before he could stop himself. 'Sorry to be blunt.'

'Don't worry,' she said. 'Disappointment happened. My brother studied at Glasgow University, English Literature. Was very good at it, even got a first-class honours.'

The shock must have been written on McCoy's face.

'Not what you were expecting to hear, I imagine. He was a brilliant young man, Mr McCoy. Everyone had high expectations, thought he would become a lecturer at the university, but he didn't want to do that. He spent the next two years writing a novel. Put all he had into it. Every publisher told him how brilliant it was but none of them would publish it.' She smiled again. 'These were the days before the *Lady Chatterley* trial. My brother's book dealt in sexual obsession, pulled no punches. They asked him to amend it, tone it down a bit, but, ever the artist, he refused. Eventually he got it published by Olympia Press in Paris. Do you know them?'

McCoy shook his head.

'They published the more controversial novels: Alexander Trocchi, Henry Miller, that sort of thing. They also published books with the sexual content but none of the art. Those ones financed the books they thought were of literary value. My brother's was one of the artistic ones. *The Love Chamber* it was called.'

She opened her bag, got out a scalloped hanky and dabbed her eyes.

McCoy gave her a minute. 'What happened then?'

'That's just it,' she said. 'Nothing. There were good reviews, kind words from his peers, and then the circus moved on. Nobody bought it.' She shrugged. 'So my brother took up drinking and tried to write another novel. Started distributing the Olympia catalogue in Britain to make some money. Soon realised the only money to be made was in the racy titles. Then he realised the real money was in titles with no artistic merit whatsoever. From there it wasn't long until he was just dealing in pornography, the high-class collectors' stuff, at first, the specialised market, and then he was drinking more and more and he ended up in the less collectible commercial kind of pornography. Hence Paddy's Market.'

'I'd never have known,' said McCoy. 'Fancy, Ally an author.'

'His book is highly collectible these days. Copies go for a lot of money. If you can find one that is – they're as rare as hen's teeth.' She smiled. 'Forgive me, I'm not here to tell you Ally's life story. I'm just trying to understand what drove him to do what he did.'

'Did he have any enemies?' asked McCoy.

'Not that I know of,' she said. 'But I only saw my brother every few years. He liked to keep to himself. I probably wouldn't know if he did. Why do you ask?'

'Apparently he was being harassed. His stock being damaged, being threatened.'

'Who by?'

'I don't know, but he was scared enough to move out his flat, to stay at the Great Northern so nobody would know where he was.' He dug in his pocket and took out a key. 'I should give this to you, really. It's the key to his lock-up at the market, the stall holder next door gave it to me.'

She shook her head. 'Much as I loved my brother, I have no wish to dig around in the contents of his stock. I consider myself a woman of the world, but I don't doubt it would make my hair curl. Will you find out who was harassing him?'

'I don't know how to say this, Miss Drummond, but now that he's dead, it's not a police matter. He killed himself. What happened before isn't really relevant now – to us, I mean.'

She nodded. 'I understand. Maybe I should just do the same. Move on, as they say. But the thought of my brother jumping off a building because someone was threatening him is heart-breaking. For all his bluster, he was a fragile man. Sensitive, as Mum used to say.'

McCoy tried to stop himself saying it. Watched her hand shake as she raised her cup of tea to her mouth. Couldn't. 'I'll keep the key. If I'm down that way in the next couple of days, I'll have a look, eh?'

'That's very kind.' She rooted around her handbag again and came out with another key. 'The key to his flat,' she said. 'His lawyer gave it to me in case I wanted to take anything. Too early for me to go there though. I can't face it at the moment. Maybe having a look there might help?'

McCoy took it. Looked at the paper label attached to it with string.

Lawson & Dobson, Solicitors
Alistair Drummond flat
14 Dolphin Road
Maxwell Park
Glasgow

McCoy looked back at her.

'I know. It was quite a surprise to me too. Last thing I knew he was renting a bedsit in Townhead, not a two-bedroom flat in one of the best areas of Glasgow.'

SEVENTEEN

Dolly McEwan, 31; Nicola McEwan, 6; Claire McEwan, 5; Anne Strang, 33; Carole Lownie, 20. McCoy pushed the files away from him, sat back in his chair and lit up. Realised Claire McEwan was staring up at him from her photograph. Looked like it had been taken at school. Bland light blue background and a wee girl with her hair in a ponytail smiling at the camera. He put a sheet of paper over it and she disappeared.

She was still alive, Claire. In the Royal. Not expected to live. The others had all died at the scene apart from Carole Lownie who died in the ambulance on the way to the hospital. McCoy wasn't sure what he would gain from reading the interim reports, but he'd thought he should and now he felt like shit. Nothing there that was going to help him, no clues as to why they had been killed, just the weight of carrying the information around with him now. But maybe he should have it sitting at the back of his mind. The ghosts of the dead urging him on to find out who'd killed them, and why.

Like the women in the Big Glen had said, they were just ordinary folk. Maybe it was all just a horrible accident and the boys had set fire to the place expecting no one to be there.

Maybe they didn't even know they'd killed anyone until they'd been arrested. Didn't make them any less guilty of their deaths but it was one way to explain what had happened.

He searched back in the files, found the photo of Dolly's Salon. It had been taken a couple of weeks ago at a re-opening party after it had been redecorated. The whole front of the shop was glass. Didn't seem possible they wouldn't have seen the people inside. Yet they'd still poured the petrol through the letterbox, set fire to a rag and pushed it in. Were halfway down the street when the shop exploded behind them.

McCoy rubbed at his eyes, looked at the clock on the wall. Half six. Almost time to go and meet Stevie. He wasn't getting anywhere with the salon fire. Didn't really know much more than he had yesterday. Three boys with no apparent connection set a fire, got arrested almost immediately, then were freed in a smash-and-grab raid. None of it made much sense. Stakes were all too high. He was missing something.

'You want a lift?' Wattie was putting his jacket on. 'Picture should run in all the papers tomorrow,' he said. 'Hopefully that'll give us something.'

'Right. Don't worry, I'll walk. Rain's off now.'

Wattie nodded, said he'd see him tomorrow. Picked up Faulds's report. He'd interviewed the prison van driver, seemed kosher. No real reason to believe he had anything to do with it. Same with the court officials. Mind you, it would be hard to prove they had. All the driver had to do was make sure he went the way he was supposed to, forget to double-lock the doors. All the official had to do was make one phone call: 'They're on their way.' They would be told not to spend any money for a couple of months, by which time no one would notice or care about the shiny new car in the driveway, or the tan from the holiday abroad.

McCoy couldn't bring himself to open the autopsy reports. That was more than he could deal with. He had just read the cause of death on the front page. Smoke inhalation. All the hairsprays and nail varnishes and bleaches going up would have made the air toxic in minutes. Had no idea how one wee girl was still alive. Maybe she'd been in the back. The fire hadn't got there so quickly.

He flicked through the files again. Stuart McEwan, aged 35, was now a widower with one dead daughter and probably a second very soon. A joiner. Arrested once for fighting when he was eighteen. A mass brawl outside the Glen in Auchinairn after an Old Firm match. Not exactly a hardened criminal. Apparently he hadn't left the wee girl's side, was sleeping next to her in the hospital. Poor bastard.

McCoy kept reading through the files. Stuart McEwan worked for McCauley Builders, out on a new site in Bishopbriggs. Did the fact he worked for McCauley's mean anything? Seemed a bit of a stretch, McCauley probably employed hundreds of joiners. McCoy turned the page and smiled. Hughie Faulds was ahead of him. McEwan had only worked there for two months, had never even met McCauley.

McCoy gathered the files up, stacked them in a pile. Whatever he was looking for, he wasn't going to find it in there. He looked at the clock. Ten to seven. Time to go. He stood up, put his jacket on, took a swig of the dreaded Pepto-Bismol and put the bottle in his pocket. He needed a drink and he was going to have one, no matter what his stomach said about it. Wouldn't sleep tonight if he didn't. All he would see were the faces of the women and the wee girls and he really didn't want that. He'd enough ghosts in his head, last thing he needed was more.

EIGHTEEN

Not only did the Muscular Arms have half a mad car coming through one of the walls, it had huge blown-up stills from old cowboy films on the walls, painted rainbows and clouds on the ceiling and a papier-mâché Oor Wullie sitting on his bucket. The clientele seemed split into two groups. Rich-looking thirty-year-olds with sharp suits or clingy dresses all drinking cocktails, or eighteen-year-olds nursing beers and dressed up like pop stars. No wonder Paul Cooper was hanging about in here. The fact there were lots of good-looking girls probably helped too.

The younger customers were doing their best to live up to the décor. Bowie boys in red brush cuts, girls in forties-style dresses, even a guy in a sailor top sitting in the corner winching a girl dressed like a Wren. Music was almost deafening, 'Virginia Plain' blasting out from a jukebox in the corner.

McCoy shouted over the bar, managed to get two cans of some American lager. Didn't serve draught. Had the feeling that as soon as Cooper heard that, they would be off somewhere else. Despite the strangeness of the place McCoy couldn't help smiling. At least it was something different. Better than the usual Glasgow pub full of miserable men knocking back pints and waiting for a fight to start.

He took a slug of his beer, ignored his stomach and found a table as far from the jukebox as possible. Was just lighting up when he realised someone was standing over him.

'What is this place?'

Cooper did not look happy. McCoy handed him the can as fast as he could and he sat down.

'Good, isn't it?' he said. 'Makes a change.'

Cooper didn't look convinced. Strange thing was he looked like he belonged, his usual James Dean get-up fitted right in. Looked like a regular. Albeit one that liked a fight.

'You seen him?' Cooper asked, looking round.

'No, just got here. You have a look around. I'm off for a pee.'

McCoy moved before Cooper could object, and headed for the toilets. The interior decoration kept going inside. The whole place – walls, floor, ceiling – was painted silver. It was empty but for a guy in an American ten-pin bowling shirt combing his quiff in the mirror above the sinks.

McCoy had just buttoned up his fly, was heading to the sinks to wash his hands, when two guys came out the cubicle, one wiping his nose, the other pushing some notes into the pocket of his jeans. He looked up, saw McCoy and grinned.

'Mr McCoy! Didn't think I'd see you in a place like this.'

McCoy shook his head. 'Spider bloody McKenzie. Funnily enough, this is exactly the kind of place where I thought I'd see you. How's it going?'

'Good.' Spider moved to the mirrors, adjusted his black and silver tie, fluffed up his blond feather cut. 'What can I interest you in, this fine evening? I've got black bombers, sulph, mandies, couple of tabs left—'

'Information,' said McCoy. 'You know this guy?' He got the photo strip out his pocket, handed it over. 'Guy in the bottom photo, blond hair.'

Spider took it, peered at it, handed it back. 'Paul Cooper. Aye, what about him?'

'You know the girl?'

Spider shook his head. Turned as the toilet door opened and a young guy with a Holy Fire T-shirt came in. 'Need to excuse me a minute,' he said. 'Work calls.'

Spider and the young guy disappeared into the cubicle and McCoy leant back on one of the sinks, waited for the deal to be done. Two minutes later the young guy emerged looking happy, Spider behind him.

'What did he buy?' asked McCoy.

'Speed,' said Spider. 'Want any?'

McCoy thought for a second. Said yes and Spider handed him a small cellophane bag of black pills. 'On the house.'

'You know where I can find him?' asked McCoy.

'Paul?' asked Spider. 'He's in here most Friday nights. Think he's staying up in the Red Road.'

'The Red Road?'

Spider nodded. 'Don't know if you know, but lately he's running with Dessie Caine's young lads. There's a flat they all share up there. If he's not there, they'll know where he is.'

McCoy thanked him, walked back into the pub. Music had changed to Mott the Hoople now, still as loud. Looked round, trying to see Cooper. Saw him sitting at a table under a picture of Mickey Mouse, two girls dressed as bobby-soxers, short skirts, ankle socks and gym shoes, chatting away next to him, can in each hand.

'Need to go,' said McCoy, approaching the table.

'Fuck sake! I'm just starting to enjoy myself,' said Cooper. 'Don't mind this place after all.'

'I know where Paul is. We need to go.'

Cooper sighed, stood up, said goodbye to the girls, and they walked out the pub onto West Nile Street. They lit up, looked about for a taxi.

'Where is the wee bugger?' Cooper asked.

'Red Road Flats,' said McCoy, waving at a taxi.

'Great,' said Cooper. 'Why'd he have to be away up there? Think we'll be back for closing time?'

'What? Want to get back to your new pals? If you hurry up and get your arse in gear, we might. Now, come on.'

NINETEEN

Red Road Flats consisted of eight huge blocks in Balornock. So tall you could see them from anywhere in the city. Home to five thousand or so people. When people first moved in, they loved it, glad to be away from derelict tenements with cold water and no indoor toilets. Bloom came off the rose pretty soon. Didn't take long to realise they were living in another kind of slum. Damp on the walls, broken lifts, no neighbours to chat to, everyone trapped behind their own front doors.

The taxi worked its way through the city heading north. City seemed quiet, rain back on, not many people about.

'What's he doing up there?'

'Staying with some other lads. Dessie Caine's lads,' said McCoy.

Cooper looked at him.

'It'll be fine. They're just young lads. Nothing for you to worry about.'

'It's not them I'm worried about, it's me.'

'Why? You can take care of yourself.'

'Because if one of them starts something, I'll have to finish it and that'll get back to Dessie and the whole fucking circus will start up and I haven't got the manpower for it.'

'Just keep calm,' said McCoy. 'It'll be fine. We've come to talk to Paul, that's it.'

'Easy for you to say,' mumbled Cooper.

The taxi stopped on Red Road and they stepped out into the drizzle. The flats loomed above them, lights from the windows shining out into the mist. Looked more like some kind of huge castle or prison block than a place people lived.

'What number?' asked Cooper.

McCoy nodded over at the Broomfield Tavern. 'That's what we're about to find out.'

The Broomie was a locals' pub. The only one near the flats. Could be violent if you were a local, definitely was if you weren't. Best thing was to get in and out, quick. The pub was long and low, white pebbledash and burgundy paintwork.

McCoy pulled open the door and they went in.

It was bright, striplights in the ceiling, bar at the right, seats at the left. Before they even made it to the bar McCoy saw a young guy in a denim jacket clock Cooper, face lit up as he hurried past them out the pub. No doubt on his way to spread the news. McCoy ordered them a couple of pints, glanced at a table by the door. Cooper was already in fight mode, hands by his sides in fists, eyes scanning the pub, that don't-fuck-with-me look on his face.

They sat down, backs to the wall, eyes on the entrance, and had a look around. The bar was lined with single guys nursing a pint, most wearing work clothes, boiler suits, painters' overalls. The seats seemed to be mainly reserved for couples and groups of women chatting away over gin and tonics and packets of crisps. The young team were by the toilets at the back. Group of twenty or so boys and girls in their late teens drinking pints, smoking away, waiting for their turns on the puggy or the pool table.

'Need to go and speak to them,' said McCoy. 'You okay to stay here?'

Cooper nodded. Eyes fixed on the door. Suddenly occurred to McCoy that he was probably carrying a knife. They really did need to get out of here quick. McCoy stood up, started walking towards the young team. A few elbows dug into each other, taps on shoulders, and by the time he got over to them they were all facing him. Waiting.

'Any of you know Paul Cooper?' he asked.

Silence.

Then a broad lad, leather jacket and a face full of acne stepped forward. 'Who wants to know?'

'Me,' said McCoy.

One of the girls laughed, quickly squashed it down.

'You want to fuck off?' asked the boy. 'Now's your chance. And I'm only going to ask once.'

McCoy sighed. Knew it wasn't going to be easy. Decided he was sick of wee boys playing hard. Speed from the bomber he'd swallowed in the taxi surged through his bloodstream.

'C'mere, you wee cunt,' he said. 'Now.'

The boy looked at him, wasn't expecting that. Right hand went into his jacket and McCoy flew at him, kicked him hard in the balls and once more in the stomach as he went down. He crumpled to the floor and McCoy was on him, knees on his shoulders.

'Where is he?' he asked. 'And that's the last time I ask nice.'

The boy's eyes were wild, looking round, realising his pals weren't going to come to his rescue. 'Tower four,' he managed to get out. 'Tenth floor, flat four.'

McCoy leant in, whispered in his ear. 'Now, me and my pal are going to finish our pints, and if I see any of your wee pals running off to tell him we're coming, I'll come back over and finish what I started. Got me?'

The boy nodded. McCoy let him go and stood up, walked back across the pub. Most people hadn't even noticed what had happened. Those who had had their faces down, didn't want to catch his eye.

'Did I just see what I thought I saw?' asked Cooper.

'He started it,' said McCoy. 'Tenth floor, tower four, flat four. Come on.'

Cooper shook his head. 'And I thought I was supposed to be the mental one.'

TWENTY

They came out the pub into a soft drizzle that made everything look smudged and out of focus. Walking towards the towers, there was no noise, just the distant traffic on Broomfield Road and a dog barking. Whole place felt eerie.

'Why do I feel like I've been dropped in behind enemy lines?' asked McCoy.

'Because you have,' said Cooper. 'So no more fucking wide stuff, keep yourself to yourself. I'll handle any bother.'

McCoy saluted. 'How come you and Dessie are at each other?'

'We're not,' said Cooper. 'If we were, I'd be lying on the ground with a knife coming out me by now. This is just business stuff. I'm on his turf and he'll want to know why. Just like I would if he was sniffing about Springburn. What tower was it again?'

'Four,' said McCoy. He was about to point to the high flat emerging from the gloom when they heard a shout.

'Cooper!'

They turned, and Tosh Burns, Dessie Caine's number two, was standing there, two big lads flanking him. Not that he really needed the support. Tosh was big enough and ugly enough to take care of himself and anyone else if the need arose.

'Tosh,' said Cooper evenly, hand on McCoy's arm to let him know he was going to deal with it.

'What you doing up this way, Cooper?' asked Tosh.

Cooper held his hand up. 'Just a wee visit, Tosh, means nothing. Be in and out in twenty minutes.'

'That's not what I asked,' said Tosh. 'I asked what you were doing here.' He came closer, peered at McCoy. 'That your wee polis pal you've got with you, is it? Should you no be out trying to find they three boys instead of following Cooper about?'

'Not my case,' said McCoy.

'Should be all your fucking cases if you ask me. Those boys need to get what they deserve.'

Cooper sighed. 'You got boys, Tosh? Sons?'

'Two,' said Tosh.

'Well, that's why I'm here. Need to speak to my boy, father to son. You understand that, eh? That's it, that's all I'm here for.'

Tosh looked at him, deciding. He'd been slashed a couple of times in his younger days, scars were faded now, almost hidden beneath the thick black stubble on his chin. Nodded. 'Be the fuck out of here in half an hour.'

Tosh and his boys disappeared back into the mist, orange streetlights lighting the way.

Tower four was one of the single blocks, twenty-four floors high. Walkway up to it took them through a kids' play park, past a few parked cars and what looked like the remains of someone's smashed-up kitchen piled by a wall. No people about, rain keeping them inside. Concierge was in his wee glass-walled office, surrounded by geranium plants, head down, paper spread out in front of him.

McCoy pressed the lift button and they watched the numbers descending. 'Think Tosh'll keep his word?'

'Soon find out if he doesn't,' said Cooper. 'Depends if he

finds out about your wee temper tantrum in the pub. What's up with you anyway?'

McCoy shrugged. 'Sometimes you've just had enough. Besides, what was I supposed to do? Wait until he got his blade out and get slashed?'

The lift doors opened, and they went in.

Wasn't any need to knock on the door of flat four. It was ajar and there was a smell of hash. 'Set The Controls For The Heart Of The Sun' blasting out. McCoy pushed the door open. The hall was dim, the only light coming from spluttering candles on the floor. McCoy tried the switch but there was no bulb, just an empty socket hanging down from the ceiling.

The living room, the source of the hash smoke and the music, was down the bottom of the hall. More candles. Two teenage boys sitting passing a joint, a girl who looked about fourteen asleep on a battered couch. Walls were covered in graffiti – YOUNG TEAM NO SURRENDER. Window at the back looking out over the lights of the city below.

The boys were so stoned it took them a minute to realise McCoy and Cooper were there. Cooper went over to the record player, kicked the arm off *A Saucerful Of Secrets*, and the room was suddenly quiet. One of the boys went to stand up. Took a look at the two men, sank back into the couch again.

'Looking for Paul Cooper,' said McCoy.

'You won't get any sense out of them,' said a young guy with red hair and a Simon shirt standing in the doorway. 'They've been smoking that shit since lunchtime.' He stepped forward. 'Name's Deke.'

'I'm McCoy,' said McCoy. 'This is—'

'I know who he is,' said Deke. 'Stevie Cooper.'

'We're looking for Paul,' said Cooper.

'Not the only one. He's no been here for three or four days. I cannae find him anywhere. Asked about, naebody seems to know where he is.'

'Any idea why he's disappeared?' asked McCoy.

Deke shook his head. 'Wish I bloody knew. Last time I saw him was Saturday. Said he was going into town, needed to see someone, and that was it. You want to see his room?'

McCoy nodded and they followed Deke into a bedroom next door. 'Bedroom' might have been pushing it. There was a mattress in the corner, with a couple of blankets over it. Beside that was an upturned cardboard box with a candle stub and a half-drunk bottle of Irn-Bru on top. Poster from *Dark Side Of The Moon* on the wall.

'Christ,' said Cooper. 'This it?'

Deke nodded.

McCoy sat down on the mattress, smell of unwashed bed clothes. There was another cardboard box at the end of the bed. McCoy had a root around in it. A pair of Levi's, socks and underpants, a copy of *Penthouse*, a picture in a broken frame. Looked like it had been taken at Christmas. People round a table, party hats on. He peered at it. Held it up to Cooper.

'That you?'

Cooper took it. Had a look. 'Aye. Never seen this before. That's in Ireland. My Aunty Cathy's.' Looked at McCoy. 'What's he got that for?'

'What do you think?' said McCoy. He stood up. There didn't seem to be anything here that would help them.

'We better go,' he said to Cooper. Turned to Deke. 'If Paul turns up, we need to talk to him. It's nothing bad, he's not in trouble, just need to talk to him, okay?'

'Okay.' Deke turned to Cooper. 'Can I speak to you a minute, Mr Cooper?'

'Stevie, it's past half an hour. We need—'

'I'll be two minutes. Off you go.'

McCoy left them there, Deke looking nervous, and took the lift back down. Had no idea what Deke wanted. Whatever it was, he wasn't telling him about it. McCoy stepped out the lift and into the foyer, concierge still reading his paper.

He peered out into the rainy night, couldn't see Tosh or his boys, hoped Cooper would hurry up. He got out his fags and lit up. He heard the lift ping and Cooper got out.

'Anyone around? Tosh?' he asked.

McCoy shook his head. 'Don't think so.'

A taxi drew up and two women slightly the worse for wear got out. McCoy flagged it and they got in.

'Good timing,' said Cooper.

McCoy told the driver to head back into town. Sat back in his seat. Listened to Cooper humming 'House Of The Rising Sun'. 'You want another drink?'

Cooper nodded. Speed needed calming down. He leant forward. 'Crownpoint Road.'

22nd May 1974

TWENTY-ONE

McCoy sat in the back of the panda car trying to decide whether a cigarette would make him feel better or worse. To his surprise, he didn't feel quite as bad as he thought he would. They'd stayed at the Shebeen until about one, McCoy alternating his drinks with mugs of milk. Seemed to have helped a bit. Stomach was only sore, not the expected agony.

He'd managed to persuade Cooper to have an ask about, see if anyone knew anything about the fire. He'd said no at first, no way was he acting as some kind of tout. But after McCoy had laid it on thick about the women and the wee girls and what had happened to them, he said he'd do it. Just this once.

The panda car turned into Cathedral Street. Drizzle still on, people huddled in bus shelters or making their way to work under umbrellas and raincoats. He'd been woken up at seven by somebody banging at the door. He'd got out of bed, realised he still had his vest and trousers on, and opened the door to see Smythe or Smith, whatever his name was, standing there. Look on his face showing exactly what he thought about people who weren't up and dressed by seven in the morning.

'Mr Murray sent me,' he said. 'Needs you right away.'

McCoy could tell something was up when they turned into Royston Road. A traffic policeman was diverting the traffic up by Charles Street, buses being stopped and the passengers ushered off. Soon saw what it was. Royston Road had been closed at Provanhill Street. Wooden trestles and ropes blocked the road. Two panda cars parked across the middle of the road just to make sure people got the message.

A line of people, some curious, some just trying to get to work, stretched across the road. Mounted policemen were keeping them back, their horses' breath clouding as they tossed their heads and pulled at the reins. McCoy could see the same set-up about five hundred yards up the road blocking anything coming the other way.

Smythe stopped the car. 'That's you, sir.'

'What's going on?'

'All I know is I was told to bring you here.'

McCoy stepped out the car. Could see a huddle up ahead. Murray, Phyllis the medical examiner, the police photographer, a couple of ambulancemen. A uniform stopped him at the barrier, said sorry after he saw his card. As he came through the cordon, Hughie Faulds turned away from the group, saw him and waved. Starting walking over to meet him.

'What's going on, Hughie?' asked McCoy. 'No expense spared by the look of things.'

'It's a body,' said Faulds in his broad Belfast accent. 'Knowing what you're like, you'd better stay back, Harry. It's bloody gruesome.'

McCoy's stomach lurched. He never had been good with the sight of blood and it seemed to be getting worse as he got older.

'Don't think I'm allowed,' said McCoy. 'Murray sent a car for me.'

'Okay, well, don't say I didn't warn you.'

They walked over to the group, and as they got closer McCoy could see what looked like an arm and the side of someone's body through everyone's legs. Felt his pace slowing, couldn't help himself.

'McCoy!' shouted Murray. 'There you are. Get over here.'

Wasn't much he could do, just had to hope for the best. He moved in, kept his eyes up and away from whatever was on the ground. Could see people hanging out the windows of the flats above the wee row of shops. Faces white, whispering to each other. He pushed in beside Murray and realised they were standing in front of the burnt-out façade of Dolly's Salon. He felt Phyllis take his arm. She whispered, 'Just breathe,' in his ear and he looked down.

A young man was lying on the road. He was naked apart from one sock and shoe and a pair of blue underpants. His face was battered and broken, nose flat to his face, one eye socket crushed and empty. Hair was thick with dried blood from various cuts and hacks on his scalp. McCoy made himself keep looking, tried to breathe slowly through his nose.

The body was mapped with more cuts, what looked like cigarette burns, stab wounds and a large red patch on his side where his skin had been cut off. His blue underpants were almost totally black with dried blood. One of his knees was crushed completely, flattened, a bone sticking out. Beside the body there was a bit of white cardboard, marked with black felt pen: *One down, two to go. Justice for the victims. Exodus 21:25.*

Next to the cardboard note, there was a cassette tape in a clear box. Yellow, BASF C60 printed on it.

McCoy forced himself to take another look at the boy, made sure he looked from head to toe and tried to take it all in because he knew he wasn't going to look again. He turned away and went to sit on the kerb opposite the shop. He took his cigarettes out, put one in his mouth and tried to light it, but his hands were shaking too much.

'Here.' Faulds held a lighter in front of him. McCoy lit up, drew the smoke deep into his lungs. Faulds sat down beside him, put his lighter back in his pocket. 'You okay?'

'Think so,' said McCoy. 'What happened?'

'Got a call about half six. Guy that owns the newsagent along the road was opening up, saw a car stop outside the hairdresser's. Two guys got out, got the body out the boot and dumped it in the street, left the message and drove off.'

'Did he see them?'

Faulds shook his head. 'Was too fast,' he said. 'Saw a red car. That was all he could really be sure of.'

'I'm assuming it's one of the boys. The salon boys?' said McCoy.

'We think it's Colin Turnbull but not confirmed yet. Need to get fingerprints or get his foster parents to do an ID, but I'd rather spare them that.'

'So whoever took the boys wasn't interested in rescuing them,' said McCoy. 'We got it wrong.'

Faulds nodded. 'The opposite. Wanted to get them so they could do that to them. Make their last hours agony, then kill them. Some kind of revenge thing.'

'Are there people like that?' asked McCoy. 'Vigilantes? I thought that was only in the Westerns.'

'Don't know,' said Faulds. 'I do know one thing from Belfast though. Never be surprised what ordinary people will do to each other.'

'What is Exodus whatever it was?'

'Exodus 21:25. It's the eye-for-an-eye one. That verse is "burning for burning, wound for wound, stripe for stripe".' Faulds smiled. 'Having a Baptist minister for a father finally came in useful.'

'What happened to him exactly?' asked McCoy.

Faulds sighed. 'You know Phyllis – won't be drawn until she's done the autopsy. Looks like he's been beaten and stabbed.

Burned. Tortured. Not sure I want to know what happened with the missing skin on his side.'

McCoy's stomach lurched again, tried to breathe it out.

'Think the cause of death was probably the two knife wounds in the chest. How much of the other stuff happened before or after that is down to Phyllis.'

'Christ,' said McCoy. 'What about the other two?'

'One down, two to go, according to the note. Looks like what happened to him is going to happen to the others. God help them, no matter what they did.'

'Unless we find them first,' said McCoy.

Faulds stood up. 'There's people in this town that won't want us to find them. Plenty will be happy with what's happened. Will think they deserved everything they got. Not going to be easy. And this is going to make it a hell of a lot harder. People that know something might not come forward now. Scared the same thing will happen to them if they do.'

'Or maybe just say nothing, wait until the three boys are dead. You saw all those people outside the court, the signs, the expression on their faces. If one of them or someone like them knows anything, they're just going to sit tight, rub their hands and wait for justice to be done. An eye for an eye.'

Faulds nodded. 'Better get back.'

He stood up and walked towards the group around the body. McCoy watched him go. Couldn't believe it. They'd all got it wrong. Taking the boys from the police van wasn't a rescue. It was a kidnap. They could take their pick from all the villains and all the vigilantes in Glasgow. There wasn't one of them who didn't want those boys dead. A difficult case had just got a hundred times worse.

TWENTY-TWO

McCoy, Murray and Faulds stood in the interview room staring at the cassette player on the table. It was a wee thing, the kind people had in their houses for taping songs off the radio. A rectangle with buttons along the bottom, space for the cassette and a speaker. Philips logo in silver plastic.

'You know how to work it?' asked Murray.

Faulds nodded. 'The kids have got one.' He put on a pair of disposable gloves, took the tape box from the evidence bag, got the yellow cassette out and put it in the machine. 'Ready?'

McCoy had never felt less ready for anything in his life.

Faulds pressed *play*. Loud click echoing in the empty room.

Nothing for a couple of seconds, just tape hiss and the little wheels turning round. Suddenly the sound changed, and they could hear noises in the background, shuffling, someone breathing. Then a voice. Glaswegian. Rough.

'Say it, you wee prick.'

Nothing. Then what sounded like a chair being pushed back. Someone being slapped, a moan. Then a different voice. Younger. Scared.

'Please, please, I'm sorry, I'm sorry, I didn't kn—'

Another slap. Harder. A moan.

McCoy winced, looked at Faulds. Knew it was only going to get worse.

'Fucking say it.'

McCoy tried to hear an accent, anything that would give them a clue, but it just sounded like every other Glaswegian man.

'My name is Colin Turnbull. I am . . .'

The voice dissolved. Another slap. A cry. Someone in the background saying what sounded like 'just fucking hit him'.

'Please, I'm sorry. I am sorry, please, I'll do anything. I don't want you to do that. Can I just ask you to stop, please, please. I'm sorry, please, I don't—'

The noise of something heavy hitting flesh. Another cry. And another.

'Fuck sake,' said Murray. 'This is hellish.'

'Sorry, please stop, please, please, I'll say it! I'll say it!'

A pause, someone trying to talk through sobs.

'My name is Colin Turnbull. I set the fire—' Sobs took over. 'I set the fire at the . . . Wait! What's that? Please. Please don't. Please put that away. I'm sorry. I'm very sorry. I'm s—'

A scream. The worst scream McCoy had ever heard.

A click on the tape. Silence for a few seconds then the sound of people breathing. Someone sobbing.

'Ready?'

A pause. Voice not much more than a whisper.

'My name is Colin Turnbull. I set the fire at the salon with Danny Walsh and Malcolm McCauley. May God forgive—'

Another click and then silence.

McCoy pulled out a chair and sat down. Put his head in his hands. Was trying hard not to pass out, felt dizzy, too much saliva in his mouth.

Faulds took the tape out the machine, put it back in its case.

Took his gloves off, sat down beside McCoy, got his cigarettes out.

Murray was leaning against the wall of the interview room. McCoy had never seen him so white. He was staring into space, hands patting his pockets looking for his pipe. 'I'll make sure someone listens to the whole thing again, just in case there's more.'

McCoy said what they were all thinking. 'One down, two to go.'

Murray sat down at the table, looked across at the two of them. 'Listen to me. That is not going to fucking happen. I'm not having another boy tortured to death on my watch, no matter what he's done. We're going to stop this now. Faulds, get back to the crime scene, get the door-to-doors started. Someone must have seen that car and the two men. McCoy, find out if there's anything we can pick up from the tape that'll tell us where it happened. Try out technical guys. If they're no use, try the university. Find someone that can make it clearer. How are you getting on with the lowlife?'

'Should have something by tonight,' he said, hoping Cooper would come through.

Murray nodded. 'Faulds, once you've got the interviews started, pick me up at Stewart Street.'

'Where are we going?'

'Pitt Street. I've got a horrible feeling this won't be the only copy of the tape.'

'Press?' asked McCoy.

'If they get hold of it, all hell will break loose. Need to be ahead of the game. And, McCoy? None of your shite. We don't have time for it. You say you're well enough to work, so bloody show me you are. I need you to make sure the body gets over to Phyllis soon as it can. See if she can find anything that'll tell us where it happened, and if I hear you're hanging about outside the morgue too scared to go in, you're out on your ear. No excuses. Got me?'

McCoy nodded.

'Good. Remember. This can't happen again. We're not going to let it.' He stood up. 'Let's go.'

TWENTY-THREE

'He phoned you?' asked McCoy, hardly believing it.

Phyllis finished washing her hands in the big sluice. Started putting on her gloves. 'He's got a point, you know. Being scared of blood is not ideal in your profession.'

'I know,' said McCoy. 'But fuck sake, you saw the body!'

'Sadly I did. Tell you what,' she said. 'You can sit in the corner so you don't have to look, just listen. How's that?'

'I owe you,' said McCoy. 'Big time.'

McCoy pushed the chair into the furthest corner of the examination room and sat down, watched Phyllis and her assistant prep the body. Tried not to think about what the boy had gone through. Was still thinking about what they'd heard on the tape. Wondered if the other two knew what was going to happen to them if McCoy didn't find them in time.

'Subject is male. Five foot eleven. Weight is eleven stone and three pounds. Age eighteen. Apart from the obvious injuries he seems to have been quite healthy, no indications of . . .'

His mind drifted off as Phyllis ran through the basics. Suddenly thought. 'Phyllis, do you know anyone who works with cassette tapes, sound recordings, that sort of thing? Maybe someone at the university?'

Phyllis stopped, scalpel in hand. 'Not that I can think of. The facilities didn't mix much. Not a lot of crossover. You would need someone who studied . . .' She stopped. 'Hang on. Maybe Moira Banks.'

'Who's that?'

'She went to Park School with me. She was a nice girl, if a bit eccentric. She works at the BBC now. Does something with recording sound for the news, I think. If she doesn't, she should know someone who will. Looking for someone to enhance the tape?'

McCoy nodded.

'What was on it?'

McCoy looked over at Turnbull. 'Him. Confessing. And getting tortured.'

'Ah,' said Phyllis. 'Wish I hadn't asked. Did he do it? Set fire to the salon?'

McCoy shrugged. 'Probably. It's why that's the question. The BBC in Queen Margaret Drive?'

'Yes. I'll tell you what. I've still got quite a bit of preparation to do. Won't be able to tell you much for a couple of hours. Not much point you sitting here when you could be at the BBC.' She looked at the clock. 'Be back here at two and no one will know you've gone. If Mr Murray calls, I'll say you popped out for a smoke then start asking him where he wants to go for dinner tonight. Should put him off.'

McCoy stood up, headed for the door.

'Two o'clock,' she shouted after him. 'No later!'

*

He made it back for quarter to two. Phyllis was washing her hands in the sluice when he walked into the examination room. Colin Turnbull lay on a trolley, dark green sheet over him.

· 115 ·

'You weren't bloody joking,' said McCoy.

'About what?' asked Phyllis, turning around.

'Your pal. She wasn't just eccentric, she was howling at the moon.'

'Yes, she always was a bit of an oddball. She used to refuse to look at the teachers if they spoke to her. I haven't seen her for a few years to be honest with you. Had the feeling she might have got worse.'

'You're not wrong. She lives in a wee tucked-away studio. Had to ask about five people before anyone knew who I was talking about. Then I had to write down what I wanted on a notepad, wasn't allowed to just tell her. She disappeared into her studio with the cassette and came out about twenty minutes later, handed me it and an envelope.'

'Ah,' said Phyllis. 'She definitely seems worse. Was she any help?'

McCoy dug in in his pocket and brought out a bit of paper. Started reading.

Length of first recording one minute and forty-six seconds. Length of second recording two minutes and eleven seconds. Two primary voices. Voice A, the one asking the questions, is approximately thirty to forty years old, brought up in Glasgow, the north most likely. Voice B, the one answering, is younger, late teens or early twenties. Accent harder to identify, seems to have been brought up in various places in the Central Belt.

'My goodness,' said Phyllis. 'She seems to know her stuff.'

'Next bit is a transcript with annotations. Do you want to hear it?'

Phyllis shook her head. 'Not really, but I suppose I should.' McCoy nodded. Started to read.

Microphone seems to be indoors, echo indicates a large room or hall. Likely on a table between the two main subjects. Sounds of breathing. Provisional thought is three to four people present. A cough from someone further away from the microphone. Traces of low-level traffic noise.

Voice A says, 'Say it, you wee prick.'

Chair being pushed back. Sound of someone being slapped on head or face. Voice B moans, 'Please, please, I'm sorry, I'm sorry, I didn't kn—'

Cut short by the sound of another slap, harder this time. Another moan from Voice B. Seems to be in more pain.

Voice A says, 'Fucking say it.'

Voice is threatening. Definitely North Glasgow. Working-class. In the far background there is the sound of air brakes. A lorry or large van.

Voice B says, 'My name is Colin Turnbull. I am . . .'

He becomes overtaken by sobs. Another slap. Very hard this time. Voice B starts to cry. A background voice says, 'Just fucking hit him.' Chairs being moved back against a wooden floor. Noise of a blow. Likely to be something heavy. Iron bar or wooden stave against flesh. Three more blows, a cry after each one. Very faint noise of an ambulance going by outside.

Voice B says, 'Please, I'm sorry. I am sorry, please, I'll do anything. I don't want you to do that. Can I just ask you to stop, please, please. I'm sorry, please, I don't—'

Voice B interrupted by what sounds like more blows. He screams, starts to talk again. 'Sorry, please stop, please, please, I'll say it! I'll say it!'

At this point his voice has become high-pitched, with an element of panic in it. Faint noise of a door opening, very faint noise of a tap running.

Voice B says, 'My name is Colin Turnbull. I set the fire—'
Sobbing.

'I set the fire at the . . . Wait! What's that? Please. Please don't. Please put that away. I'm sorry. I'm very sorry. I'm s—'

Voice B stops abruptly, starts to scream. What sounds like the noise of a large knife being sharpened against a stone. Noise of air brakes again.

Tape is stopped. Forty-six seconds later it is restarted. No reason to believe area where microphone is situated has changed. Sounds of breathing. Approx. five or six people. Quiet sobbing, presumably from Voice B.

Voice A says, 'Ready?'

After a five-second pause, Voice B says, 'My name is Colin Turnbull. I set the fire at the salon with Danny Walsh and Malcolm McCauley. May God forgive—'

Tape finishes.

McCoy looked up. Phyllis, wiping her eyes, turned away quickly.

'Sorry. Should have warned you. It's grim stuff.'

Phyllis blew her nose, turned back to McCoy. 'Does all that help?'

'Maybe,' he said. 'Tells us more than we knew before.' McCoy looked over at the body under the sheet. 'How did you get on?'

'Probably going to tell you what you already know. He died of two deep stab wounds to the heart, inflicted very closely together. Unfortunately, all his other injuries took place before that. He has gouges and cuts to his scalp. Extensive bruising over sixty per cent of his body caused, as Moira said, by a heavy object. Numerous burns from cigarettes. A lighter, or some sort of flame, seems to have been held to his penis at one point. One of the blows he received ruptured his spleen. If the knife wounds hadn't killed him, that would have. His left knee was crushed. It looks like a very heavy object, a concrete block going by the dust in the wound, was dropped on it repeatedly. Superficial knife wounds an inch or so deep on his chest and torso.'

'Christ,' said McCoy. 'What didn't they do to him?'

'Not much. Whoever it was seemed determined to cause him as much pain as possible before his death. The poor boy must have been in absolute agony. And terrified, absolutely terrified.'

'What about the . . .' McCoy pointed to the boy's side.

'I'd hoped you weren't going to ask about that,' said Phyllis. 'They seem to have removed a patch of his skin approximately four inches square, using a straight sharp blade.'

'A knife?'

Phyllis shook her head. 'I suspect it was something more like a potato peeler.'

'Fuck sake,' said McCoy, wave of nausea hitting him.

'As I said, they were intent on inflicting as much pain as possible. There was also a large amount of salt in and surrounding the wound. Looks like they rubbed it in. Literally.'

McCoy sat back in his chair, tried to breathe slowly. Could feel his stomach doubling over itself.

'You okay?'

He nodded. 'Yep.' Lied. 'Anything on the body to tell us where this happened?'

'Not so far. There was some matter on the bottom of his shoe. I'll send that off to be analysed. There was blood under his fingernails but I suspect that will all be his own. Didn't look to be anything unusual on the underpants or sock. Hair is full of dust and fibres, as if he's been lying on a carpet or been wrapped up in one at some point. We'll do what we can do but I wouldn't hold your breath.'

McCoy said goodbye to Phyllis and stepped out the door of the morgue onto the Saltmarket. Rain had stopped, was even a rainbow in the sky over Glasgow Green. Wondered what the last thing Colin Turnbull had seen was. The faces of his torturers? The lights in the ceiling as he lay dying? Whatever it had been, it was nothing a eighteen-year-old boy should have to see, no matter what he had done. Could only hope they would find the other two before they had to look at the same thing.

TWENTY-FOUR

McCoy had never seen the station so busy. The usual cloud of cigarette smoke was thicker than ever, didn't even need to light up, could just breathe it in. All the Stewart Street lads were gathered on one side of the room, the Tobago Street lads on the other. Both sides looking shifty, sticking to themselves. All of them waiting for Murray to come and put them out their misery.

'It's like being back at school doing Scottish country dancing,' said Wattie. 'Boys one side, girls the other.'

'Anything happen with the picture of the girl in the paper?'

Wattie shook his head. 'Not yet. It's like she never existed. You have any luck finding Cooper Junior?'

'Nope. He's done a runner from his flat.'

'Christ, we're doing well. Any idea what we do next? Maybe we—'

'Gents.'

Murray had come to stand at the far end of the office, Faulds at his side. Murray looked round the room, made sure everyone was quiet, all attention on him. He started talking slowly and deliberately, wanted every word to be understood.

'This morning the body of Colin Turnbull was dumped in the street outside Dolly's Salon on Royston Road. He had been severely tortured, kept alive so he could suffer, before being killed by two knife wounds to the heart. As you know, he was one of the three boys charged with the murder of the women and girls at the salon. With him was a note saying, "One down, two to go". I don't have to tell you what that means.'

He stopped, let it sink in.

'Vigilantism is never acceptable. It's part of the very reason we have a police force, the reason why we strive to do our jobs to the best of our abilities. Vigilantism is just mob rule. People with no authority deciding to set themselves up as judge, jury and executioner. Whoever did this to Colin Turnbull may try to use retribution as an excuse or a reason but it's not. What happened to Colin Turnbull is murder, plain and simple. And it's up to us to stop it happening again. As of today, we—'

Murray stopped, stared at the Tobago Street side of the room. Pointed. 'You,' he said. 'What did you just say?'

The whole room turned to look.

'Who's he talking to?' asked McCoy, trying to see.

'Alec Stones,' said Wattie. 'Detective at Tobago Street. A wanker's wanker.'

Stones, an untidy-looking guy in a white shirt with faint brown sweat stains under the armpits, shook his head.

'I asked you what you fucking said, officer,' said Murray, voice slow and menacing. 'Answer me.'

Stones stood up. Looked belligerent. 'Just said what we're all thinking. That wee bastard deserved it.'

There was silence, everyone's eyes on Murray. The terrible thing was that what Stones said had a grain of truth in it, as far as McCoy was concerned. He knew that at least half the coppers in the room felt the same. Justice was being done. An eye for an eye. Who cared how it came about?

'Anyone else feel like Mr Stones?' asked Murray, looking round.

Low murmurs. Two other guys from Tobago Street stood up. Dunbar and some guy whose name McCoy couldn't remember.

'You've seen the pictures, they women and they wee lassies,' said Dunbar. 'And we're supposed to feel sorry for the wee fucker who did it? Far as I'm concerned whoever did him over did us a favour.'

Murray nodded. Even from the back of the room McCoy could see his ears going red. Knew what that meant. An explosion. But it was worse. Murray was too angry to even shout.

He spoke quietly, trying to restrain himself. 'You three excuses for police officers get the fuck out this office before I do something I shouldn't. Don't bother coming in tomorrow. You're fired. And if you're still in this station when I finish this briefing, I won't be held responsible for what I'll do to you.'

The room was still, everyone tense, waiting.

Then Murray roared, 'Are you fucking deaf? Now, I said!'

The three of them hustled out, Stones trying to look defiant, the other two just shell-shocked.

'Anyone else want to join them?' He looked at every individual in the room, made sure he caught their eye. 'Now, if I hear anything like that from any of you at any time on this investigation, you'll be gone. The motto of this police force is "Semper Vigilo" – Always Vigilant – and that is what we do. Irrespective of who those people are and what they may or may not have done, we keep people safe. That's our job. It's not for us to decide who is guilty and who is innocent. That's the job of the judiciary. We leave that up to them. Understand?'

A few mumbles of 'yes'.

'I said, do you understand?'

A chorus of 'yes, sir'.

'Right. Let's get on with our fucking jobs. We need to find those boys as quickly as possible. Faulds here is going to take you through how we're going to do that and how the work will be divided. I'm going to say one final thing. Whoever did this to Colin Turnbull is going to pay for it. No one is getting away with cold-blooded murder on our patch. Don't let me down.'

And with that, Murray exited the room. Faulds took over, left with the task of telling everyone what they were supposed to be doing, and who with. Didn't take long for McCoy to drift off as Faulds ran through everyone's assignments. McCoy was pinning all his hopes on Cooper, was all he had to contribute. Wasn't going to see him until this evening, which left this afternoon to worry about Wattie's case and the girl. Only real lead they had about who she was was Paul Cooper, and nobody had any idea where he had disappeared to.

Kids disappeared all the time in Glasgow. Ran away from home to the big city or from Borstal or from wherever they didn't want to be, had to go somewhere. He tried to remember some of the stories from when he was in the home. They were probably out of date by now but the same principle applied. Teenage kids with no money and nowhere to go only had one thing that was of any value. Themselves.

Realised Faulds was winding up his briefing. Nudged a half-asleep Wattie. 'Come on, you. We need to get to Paddy's Market.'

TWENTY-FIVE

'Do you think there are rats round here?' asked Wattie.

'This near the river? Absolutely.' McCoy realised Wattie was looking glum. 'You're not worried about rats, are you? You must have seen plenty of them when you were doing beat duty?'

'They were Greenock rats though. Different thing. They eat grain and stuff like that.'

McCoy looked at him. 'Sometimes you amaze me, Wattie. And sometimes I think you're just two pennies short of a shilling.'

They were at Paddy's Market. Not at the market itself, but right up the back where the stall holders stored their stock. If the smell at the outdoor part was distinctive, way back here, deep under the railway arches, you could just about taste it. Old clothes that hadn't been washed, the smell of stale fat used to fry dodgy burgers, and the walls wet from leakage from the river.

McCoy dug in his pocket for the key to Dirty Ally's cupboard.

'What are we looking for exactly?'

'Fucking thing,' said McCoy. Couldn't get the key to turn in the lock of the big wooden cupboard. Was scared to push it in too hard in case it snapped in the lock. Tried again. 'Fucking fucker.'

'Jesus Christ!' said Wattie. 'Give it to me before you break the bloody thing.'

McCoy handed the key over and sat down on a metal office chair with a ripped foam seat. Had a look around. Piles of junk everywhere: old bikes, car engine parts, boxes of 'Quality Dog Food'. A pile of cardboard boxes full of Vim sink cleaner sat beside him. By the look of the labels, they had been manufactured in the fifties. Probably been dumped there then and never looked at again. Least he knew now where to hide the body if he ever killed someone.

'You listen to the tape?'

'Nope,' said Wattie. 'I couldn't face it. I read the transcript that the woman from the university did though. Poor bastard.'

'Any idea where it could have taken place?'

'Could be anywhere,' said Wattie, fiddling with the key. 'Traffic in the background, people breathing, not much to go on. There you go.' He pulled the door open. 'Fuck me.'

They were looking at piles and piles of scud mags. Must have been thousands of them. Each cover more lurid than the one before.

Wattie pulled one out. *New Swedish Erotica*. Had a flick through. 'Is this stuff legal?'

'Not sure,' said McCoy. 'Anyway, that's the vice squad's problem, not ours. We're looking for photo sets. The home-made stuff.'

'That what turns you on, is it?' asked Wattie.

McCoy ignored him and pulled a cardboard box down from the top shelf. Put it down on the chair. 'Think this is what we want,' he said.

The box was full of brown hardback envelopes. He picked one out. 'Lusty Wives' written on it in ballpoint pen. Inside were a dozen black-and-white photos of a middle-aged woman at the beach, legs akimbo, wearing nothing but a smile and a black lacy bra. Next one was entitled 'Naughty Schoolgirl Gets The Cane'. It was exactly what McCoy imagined it would be. Girl looked about the same age as the girl in the graveyard, but it wasn't her.

'You really think this is what happens to kids with nowhere else to go?' said Wattie. 'End up letting dirty old men take their pictures?'

McCoy nodded. 'No other way to earn money.'

'Come on, there's lots of other ways,' said Wattie.

McCoy looked at him. 'That right? Know much about being a thirteen-year-old kid on the streets with nothing and nobody, do you? No money, not even any food or anywhere to stay the night? What were you doing when you were thirteen? Going to school, having your dinner, worrying if Mary in the maths class liked you?'

'All right, all right. What's up with you?'

'Nothing. Keep looking,' said McCoy, handing him a pile of photo sets.

Wattie started looking through them, kept quiet. McCoy did the same. Trying to keep the peace.

'If I say this, don't go mental,' said Wattie. 'You gave me a row the other day for automatically thinking the girl in Sighthill Cemetery was a working girl. You don't think you're being just as bad?'

'What?' asked McCoy, starting to get angry. 'What do you mean?'

Wattie looked at him nervously. 'Well. You grew up in a certain way, children's homes and that. Lot of kids there end up in bad situations. Maybe that makes you always think the worst things that can happen to people always do. That they'll end up in Blythswood Square or in these bloody photos. I don't think that's always what happens to runaway kids. Most of them end up going home after a while or just getting a job in a different town.'

McCoy put the box down, sat on the chair. Maybe he was as closed-minded as the rest of the polis in Glasgow, just in a different way. Had never really thought about it.

'Let's say you've got a point,' he said. 'And I'm not saying you have, but if you were a runaway, what would you do?'

'I'd try and get a job. Any kind of job. Potman in a bar, picking up stock at the fruit market, sell papers, that sort of thing. Maybe join the army.'

'And if you were a girl?'

'Maybe work in a shop, waitress in a cafe, a baker's, something like that.'

McCoy took his cigarettes out, lit up. Smell of the market was starting to get to him. 'Wouldn't someone miss you if you disappeared from a job like that, call the polis?'

'Not necessarily,' said Wattie, picking up another pile of buff envelopes. 'You've run away once, maybe they'd just think you'd done it again.'

McCoy looked at him.

'What?'

'Nothing,' said McCoy. 'Just wondering how someone so stupid-looking could suddenly say something that made sense. You're right. But we're here now so just indulge me and let's look at all these bloody photos, eh?'

Half an hour later the box was empty. McCoy sighed, started gathering up the envelopes.

Wattie sat on the chair and watched him. 'Don't think I've ever seen so many candlewick bedspreads in my life. Not sure I'll ever look at a cucumber the same way again either.'

'But no girl from Sighthill,' said McCoy.

'Nope,' said Wattie. Looked at McCoy.

'You're going to make me say it, aren't you?'

'Too right.'

'I was wrong. You were right. That's us even. Happy?'

'Yep,' said Wattie. 'Let's get out of here. Smell of this place is giving me the boak.'

McCoy agreed, put the box back in the cupboard, and locked it. They started walking through the boarded-up stalls and the storage boxes heading for the outside and the fresh air. Was only when they stepped out into the light that McCoy noticed the magazine in Wattie's back pocket.

'What have you got that for?'

'What do you think?' said Wattie.

'Dirty bugger.'

'I wish,' said Wattie. 'Between a teething baby keeping me up all night and a hormonal wife who works all the bloody time, this magazine's going to be the closest I'll get to a sex life in the next few weeks.' He yawned, stretched. 'Where you off to now?'

'Going to see Stevie Cooper, see if he's found anything out about the fire.'

'Let's hope so. I'm away home. I'll see you tomorrow.'

'Magazine burning a hole in your pocket, is it?'

Wattie grinned. 'If I leave now, I'll get home a good twenty minutes before the wife and the wee man. More than enough time.'

TWENTY-SIX

McCoy sat in a deckchair at the side of the pool watching Cooper power his way up and down. He'd stopped counting how many lengths he'd done at twenty, must be on thirty-odd by now. McCoy pulled at his tie, undid his top button. Atmosphere was hot and humid, stink of chlorine and bleach. The rain was drumming on the row of skylights above the pool, and it made him think of the one holiday he could remember being on when he was wee. A caravan in Arbroath for the weekend. Rained every day.

Arlington Baths was in Woodlands, mostly full of old boys in the sunroom reading the paper. Retired professors and doctors, this was a private club after all. God knows how Cooper had managed to wangle a membership. Better not to ask.

'Fifty!' Cooper pulled himself out the pool, breathing hard. He walked over, towel in hand. 'I try and do fifty a day,' he said. 'Good exercise.'

McCoy nodded. Noticed a new addition to Cooper's collection of scars. Pointed. 'What's that?'

Cooper looked down at his torso. There was a cut, stitches still in, stretching up out his swimming trunks. 'My business,' he said.

McCoy shrugged, stood up. 'You find anything out about the fire?'

Cooper rubbed at his hair with the towel. 'Might have, might not. We'll have to see. Need to go to the Bells and find out.'

An hour later McCoy was sheltering in the entranceway to the Bells watching the rain fall. Water from a blocked drain was gushing like a river down the middle of Springburn Road, wobbly reflections of streetlights and shop signs shining up at him. McCoy had to confess he was quite enjoying the downpour. He liked it when the weather was something – torrential rain, snow, a heatwave. Was better than the usual dull Glasgow drizzle.

He'd come out the pub to get some fresh air. The fact he hadn't really drunk anything for a month was hitting him hard. Two pints of Guinness and he was half cut. Stomach seemed to be behaving itself so far, just the occasional grumble.

He could see Jumbo sitting in the driver's seat of a Zephyr parked across the road. Must be reading something, head was down, mouthing the words. Couldn't imagine Jumbo had a driver's licence but that wouldn't matter much to Cooper. He'd run them both up from the baths, driven well enough. At least Cooper was smart enough to have someone with him all the time now. He was getting to the age and status where some up-and-coming wide boy might have a go, try and make his mark. He knew Cooper could take care of himself, but he was glad he had the build of a Jumbo to back him up. Might help if he was looking around for them rather than reading a comic though.

He was just about to open the pub door and go back in when it swung open and the man himself was standing there.

'What the fuck are you doing out here?' he asked.

'Nothing,' said McCoy. 'Just getting a bit of fresh air. That okay with you?'

'Christ, that ulcer's changed you, McCoy,' said Cooper. 'Got any fags?'

McCoy gave him one.

Cooper dug in his pocket and got his lighter out, was just raising it up to his mouth when he stopped, took the cigarette out his mouth. 'All right, Deke?'

McCoy looked up, and the boy from the Red Road Flats edged into the doorway beside them.

'It's like a bloody monsoon,' Deke said. 'Never seen anything like it.'

'Is this who we were waiting for?' asked McCoy.

'New recruit,' said Cooper. Seeing McCoy's puzzlement, he added, 'Need to build things up again.'

'So that's what you stayed behind for the other night?' asked McCoy.

Deke grinned. 'Made him an offer he couldn't refuse.'

McCoy smiled, not sure poaching one of Dessie Caine's young lads was Cooper's best idea, but he'd done it now.

Cooper flicked his cigarette into the gutter, and it was immediately whisked away on the stream of water. 'Let's get a drink and see what Deke here's got to say for himself.'

Back inside the Bells, McCoy and Cooper sat down and Deke went up to get the drinks. McCoy watched him go, supposed Cooper had a point. He was young, seemed capable, obviously wanted to move on. And Cooper needed someone to replace Billy.

'How's Jumbo taking to the new recruit?'

'Deke bought him two *Commando* comics he didn't have. Jumbo was made up. He's his best pal now.'

Deke appeared with the drinks and sat down. 'Dessie Caine owns Dolly's Salon,' he said. 'He's nowhere on the books but it's his all right.'

'You sure?' asked McCoy, surprised. 'I didn't know that.'

'Nobody does. Owns most of that strip in Royston. The

butcher's. The fruit shop. Only place he doesn't own is the Galbraith's.'

It was all starting to make sense to McCoy.

'So that's why the salon got torched then? Johnny Smart did it?'

'That's your job to find out, not mine,' said Cooper. 'Him and Johnny Smart have been firing guns across each other's bows for a month or so. Looks like Johnny decided to up the ante. And you know what Johnny's like.'

'A nutter,' said McCoy.

'That's one word for him,' said Cooper. 'He's a piece of work, Johnny Smart. Soon as he gets angry, all bets are off, you've no idea what he'll do. Looks all nice and respectable with his suits on, but I've seen him slice someone's ear off, stuff it in the guy's mouth and make him eat it.'

'Lovely,' said McCoy. 'But would he up the ante that much? Four people dead. That's a big up.'

'I told you. Nothing about Johnny Smart would surprise me.'

'Dessie's not that much better. He's not going to let this go unanswered, is he?'

Deke shook his head. 'Wouldn't think so.'

'Christ, if those two really go at each other all hell will break loose. It'll be a war.' Realised Cooper didn't look that interested. 'You not bothered?'

'Me?' asked Cooper, putting his pint down. 'Why would I be? If the two of them start knocking fuck out each other, then it's all the better for me.'

McCoy sat back, watched as Cooper and Deke got up to play the puggy. There was no way Johnny Smart would ever admit to starting the fire. If he did, he'd be public enemy number one, never live it down. And now he was making sure the boys weren't able to talk to anyone about who had put them up to it. Making it look like some nutter vigilantes had got hold of them. He was clearing house and quick. Trying to make the whole thing go away before it connected back to him.

He looked up at the sound of coins pouring out the puggy, Deke trying to gather them up from the tray and the floor.

Wasn't sure there was much point going to see Johnny Smart. He was famous for hiding behind his big lawyers, saying nothing to no one, least of all the police. Even if McCoy tried to see him, the lawyers would be all over him asking for a reason for the interview request, and Stevie Cooper telling tales wasn't something he was able to tell them or anywhere near good enough.

Cooper had got a pint glass from the bar and they were filling it up with the fifty pences from the machine. Had to go back and get another glass, they'd won so much.

Maybe he was looking at this the wrong way. If Johnny Smart was a dead end, maybe he should be going to see Dessie Caine, see what he had to say about it. Maybe he'd be angry enough to get the boys back, make sure they testified that Johnny had asked them to set the fire. Was a bit of a longshot, but it was all he could think of to keep things moving forward. Wasn't holding out much hope of Murray and Faulds finding them. Not in time anyway.

Cooper dumped the two beer glasses full of money on the table. 'Don't think that thing's paid out since 1969. We're going to go and spend it at the casino. Fancy it?'

McCoy shook his head. The two drinks he'd had were causing his stomach distress, didn't want to risk any more. 'I'll leave you boys to spend your ill-gotten gains.' He stood up. 'Dessie still at Forge Street?'

'Far as I know,' said Cooper.

'I'll go and see him tomorrow. Shake his tree.'

'Rather you than me,' said Cooper. 'I mean it, Harry. He comes across all holy these days, but Dessie Caine is still Dessie Caine.'

'What do you mean?'

'You no know about him?' asked Cooper, stuffing the coins into his pockets.

McCoy shook his head.

'Thought you polis were supposed to be all over these guys,' said Cooper. 'You're bloody useless. When he was nineteen, twenty, he waded into the Cumbie, in Gallowgate, and slashed five men in one night. The place was running with blood. And that was just the beginning. He's a fucking animal, Harry. Watch yourself.'

23rd May 1974

TWENTY-SEVEN

Dessie Caine lived at the corner of Forge Street and Stroma Street, a four in a block at the top of a hill. He could look out his front window and survey his domain of Royston below. They had been stopped by two lads in the garden, sullen fuckers who'd blocked their way, asked what they were doing there. Two police badges and an assurance they would lift them if they didn't fuck off later, they were knocking on the door.

It was answered by a woman in a black dress with a small crucifix around her neck. She was probably only late thirties but the dress and her scraped-back hair made her look older. She stood in the doorway for a second, looked surprised to see anyone there.

'Can I help you?' she asked. Remains of a southern Irish accent.

'I'm Detective McCoy and this is my colleague Watson. We'd like a word with your husband if we could, Mrs Caine.'

She nodded. If it wasn't nine in the morning, McCoy would swear she was holding onto the door frame to stop herself swaying. 'Dessie, you mean. Everyone calls him Dessie. Come away in.'

She pulled the door open, pointed at the holy water font on the wall. McCoy dipped his fingers in, crossed himself. Wattie copied him. No real idea what he was doing.

'Splendid,' she said, assured they were of the one true faith. 'Now come away upstairs.'

They followed her up a set of carpeted stairs to the top landing. That's where things got strange. There were too many rooms, too many big rooms for a cottage flat. Took McCoy a minute to work out why. The top two flats had been combined, the dividing wall knocked through. There was what looked like an office off to one side, a dapperly dressed wee man spreading out blueprints of a building onto a table. He looked up and smiled as they passed. McCoy had the vague feeling he'd met him before, couldn't work out where.

Mrs Caine ushered them through into the double-sized living room, a row of windows looking down onto Glenconner Park and the Charles Street flats in the distance. Shouldn't have been surprised Dolly's Salon was Dessie's, could just about see it from here. The room bore more than a passing resemblance to a gift shop at Lourdes or Carfin. The walls were lined with various pictures of Jesus and Mary. Jesus with his bleeding heart. Mary with the infant Jesus. Jesus on the cross. Mary with the bleeding Jesus across her lap. In between these were representations of various saints and pictures of Dessie trussed up in a suit and tie standing beside different priests at functions. Charity auctions, Knights of St Columba dinners, keystone ceremonies for various chapels.

At a table by the widow, Tosh and some other young heavy were sitting, full ashtray and empty breakfast plates in front of them. Tosh looked at McCoy, belched loudly, started picking his teeth with a matchstick. There was a dog under the table, big, angry-looking thing, kept its eyes on Wattie and McCoy, growled.

The young heavy was counting money, a mound of pound notes and fivers, putting them into piles then wrapping elastic bands round them. Noticed McCoy watching. 'Fuck you looking at?' he said.

McCoy turned away, looked down towards the end of the room. Dessie Caine was sitting in an armchair wearing a pair of pyjama bottoms, slippers and a vest. Thick greyish hair covered his shoulders and sprouted from the back of his vest. He was a heavy-set man, not fat, just heavy, muscle that had settled in an older man's body. He had a plate in his hand, strips of fatty, barely cooked bacon on it, and he was lowering them into his mouth one by one. Didn't look like he was going to acknowledge McCoy and Wattie's existence until his breakfast was done.

'He'll not be long,' said Mrs Caine. 'Doesn't like to be disturbed when he's eating.' She seemed at a loss, looked at them. 'Can I get you a tea?'

'That'd be lovely,' said McCoy. 'Very kind of you.'

She stood there for a second. McCoy smiled at her.

'Sit yourself down,' she said. 'I'll not be a minute.'

They lowered themselves into antimacassar-covered armchairs along from Dessie, who was still ignoring them, still lowering the fatty bacon into his gullet.

A man appeared at the door. 'Blueprints?'

'Have to deal with this first. Twenty minutes?'

'No problem,' said the man. Disappeared.

'Who's that?' asked McCoy.

Dessie finally looked at them. 'Not know him? Man's a genius. Designing our new chapel for us.'

'Us?'

'Royston Diocese. I help with the charity drive.'

'Very noble,' said McCoy. 'Do a lot of charity work do you, Mr Caine?'

Dessie finished his last rasher and sat back in his chair. 'Something I can do for you two gentlemen?'

'We're investigating the fire at Dolly's Salon down the road,' said McCoy.

'A terrible tragedy,' said Dessie and crossed himself. 'Those poor women.'

'Must have been especially difficult for you too,' said McCoy. 'You owning the salon and all.'

'Here we are!'

Mrs Caine wobbled in, carrying a tray with a teapot, three cups and matching saucers, and a plate of biscuits. Wattie stood up and took the tray as she approached, must have noticed the state of her too. There was silence as she dished the tea things out, cups and saucers rattling as she handed them over with shaky hands. She finished arranging and pouring and eventually left again.

Dessie picked up a small china cup with flowers on it. 'Right. So what the fuck are you talking about?'

'Sorry,' said McCoy, picking up a biscuit. 'We understood you owned the premises. Are we wrong?'

Dessie sipped his tea, put the cup down on the arm of his chair. 'Now why would you think something like that?'

'Sources,' said McCoy. 'Anonymous sources. This shortbread is great by the way. Homemade?'

'Maybe you should tell your *sources* to get to fuck,' said Dessie. 'I don't own any hairdresser's.'

'Really?' asked McCoy. 'Not sure Johnny Smart sees it that way.'

And that was that.

Dessie bellowed, and Tosh and the other guy were up and at them, dog barking and baring his teeth.

'Get these cunts out of here,' said Dessie. 'Now!'

Tosh went to grab them and McCoy held his hands up to stop him. 'We can manage ourselves,' he said, turning back to Dessie. 'Johnny Smart's got those boys hidden God knows where. He's going to make sure no one knows why they attacked the hairdresser's. Make sure nobody knows he was going at you. You happy with that?'

McCoy just managed to step back before Dessie jumped up from his chair, meaty fists flying. He stood there glowering.

'Thanks for the tea, Dessie,' said McCoy. 'See you around, eh?'

They left before Dessie could have another go.

Back in the garden, the two lads threw them dirty looks as they stepped aside. McCoy stood by the car, got his cigarettes out. Lit up, threw the match into the gutter.

'Was it my imagination,' said Wattie, 'or was Mrs Caine completely pissed?'

'She was definitely something. Not there half the time.' He pulled the car door open. 'Not sure I blame her either. Living in a house like that would be enough to send you to the nuthouse.'

'Or the off-licence,' said Wattie. He opened the door. 'Where now?'

'Can you drop me at Tobago Street?'

Wattie nodded, got in the car. 'Rather you than me.'

TWENTY-EIGHT

McCoy watched Faulds push the last bit of toast into his mouth and start chewing. Was getting a bit tired of watching people eat their breakfasts. 'That all you ever eat, fry-ups? Northern Irish thing, is it?'

Faulds crossed his cutlery on the empty plate in front of him. Sighed. 'It's breakfast time. That's why I'm eating it. Now are you supposed to be briefing me or criticising my eating habits?'

They were in the Milk Churn on London Road, not too far from Tobago Street. A dairy owned by two sisters that did breakfasts and soup all day. Rain was running down the front window, turning the street outside into a blurry mess of green-and-yellow buses as they went past heading into town. They'd arranged to meet there: neutral ground. No way was McCoy setting foot in Tobago Street if he could help it.

'Word is Dessie Caine owns Dolly's Salon,' he said, eyeing an uneaten bit of bacon on Faulds's plate.

Faulds thought for a minute. 'Makes sense, it's on his patch. How do you know?'

'Wee birdie told me,' said McCoy. 'Not common knowledge at all. And him and Johnny Smart have been squabbling. The both of them want Haghill. Christ knows why, mind you, it's a dump.'

'That all, gents?' Linda, one of the sisters, had come over, picked up Faulds's plate before McCoy had a chance to nab the bacon.

'Two coffees, please, Linda,' said Faulds as McCoy watched Linda and the bacon disappear into the back shop.

'You think Johnny set the fire then?' said Faulds.

'If he did, all of Glasgow will be after him. So he'll be making sure nobody knows, hence the boys disappearing.'

'Christ,' said Faulds. 'Does Murray know about this?'

McCoy shook his head. 'Was leaving that pleasure to you. I saw the paper this morning. Has he killed anyone yet?'

'Not yet, but I'd give it until lunchtime. He was absolutely fucking beeling this morning. I got out of there as fast as I could.'

'Don't blame you. It's a leak, is it?'

'Yep. It's the transcript you got that woman to do pretty much verbatim.' Faulds held up his paper. 'And now it's splattered all over the front page of the *Daily Record*.'

McCoy winced. 'So it definitely came from us?'

'Had to. It'll be like the bloody Spanish Inquisition over there the day.'

Coffees arrived. McCoy had a sip and put it back down. Instant twinge. He got the bottle of Pepto-Bismol out his pocket and took a swig.

'Thought you were all better?'

'I am,' said McCoy. 'Just developed a taste for it, that's all.'

'My arse,' said Faulds. 'I'll try and set up an interview with Johnny Smart, see if I can make it through the lawyers.'

'Good luck,' said McCoy. 'But I don't think you'll get anywhere near him.'

'Probably not. But I have to try. Is it still Lomax?'

McCoy shook his head. 'Not any more. Now it all goes through some advocate in Edinburgh, offices in the New Town and "sir" in front of his name. Must be costing a fucking fortune, but Johnny's got the money, I suppose.'

Faulds drew a cheque in the air and Linda nodded. 'What you doing today?'

'I was going to go into the office but fuck that for a game of soldiers. I'm not getting the third degree from Murray. I'm going to go and have a think. I'm getting nowhere with Wattie's case. Really need a breakthrough.' He sighed. 'So, back to the beginning, see if we missed anything. Where would a runaway fifteen-year-old kid with no money go? Our only lead has disappeared off the face of the earth.'

Faulds took a sip of his coffee and grimaced. 'Cold,' he said. 'You tried Sister Jimmy?'

McCoy shook his head. 'Not sure I can face it.'

'Might be worth it. If anyone is going to know, it'll be him.'

'Where is he these days?'

Faulds looked at his watch. 'This time of the day, God only knows, but he usually turns up in Equi about lunchtime and tries to drown his hangover in coffee. Assuming he's got up by then, that is.'

McCoy got out his cigarettes and lit up. More stomach pain. Brought up the subject the both of them had been avoiding. 'You think you're going to find the boys before . . . you know?'

Faulds's face clouded. He shrugged. 'I hope so, but to be honest, Harry, we've got fuck all. We're running out of time. Doesn't look good.' He shook his head. 'And you know the worst thing? Plenty of people in this town are happy for it to happen, just waiting for the next boy to be dumped fuck knows where. You heard the wee girl died last night?'

'Shite,' said McCoy.

'More fuel to the fire if you'll pardon the expression. She'll be front page of the afternoon papers. They'll go over it all again. Killed as she got ready for a party, Communion photo, the works. For a lot of people that's even less motivation to help us find the boys. Far as they're concerned, the fuckers deserve what's coming to them.'

Faulds stood up. 'Better get going.' He put his coat on, paid the bill and left.

McCoy sat for a bit, stirring the spoon in his cold coffee. Picked up Faulds's paper. The transcript story went all the way through to page seven. Turned it over. Picture of Tom McCauley and his wife pictured in front of their nice big house.

PLEASE HELP US FIND OUR SON.

Skimmed the article. Had a feeling the journalist was only just managing to stop himself saying whatever the bastard gets he deserves it. Probably what most of the readers thought too. Was about to get ready to go when he heard a horn, looked through the window, and Wattie was sitting in an unmarked Viva waving him over. He left the paper on the table, Tom McCauley looking up at him, and walked out the cafe. Money could do lots of things, but it couldn't keep your kids safe, no matter how much of it you had.

TWENTY-NINE

McCoy got in the car, still annoyed he hadn't grabbed that last slice of bacon.

'How was your breakfast?' asked Wattie, starting the engine.

'Didn't have any,' said McCoy. 'Just watched Faulds eat his.'

'Nae joy. How's he getting on?'

'Going to try and get an interview with Johnny Smart, see if he can press him about the fire.'

'He'll be lucky,' said Wattie, turning off London Road.

'Speaking of lucky, how come you escaped the grand inquisition?'

'Murray started off, then he says to me, "I'm wasting my time here, Watson. You have neither the guile nor the gumption to leak anything to the bloody press." Didn't know whether to be pleased or offended.'

'Both, I think. Where we off to?'

'To see what Dessie's boys have been up to. Didn't take them long, we only left there an hour ago.'

Twenty minutes later they were standing opposite what was soon to be the Open Arms pub – until a few hours ago that was. Now it was a mess. The low one-storey building, due to open in a week, had only just been finished. Now, every shiny new window had been smashed, glass all over the car park. Black paint had been thrown all over the white roughcast walls. The door had been kicked in and was now hanging at an awkward angle. The gutters had been pulled down and strewn all over the street, the drainpipes lying beside them. And, in a finishing touch, the big sign saying *Opening Soon!* now had three big black words painted on: IS IT FUCK.

'Nice to see vandals have a sense of humour these days,' said McCoy.

'Wasn't all laughs,' said Wattie. 'Apparently Dessie knocked fuck out the two bar staff that were setting up the place. One of them's in hospital with a cracked skull and the other got his face rubbed up and down the roughcast wall. Worked like a cheese grater apparently. He's going to need skin grafts and all sorts.'

'Let me guess, neither of them saw who just about killed them?'

Wattie shook his head. 'They came up behind me, officer.'

A Jaguar pulled in and Murray got out, looking exasperated.

'Sir,' said Wattie, walking over to greet him. Was soon stopped dead in his tracks.

'Any progress on your case yet?' barked Murray. 'Do we know who the girl is?'

'Well,' said Wattie looking flustered, 'things are going a bit slower than I'd hoped, so—'

'No is the answer. So what the fuck are you doing here? Go and make some bloody progress instead of wasting your time.'

Wattie scuttled off, Murray glowering after him.

'Don't need to ask what kind of mood you're in then,' said McCoy.

'You surprised? Take it you heard about the leak?' asked Murray.

McCoy nodded.

'I swear to God, when I catch the bugger that did it, their life won't be worth living.'

McCoy debated whether to say it. Quickly decided Murray's mood couldn't really get any worse. 'I know it's not my business, but it seems pretty obvious who it was.'

'Who?'

'Got to be Colin Stones,' said McCoy. 'You sacked him in front of all his pals. This is the perfect way to get revenge and some money at the same time, and he's the type to do it.'

Murray didn't say anything. Started looking for his pipe.

'Not much you can do about it now though, if he did. He's had his jotters already. Might as well call off the witch hunt.'

Murray couldn't find his pipe in any of his pockets. Swore. Stopped looking. 'I shouldn't have done it, should I? Sacked them?'

McCoy shrugged. 'Maybe could have waited until you had the three of them alone.'

Murray looked round, walked over to the low wall surrounding the pub and sat down. McCoy sat down beside him. A few boys on bikes were circling, no doubt waiting for the opportunity to get through the smashed door and see what they could take.

'Managed to make a good job of destroying the place,' Murray said, nodding over. 'Give us one of your bloody cigarettes.' McCoy gave him one and he lit up. Grimaced. 'These are bloody awful. I don't know how you smoke them.' He took another drag, dropped it on the ground and stamped it out. 'It's a lot of work. Running two stations, these bloody boys, trying to keep on top of everything.'

McCoy nodded.

'Phyllis told me not to take the other station on.' He smiled. 'She was probably right. Appealed to my vanity, I suppose. Only I can sort things out. And look where we are now. Tobago Street's in bloody mutiny, time is running out for those boys,

I'm firing people left, right and centre, and now you've got me sitting in front of a wrecked pub in the back arse of Riddrie.' He looked over at the pub. 'So why am I here?'

McCoy pointed. 'This pub belongs to Johnny Smart, not that you'll find him anywhere near the paperwork. Him and Dessie Caine have been snapping at each other's heels over who runs Haghill.'

'Haghill?' said Murray. 'Really?'

'I know. But territory is territory, I suppose. Anyway, turns out Dessie owns Dolly's Salon.'

'Does he now? That's never come up.'

'Well, just like Johnny Smart and this pub, his name's nowhere near it, but it's his. So, I'm thinking maybe all this — the fire, the dead women, the kidnapped boys — is all the beginning of another turf war.'

'Christ,' said Murray. 'You sure Johnny Smart ordered the fire at the salon?'

'Nope,' said McCoy. 'But if he did, maybe he thought it was going to be empty, didn't mean to kill anyone. Then he finds out he's got blood, a lot of blood, on his hands. Needs to move fast to stop everyone knowing he's the bastard that did it and hanging him from the nearest lamppost. So he starts cleaning house. Getting rid of the boys before they could tell anyone why they did it. Makes it look like some vigilante revenge thing.'

Murray took his hat off, ran his hands through what was left of his reddish hair, put it back on. 'All this to run fucking Haghill? All these people dead for that shithole?' He shook his head. 'It doesn't make sense.'

'Not everything does,' said McCoy. 'We spend our days trying to find out who did what, why they did it, what their motive was. Trying to tie everything up into neat little parcels. No unanswered questions, no loose ends. Sometimes things just aren't that neat. We want the death of five people in an arson attack to mean something, to have a reason, to find the person that did it, get them jailed. It's what we're trained to do. But maybe it was just a stupid accident, maybe they were just in the wrong place at the wrong time.'

McCoy realised Murray was looking at him. 'What?'

'Since when did you turn into a bloody philosopher?'

'Sorry,' said McCoy. 'Got a bit carried away.'

Murray looked serious. 'Doesn't matter why Johnny Smart did it. If he ordered the fire, he's responsible for what happened, and if you're right, he's responsible for trying to cover it up as well. We got anyone on his payroll?'

McCoy shook his head. 'He runs a tight ship. No leaks, no touts, as far as I know.'

'Great,' said Murray. 'So we have to deal with his bloody Edinburgh lawyer. With no evidence to question him. Who's your source about Dessie owning the salon?'

'Stevie Cooper.'

'Fuck sake!' said Murray. 'Not exactly what you'd call a reliable witness. Besides he's got skin in the game. Seeing Johnny Smart go down would suit him just fine.'

'I don't think he's making it up,' said McCoy. 'Spoke to a young guy who used to work for Dessie.'

'Maybe he is, maybe he isn't. Either way it doesn't help us. We need corroboration, someone else who knows about the salon. You get me that and we'll go after Johnny Smart all guns blazing.' He waved over the uniform standing beside his car smoking. 'Meanwhile I'll get Faulds on Johnny Smart's wee hidey-holes. His pubs and his lock-ups and his warehouses. Those two boys must be somewhere. You want a lift to the station?'

McCoy shook his head. 'Got to go and see someone for my sins. He's a toerag but he might help us figure out who the girl is.'

'Is Watson doing a decent job?' asked Murray. 'I worry about him.'

'I know you do,' said McCoy. 'But he's doing everything he's supposed to be doing. It's all a bit by the book, but that's just inexperience. He's getting there.'

Murray didn't look convinced.

THIRTY

Equi was an Italian cafe on Sauchiehall Street. Bright blue sign on brown mosaic. Looked like it belonged in Naples rather than Glasgow. It sold pasta, ice cream and frothy coffee to students from the art school, shoppers and office workers. Single cups of tea to old women who took an hour to drink it, really just there to enjoy the warmth and the company.

McCoy pushed the door open and went inside. Ordered a coffee at the counter and made his way to the back where Sister Jimmy was sitting in his usual booth. He looked like he hadn't been home yet. Jet-black hair in a Bryan Ferry quiff, silver jean jacket and chipped black nail varnish. He looked up, saw McCoy and let out an audible moan.

'No the day, McCoy, please God. I'm hanging. Can you no see I'm dying here?'

McCoy could. Sister Jimmy had black bags under his eyes, reeked of booze and cigarettes, and his platform-booted foot was drumming on the lino floor. Wasn't hard to picture the previous twenty-four hours.

McCoy sat down, took his jacket off and looked at him. 'Let me guess,' he said. 'Spider's black bombers. Enough rum and Coke to sink a battleship. Forty Regal. Couple of joints to try and calm down, which haven't worked. The Muscular Arms then Vintners then Clouds then someone's flat in the West End, then a couple of pints at the Empire Bar at eight this morning when it opened. How am I doing?'

Sister Jimmy put his head in his hands and groaned again. 'Too bloody well. Don't remind me. You tried they black bombers of Spider's? He's punting them cheap out the toilets in the Arms. Now I know why.'

'Yep,' said McCoy. 'They blow your bloody head off. Made me leather some kid in the Broomie.'

The waitress approached with two coffees and a Coke. Sister Jimmy drank the juice down in one, burped and started ladling sugar into his coffee.

'I think I'm going to puke,' he said. 'Don't have any of they black bombers left, do you? Kill me or cure me.'

McCoy dug in his pocket and put the pills on the table. Sister Jimmy reached for them, but McCoy blocked his hand. 'Not until you tell me what I need to know.'

'Jesus Christ,' said Sister Jimmy. 'That's pure torture. You should be ashamed of yourself.' He lit up another Regal, blew the smoke in McCoy's face. 'If you don't give me them, then you and I are going to fall out.'

'I'll live,' said McCoy. He got the photo strip out and laid it next to the pills. 'Boy in the bottom picture. Blond hair. You seen him around?'

Sister Jimmy looked at it, shook his head.

McCoy sighed. Really didn't have time for this. 'He's a good-looking fifteen-year-old boy floating about town with no money and nowhere to stay. It's got you written all over it. Now, where is he?'

'I don't know what you mean,' said Sister Jimmy with all the hauteur of an elderly dowager. 'That boy swore to me he was eighteen. I was framed.'

'That right?' said McCoy. Tapped the picture. 'I don't give a fuck about that. Just tell me where he is.'

Sister Jimmy sipped his coffee, smoked his cigarette, didn't say anything.

'Let me make this easier for you. He's called Paul Cooper, as I'm sure you know. What you probably don't know is he's Stevie Cooper's son and unless you start talking, I might have to forget myself and let slip to Cooper that you've been hanging about with him.'

McCoy didn't think it was possible, but Sister Jimmy's face suddenly went even whiter.

'You wouldn't do that.'

'Yes, I would,' said McCoy. 'And you know it.'

Sister Jimmy sighed. 'He's staying at the Big House.'

'What's that?'

Sister Jimmy looked quite pleased with himself. 'You don't know? My, my, McCoy, you're slipping. Used to be a time when you knew everything that was going on. It's a squat in Garnethill Street. Hippies, Hare Krishnas.' He sniffed. 'Not exactly my scene but that's where he is. All a bit dirty finger-nails and mung bean stew for my liking, but they take anyone in. Well, that's where he was . . .'

'What does that mean?' asked McCoy.

'Doubt he's still there. They were threatening to throw him out. Beat one of the hippies up. Not exactly peace and love. They were having a house meeting about it last night. Can you imagine? I'd rather be boiled in oil.'

'And if he's not there?'

Sister Jimmy shrugged. 'Your guess is as good as mine. God knows he's a good-looking boy, but he's a bit wild even for me, and I like them rough, got the bruises to prove it. Makes sense now, Stevie Cooper being his dad. They're not that different.'

'What about the girl?' asked McCoy. 'Recognise her?'

Sister Jimmy looked at the picture again, shook his head. 'I'm not very good with girls, not my area of interest, to be honest.'

'You know Dirty Ally's dead?'

Sister Jimmy raised his eyebrows.

'Killed himself.'

'That's a shame. For a dirty old lech he wasn't the worst.'

'You ever supply him with models?' asked McCoy.

More raised eyebrows. 'Well, I may have steered a few aspiring young people his way. He paid good money, you know.'

'The girl and Paul. Would he have been interested in them?'

'You kidding?' said Sister Jimmy. 'Two lookers like that? He'd have been all over them like a cheap suit.'

McCoy pushed the two pills across the table. Sister Jimmy picked them up, swallowed them over with a gulp of his coffee.

'Gracias,' he said. 'You've saved my life.'

McCoy stood up, went to go.

'Harry?' he said. 'Don't tell Cooper anything. Please. My life's fucked up enough without him after me.'

McCoy nodded, headed out the cafe. Was still making his mind up.

THIRTY-ONE

Dolphin Place was in genteel Pollokshields. A wide road of red sandstone flats near Maxwell Park, which meant it had taken McCoy and Wattie far longer to find than it should have. The Southside was a mystery to both of them: wasn't their patch, wasn't where they lived, wasn't somewhere they ever went.

McCoy pulled in by number 16. Took the key out the ignition and the engine died.

'At long bloody last,' said Wattie.

'Stop your moaning,' said McCoy. 'You're supposed to be the navigator.'

'First I've heard,' said Wattie. 'And how the fuck would I know where it is? I'm from bloody Greenock.'

'And you'll be going back there if you keep up that insubordination. I'm your senior officer and I should be treated with respect.'

Wattie snorted and got out the car.

The close was wide and cool, ornate tiles halfway up the walls and curved wooden banisters. A cat was sitting on the first step. Wattie bent down to pet it and it started purring.

'You know this is going to be a waste of time?' he said. 'Just like the cupboard at Paddy's Market. Don't know why you're still so convinced the girl from the graveyard is going to be in some dirty pictures.'

'Stop complaining,' said McCoy as they started to climb the stairs. 'We've got fuck all other leads and at least you'll get another scud mag out of it.'

'No, I won't,' said Wattie. 'Mary found the other one.'

'Oops. Did she batter you with it?'

'Worse. Gave me a bloody lecture about disrespecting women and exploitation and God knows what. Went on for about half an hour until the wee man started bawling. First time I've been glad he's teething. This it?'

McCoy nodded. They'd arrived at a green-painted door with a stained-glass window depicting some sort of country scene. Half of it was covered by a board taped on from the inside. A brass name plate saying *Drummond* was on the wall next to the bell.

'I thought he'd be living in some bedsit surrounded by scud mags and chip wrappers,' said Wattie. 'This is too posh for him.'

McCoy turned the key in the lock and pushed the door open. First thing they saw was a grandfather clock ticking away, weight swinging back and forward. The next was books, loads and loads of books. The hall floor was covered in them. Open, shut, half ripped apart. The bookshelves lining the walls were empty. Dark rectangles on the walls showed where pictures had been pulled off and dumped on the floor. There was a dresser, drawers pulled out, and what looked like bed linen and tablecloths strewn everywhere.

'Christ,' said Wattie. 'What a mess.'

They picked their way through the books, couldn't avoid standing on a few, and McCoy pushed open a wooden door with another stained-glass scene. There was a round Victorian table in the window bay, huge crystal vase full of lilies smashed on the floor beside it. Two armchairs and a settee had been slashed over and over again, most of the stuffing joining more books on the floor. There was a piano at the other end of the room that looked as though someone had drawn a knife across it a few times, deep gouges in the shiny wood. Smashed Wally dugs in the fireplace, radiogram on its side, records and their sleeves everywhere.

'I know it's a fucking mess now but how did Dirty Ally afford this kind of place?' asked Wattie. 'And if he had all this, what the fuck was he doing selling old scud mags at Paddy's Market?'

'I've no idea,' said McCoy. 'Not what I was expecting at all.'

They went through the rest of the flat and it was all much the same. What once had been a beautifully furnished and cared-for home was now in ruins. Everything that could have been smashed had been. Every cupboard and drawer emptied onto the floor. Whatever it was the men who had broken in had been looking for, they had to have found it. McCoy had never seen anywhere so comprehensively turned over in his life.

They sat down at a table in the kitchen, the room with the least damage. McCoy noticed a miraculously intact half-full bottle of Johnnie Walker Black Label on top of the fridge.

'Don't think Ally would grudge us,' he said. Picked up two cups from the floor, gave them a rinse and poured a good measure into each.

'Don't think there's going to be many photo sets of randy housewives here,' said Wattie, taking a gulp.

'Nope,' said McCoy. 'Here and Paddy's Market. It's like two different worlds. Doesn't make any sense at all.' They sat for a minute listening to the ticking of the grandfather clock in the hall. Stripes of sunlight across the kitchen wall. 'There's no way his Paddy's business paid for all this. So what did?'

'Family money?' said Wattie.

McCoy shook his head. 'His sister was as surprised he lived here as we were. Needs to be something much bigger.'

'And illegal, no doubt,' said Wattie. 'Maybe that's why he

kept the Paddy's Market stuff going. So no one would suspect.'

'That, Watson,' said McCoy, 'is a very good point.' He stood up. 'I'm going to take one more poke about. Care to join me?'

'Nope,' said Wattie. 'I'll just sit here enjoying this whisky I'll never be able to afford in this flat I'll never be able to afford because I'm a fucking polis and not a scud bookseller.'

McCoy opened the door to Ally's bedroom. He sat on the bed and looked at the few books remaining on the bookshelf in front of him: André Gide, Ford Madox Ford. Kept scanning along until he found an author he knew. Charles Dickens, *Dombey and Son*. Had heard of Charles Dickens, but not that book.

He stood up, walked over to the desk on a carpet of hardbacks, righted the chair and sat on it. There was a picture in a silver frame. Smashed glass. He peered at it, made out a sunny garden, two little kids squinting in the sun, looked like Ally and his sister. McCoy looked through the open desk drawer. A selection of fountain pens, Ally's passport, a bottle of pills, a certificate of graduation rolled up in a tube. *Alistair Drummond, First Class Honours in English Literature, University of Glasgow, 1954*. He rolled it up, put it back in the tube. Wasn't getting anywhere.

He looked under the bed. Nothing. Opened the wardrobe. Cord trousers, tweed suits, Tattersall shirts. Stuck his hands in the suit pockets, found a fiver, pocketed it. Sat back on the bed. If Ally had anything to hide, where would he hide it? Could hear Wattie pouring himself another drink in the kitchen. Could hear the ticking of the grandfather clock.

McCoy stood up again and walked through to the hall. Stopped in front of the clock. He opened the glass-panelled door and the ticking got louder. He put his hand out to stop the weight and the ticking stopped. He felt behind the weight. Right down at the bottom he could feel something like a rolled-up bit of leather. He pushed his hand in, and pulled it out. It was about a foot long, and it felt like there was something metal inside. A gun? He unrolled it and two spare clock weights fell out onto the carpet.

McCoy swore, rolled them back up and put the leather bundle back in the clock case. He realised he was standing on a copy of Ally's own book, *The Love Chamber*. Picture of an angst-ridden young man on the front, what looked like a mansion in the background. He picked it up and felt something shift inside. Had to pull hard to open it, seemed the front cover had been glued to the pages. Managed to get it open and realised why.

The pages of the book had been hollowed out and in the cavity was a large key with a square hoop of metal at the top and two other little keys attached to heavy oblongs of plastic by a circle of wire. The oblongs were orange with black writing. One said *Happiness Hotel, Room 1*. The other, *Happiness Hotel, Room 2*. McCoy put the three keys in his pocket and dropped the book. Called through to Wattie, told him they were going.

THIRTY-TWO

'I don't get it,' said Wattie. 'He was staying at a hotel as well as the Great Northern?'

'Maybe,' said McCoy. 'But why two rooms?' He looked up from his desk. 'You heard of the Happiness Hotel?'

'Nope,' said Wattie. 'Hang on.' He walked over to the filing cabinet next to Thomson's empty desk and came back with a *Yellow Pages*. He put it down on McCoy's desk and started flipping through.

'There's a Hazelbank Hotel, a Hillview guesthouse.' Looked up. 'That's about it. Maybe it's just a souvenir thing he brought back from his holidays.'

'But why hide it in a book? And what's the other key for?'

'Fuck knows. Whatever they are, they're no helping us.'

McCoy lit up. Wattie was right, they were getting precisely nowhere. Still no Paul Cooper, still no idea who the girl was. Wondered how Faulds and Murray were getting on with Johnny Smart and his Edinburgh lawyers. Johnny Smart was a weird one, had almost made it into being legit. Had garages, a taxi company, accountants to cover his tracks. The gangster's dream. Trouble was you had to spend as much time maintaining the lie as it took you to get there. Would he really want to get involved in a turf war at this point? Probably. Just like all the others, he couldn't quite let it go. People like Johnny Smart never really went legit, just spent a lot of time and money trying to pretend that they had.

Just then Faulds came through the office door.

'Speak of the devil,' said McCoy. 'How'd you get on?' Faulds came over and sat down. Didn't look good, looked tired and downtrodden. McCoy had forgotten how much being on the front line of a big investigation took out of you. No sleep, constant pressure. Worse when you weren't getting any results. 'You want a cup of tea?'

Faulds nodded.

'No worries. Wattie, three teas, please.'

Wattie swore and wandered over to the kitchen.

'How'd it go with Johnny Smart?'

'Lawyers wouldn't let us see him. Said we didn't have adequate reason for an interview. The bugger's right.'

'Christ,' said McCoy.

'That's not all. Sent us away with a flea in our ear. Made it perfectly clear if we mention any kind of connection between his client and the salon fire, he will sue us for all he's worth. Defamation.'

Wattie appeared a few minutes later with the teas, put them down. 'Billy's eaten all the biscuits.'

Faulds yawned, took a sip of his tea.

'How's Murray?' asked McCoy.

Faulds shook his head.

'That bad?'

'Left him marching up and down outside Pitt Street trying to calm down before he goes in.' He pulled an *Evening Times* from his jacket pocket. 'And this isn't exactly helping.'

McCoy unfolded the paper. Front page. Big black headline. WHERE ARE THEY?

He skimmed through the article. Usual rehash of the salon fire then a gory description of what had happened to Colin Turnbull and questions as to why the police hadn't yet found the other two boys.

'Great,' said McCoy. 'Always nice to have the press on your side.'

Faulds put his mug on the desk, looked like he was about to fall asleep.

'Look, Hughie, you're dead on your feet. Away home and get a couple of hours.'

Faulds nodded, yawned again. Went to make for the door.

'I'll come with you,' said Wattie. 'Need to go and get fags.' He turned to McCoy. 'You want anything?'

McCoy shook his head. Thought. Called after them.

'Get me a bar of Fruit & Nut!'

Chocolate and Rich Tea biscuits were about the only things he could eat these days. He'd soon be putting the weight back on, at least. He flicked through the rest of Faulds's paper. More bombs in Belfast. A wee toerag whose picture he recognised jailed for robbing a pensioner. Bruce Forsyth opening a supermarket in Kilmarnock. Poor bugger. Stopped. There was a picture in the top half of page five. Home news.

Three men standing behind a table with a model of a chapel that looked like a bunker. Read the caption. *Diocese announce new chapel in Royston. Father Samuel McKenna and leader of the fundraising committee Desmond Caine discuss plans with the architect.*

And there he was. Dessie looking sweaty in a new suit, smiling at the camera. McCoy read through the article. Father Samuel McKenna, soon to be crowned Archbishop of Glasgow, acknowledging Mr Caine's sterling fundraising actions and his determination that Royston should have a new chapel. A quote from the architect blabbering on about modern places of worship for a modern city and Dessie thanking all his donors.

McCoy sat back in his chair. Dessie was becoming a Holy Roller right enough. And just like Johnny Smart, he was going to have a job of making sure the mask didn't slip. Especially now he was big pals with McKenna.

Glasgow was changing. All the old boys were scrambling about, desperate to get legit. One minute you're slicing someone's nose off with an open razor, next minute you're in the Knights of St Columba, eating Chicken Balmoral at a charity dinner and exchanging chit-chat with the Archbishop.

The stakes were getting raised. Everything they wanted now, Johnny Smart and Dessie Caine, depended on one thing. Staying out of trouble, or, more accurately, making sure they couldn't be connected to trouble. McCoy stood up, picked up his cigarettes and headed for the door. Wondered exactly how far they would go to make sure that didn't happen.

This wasn't about taking over a rival's pub or getting one up on each other any more. It was way past that. McCoy had a feeling that there wasn't much either of them wouldn't do now. Didn't matter if it was to each other or to anyone else who got in the way. This was about survival.

24th May 1974

THIRTY-THREE

The call had been made half an hour ago, at six forty-five. A milkman this time. Just finishing his round when he saw a car pull up and dump what he thought was a rolled-up carpet on the pavement. Went to have a look. Threw up when he realised what it really was.

The body had been left outside 18 Wellshot Road, a main-door flat opposite Tollcross Park. McCoy was just about to ask one of the uniforms if they'd seen Murray when the door of the flat opened. A young woman being supported by a female police officer appeared. She'd blonde hair poking out a headscarf, head was down, crying, looked like she was holding onto the officer for dear life. The female officer was shushing her, arms around her, telling her it would be all right. She didn't look like anything would ever be all right again.

'Who is she?'

Wattie looked at his notebook. 'Helen Glen, aged twenty-eight, works at Frasers in town, make-up counter. Lives by herself.'

'So why did they dump the boy here?' asked McCoy.

'Her sister's funeral is today.'

They turned and Murray was standing there, empty pipe in his mouth. 'The funeral is supposed to leave from here this afternoon. And instead of offering our sympathies we're standing here looking at another dead boy taken on our watch.'

'You tried,' said McCoy.

'Not hard enough,' said Murray. 'Imagine that was your son. You think "you tried" would satisfy you? Not even a bloody trial to decide whether they did it or not, just a vigilante mob and a dead body dumped in the street.'

McCoy looked over at the tent that had been erected over the boy's body. Could see Phyllis changing into her overalls, uniforms setting up rope barriers around the front of the house. Tried not to look at the blood pooled on the street.

'So is this some sort of reward thing? Here's the boy who killed your sister?'

Murray took the pipe from his mouth. 'Looks like it. They knew what was going to happen today. Everybody does. Picked their moment. This funeral is going to be huge. They had to move it to the cathedral to try and accommodate all the mourners and they're still expecting thousands more outside. Archbishop is doing the service, last one before he retires.' He nodded over at a line of bored men. 'Press boys tell me all the big papers are sending people up from London.'

'Which one of them is it?' asked McCoy.

'Danny Walsh,' said Murray. 'What's left of him.'

'Was there a note like before? A tape?' asked McCoy.

'Note said, "Two down, one to go", same biblical thing as last time and another yellow cassette. In the boy's mouth this time.'

'And the boy? What happened to him?'

'You'd know if you went and had a bloody look.'

'Come on, Murray, give me a break.'

'Same as the last one. Battered and burned and knifed, except

· 168 ·

this time they decided to cut some of his fingers off. He's only got six left. Rest are in the pockets of his jeans.'

McCoy's stomach lurched. He turned away, tried to breathe slowly.

'Phyllis is going to take the body back to the morgue as soon as she can. I want you to be there when she does her report.'

McCoy was about to object, saw the look on Murray's face, didn't.

'Watson?' said Murray.

'Sir?'

'Make yourself useful. Go and check how the door-to-doors are getting on. See if anyone saw them dump the body.'

Wattie nodded, set off towards the flats.

'She didn't look too pleased about what had happened,' said McCoy. 'The sister.'

'No,' said Murray. 'That's one good thing. Last thing we need is her saying justice has been done and congratulating whoever did it. Would send the mob into a bloody frenzy.'

'Might still come,' said McCoy. 'Once she gets over the shock. And the press gets hold of her.'

'That's why I'm off to see the Archbishop. Going to ask him to make his speech about he who casts the first stone et cetera. Hopefully quieten the crowd down.'

'You met him before?' asked McCoy.

'Civil dinners, charity things. Usual bloody roundabout of civic nonsense.'

'You met the new one?'

'Father McKenna? Couple of times. Very much the coming man, I believe, on the fast track. Archbishop of Glasgow just another stepping stone. Why?'

'Saw a picture of him in the paper the other day. With Dessie Caine.'

Murray rolled his eyes. 'Ah. The sainted bloody Dessie. You know they tried to sit him next to me at a Knights of St Columba dinner once? I told them exactly where to shove that idea, made sure he heard me too.'

'You not buying his transformation into model citizen then?'

Murray snorted. 'Not a bit of it. He's an evil bastard, always has been, always will be.'

McCoy got his cigarettes out, started counting on his fingers. 'First body was dumped on Wednesday. Today's Friday. I bet the next one will be dumped on Sunday. One every two days.'

'Christ.'

'We've got forty-eight hours to find Malcom McCauley. And we've got no fucking clue where to look.'

A uniform walked over from the tent. Brown paper evidence bag in hand. Gave it to Murray.

'What's that?' asked McCoy.

'The tape,' said Murray. 'You, me and Faulds are going to go and listen to it. No transcripts this time. Not making that mistake again. You ready?'

McCoy nodded. Never been less ready for anything in his life. Between the body, the tape and the morgue, today was turning into a very bad day.

THIRTY-FOUR

It was the sound of the boy's second finger being cut off that did it. The slice of the garden shears followed by half a second of silence then the worst screaming McCoy had ever heard. He grabbed the metal wastebasket, held his head over it. He retched a few times, hadn't eaten enough to actually throw up, and tried to calm down, tried to breathe.

Murray was shaking his head. 'Finished with the bloody histrionics?'

McCoy nodded.

'Come on, Murray,' said Faulds. 'It's fucking brutal. Feel a bit queasy myself.'

'That's no excuse. We're police officers, no bloody school-children. You ready?'

Faulds nodded and Murray pressed *play* again.

The scream died out, replaced by sobbing and whimpering. And then the voice of Danny Walsh.

'I'm sorry, I'm sorry, please don't hurt me, please, please, please don't, I'm sorry, I'm sorry, I can't . . .'

He dissolved into sobs. Noise of someone laughing in the background. Then something that sounded like music in the background.

'Can you play that bit again?' asked McCoy.

Faulds rewound the tape.

'Can you make out what it is?' asked McCoy.

'Sounds like "Danny Boy",' said Faulds.

'Eh?' asked Murray. 'You sure?'

Faulds shook his head. 'Too faint to be sure. The boy's crying too loud.'

Tape kept going. Sound of someone scissoring the garden shears open and closed. High-pitched scream from Danny Walsh, broken, terrified, no doubt knowing how this was going to end. McCoy looked at Faulds. He was suffering too. His normally ruddy face was grey, and when he brought his cigarette up to his mouth, his hand was shaking. Tape kept going, spinning round on the little wheels.

Another voice. 'Say it.'

Danny Walsh again.

Johnny Smart gave us money to set fire to the hairdresser's. Said he wanted to get at Dessie Caine.'

Distant sound of traffic and air brakes. Sound of someone walking away from the microphone, a door opening and closing. Then Danny Walsh again.

'Is that it? Is it finished? Please, I can't. What's that? My dad's got money, he'll . . . What's that? Our Father which art in heaven hallowed . . . please, God, please! Please!'

A terrible scream. The scream of someone who knew they were about to die. Noise like someone cutting into a melon, more screams.

'For fuck sake, Murray!' said McCoy. 'Turn it off!'

Murray pressed the *stop* button and the three of them sat in silence. Faulds lit up again. Murray looked for his pipe in his pockets and McCoy held onto the wastebasket. Couldn't trust himself not to be sick. The room seemed to be getting smaller, closing in. He couldn't breathe. He stood up and walked out the interview room, Murray calling after him.

The rain was back on, but he didn't care. Just wanted air and to be away from that room and that tape. He sat down on the wall opposite the station and lit up. Stomach was in knots, wasn't sure if it was from his ulcer or the tape. Probably a bit of both. Tried not to think about it but he couldn't help himself. What must it have been like walking into that room, knowing what was going to happen to you, knowing you were going to be tortured. What age was Danny Walsh? Sixteen? Seventeen? Who could do something like that to a boy that age, no matter what he had done?

The station door opened. Murray looked around for McCoy, saw him and walked over. McCoy swore. Just what he needed, another bollocking for not being up to it.

Murray sat down beside him. 'You okay?'

'Been better,' said McCoy.

'Nobody wants to listen to that, McCoy. It's not just you. But we have to. You have to.'

McCoy nodded, knew Murray was right. 'As long as you don't make me listen a second time.'

Murray shook his head. 'Once is enough for any man. You notice anything on it?'

McCoy thought. 'Sounds like the same place as last time, the traffic, lorries. Whoever was asking him to say it left before he was killed.' He smiled weakly. 'Maybe he's squeamish too.'

'A neat confession,' said Murray. 'I never like those.'

'It's pointless,' said McCoy. 'I'd confess to shooting JFK if someone was doing that to me. Even if it's true it's no use. Johnny Smart's lawyers will tell us where to go. You going to try them anyway?'

Murray seemed miles away. 'They're going to do the same to the last boy, aren't they?'

McCoy didn't say anything.

'And we can't do anything to stop it.'

'You don't know that, Murray. We might catch a break, we're due one.'

'From where? We've been blindsided by this thing since it happened. Two steps behind the pace, flailing about, making a noise, pretending we're on top of it. Truth is we're nowhere.'

'Come on, Murray. I'm supposed to be the miserable one, not you.'

'I've got no choice,' said Murray. 'Can't kid myself on any longer, jolly up the troops. After listening to those tapes, I don't have it in me any more. Nigh on thirty years I've been a polis and I've never heard anything like that in my life.'

'You've got to,' said McCoy. 'If you fall, we all fall. You're the only thing keeping this investigation going forward. We might not be there yet, but we don't stand a chance if you give up. We're the only hope that third boy has got.'

Murray nodded. Stood up and walked back across the road and into the station. McCoy watched him go. For the first time in his professional life, he felt adrift. Murray had always been the rock, the one telling him to keep going, to do better. Wouldn't have been a detective without Murray. Wouldn't be half the man he was. No way he was going to let him down now. Swore he'd find that last boy before they killed him. Trouble was he had no idea how to do it. He was as lost as everyone else.

THIRTY-FIVE

'It's hard to believe, but you actually look worse than you normally do when you come here,' said Phyllis as McCoy came through the door to the examination room.

McCoy replied while trying to avoid looking at the blood or whatever gunk was smeared down the front of her gown. 'There was another tape. That poor bugger. Just listened to it. Worse than the last one.'

'Ah, I don't envy you that,' said Phyllis.

'Think I'll watch from over here if you don't mind,' said McCoy, sitting down by the door.

'You won't see much from there.'

'That's kind of the point.'

Phyllis shook her head, went back to the body on the slab.

McCoy listened to Phyllis dictating to her assistant for a couple of minutes, then tuned out. Smell was getting to him too. Bleach and something much worse.

'McCoy?'

Phyllis was standing with her gloved and bloody hands in the air, the opened-up body of Danny Walsh laid out in front of her. He looked away quickly.

'Something here that might interest you. Do you want to come and see?'

'Nope.'

'Well, I'm not shouting over there so you're going to have to come a bit closer.'

McCoy sighed, got up, took a couple of steps. Kept his eyes firmly on the floor.

'This is something you don't often see,' said Phyllis. 'It seems his left foot has been immersed in boiling water.'

McCoy winced. '"Burn for a burn",' he said. 'The Bible quote.'

'The skin's peeled off, as has most of the next layer of flesh. I'm hoping he lost consciousness during it.'

'Lovely,' said McCoy. 'Tell me more.'

'Well, the metatarsals are—'

There was a knock, the examination-room door opened, and Joe, the bloke who worked on reception, was standing there, sheet of paper in his hand.

'Harry McCoy! Don't often see you in here. How's things?'

'Great,' said McCoy. 'Just having a chat about how sore it is to have your foot boiled.'

Joe held out the paper to Phyllis. 'Bloke said this was urgent. Hope I've written it all down right.'

Phyllis held up her bloody gloves. 'McCoy, could you?'

McCoy took the note from Joe and started to read. 'It's from someone called Professor McKay.'

'Ah, been waiting for this. Professor McKay was analysing the organic matter on the bottom of Colin Turnbull's shoe for me.'

'Oh yes,' said McCoy, pretending he hadn't forgotten all about that. Held the note out in front of Phyllis.

She peered at it. 'Apparently it was a raisin.'

'Great,' said McCoy. 'Must have had a bar of Cadbury's Fruit & Nut before they killed him.'

'A raisin and . . .'

'And?'

'And mushed into it was the lower half of a Trichonephila clavipes.'

'A what?' asked McCoy.

'Commonly known as a golden silk orb-weaver. It's a kind of spider.'

'Not sure the fact that Colin Turnbull stepped on a spider after he ate his chocolate is going to help us find the buggers who did it.'

Phyllis kept reading, then looked up. 'That, Harry McCoy, is where you may be wrong. It says here that the golden silk orb-weaver is native to Central America. They live in banana plants, sometimes found when the crates are unpacked.' She skimmed down the rest of the note. 'That's it.'

McCoy lowered the paper, headed back to his seat. Tried to think. Had Colin Turnbull been in a fruit shop before he was killed? What would he have been doing in there? Didn't make much sense.

'Not my job of course,' said Phyllis.

'But . . .' said McCoy.

'Were I a detective I would deduce that poor Colin Turnbull was kept or killed at a place where they unpack bananas.'

McCoy thought for a minute. Looked at Phyllis and grinned. 'Air brakes! Makes sense now.'

'What does?' asked Phyllis, but she was talking to his back. McCoy was halfway out the door already.

THIRTY-SIX

Four police vans, three single-deckers hired from Caledonia Buses, six pandas and a van providing teas. The fruit market car park was full when McCoy turned up. Looked like a police invasion. He could see Wattie wandering about with a clipboard in his hand pointing at various areas of the warehouses, sending teams of six uniforms off to each one. The dog handlers were off to the side, restless Alsatians straining at their leads and barking.

The fruit market had moved from the city centre to Blochairn in the north, with its better road access to the new motorway. It was a collection of warehouses and refrigerated units covering a couple of acres. A few burger vans dotted about, the stink of rotting fruit and fish from the adjoining market. Against a lot of opposition, Murray had managed to get the whole place evacuated. The workers who had been turfed out were huddled together, smoking away, didn't look happy. A long line of huge lorries had formed near the entrance, no place to load or unload, drivers standing by the open doors of their cabs watching what was going on.

McCoy walked over to Wattie. 'Stinks here,' he said. 'How's it going?'

'Count yourself lucky it's not a hot summer's day, it's a hundred times worse then. We're getting there. It's a big bloody place though. How was the autopsy?'

'Don't tell Murray but I left before it was finished. Had to tell him about this.'

'Yeah, right. How long did that take? Two minutes? You could be back there now.'

'Aye, and I could punch you in the neck. So what's the plan?'

'Uniforms are divided up into teams of six, working left to right across the bays. Nightmare getting the bodies, half the force is at that big funeral this afternoon.' He pointed over at the rows of warehouses. 'Size of this place means it will probably take us a few hours to cover it. All this for a bloody spider?'

'Don't knock it. It's all we've got. The autopsy this afternoon isn't going to tell us anything we didn't know. Tortured then stabbed in the heart twice, just like the first one. Poor bugger must have been in agony, they even boiled—'

'Sir?'

Smythe was standing holding a plastic Marks & Spencer's carrier bag. He held it out to them.

'At last!' said Wattie, taking it. 'C'mon,' he said to McCoy and started walking towards the dog handlers.

'What's in there?' asked McCoy, hurrying to catch up.

'A pair of Danny Walsh's socks and his underpants.'

'Lovely,' said McCoy.

'To us, fucking bouffing. To the dogs it's Christmas come early.'

'That it?' asked one of the dog handlers coming towards them, Alsatian wagging its tail beside him.

Wattie nodded, gave him the bag. The handler took one of the socks and knelt down by his dog, covered his nose in it and started talking into his ear. The dog seemed to be listening, suddenly broke away, started barking.

'That's it,' said the handler. 'He's got the scent now. I'll blow the whistle if we find anything.'

He walked off towards the warehouses, dog pulling at the lead.

'Think it'll work?' asked McCoy.

'Fuck knows. Think we've got a couple of hours with the market cleared, can't stretch it much further than that. If we don't get anything by then, the game's a bogey. You sticking around?'

'May as well. It's this or the autopsy.'

'I'd better go back and see how the hand-to-hand is going.'

This was the stuff Wattie was good at. Organising things, handling big groups of people. He wasn't a bad detective at all, just different to McCoy. Liked the things he didn't. Different styles. Should really speak to Murray about it. Maybe there was a better role for Wattie than following him about all day.

An hour later McCoy was lighting his tenth cigarette of the day, trying to ignore the grumbling of the lorry drivers and work out how the fuck they could find Paul Cooper. He watched a couple of guys unloading big cardboard boxes of tulips from a lorry with Dutch number plates. They just piled them by the side of the road, nowhere else to put them, he supposed.

McCoy wasn't sure why, but he felt that Dirty Ally, the girl and Paul Cooper must be connected. Maybe if he knew what the bloody hotel keys were for, he could find out how. Wondered if there was a way of going in reverse, showing some expert the keys and them telling you what kind of lock they fitted. Might help narrow things down a bit. He dropped his cigarette on the ground, was just about to stamp it out and go and find Wattie, ask him if he'd heard of such a thing, when he heard a police whistle and started running.

THIRTY-SEVEN

'Fuck!' Murray kicked at a cardboard box in the corner of the room.

McCoy couldn't blame him, looked like all their work had been for nothing. Close but not close enough. They were standing in a storage unit at the east end of the fruit market. It was basically a big white box, concrete floor, plaster walls, about twenty feet square. In the corner were two mattresses, a bucket full of piss, the wrappers from fish and chips and a couple of empty Irn-Bru bottles.

The sniffer dog was whining, probably wondering why everyone wasn't happy with what he'd found. McCoy walked over to the corner, poked the chip wrappers with the toe of his shoe, revealed a Mars Bar wrapper underneath.

'Whose is it?' asked Murray.

'Nobody's,' said Wattie. 'Hasn't been rented for a couple of years. Last tenant was an old Italian guy. Imported tinned tomatoes, retired years ago.'

'Why move them?' asked McCoy. 'This looks like a pretty tight set-up.'

'Maybe something spooked them,' said Wattie. 'Worried about being discovered.'

'There's three fish and chip wrappers,' said McCoy. 'This must be where they brought them at first.'

'You called the lab boys?' asked Murray.

Wattie nodded. 'On their way.'

'Maybe they'll find something.' Murray's anger seemed to have subsided into a kind of resigned exhaustion. 'Need to find that boy before something happens to him. Maybe we—'

'Is he here?'

Tom McCauley was standing in the doorway, the bulk of him blocking out most of the light.

McCoy shook his head.

McCauley looked like he'd been punched in the stomach. He let out a moan, held onto the wall.

'Can I ask you what you're doing here, Mr McCauley? Or rather, how you knew we were here?' said Murray.

McCauley wiped at his eyes with his shirt sleeve, tried to pull himself together. 'I've got a haulage company. Some of the boys work out of here. They called me when they realised what was going on.'

McCoy rolled his eyes. Last thing they needed was a distraught father wandering about.

'Is that where they were?' asked McCauley, pointing at the mattresses.

'We think so,' said McCoy.

'Where is he now?' asked McCauley.

McCoy and Murray looked at each other.

'Tell you what, Mr McCauley,' said McCoy. 'You come with me and we'll get you a cup of tea, eh? I can tell you what we think has happened.'

McCauley nodded, eyes stuck on the mattresses in the corner.

McCoy took his arm. McCauley held onto him like a lost child as they walked out the door.

'Do you have any idea what me and his mother have been going through?' asked McCauley as they sat on a bench by the burger van.

McCoy handed him a mug of tea. Answered truthfully. 'I can't even imagine.'

'When the news came in about the first boy I thought his mother was going to go mad, or kill herself or something. I've never seen someone in such pain in my life. I couldn't talk to her, couldn't touch her. She hasn't eaten since he's been gone, she's running on her bloody nerves, paces the house all night, sits on his bed, one of his jumpers in her hands and bawls her eyes out.' He looked at McCoy. 'I don't know what to do any more.'

McCauley was nothing like the angry big man he'd been when they'd visited his house and somehow that made it all the worse. A man like that reduced to a shell of what he'd been, all he had left was fear. In a way, it might have been easier if Malcolm had been the first. At least then he and his wife wouldn't have had this terrible wait.

'I'm sorry,' said McCoy. 'I wasn't at my best when we came to see you. You didn't deserve it.'

'That's okay. I know how I come across. I started out as a day labourer on building sites. I came from nothing, had to fight every day to get ahead. Sometimes I forget I'm supposed to be a well-mannered man now, pillar of the community. Can't quite leave it all behind me.'

'When Malcom disappeared,' said McCoy, 'did you ever know where he went?'

'Sometimes,' said McCauley. 'We'd get a phone call. *I need money. I owe money. I want money.* Sad thing is his mother and I were so desperate to see him that we went every time. Was usually somewhere round Garnethill, Woodlands, whatever rundown flat or squat he was living in.'

McCoy had an idea. There was someone else living like that. 'He ever mention a Paul Cooper?'

McCauley shook his head. 'Apart from asking for money, he couldn't bring himself to talk to us.'

McCoy dug in his pocket, took out the photo strip and handed it to McCauley. 'Recognise the boy at the bottom?'

McCauley looked at it. Handed it back, puzzled. 'Of course I recognise him.'

'That's Paul Cooper,' said McCoy.

'That one's my son. That's Malcolm. He's not facing the camera but it's him all right.'

'What?'

'Malcolm, that's him at the bottom, looking to the side,' said McCauley.

'You recognise the other two?' asked McCoy.

McCauley looked at it again. 'Think so,' he said. 'Last time we saw Malcolm he was waiting for us outside a flat in Hill Street.'

'Can you remember the number?'

McCauley shook his head. 'Was a main-door flat, that's all I remember. It was a nice night, him and those two were waiting on the step, think it was them anyway, passing a joint bold as you like. Girl had her arm round the boy with the short hair. Had bare feet, the wife couldn't get over it. Bare feet on a Glasgow street. She tried to talk to Malcolm, but he was gone, high as a kite. We just gave him the money and left. What's the other boy's name again?'

'Paul. Paul Cooper.'

'I remember him because he didn't look like Malcolm's usual pals. They were all hippie types, peely-wally, skinny, long hair. That boy looked more like a boxer.' He tried to smile. 'Looked like me when I was young.' He looked at McCoy. 'You know what I should have done? Bundled him up no matter how much he argued, thrown him in the back of the car and taken him home.' His face crumpled. 'He's still my wee boy.'

And then he started crying, sobs that shook his whole body. McCoy moved along the wall, put his arm around him and McCauley buried his face in McCoy's shoulder and wept.

THIRTY-EIGHT

Couldn't help himself. He had to see it. The crowds had already filled up the cathedral, spilled outside onto the square in front. All of them looked sombre, most dressed in black, umbrellas and raincoats against the drizzle. There were TV vans parked off to the side, cameramen on top scanning the crowd waiting for the funeral cortège to arrive.

McCoy stood in the lee of the Provand's Lordship across the road and lit up. Wondered if there would be a funeral like this for the two dead boys. Didn't think so somehow.

'All right, McCoy?'

Mary was wearing a plastic see-through raincoat over a dark suit, had even gone easy on the make-up for once. 'Come to gawp, have we?'

'Yep,' said McCoy. 'You working?'

'Supposed to be. "Gathering incidental colour" as our esteemed editor calls it. Wandering about in the bloody rain I call it.'

'Hear they've got the Archbishop to do the service,' said McCoy.

Mary sighed. 'His final duty before retirement. Stupid old arse.'

'Not a fan, then?'

Mary snorted. 'Why would I be? I'm a woman.'

'Fair enough,' said McCoy. 'The new one any better, is he?'

She shrugged. 'He's been briefed, talks the right talk, but he's still telling me what I can and can't do with my body so he can go and fuck himself.' She looked at the crowd. 'I better go and see if I can find anyone who's come all the way from Canada for this or who went to school with her. If you see Wattie, tell him I'll no be home until late and to go and get the wee man from my mum's.'

McCoy nodded and watched Mary walk off towards the crowd. He looked at his watch. Had arranged to meet Cooper to go to the Hill Street address at seven. Wasn't quite sure what to do until then. McCauley had unnerved him. Wasn't used to grown men sobbing in his arms. Wished he'd been able to tell him they were hot on the trail, that they would find his son soon.

He was just getting the Pepto-Bismol out his pocket when the hearse, followed by a line of black funeral cars, came round the corner and started up the hill. The coffin was completely covered in flowers, all of them white. Driver of the hearse stared straight ahead, cap on. Turned right, towards the cathedral.

The next car was a Jaguar limousine, a white-faced man and a little boy dressed up in black in the back. Both of them looked terrified.

Flashbulbs had started popping at the cathedral entrance, cameramen zooming in as the hearse arrived. Six men, the pallbearers, stepped out the cathedral entrance and lined up at the back of the limo. The man and the boy got out the car, stood there looking bewildered as the flashbulbs went off. The boy put his hands over his face, started crying.

McCoy had seen enough, was just turning to walk up Cathedral Street when the last of the funeral cars pulled up beside him, joined the queue to get to the cathedral. The window rolled down and Dessie Caine leant out, lit up a cigarette. Could see the new Archbishop in waiting behind him. Dessie took a few hurried puffs, dropped the cigarette onto the wet road, started to roll up the window. Realised McCoy was looking at him. Stared back until his face disappeared behind the misty window.

It took McCoy twenty minutes or so to walk to Dolly's Salon. Couldn't get the image of Dessie Caine out his mind. Face framed by the car window, Father McKenna beside him. Whatever Dessie was up to, it seemed to be paying off. He was deep within the belly of the beast. Hair combed and parted, dark suit and black tie. Just like all the other city dignitaries come to pay their respects. Wasn't sure Murray would be able to avoid sitting next to him at fancy dinners much longer. Dessie was transforming himself, and it didn't look like anyone or anything would be able to stop him.

THIRTY-NINE

There were more flowers outside Dolly's Salon, Mass cards, handwritten notes. Little pictures of them cut out from the paper and glued onto cardboard. Three women, two little girls. He picked up one of the bits of cardboard. A picture of Dolly at some Christmas party. Paper hat on, big smile. Looked like a child's handwriting beneath it.

Aunty Dolly, I know you are in heaven now. I love you. Caitriona XXX

He looked at Dolly's for a while. Suddenly it seemed like they had been travelling down one track the whole time. Gangsters and turf, had been all about them. The women killed accidentally. But maybe the fire was about the women after all. Everybody had been so keen to blame it on Dessie Caine and Johnny Smart. He'd been no different, as blind as the rest. The same attitude he had been giving Wattie a hard time about. Should be ashamed of himself.

Took him a minute or so to remember the name of the woman he'd spoken to, the one who'd taken him to the pub. Remembered. Una, worked in Galbraith's. He put the card back, hurried up the road.

'She's no here, son,' said the woman behind the counter. 'We shut at six. You only got me because I'm running bloody late as usual.'

'Any idea where she lives?'

The woman nodded, caused a ripple down her many chins. 'Aye, but she'll no be there either. She goes to six o'clock Mass, up at St Roch's. You'll catch her there.'

McCoy thanked her, bought a packet of Rich Tea biscuits and a pint of milk. Started working his way through the biscuits as he walked up the road towards the chapel. All the shops were closed except for the off-licence which seemed to be doing a roaring trade. There was a group of teenage boys hanging outside, all baggy trousers, star jumpers and scuffed platform shoes.

One of them broke away, came up to McCoy. 'Gonnae go in for us, mister.'

McCoy looked at him, couldn't have been older than thirteen or fourteen. 'Aye, right,' he said. 'Chase yourself.'

The boy shrugged, stood aside as McCoy walked past. Waited until he was further up the road before he shouted 'wanker' after him. Fair enough.

Mass seemed to be about halfway through when he opened the chapel door and went in. He stood at the back, scanned the crowd for Una, and eventually recognised the back of her head a couple of pews from the front. Turned to go and wait outside when he noticed a table set up at the other side of the chapel.

The model chapel he'd seen in the paper sat in the middle, mossy trees and toy cars around it to give a sense of scale. Neat little sign by it: *Proposed New St Roch's Chapel designed by Gillespie, Kidd & Coia Architects.*

There were photos and drawings on the wall behind. What the interior would look like, where the chapel would be, roughly opposite the building they were in now. A set of photos with

Dessie holding various big cardboard cheques. Donations to the building fund. Five thousand pounds from Glasgow Corporation, eight thousand from the Diocese, and twenty thousand from Mr and Mrs Caine. Dessie and his wife handing a cheque to Father McKenna. Big smiles on everyone's faces.

A rustle behind him, people shuffling along pews as the priest started the communion. McCoy watched the congregation line up, then headed for the door.

He sat down on the wall of the primary school opposite the chapel, pulled the foil top off his bottle of milk and took a swig. He didn't like milk much but the combination of that and the Rich Tea biscuits seemed to work. Stomach was quiet for once. The chapel was an unassuming brick building. Wondered if that was why Dessie Caine wanted to build a new one, wasn't good enough for his Kingdom of Royston.

Supposed that was what laypeople did to impress the church. Raise money, be a good boy and your passage to heaven was guaranteed. No matter what Dessie Caine did now, heaven was surely the last place he'd be heading. McCoy popped the last biscuit into his mouth and watched as the big door opened and the congregation filed out. Una was one of the last to appear. She recognised him, waved and came over.

'Can I ask you a few more questions?' McCoy asked.

'Aye. As long as you don't mind walking with me, got to be getting home.'

'No problem. Just wanted to ask you about the women. Think they've got a bit lost in all this.'

Una scrabbled around in her bag, found a Rainmate and put it on. 'They wouldn't even have been there normally. Was all because they were getting ready for the party. Anne's sister. Her fortieth. She'd booked the function room at the Royston up on Blochairn Road. They were just in there to get ready, get their hair done and that. Have a few drinks before they went.'

'The kids?' asked McCoy.

'The kids shouldn't have been there either. Dolly's babysitter fell through, so they were just there until their dad got off work and came to get them . . .'

'No one would have wanted to hurt them, would they?' he asked. 'No angry husbands finding out they had someone on the side?'

Una shook her head. 'This is Royston, not Hollywood. They were just ordinary women. Worked, went out for a drink every so often, looked after their kids. Tried to do their best.'

They were back at the off-licence now. A dirty look from the boys outside.

Una stopped. Suddenly occurred to her. 'What, you think they were the target? Is that it?'

'I don't know,' said McCoy, walking on. 'I'm just trying to make some sense of what happened, to work out why those boys did it. Just seems like there's no real explanation other than a horrible accident. Like you said, any other night the place would have been empty.'

'Not empty,' said Una. 'Carole would have been there.'

'Carole?'

'Carole Lownie.'

'Sorry,' McCoy said, 'why would she have been there?'

Una sighed. 'I don't know how to say this in a nice way. Carole was a bit slow, if you know what I mean. Nice girl but she wasnae right. She had a job in Dolly's, would go in every night from six to seven to tidy up, wash the floor, that sort of thing.' She smiled. 'Think she had the job because Dolly felt sorry for her. She wasn't really needed but she was so proud of it. Told everyone she met that she was working. Maybe made her feel more like a normal girl, you know?'

McCoy nodded.

Una took a hanky out her coat pocket, blew her nose and wiped her eyes. 'When I think about it, I just . . .'

'Sorry for bringing it up. I should have thought.'

'Those boys they got?' said Una. 'No matter what they did, they didn't deserve what happened to them. Just more pain for everyone. When I think of their poor mothers . . .' She wiped her eyes again, pointed to a close a few yards up. 'This is me.'

'Thanks, Una.'

'If you really want to thank me, find that last boy before they get him, eh?'

McCoy watched her walk up the street and disappear into the close. Wished he could tell her that he would.

FORTY

Cooper was waiting for him at the end of the street.

'You ready for this?' asked McCoy.

'Why wouldn't I be?' said Cooper. Voice sounded normal but his body language betrayed him. Foot was drumming on the ground, Zippo turning through his fingers.

'I need to speak to him, Stevie, so don't come over all angry father and chase him off. Okay?'

'Fuck off, McCoy. Let's go.'

They walked along Hill Street looking at the main-door flats. Stopped at number 72. It had a poster of Jimi Hendrix in the window, Pink Floyd blasting out. Had to be it. Cooper looked at McCoy, nodded at the door. McCoy knocked. Nothing. Knocked harder, tried to make sure he was heard above 'Fearless'. Was just about to knock again when the door opened, and Paul Cooper was standing there. He looked from McCoy to Cooper, turned and ran, disappearing into the dark of the house in seconds.

'Shite,' said McCoy.

'Hang on.'

'What do you mean? He's going to bolt through the back door!'

'No, he's not,' said Cooper. 'Wait.'

Wasn't long until Paul reappeared in the hall. He was being held around the waist by Jumbo, Deke trailing behind them, rubbing at his chin.

'I got him, Mr Cooper,' said Jumbo. 'He hit Deke but I got him.'

Paul gave up struggling, was just standing limp in Jumbo's grip, looking at them. 'Who's he?'

'McCoy,' said Cooper. 'A pal, polis. Needs to talk to you.'

McCoy stepped forward. 'You're not in any trouble, Paul. We're just trying to find out what happened to this girl.' He held out the photo strip and Paul looked at it.

'Where did you get that?'

Suddenly struck McCoy that he might not know. 'Her purse. She's dead, son.'

Paul frowned. 'Thought she was.'

'If I get Jumbo to let you go, you'll no do anything stupid?' said Cooper.

Paul nodded and Jumbo let him go. He sat down on the step and put his head in his hands. Really did look like his father. Same blond hair, same muscular build. Cooper sat down next to him. Tried to put his arm round his shoulder but Paul shrugged it off. Cooper tried again and this time he let it stay.

'C'mon,' he said. 'Let's get a drink.'

They walked up the road, heading for Macintosh's. McCoy and Paul were at the back, trailing a bit.

'Do you think she was in pain?' Paul asked.

McCoy didn't know what to say. 'Probably, but only for a minute or so. Would have been over quick.'

'Paul!' Cooper was walking backwards, shouting. 'C'mere. Need to talk to you.'

Paul trotted up the road towards him. McCoy watched him go. Was hard to believe Cooper's son was only fifteen, looked older. He was dressed in a pair of cords, white T-shirt and a denim jacket, crew cut. Looked every bit the young gang member on the rise. Maybe he would be soon.

When they got to Macintosh's, Cooper told Jumbo and Deke to wait inside by the door and sat down next to McCoy by the bar. Paul sat next to them, eyes red from crying.

'You all right, son?' asked McCoy.

Paul nodded. Cooper called over to Deke, told him to get the drinks in.

'What was her name?'

'Trisha O'Hara,' said Paul. 'Well, it was last week. She changed it a lot. No idea what her real name was.'

'Why'd she do that?'

Paul shrugged. 'Said there were people she wanted to avoid. Didn't want them coming after her.'

'What kind of people?' asked McCoy.

'Landlords she'd stiffed mainly. She moved a lot.'

Deke appeared with the drinks and Paul took a long slug, wiped his mouth. 'You working for my dad now?'

Deke smiled. 'For my sins.'

'What happened to her?' Paul asked McCoy.

'Son . . .' said Cooper.

'I want to know,' said Paul. 'I've got a right.'

'She was strangled,' said McCoy. 'Found in Sighthill Cemetery on Sunday morning. When did you last see her?'

'Friday,' said Paul. 'That's when we got the photos taken. In Central Station.'

'Where did she go after that?'

'I don't know. She wasn't one for keeping you informed. Appeared and disappeared. Didn't want to be held down. Do you know who did it? Who killed her?'

McCoy shook his head. 'We were hoping you could help us find out. What else can you tell us? How did you meet her?'

'In the Arms,' said Paul. 'She asked me for a light, and we got talking.'

'When was that?'

'Couple of months ago.'

'Where did she live?'

'Sometimes with me, in whatever flat I was staying. Red Road for a while. Sometimes she'd disappear for a week or so. She'd a pal in Edinburgh, said she'd been there.'

'Where did she come from? Where's her parents?'

'Didn't have any,' he said. 'Said she'd lived all over the place when she was wee. With aunties, her gran before she died. Been at a boarding school for a while.' Paul took another big slug of his pint. Finished it.

'Look, I can tell you all this, but I don't know how much of it is true. She liked to spin tales. Heard her tell someone once she was related to Paul McCartney, was always saying stuff like that. You never really knew what was true and what wasn't. She didn't mean any harm, she just liked things, herself, to seem exciting, special. Not just be another ordinary girl.' He smiled. 'She definitely wasn't that.' His eyes started to well up again. 'I'm just going to go to the gents for a minute. Wash my face.'

He stood up and Jumbo stood up too, ready to go with him. Cooper shook his head and he sat back down again. Paul headed for the gents, disappeared behind the door.

'Christ,' said McCoy. 'Not sure if that helps or makes it worse. Sounds like he didn't really know who she was either. What did you say to him?'

'Told him I wanted him to come home,' said Cooper. 'That there was a room for him in Memen Road and a job if he wanted it.'

'What did he say?'

'Said he was going to come with me tonight. He's a big lug, makes you forget he's only fifteen. Think he just wants someone to look after him for a while.'

McCoy smiled. 'Big Daddy Stevie. Who'd have thought it?'

'Fuck off, McCoy,' said Cooper. 'Think he wants another pint?'

'Probably,' said McCoy, digging in his pocket for his cigarettes while Cooper waved Jumbo over.

'Go and check what Paul wants, then go to the bar.'

Jumbo nodded, headed to the back of the bar. Was back a minute or so later.

'He's not in there,' he said. 'He's gone.'

FORTY-ONE

McCoy had seen Cooper angry before, lots of times, but never like this. This was personal. Paul had told him exactly what he'd wanted to hear, that he was coming home, that he wanted his dad to look after him, and then he'd disappeared. He'd lied to him. Lied to his face.

Jumbo was sitting by the pub door with a look on his face like a dog that knows it's done something wrong. Deke just looked terrified.

'Maybe it was all too much for him,' said McCoy. 'Maybe I pushed him too hard.'

'Shut the fuck up,' said Cooper.

McCoy held his hands up in surrender. Cooper was looking round the pub, for someone or something to vent his anger on. The few customers had sensed something was wrong, were keeping their heads down. Cooper's eyes settled on Deke. 'What the fuck are you looking at?'

McCoy's heart sank. He'd found someone.

Deke shook his head. 'Nothing, Stevie.'

Cooper stood up. 'Stevie?' he said. 'What? You think you can call me that? You work for me, son, we're no fucking pals.'

The look on Deke's face said it all. He knew whatever he said would be wrong. 'Sorry, Mr Cooper. I didn't mean anything.'

'C'mere,' said Cooper.

'Come on, Stevie,' said McCoy. 'The boy didn't mean any harm.'

Cooper turned to him, looked him in the eye. 'I thought I told you to shut the fuck up.'

Deke walked over to Cooper, stood in front of him. Cooper kicked a chair out. 'Sit,' he said. As soon as Deke sat down, Cooper grabbed him by the throat, fingers pressing into his windpipe, knuckles going white at the pressure he was using. Pulled Deke's face close to his. Deke's eyes were watering, face going redder. His hands were pulling at Cooper's but his hand wasn't shifting.

McCoy knew he had to do something quick. Cooper's eyes had gone blank and McCoy knew what that meant. He wasn't going to stop until Deke was hurt. Badly hurt. He turned round to look at Jumbo but he was staring at the wall in front of him, muttering something under his breath. A prayer by the sound of it.

McCoy only had one chance. Had to take it. 'I told him to go,' he said. 'If you've got a problem, it's with me.'

Cooper seemed to come to. Looked at him. Let go of Deke's neck and Deke fell off his chair onto the floor, coughing and spluttering.

'What?'

'When we were walking down from his flat, I told him he had to do a runner, not tell anyone.'

'You did what?' said Cooper 'Why the fuck did you do that?'

'Because if he didn't, I'd have to take him in. He's a suspect in the girl's murder. Last person to see her and he's her boyfriend. It's textbook stuff. I know he didn't do it, but I'd have to get him into the station for an interview and that's the last thing he needs. I want him out there, trying to find out what happened to her. He's got a better chance than I have.'

Cooper grinned and the fear went out the room like air from a balloon. 'Crafty wee bastard. Didn't even say a word. I knew he had a reason to disappear.'

McCoy nodded. 'Just want him to keep an ear out, ask about, see if anybody knows anything.'

Cooper leant over, pulled Deke off the floor and sat him back on the chair.

'No hard feelings, son? Okay?'

Deke said yes but looked shell-shocked.

Cooper slapped his back. 'Good man. Jumbo, away and get us a round. Brandy for Deke as well, help him get over his wee fright, eh?'

Jumbo jumped up, headed for the bar, look of relief on his face.

'I'm just going out for some air,' said McCoy. 'Stomach's playing up.'

Cooper nodded, was helping Deke get the collar of his shirt straight again.

McCoy opened the door and stepped out onto Cambridge Street. Lit up. The streetlights came on, reflecting on the wet street. A woman and her pal, both the worse for wear, were weaving up Parliamentary Road, arms linked together, helping each other not fall over.

He blew a line of smoke up towards the streetlights. Wondered why Paul had run. Wondered what would happen when Cooper found out he'd lied to him, that he hadn't told Paul to run at all. Hoped he wouldn't be there when he did.

FORTY-TWO

'Where is he?' asked McCoy.

'How would I know?' sniffed Sister Jimmy, fixing his hair in the gents in the Muscular Arms. 'You're getting like a bloody broken record, McCoy. Paul Cooper on the brain.'

'How would you know?' asked McCoy. 'Because you know every shithole flat and squat in Garnethill as you were keen to point out but somehow you didn't know Paul was staying at Hill Street? Fuck off!'

'What's it got to do with you what—'

Sister Jimmy didn't have time to finish his sentence. McCoy had grabbed him by the neck and pushed him up against the wall mirrors.

'Come on, McCoy,' said Spider. 'That's not—'

'And you can fuck off too, Spider,' said McCoy to his reflection. 'Away back to your office.'

Spider held his hands up, retreated into his cubicle.

'Where . . . is . . . he?' asked McCoy. 'I swear, Jimmy, you tell me now, or I'll splatter you all over these fucking walls.'

Sister Jimmy's face was starting to go red. Eyes darting from side to side. He held his hands up and McCoy let him go, spluttering and coughing onto the tiled toilet floor.

'Now,' said McCoy, standing over him.

'He said he was going to the Happiness Hotel,' said Sister Jimmy between coughs.

McCoy wasn't expecting that. The name on the keys in Ally's book. 'What? What's that?'

'That's what I said. He didn't answer me, just said it would be safe now, no one in it any more.'

McCoy raised his foot and held it over Sister Jimmy's face. Look of terror.

'I mean it, McCoy, please. I'm no lying. Please!'

McCoy stamped his foot down onto the floor next to Sister Jimmy's head. Sister Jimmy let out a scream and McCoy squatted down beside him.

'If I find out you're lying, next time it'll be your face. Got me?' Sister Jimmy nodded. 'You see him, you tell him to find me. He's not in any trouble, I just want to speak to him. If he doesn't want his dad to be there, that's fine, it'll just be me. And if you don't find him and get him to come and see me, I'll make sure Stevie Cooper knows about it.'

McCoy stood up. Battered on Spider's office door. Spider opened it, saw Sister Jimmy on the floor. Looked scared.

McCoy held his hand out to Spider palm up. 'Give.'

Spider rooted in his pockets, took out a bag of black bombers and put them in McCoy's hand. McCoy put them in his pocket, walked out the toilets. Never knew when they might come in handy.

He walked out into the rainy night. Decided to walk a bit, try and calm down. No real question now, Ally and Paul Cooper were connected. And chances were that Trisha O'Hara was caught up in it too. Despite what Wattie said, he could only think of one thing that would connect them. Plenty of people Ally knew would be more than interested in pictures of Paul and the girl. But why were Ally and the girl dead now? There were loads of dirty pictures floating about Glasgow, other guys like Dirty Ally, other girls like Paul's girlfriend. What had happened to make them different?

He saw a taxi turn into Wellington Street, held his hand out. One thing he did know: if Ally had killed himself and the girl was dead too, then maybe Paul Cooper was better off in the Happiness Hotel, whatever the fuck that was. Better off where nobody could find him.

He got in the cab. Told the driver he was going to Gardner Street. Home.

25th May 1974

FORTY-THREE

It was beginning to feel like McCoy was never out of Royston. Wattie pulled up in the car park by the Charles Street flats and took the key out the ignition. McCoy looked up at the towers, wondered if the woman was up already, selling whatever it was in the Irn-Bru bottles to the men from the Model across the street. Seven o'clock in the morning might be too early even for her.

He yawned, stomach had got him up at five again. Couldn't get back to sleep. Kept thinking about time running out. It was Saturday morning now. They had to find Malcom McCauley alive today or they'd likely find his body tomorrow.

'No luck with Trisha O'Hara,' said Wattie. 'Got them to run it this morning. One Trisha O'Hara lives in Knightswood, arrested for shoplifting four years ago. Aged fifty-one at the time.'

McCoy tried to get his mind off Malcom McCauley. Pay attention. 'Wasn't holding out much hope. Paul said she changed her name all the time.'

'And now he's run off again? Not an easy man to pin down, young Paul Cooper.'

'Told Sister Jimmy to find him last night,' said McCoy. 'Made it clear his dad wouldn't be happy if he didn't.'

'Makes sense. Did you know this was called Glenconner Park?' asked Wattie, pushing his arm into the sleeve of his raincoat.

McCoy shook his head. 'Always just thought of it as the patch of grass by the school.'

'Me neither,' said Wattie, raincoat now successfully on. 'Had no idea what the guy was talking about when it was called in.'

'Don't tell me it was another bloody dog walker?' asked McCoy, getting into his own overcoat. Not the easiest manoeuvre in the front seat of a Viva.

'Not this time. Postman going for a pee. You ready?'

'As I'll ever be.' McCoy opened the car door and the wind almost pulled it from his hand, stepped out into the pouring rain.

By the time they'd walked across the car park and the football pitches they were soaking. A wild wind was driving the rain sideways and right into their faces. Up ahead, in the trees, a corner of the canvas that had been erected over the body had come loose, was flapping wildly. A uniform was trying to grab it, not having much luck. McCoy and Wattie ducked down under it, grateful for whatever shelter it afforded, and had a look at the reason they were in Glenconner Park.

A middle-aged man was lying on the grass staring up at them. A livid red line slashed across his neck, blood on his wet shirt. An ordinary man. He was wearing a pair of suit trousers and a pale blue shirt, black slip-ons. Clothes were soaking, stuck to him, could see the outline of his vest under the shirt. His face looked familiar for a second and then it was gone. Probably just looked like every other working man in Glasgow. A uniform handed McCoy a wallet. He opened it up, unfolded the driving licence. Read it out. 'Ian Barrett.'

McCoy looked through the wallet. Couple of photos of what looked like his mum and dad at the front at Blackpool, pools coupon, found a wage slip. 'Worked for the Corporation,' he said. 'Janitor at Atholl House.'

Wattie looked blank, the first uniform shook his head.

'Atholl House?' They turned to see the other uniform had managed to tie the canvas down. 'It's a mother and baby place, up in Partickhill.'

McCoy could feel the rainwater seeping into his socks and down the back of his shirt.

'We're not that far from Sighthill Cemetery,' said Wattie, voicing what McCoy was thinking. 'He's been strangled as well.'

McCoy glanced at him. 'Not much in common with the girl though. This guy is a working stiff, a man, middle-aged.'

'Maybe what they had in common wasn't physical.'

'Hurts me to say it but you're getting better, Watson.' He looked at the uniform. 'The postman have anything to say?'

'Not really. Had just done the flats and was going across to the primary school, was desperate for a pee so he came into these trees. Found him lying there.'

McCoy looked around. Traffic was busy on Royston Road, but in the dark it would be easy to turn up the wee road to the football pitches, unload a body, dump it. 'Need to organise a door-to-door of any of the flats that overlook the park,' he said. 'See if anyone saw anything, a car parked here maybe, anything like that. He have anything else on him?'

The uniform opened the brown paper evidence bag he was holding. 'Just under a pound in change, packet of Regal and a box of matches, a snotty hanky and a key.'

'A key to what?' asked McCoy.

'No idea,' said the uniform, digging in the bag. 'Funny-looking thing.' He pulled his hand out and held the key up.

McCoy couldn't believe it. It was a large iron key with a square hoop at the end. The same as the one they had found in Dirty Ally's flat.

'Fuck,' said Wattie. 'What's that doing there?'

'Put that in a separate bag and then give it to me,' said McCoy.

Uniform nodded, wandered off out the tent in search of the crime kit.

'That's the same as the other one, isn't it?' asked Wattie.

'Yep.'

'Why have him and Dirty Ally got the same key? Did they know each other?'

'Must have done,' said McCoy. 'And now they're both dead.'

'And he's been killed the same way as the girl in the cemetery. You think it's all connected?'

McCoy looked across the road at the Great Northern, grey and dark in the morning gloom.

'Yes,' he said. 'Oh yes . . .'

FORTY-FOUR

It didn't take long to find Bert Cross. He was sitting in the same chair as last time, same raincoat on, same magazine for all McCoy knew. He looked up, flicker of fear in his bright blue eyes. 'All right, son?'

'Not really,' said McCoy. 'C'mon, we're going to take a walk.'

Cross sighed, got himself out his chair, and McCoy led him downstairs to the office.

'This is most irregular,' said Swan as McCoy, Wattie and Cross settled themselves into seats. 'Maybe I should stay here and be a witness to what is happening.'

'No need, sir,' said Wattie. 'Just a friendly chat. If you could shut the door on the way out, that would be much appreciated.'

Swan hesitated for a moment, realised he'd been beaten and left.

'What's this all about, son?' asked Cross. 'I told you all I knew last time.'

'Don't think you did, Bert,' said McCoy. 'How much did he give you?'

Cross sank back in his chair, looked like what he was, a frightened old man. 'I don't know what you're talking about, son.'

'Let me make it easy for you,' said McCoy. 'We can have a wee chat here, goes no further, and you can go back upstairs and finish your *People's Friend*. Or I can charge you with wasting police time and take you down to the station, put you in a holding cell, and forget you're there for a couple of days. Your choice.'

Cross blinked, realised he didn't really have an option. 'A fiver. He gave me a fiver. You don't have a fag, do you, son?'

McCoy dug in his pocket, handed over a packet of Regal and his lighter. Cross took them in his shaky hands, lit up, breathed in deep.

'Just tell me what happened that morning,' said McCoy. 'Take your time.'

'I get up early, always have done. Haven't worked for near on twenty years but I still get up at half six. Up and about before everyone else, that's me. So I'm scrabbling about the yard like I do most mornings. Sometimes there's ginger bottles in the bins, can take them back for money, sometimes there's something to sell.' He smiled. 'Never thought I'd end up as a bloody bin raker but there you are. Christ, if my mother could see me now she'd—'

'Bert. That morning.'

Bert held his hands up. 'Sorry, son. Anyway, I'm out there doing that and a bloody slate lands beside me, smashes into smithereens, could have bloody killed me, so I look up and there's two people on the roof. I recognise Ally but not the other guy.'

'And?'

'The other guy is standing right beside Ally, looks like he's talking to him, and Ally's shaking his head, trying to get away from him, but the guy's got hold of his arm. Next thing, he's got Ally round the waist and he's dragging him to the edge of the roof . . .'

'What happened then?' asked McCoy.

Cross shook his head. Looked determined. 'I'm no doing it.'

'Doing what?'

'I'm no saying any more. The worst you can do is put me in the jail for a couple of nights. Compared to here that's no much different. I've been in before, I'll live. But . . .'

'But what?' said McCoy.

'But what if that guy finds out I've tell't. Who's to say he'll no come after me next.'

'For fuck sake,' said McCoy.

Cross sat there looking defiant, cigarette in his trembling hands.

'You're not going to tell us what he looked like?'

He shook his head.

'Okay. Your choice. Fuck off.'

Cross looked surprised.

'Now,' said McCoy. 'Get to fuck.'

Didn't need to be told twice. Was off and out the door in seconds.

'You're letting him go?' asked Wattie.

'What else can I do?' said McCoy. 'I can't beat it out of him. If he gets anywhere near a judge, he'll suddenly become even more forgetful than he already is.' He sighed. 'Far as he's concerned, he's doing the right thing. Hard to argue.'

'From what he said, Ally was chucked off the roof?' said Wattie.

'Sounds like it. Or frightened so much he jumped. Whatever, he ended up dead.'

'So that's Ally, the girl and the bloke this morning. All killed. And we still don't know why, or who did it.'

'There's someone who might have a good idea,' said McCoy. 'Paul Cooper. Let's give Sister Jimmy until the end of the day to find him.'

'And if he doesn't?'

McCoy stood up. 'Fuck knows. We'll worry about it then. Now let's go and see who this bloody janitor is.'

They walked out the door of the Great Northern, headed up the road towards the car. Two guys sheltering in a bus stop stepped out as they passed. Both were sixty-odd, battered by life, no doubt staying at the Northern.

'Can you spare some change, son?' one asked. Held out a grubby hand.

The other one, torn blue jumper under a suit, smiled at them both, front teeth missing. Seemed to be somewhere else.

McCoy stopped, got his wallet out, pulled out a fiver and handed it to the one with the blue jumper.

'Christ. Thanks, pal, thanks a lot. I'll remember you in my prayers.'

McCoy said nothing, started walking towards the car.

'What's up with you, Daddy Warbucks?' asked Wattie.

McCoy stopped, looked back round at the two men hurrying up the road, no doubt heading to the nearest off-licence. Turned back. 'See the one with the blue jumper?'

Wattie nodded.

'That's my dad.'

FORTY-FIVE

'You okay?'

McCoy continued staring out the windscreen at the wet road ahead.

'Are you?'

'Just drive the fucking car.'

Wattie sighed, did just that. They were headed for the West End and Atholl House to try and find out what the dead janitor's story was and why he had the same bloody key as Ally. McCoy watched the windscreen wipers go back and forward. That was all he felt like doing, anything to avoid thinking about the man in the blue jumper.

They turned into the gravel drive of Atholl House. It looked like it had once been a private house. One of those big sand-stone villas that shipyard or industrial tycoons had built on the tranquil banks of Partickhill. Enough room for the family, the cars, the servants up in the eaves. Now, like Partickhill itself, it had seen better times.

New houses had been built in the spaces between the old villas, gardens sold off bit by bit to pay for the expenses of running a big house. Whatever money had been made hadn't been spent on upkeep. The house had moss growing out the gutters, a couple of broken windows repaired with board, and a garden that looked neglected and overgrown.

Wattie parked the car and they sat for a minute.

'Don't ask me again,' said McCoy. 'I'm fine.'

Wattie nodded. 'Okay. Let's go.'

'Dead?' The woman behind the desk looked at them blankly. 'Ian Barrett is dead?'

McCoy read the name on the wooden sign on the desk in front of her. Had forgotten her name as soon as she'd told them it. Mrs L. Black. Matron. Still thinking about his dad.

'I'm afraid so, Mrs Black. What can you tell us about him?'

'How did he die?' she asked.

'Not at liberty to say at the moment,' said McCoy. 'Barrett?'

Mrs Black tried to get a hold of herself. Took a deep breath. 'He was the janitor here. I've been here almost ten years and he was here when I arrived. Knows the building, the heating, inside out. We'd be lost without him.' She stopped. 'Will be lost without him. I can't believe it.'

'Family?' asked Wattie.

She shook her head. 'He had an elderly mother, but she died a few years ago. Other than that, nobody.'

'Did he live on the property?' asked Wattie.

Mrs Black nodded. 'Wasn't supposed to but he did. He lost his flat a couple of years ago.' She stopped, reduced her voice to a whisper. 'Had a gambling problem for a while.' Waited for McCoy and Wattie to nod their understanding. Carried on as normal. 'So he set himself up in a wee space by the boiler room. Was only supposed to be for a few days but he's still there. It suited us and him. He was always here to tend to things. Wasn't much of a life but he seemed happy here. Used to call it his home.'

McCoy looked up, realised Mrs Black and Wattie were staring at him. 'What?'

'Cup of tea? Can I get you one?' Mrs Black asked.

McCoy hadn't heard, had been miles away. Back in Springburn aged six, waiting for his dad to come out the Glen, hoping he'd have some money left to buy them chips.

'No, thanks. Mr Watson, can you continue the conversation? I'd like to have a look at Mr Barrett's living quarters.'

Mrs Black gave him directions and Wattie gave him a strange look. McCoy wasn't sure he knew what he was doing either but he knew he would be no use in this interview. Couldn't concentrate. Couldn't think straight.

He left the office, shut the door behind him, and stood in the hallway. Tried to get his mind back on track. All he really wanted to do was walk out the door and find the nearest pub. Drink his memories and his dad away. Drink everything away. Was the last thing he or his stomach needed but he knew it would make him feel better, for a while. He walked towards the front door, pulled it open, heard a voice.

'Where the fuck are you going?'

Wattie was standing outside the matron's office.

'You checking up on me?'

'Too right I am.'

McCoy sat down on a chair by the door, poster for Gerber's baby food on the wall opposite him. Got his cigarettes out, couldn't find his lighter. Turned to Wattie. 'He didn't recognise me. He didn't even know who I was.'

And then he started to cry.

FORTY-SIX

McCoy opened his eyes. Didn't know where he was for a second. Sat up on the bed. Remembered. Barrett's living quarters. A single bed in a room not much bigger than a cupboard, low rumble of the boiler next door, smell of dirty sheets and coal. He looked over to see Wattie standing in the doorway.

'What happened?'

'Not much,' said Wattie. 'You got a bit upset so we came down here. You lay on the bed for a while and then you fell asleep. Only been out for twenty minutes or so. Feel any better?'

McCoy nodded. The old defence mechanism had kicked in. When things got too bad, he just fell asleep, couldn't help himself. When he needed to be somewhere else, away from the fear and the hurt, sleeping was the easiest way to do it. He rubbed at his eyes. Must be in a bad way, hadn't done it since he was a boy.

'Sorry,' he said.

Wattie shook his head. 'Don't be sorry. It's okay. Thing with your dad's knocked you for six. It's understandable.'

'Don't tell Murray.'

'I won't,' said Wattie. 'What am I, a bloody clype?'

McCoy smiled. 'You are many things, Douglas Watson, but a clype isn't one of them.'

He stood up. Tried to shake himself back into the present. 'Lady Bountiful have anything to say?'

'Not really. Barrett was a living saint apparently. I even showed her the key. Not for anywhere here, no idea what it was for. Had a poke around in here while you were out for the count. Piles of bloody photos all hidden away in a box behind the boiler. No wonder he didn't want anyone down here. Didn't turn anything up. Except for one thing . . .' He held out a hard-backed envelope.

McCoy took it, opened it, and pulled out six or seven glossy black-and-white photos. Trisha O'Hara sitting on the edge of the bed where McCoy was now, dressed in a schoolgirl uniform. Uniform came off as the pictures advanced.

McCoy put them back in the envelope, handed it back to Wattie. 'Shite,' he said. 'This is getting worse and worse.'

'You think she was here as a mother and baby thing?'

'Could well be,' said McCoy. 'Why don't you go and show them to Mrs Black, see if she recognises her? Maybe just the first one. Ask her what else Ian Barrett really got up to here. I need some fresh air.'

McCoy stood in the shelter of the house and lit up. Listened to the rain dripping off the trees in the garden. Looked at his watch. Half one. Sister Jimmy had the afternoon to come through and find Paul Cooper. Needed to talk to him and quick. Whether he knew it or not, Paul was in danger of ending up like Ally or Ian Barrett or Trisha. McCoy watched as a minibus came up the drive and parked beside the Viva.

Five or six teenage girls started to pile out, laughing, holding their jackets above their heads, trying to stay dry. All of them pregnant, some with bigger bumps than others.

'Excuse me?' He stopped one of them as she was going in

the door. Showed her his police card. He dug in his pocket and handed her the photo strip. 'You know this girl?'

She looked at it. 'Trisha O'Hara. She was here when I arrived. Left a few months ago. Had the baby and went.'

'Right. So when are you due?' asked McCoy, looking at her big bump.

'Any bloody day,' she said. 'Anything else? Because I'm pure bursting for a pee.'

'Ian Barrett. The janitor. What do you know about him?'

'Creepy Ian? Same as everyone else. He's a fucking lech. You learn pretty quickly to stay out his way unless you want your arse felt.' She started moving from toe to toe. 'Sorry, mister, I really need to go.'

McCoy nodded and she ran for the door, bumping into Wattie coming in the other direction.

'She was here,' said Wattie.

'Who? Trisha O'Hara?' said McCoy, grinning.

'How'd you know that? Sneaky bastard. Same as what Paul said. In and out of care and foster homes, no real family. Had a baby in December, left straight after.'

'Poor cow,' said McCoy. 'What happened to the baby?'

'Adopted by a couple in Stirling apparently. Churchgoers.'

'She say anything about the photos?'

Wattie shook his head. 'Just that she had no idea what they were or why they were behind the boiler. Was very sure the squeaky-clean Ian Barrett had nothing to do with them.'

'Not what I've just been told. Apparently, he was a right creepy bastard. A lech.'

'Wouldn't surprise me,' said Wattie. 'If he was taking pictures like that, then Trisha O'Hara probably wasn't the first or the last. Think he passed them on to Dirty Ally?'

'Yep. Stuff like that he'd get good money for on his stall. Not sure it would be enough to pay for that fancy flat of his though.'

'What did then?'

'No idea,' said McCoy. 'But I've got a feeling that whatever it was, it happened at the Happiness Hotel.'

They were walking towards the car when Wattie stopped and pulled something out his pocket. 'Got a present for you. Took it off the notice board.' Handed over a photograph folded in half.

'Not another bloody dirty picture.'

'Depends how you look at it,' said Wattie.

McCoy unfolded the photograph. Last thing he expected to see was Dessie Caine looking up at him. Him and Father McKenna presenting Christmas gifts to the girls of Atholl house. Dessie all dressed up like Santa, Father McKenna, big smile on his face, handing a parcel to a girl.

McCoy looked at Wattie. 'That who I think it is?'

Wattie nodded. 'It's Trisha O'Hara.'

FORTY-SEVEN

Murray looked at the photo, looked back at McCoy. 'It's not enough.'

'It's a connection,' said McCoy.

'No, it's not,' he said, sitting back in his chair. 'There were probably forty girls there that day. He no doubt gave a present to each one. This girl was just one of them, nothing special. You could probably find a photo of me with her if you tried hard enough. I told you before, it's a circuit, a charity circuit.'

Wasn't really any point in arguing. Murray was right. The photo wasn't a real connection with Dessie Caine, besides, as far as he knew, Dessie's speciality was knocking off the men who threatened his empire or didn't do what they were told. Not fifteen-year-old girls.

'The janitor,' said Murray. 'He seems a more likely candidate. He got any previous?'

'Two convictions for sexual assault. One a few years ago, one when he was nineteen. Spent a couple of months inside for the first one.'

Murray picked his tobacco pouch off the desk, started packing his pipe. 'Why both of them though? Him and the girl?'

'That's what doesn't make much sense. If she threatened to expose him for taking the photos, maybe he overreacted and killed her. If she'd had some sort of vengeful father and he found out about them, he could have killed him. But the two of them turning up dead?'

'Maybe they're not connected.'

'Be a big coincidence then. Both of them strangled and one with dirty pictures of the other? A very big coincidence indeed.'

Murray's phone rang and he answered it. Started talking about proposed manpower numbers for the coming year. McCoy listened for a bit then drifted off. Wondered what his dad and his pal had bought with the money. Real drink probably. Windfall like that, they'd buy Red Hackle or Lanliq. Proper drink, not meths mixed with fuck knows and sold in an Irn-Bru bottle. Tried to work out how old his dad was now. He was thirty-two, so his dad must be forty-nine now. Looked as though he was past sixty.

'What's up with you? Look like you've lost a fiver and found a pound.'

'Nothing,' said McCoy 'Just thinking.'

'Aye, right. I've known you too long for that excuse. What is it?' asked Murray, looking for his matches.

McCoy dug his lighter out his pocket. Handed it over. 'I saw my dad today.'

Murray looked shocked, then angry. 'George? He still alive?'

McCoy nodded. 'Saw him outside the Great Northern. Him and a pal.'

'How was he?' asked Murray, lighting his pipe. 'Drunk, I suppose.'

'On his way.'

'Did you tell him to stay away from you? That man ran out of second chances a long time ago.'

McCoy looked away. Didn't know why, but he felt too ashamed to tell Murray what had really happened. 'Told him to keep walking. Leave me alone.'

'Good,' said Murray. 'Well done.' He disappeared in a cloud of smoke for a few seconds.

'Lab boys turn anything up from the fruit market?' McCoy wanted the subject changed. Couldn't bear to hear Murray's usual rant about George McCoy and his failings. He'd been hearing it half his life.

'Bugger all,' said Murray. 'You know how many people work there? Over three hundred. Got to work out which warehouses overlook the storage unit, who was on shift, who could have seen anything, before we can even get the interviews going properly.'

'Get Wattie to do it. He's good at that sort of thing.'

'Is he?' said Murray, sounding surprised.

'Yep. He's good at organising big searches. I mean it, he's really good at it.'

Murray thought for a minute. Chewed on his pipe stem. 'That's not a bad idea. If he's half decent, it would free Faulds up to do something more useful.'

'Like interviewing Johnny Smart?' asked McCoy.

'Exactly. Think his lawyer's just about exhausted his excuses. You okay to keep on the girl and the janitor?'

'Will do.'

'Good.'

McCoy stood up.

'I know you, Harry, know what you're like,' said Murray. 'You'll find some way to make your bloody dad's behaviour your fault. It isn't and it wasn't. Don't forget that. George McCoy got done for child neglect umpteen times. Don't waste your time thinking about the bastard. Right?'

McCoy nodded. Walked out Murray's office. Wondered where his dad was now.

FORTY-EIGHT

McCoy needed fags. And he didn't want to be in the office. Noise of the phones and some argument between Moore and Sammy Prentice about whose turn it was to check the lock-ups was starting to turn into a shouting match. It was doing his head in.

'Want anything?' he asked Wattie.

Wattie shook his head. Looked worried. 'Murray wants to see me. What's that about?'

'Don't worry. Wants you to oversee the fruit market interviews.'

Wattie's face brightened. He put the packet of crisps he was eating down on his desk. 'Does he? Really?'

'Yep,' said McCoy. 'I told him you were good at that sort of thing so don't bloody mess it up.'

Left Wattie looking even more worried than before.

Amazingly the rain had let up for the afternoon. Was even an attempt by the sun to break through the clouds. McCoy walked to the newsagent, stopped outside when he saw the headline under the crossed wire of the *Evening Times* board.

BUSINESSMAN OFFERS REWARD FOR INFORMATION ON LAST BOY

He went in, bought the paper and his fags, sat down in the bus stop outside and opened the paper. Expected to see a picture of Malcolm McCauley, but it wasn't him staring up from the paper. It was Dessie Caine. As a 'prominent citizen' of Royston, he had donated five thousand pounds for information leading to the recovery of Malcolm McCauley and his proper trial and conviction. 'Justice must be done,' he said, 'for the families involved.'

McCoy folded the paper and lit up. Had to take his hat off to Dessie. What better way to make sure Malcom McCauley lived to tell the tale of how Johnny Smart got them to start the fire. He was upping the ante again. Wondered how Johnny Smart felt reading the paper this afternoon. Knew one thing, Johnny was being boxed into a corner, and that was not something he'd be happy about. If McCoy was Dessie, he'd be watching his back.

He stubbed out his cigarette. Wondered how long he could put off the inevitable. He had two choices as far as he could see. He could go and get drunk, and get so drunk he wouldn't think about his dad any more, or he could do what Murray had said. Stop feeling guilty about something that wasn't his fault.

To do either one, he would have to go back to where he didn't want to go. His childhood. Looked up at the sun trying to break through the clouds. Told himself he had stuff to do, had to keep working, that would keep the thoughts of his dad at bay. And if he was going to do that, he had someone to find. Sister Jimmy.

Didn't take as long as he thought it would. He tried Equi. No dice. Tried the Muscular Arms. Guy behind the bar told him it was too early for Sister Jimmy. Suggested he try Forbidden Dreams. Had to ask the barman what that was. Second-hand clothes shop up a close in Sauchiehall Street, he said. One of his pals worked there, and he sometimes spent the afternoons hanging out there.

Upstairs to Forbidden Dreams said the sign in the close. *Clothes, jewellery, accessories, all your heart's desires.* Was hard to believe a second-hand clothes shop above a pub at the wrong end of Sauchiehall Street could deliver so much, but who was McCoy to question it. He climbed up the stairs, stood into the side to let two girls dressed a bit like Alice Cooper pass, and made it to the top-floor landing. Could hear The Velvet Underground through the door, smell incense. He pushed the door open and went in.

The shop was really a converted flat. The floors, walls, ceilings were all painted black. There were racks of clothes along the walls, mannequins in thirties gear, posters of fifties horror films hanging up. McCoy made his way towards the noise he could hear coming from the big room at the front. The windows overlooking Sauchiehall Street were frosted over, room lit by candles and a few lava lamps. A stuffed buffalo head looked down on the rails and old dressers full of scarves and cravats. There was a desk at the window. A woman in her twenties, dressed like Morticia from the Addams Family, was folding what looked like old simmets. Jet-black hair, jet-black eye make-up, jet-black tight-fitting dress. She looked up. Obviously pegged McCoy as different from her regular customers.

'Can I help you?' she asked in a tone sounding like it would be very unlikely.

'Maybe,' he said. 'Looking for Sister Jimmy.'

'She's just trying something on,' she said, nodding at a curtained alcove. 'Be out in a minute.'

McCoy decided not to wait, went over and pulled the curtain wide. Sister Jimmy was half in, half out a green satin evening gown, long white gloves that went up his arms, diamanté earrings, hair slicked back in a chignon. Saw McCoy in the mirror. Looked as shocked as McCoy was. Pushed him out and yanked the curtain shut.

'Could you give me a bit of bloody privacy!' he shouted. 'I'll be out in a minute.'

McCoy was so surprised he backed off, sat on a gold chair with a red velvet cushion beside a full-length mirror and waited. Couple of minutes later the curtain was pulled aside and Sister Jimmy was there in all his glory. Dress clinging to his body and complete outfit now set off with red stilettos. Effect somewhat diminished by his deep voice and East End accent.

'I tried,' he said. 'Honest. Asked everywhere. The wee bastard's disappeared off the face of the earth.'

McCoy stared at him. Still couldn't believe it. Had to admit Sister Jimmy didn't look bad as a woman.

'And, before you ask, no bastard has ever heard of the bloody Happiness Hotel whatever it is. Okay? And if you think kicking shit out of me or clyping to bloody Stevie Cooper is going to change that, well, go ahead, but it isn't.'

'That's you told,' chipped in the woman behind the desk. 'Big time.'

A defiant Sister Jimmy dressed as a forties film star was hard to argue with. McCoy had the feeling he wasn't lying. Sister Jimmy had a lot to lose if he was, and nothing much to gain.

'How long's this been going on?' he asked, looking Sister Jimmy up and down.

'None of your fucking business,' he said. Went over to the mirror and started re-applying his lipstick.

'Maybe I could interest you in a new suit?' said Morticia. 'Looks like you could do with one.'

For a minute, McCoy almost took her up on the offer. Whole situation was so strange it seemed like not a bad idea. 'Maybe another time. You better not be lying to me,' he said to Sister Jimmy.

Sister Jimmy turned away from the mirror to look at him. 'Sure as I'm dressed as Betty Grable, I'm not,' he said. 'I wanted to be able to tell you where he is, believe me. I want you off my back, but he's not hanging about with anyone he knows. It's not just you who doesn't know where he is, nobody does. Think he's fucked off.'

'Where?' asked McCoy.

'Where does anyone from Glasgow go when they need a change? London. Cheap train ticket and seven hours later you're in the big city. Just another unknown face and no one you know breathing down your neck.'

McCoy stepped back out to the relative calm of Sauchiehall Street. Took a swig of his Pepto-Bismol. Had to admit Sister Jimmy had a point. Three quid and you could leave all this behind. What reason did Paul Cooper have to stay? His girlfriend was dead and his dad couldn't decide whether to kick his head in or take him into the family business. Made sense for him to go. Trouble was, that didn't help McCoy one bit.

He started heading for the office when a car drew up beside him. Window was rolled down. He thought someone was going to ask him directions and he leant in. Realised he was looking down the barrel of a gun.

The man holding it smiled.

'Johnny Smart would like to see you. Get in the back.'

FORTY-NINE

McCoy had been dropped off at the entrance to the Botanic Gardens, and told that Mr Smart would be sitting on a bench by the Kibble Palace. McCoy went through the park gates, walked up the wide path by the flower beds and past the women with babies in prams taking the air. The Botanic Gardens was a remnant of the city's Victorian wealth, a couple of acres of manicured park and two enormous greenhouses full of plants from around the empire.

Smart smiled as McCoy approached, stood up and held his hand out to shake.

His nickname certainly suited him. Been used for so long now people assumed it was his real name. He'd a pale grey suit on, red Windsor knot tie on a blue shirt, black brogues polished to army standard. Smart wasn't a big guy, five foot five or so, but with his attire and an aura of always being in control, he was a formidable presence.

McCoy shook his hand and they started walking. 'A gun? Who do you think you are? Al Capone?'

'He didnae have that, did he?' said Smart, looking pained. 'Stupid wee prick. I told him to get rid of it. It's only a bloody replica as well, got it on his holidays in Spain.'

'You could just have asked, you know,' said McCoy. 'We've been trying to speak to you for days.'

Johnny Smart smiled. 'This is unofficial,' he said. 'Off the books. Lawyer would kill me if he knew I was talking to you.'

'Why me?' asked McCoy. 'I'm not even on the investigation.'

'Because Murray listens to you.'

'How do you know that?'

'Because it's my job to know things like that. C'mon, let's get a seat in the Palace.'

Terminalia muelleri said the sign next to the tree beside the bench. Australian almond. Inside the pavilion it was about ten degrees hotter than outside and very humid, like an Australian rainforest, McCoy supposed. They sat down and watched a group of schoolkids in shorts and pinafores being shown all the different plants.

'I didn't have anything do with the fire at Dolly's Salon,' said Smart. 'That's what I want you to know. There is no way I'm getting held responsible for those deaths.'

'That so?' said McCoy, getting his fags out. 'Because one of the boys said you asked him to do it.'

'Ah,' said Smart. He smiled. 'The confession. My lawyer told me about that. Said it had, what was the exact phrase, zero credibility. Obtained under extreme distress.'

'Why'd he say it then?'

Smart shrugged. 'You'd have to ask whoever was torturing him.'

'And who was that?'

'No idea. That's your problem. I just need you to know it wasn't me that did it.'

McCoy lit up, was beginning to get a bit tired of Johnny Smart and his need to knows. 'I thought you and Dessie were having a wee skirmish. Something about who gets to run the People's Republic of Haghill.'

'We are. But setting fire to things isn't my style. Never was. I prefer a more direct style of confrontation. More man-to-man, if you get me.'

One of the schoolkids was getting a row from his teacher, bunch of exotic-looking leaves in his hand, guilty expression on his face.

'You know what I'd be doing if I was you?' McCoy blew out a lungful of smoke and watched it disperse.

'What's that?'

'Exactly this. I'm guessing you read the paper this afternoon, saw Dessie's wee reward announcement. It's put the wind up you, so you're doing everything you possibly can to distance yourself from the death of five people. Maybe it was an accident, maybe there wasn't supposed to be anyone there, but it still happened.'

'I didn't do it.'

'And you know what else I'd be doing? Cleaning house. Making sure there was no one left to tell tales. No boys left who knew what really happened.'

Smart didn't say anything, stared ahead, one hand spinning the signet ring on the other's pinkie.

'And because you're not a jumped-up street fighter like Dessie, you did something clever. Got a confession that everyone knows is worthless, so obviously worthless that it throws everyone off the scent. Can hear them now. Can't really have been Johnny Smart, must be someone trying to frame him.' McCoy nodded at the plants and paths in front of them. 'And this wee tête-á-tête was a good idea too. The honest thief driven to contact the polis so disgusted is he by the scale of the crime. Getting warm am I, Mr Smart?'

Smart turned. Looked him in the eye. Then spat in his face.

McCoy got his hanky out, wiped it away. 'Looks like I struck a nerve,' he said. 'You're fucked and you know it.'

'Looks like I was wrong,' said Smart. 'I was told you were a half-decent cop, someone who would listen.'

'To your fairy tale? Afraid not, Mr Smart. And if you thought I was going to trot back to Murray with your tale of woe, then you're stupider than I thought.' He stood up. 'No matter how good your lawyer is, he's not infallible. Murray will get his interview today or tomorrow and then you really will be fucked. Good luck in Barlinnie.' Turned to go, stopped. Looked back at him. 'And, by the way, if you ever fucking spit on me again, I'll break both your fucking legs.'

*

McCoy stormed out the Botanic Gardens, tried to calm down. His stomach hurt. Headed for the Boots on Byres Road. Had the feeling he was being played and he didn't like it. Johnny Smart had wound him up. Hated the idea that all those lives had been sacrificed just because someone wanted to keep their reputation as a 'gentleman criminal' and swan about Glasgow in bloody Daks suits.

McCoy bought a new Pepto-Bismol, stood in the bus shelter outside, and slugged it.

An old woman in a raincoat and matching bonnet looked at him sympathetically. 'Heartburn, is it?'

'Something like that.'

'Cucumbers,' she said. 'Avoid them like the plague. That's my advice.'

McCoy took another drink, and watched her get on a number 47 bus. He looked at his watch. It was too early to go and see how Wattie was getting on at the fruit market. Needed to do something though. Byres Road was too full of pubs, too tempting. He could cross the road and stand outside Curlers, remember the time his dad told him he'd be back out in twenty minutes. A taxi driver on the rank had given him money for chips, seen him standing there every time he came back to join the queue of taxis, felt sorry for him. His dad came out at closing time, told him he'd met a pal. That was it.

Wasn't going to do it, wasn't going to give him the satisfaction. He walked over to the taxi rank and got in a cab. Needed to do something, even if it involved ignoring everything Murray had said. Either that or he'd be in Curlers himself in five minutes, whisky in hand.

FIFTY

McCoy's taxi was inching its way along Royston Road, road-works causing the delay. They stopped by Dolly's Salon, cards and flowers all bedraggled now, spread across the wet pavement. Taxi sat there for a full five minutes before McCoy decided to walk. Forge Street wasn't that far and sitting in traffic was driving him mad again.

He paid the driver, got out, and took a quick look across the road at the Great Northern, was relieved to see no sign of his dad. Starting walking up past the Charles Street flats and headed for Dessie Caine's house. Knew he was fishing but he wanted Dessie to squirm for a bit. Was sick of him and Johnny Smart thinking they ran the show.

As it turned out, McCoy didn't need to walk as far as Forge Street. Saw one of Dessie's boys standing by the entrance to the park. Long leather coat, trying to look hard.

'Where is he?'

Guy in the coat sniffed, looked at him. 'Fuck's it got to do with you?'

McCoy sighed. Was never easy. He took out his police card, held it up to the guy's face. 'That's what it's got to do with me, you stupid prick. Where?'

The guy tried to look like he wasn't bothered, pointed into the park.

McCoy walked past him, made sure his shoulder hit him, bumped him off the path. Little victories. Petty but satisfying.

He could see three figures up ahead. The bulky one had to be Dessie, small one looked like the architect Jack Coia, tall one he wasn't sure about. Coia was pointing, seemed to be showing them where the new chapel would go, the other two listening. McCoy got nearer, and saw it was Dessie and Coia right enough, saw the flash of the tall one's dog collar. Father McKenna.

He felt the photo in his pocket, wished he'd waited until Wattie could come with him. Too late now. 'Gents,' he said. 'This where it's going to be, is it?'

'Yes, that's the plan,' said Coia. Seemed happy to explain. 'Access to a main road. Beautiful, wooded site. Hopefully we will be able to start the—'

'What are you doing here?' asked Dessie angrily. 'We're busy.'

'Just wanted to ask you a few questions,' said McCoy. 'You and Mr McKenna here. Lucky me catching you together.'

McKenna looked puzzled. 'I'm sorry, I don't know—'

'Detective McCoy. Glasgow Police,' said McCoy, holding out his badge. 'Mr Coia? Would you mind taking a wee walk?'

Coia nodded and set off towards the old chapel across the road. McCoy watched him go, took the photo from Atholl House out his coat pocket, handed it over.

McKenna took it, held it out in front of him and Dessie. 'Not entirely sure what I'm looking at. Seems to be a Christmas party.'

'Maybe give it to Dessie,' said McCoy. 'Let him have a closer look.'

Dessie gave McCoy a look that would sour milk, took it from McKenna's hand.

'The girl you're giving the present to – recognise her?'

'No,' said Dessie.

'Trisha O'Hara,' said McCoy. 'Atholl House. Ring any bells?'

Another filthy look. 'No,' he growled.

'Well, you gents met her, there it is in black and white. Either of you meet her again?'

'I'm sorry,' said McKenna. 'I'm lost. I've no idea what this is all about.'

'Fuck off, McCoy,' said Dessie. He dropped the photo at McCoy's feet. 'Before I make you.'

McCoy bent down and picked the photo up, wiped it clean. 'Reason I'm asking is that Trisha O'Hara was found dead about a mile up the road from here. Sighthill Cemetery, to be exact. A young girl you both met. A young girl murdered in your diocese, Mr McKenna, and right on your patch, Dessie, and neither of you have even heard about it. Funny that, wouldn't you say?'

McKenna's eyes narrowed. 'I think it's time this conversation drew to a close. I have no idea what you are doing here or what you are trying to imply. I meet many young people in my job, as does Mr Caine. You will forgive me if I don't remember every single one. However, I can safely say I never met this girl outside the context of this photograph. Dessie? Did you?'

Dessie shook his head. 'No.'

McCoy could see Dessie's hands were clenched into fists, colour starting to rise on his face. He should be backing off. Couldn't help himself.

'Well, that's strange, isn't it? You say you can't remember everyone you meet, yet you must have remembered Trisha O'Hara because you're certain you never met her again. How does that work?'

'Goodbye, Mr McCoy,' said McKenna.

McCoy shrugged. Went to walk away, turned back.

'The reward,' he said. 'What's that about, Dessie? Trying to wind up Johnny Smart? Or just performing your duties as the patron saint of Royston?'

Dessie didn't look at him, kept staring ahead.

'Looking a bit puzzled there, Mr McKenna, not—'

'It's Father McKenna,' he said, looking exasperated.

'Not to me it's not,' said McCoy. 'I've got one of those and, believe me, I don't need another one. You're probably looking puzzled because you don't know who Johnny Smart is. I'll tell you, shall I? He's another crook just like Dessie here. Hurts people and steals for a living, just like Dessie. Only difference is Johnny Smart is trying to go legit by acquiring businesses, not by trying to buy his way into heaven.'

Dessie had had enough. He moved towards McCoy, fists raised, temper up. 'Listen, you wee prick, I'm—'

'Dessie!'

Dessie stopped in his tracks.

'Don't let this idiot provoke you,' said McKenna. 'It's not worth it.'

Dessie stood, eyes on McCoy. Fists came down and he stepped back. 'You've crossed a line,' he said. 'Embarrassing me and Father McKenna. I won't forget that, McCoy. Believe me.'

'I asked you a question about a murdered girl on your patch. Not quite sure why that's embarrassing. Unless you've got something to be embarrassed about, that is.'

McCoy turned and walked away. Wasn't sure he had achieved anything but winding Dessie up. That was good enough for him. But he had learned something he wasn't expecting. Dessie and McKenna were a little too prepared for questions about Trisha O'Hara. Made you wonder why.

FIFTY-ONE

McCoy walked up Darnick Street, heading for the fruit market to see how Wattie was getting on. If he knew people like McKenna, he knew this: he'd be onto Murray or Murray's boss in Pitt Street within the hour telling them what a naughty boy McCoy'd been. Truth was he had been. He'd pushed too hard with no real reason, but the anger about his dad had had to come out somewhere and if it earned him a roasting from Murray he didn't much care.

If he was being honest with himself, it had all been for nothing. He knew Trisha O'Hara, Ian Barrett and Dirty Ally's deaths were connected, just didn't know how, and if Paul Cooper had disappeared off to London, he was even less likely to find out now. Felt like he'd been flailing about getting nowhere. Wasn't doing a great job of proving to Murray he needed to be back. If Barrett had been providing dirty pictures to Dirty Ally and one of the models was Trisha O'Hara, why had they all ended up dead?

Sure, it was a crime, but it was a wee grubby one. Not enough to result in three deaths. There had to be something else that connected them. He stopped, crossed Provanhill Road and noticed the Royston up ahead. Rain was getting worse.

Maybe he'd go in for one before he met Wattie. Maybe it would be more than one. He was getting nowhere with this case and he wanted to drink his dad away.

The first Guinness and double Bell's went down well, second was going down even better. Maybe his stomach was on the mend after all. The Royston wasn't somewhere he'd been before, he'd driven past loads of times but had never had the inclination to stop. It was one of those weird pubs with an early licence. Opened at eight for the fruit market workers coming off shift, served breakfast so you could get a pint. Breakfast being the same dry roll that got passed back and forwards along the bar.

He had a look along the bar. Usual collection of lonely drinkers. Just like him. There was a jukebox in the corner, looked like a Rolling Stones fan had been filling it up. 'Jumpin' Jack Flash' had just become 'Brown Sugar'. There was a framed photo behind the bar. The front of Dolly's Salon. Looked like opening day. Lots of smiles and a pink ribbon across the door. Little sign beneath it: R.I.P.

Remembered the Royston was where the party that the girls had been getting ready for was meant to take place. The barman was standing at the end of the bar, smoking a roll-up and reading a copy of the *Racing Post*. About five inches of black stitches holding together a recent slash on his cheek.

McCoy called him over, showed him his police card. 'What happened to you?'

'Cut myself shaving,' he said.

'Fair enough,' said McCoy. 'This where Dolly's party was supposed to be?'

The barman nodded.

'Why here?' asked McCoy.

'Luck,' said the barman. 'They only decided to have it that afternoon, a spontaneous kind of thing. They'd already tried a couple of places, but their reception rooms were booked. We were empty that night. Guy who'd booked it for his retirement party got hit by a car when he was coming out of Woolie's. He's still in the Royal.'

McCoy thought back to what Una had said. That the only person who would normally be in the salon at that time of night was Carole, the cleaner. Maybe a cleaner who wasn't all there wouldn't mean much to a man like Johnny Smart. Just a casualty of bigger things.

More he thought about it, more he realised that that was exactly the way the police had treated her. The public too. Didn't remember seeing many pictures of her or Mass cards outside the salon. Not much mention of her in the station or the papers. If pity had a hierarchy, the wee girls were at the top and she was firmly at the bottom. Expendable. Didn't seem fair.

McCoy realised the barman had asked him something. 'What?'

'I said, you want another?'

McCoy nodded. 'The function suite. Can I have a look?'

The barman shrugged. 'If you want, it's just an empty hall.'

McCoy followed the barman back towards the entrance and through another door. A corridor led them to the back of the building and he pushed a door open. They went through, door closed behind them, and 'Jumpin' Jack Flash' was reduced to a distant thump.

The function suite was cold, probably didn't bother heating it when no one was using it. There was a stage at one end with a sparkly curtain made of the foil they stamped milk-bottle tops from. A neat round hole every inch or so. There were a few deflated balloons bumping the ceiling, a wooden dancefloor, booths round the walls and some piled-up chairs in the corner. Looked more suitable for a funeral purvey than a birthday celebration. Thought he'd better say something.

'Nice place,' said McCoy. 'You get a lot of bookings . . .'

Stopped.

'You all right?'

'Shh,' said McCoy. Listened. He heard it again. 'Is that air brakes?'

'Yes. The lorries come down from the fruit market and go past here to get on the main road. Why?'

'Stay here,' said McCoy and ran to the door. The bar had got busier, two women were at the jukebox, change in hand, trying to decide. McCoy shoved his police card in front of them, told them to move. After a few tuts and a muttered 'fuck sake' they did and McCoy scanned the selection. The usual stuff. This month's hits, 'Tiger Feet', that wee Lena Zavaroni girl, 'Billy, Don't Be A Hero' and the big ones from the past couple of years, Beatles, T. Rex, Sweet. He kept looking but it all seemed to be recent stuff. Made himself trace down each column of selections slowly with his finger, not miss anything.

'You fucker,' he said under his breath when he saw it. 'You fucker.'

Found a ten pence in the change in his pocket, put it in and pressed in 237-A. Ran back through to the function suite.

The barman was still there looking puzzled. 'You okay, pal? You're running about like a blue-arsed—'

'Shh!' said McCoy, held his hand up—

The barman shut up. McCoy could hear distant traffic, air brakes, and in the background he could just make out Andy Williams singing 'Danny Boy'. He crouched down on the dancefloor. Dug in his pocket, couldn't find any. 'You got any matches?'

The barman took a box of Bluebell matches from his cardigan pocket, handed it over. McCoy got one out, stuck the blank end into the gap between the floorboards, dragged it along, then held it up in front of his face. The tip was dark red, flakes of dried blood clinging to it.

'Who owns this pub?'

'I do,' said the barman. 'Was my father's before me.'

'That right? Who really owns it?' He stood up. 'I know your name might be over the door and on the lease but who are you in hock to?'

The barman looked at him. 'I don't know what you're talking about. It's my pub.'

'Okay. Well, in that case you'll have to explain to Inspector Murray what this blood is doing all over your dancefloor. That okay with you?'

'That's easy. There was a fight last Saturday.'

'Must have been a hell of a fight. There's blood everywhere. Still your pub?'

The barman nodded, looked less and less sure of himself.

'Well, if I was you, I'd go and phone whoever the pub doesn't belong to, or whoever gave you those stitches, and tell him you're fucked and going to jail. He'll probably want to know.'

The barman held McCoy's gaze for a second. Broke off, hurried next door.

McCoy sat down on the floor. Was a difficult one to call. The pub was where? Germiston? Not that far from Johnny Smart in Dennistoun or Dessie Caine in Royston. Probably belonged to one of them. Pub owner falls behind on his loans, borrows money, borrows a bit more, suddenly the interest rates go up, way up, and he can't pay. Johnny Smart or someone like him takes twenty per cent to start, interest rates go up again, takes another ten per cent in lieu. Goes on until he owns the pub, and the owner is working for him. Oldest trick in the book.

The barman appeared again.

'Need you to make another call,' McCoy said. 'Away and call Stewart Street. Ask for Inspector Murray. Tell him McCoy said to get to the Royston now and bring Faulds.'

FIFTY-TWO

McCoy didn't have time to wait for them to arrive. If Malcolm McCauley was here, he needed to find him and quick. Walked back through to the bar, got there just as the barman was putting the phone down.

'Where is he?' said McCoy.

'Who?' asked the barman.

'You think I've got time for this shite? I'll ask you one more time. Where is he?'

The barman took a second, looked like he was going to tell him, then shook his head.

'Your funeral, you stupid prick. Cellar keys. Now.'

McCoy followed the barman round the back of the building, watched him unlock two padlocks on a steel door. Precautions made sense round here, cellar full of whisky and vodka would be a prime target. Locks and steel door would also make it harder for anyone trying to find Malcolm.

The door swung open and the barman stood aside.

McCoy clicked the light switch and walked down the stairs as the striplights flickered into life. Wasn't the kind of place he was expecting. The room looked more like Phyllis's autopsy suite than anything else. Whitewashed walls, whitewashed floor and banks of steel shelving holding neat piles of crates, kegs and boxes. He looked around, knew as soon as he did that Malcolm wasn't here. There was nowhere to hide him, place was a sealed white box. No doors leading off it, no hatches in the floor, nothing.

He walked back up the stairs.

Barman was standing off to the side, smoking, hand unsteady as he brought his cigarette up to his mouth. 'Seen enough?'

'Not by a long shot,' said McCoy.

Twenty minutes later he'd looked everywhere he could think of. Storage cupboards, crawl spaces, even the loft. Found rat traps, Christmas decorations in boxes, old staff rotas, but no trace of Malcom McCauley. McCoy was covered in dust, getting angrier and angrier. He had to be here somewhere. Had to be.

The barman had followed him everywhere, hovering over his shoulder, smoking for Scotland.

'When I find him,' said McCoy, 'I'm going to charge you with kidnapping, obstructing a police investigation, assault, and anything else I can think of. You'll be in prison for ten years at least. You know that?'

By the look of him the barman didn't.

'I didn't have anything to . . .'

Stopped, realised what he'd said.

'Last chance,' said McCoy.

'If I knew anything, I still wouldn't tell you,' he said. Touched the scar on his face. 'If I get sent to prison, at least I'll be alive.'

'Wouldn't be too sure about that,' said McCoy. 'You think whoever organised your face getting opened couldn't organise worse in Barlinnie? Last thing they need is you hanging about, deciding to squeal one day.'

The barman sat down on the padded bench running along the back of the function room. Put his head in his hands. McCoy didn't blame him. He was fucked either way.

'Look, you tell me, and I'll swear you didn't at the trial. I'll say you kept your mouth shut. Put in a good word when it comes to the sentencing. Get you sent to prison down south. It's your best bet.'

McCoy wasn't sure his word would make any difference, but it was all he had.

The barman looked at him. 'He's in the cellar.'

FIFTY-THREE

The barman opened the two padlocks again and swung the cellar door open, went down the stairs, McCoy following behind. He walked across the white room heading for the back wall. Stood in front of it, staring.

'Hard to find sometimes,' he said. Started running his hands over the wall. Stopped. 'Found it.'

McCoy peered at where the barman's hand was resting. Couldn't see anything. Stepped closer to the wall. 'Shit.'

There was a hairline crack going from floor to ceiling.

'He built it to store stuff,' said the barman. 'Stuff that had to be hidden.'

He took his set of keys out his pocket, got a penknife off the ring, and opened it up. Worked the tip of the blade into the crack.

'It's a pain in the arse,' he said. 'Needs to get painted over every time it's opened.'

He wiggled the blade gently from side to side. Nothing. And then the panel loosened in the wall. Barman handed McCoy the penknife. 'Hold this a minute.'

McCoy took it, and the barman lifted the panel away from the wall, carefully eased it onto the floor. It had been covering a dirty wooden door. The barman took another key from the ring, put it in the shiny lock, and opened the door.

'This is the old cellar,' he said. 'Goes back another five or six yards. They built this room inside it.'

'Who did?' asked McCoy.

The barman smiled. Didn't answer. Reached into the door-frame and clicked a light switch. 'Come on.'

He stepped into the cellar and McCoy followed. There was a path of wooden boards on the stone floor. They started walking. On either side of the path, there were piles of boxes, a rolled-up carpet with what looked like a rifle barrel sticking out the top, a wooden crate with *Property of The Glasgow Whisky Bond* stencilled on it.

'Malcolm,' shouted the barman. 'You're all right. It's only me.'

They turned a corner round a pillar and McCoy stopped dead.

Malcom McCauley was lying on a dirty tartan rug on the floor. His arms were tied behind his back, feet tied at the ankles, thick gag in his mouth. A chain round his waist was looped around another pillar and secured with a padlock. He looked at them, eyes wild.

'Jesus Christ,' said McCoy. 'Jesus fucking Christ.'

He couldn't believe it. He'd actually found him.

FIFTY-FOUR

'Two types of blood,' said one of the lab guys, pointing at the floor of the function suite. 'Type A and Type AB. I'll check if it matches the boys.'

'Not just some broken nose from a fight, is it?'

The guy shook his head. 'Between the two kinds there's enough to drown in.'

'Nice,' said McCoy. 'Thanks for that.'

The lab guy nodded, went back to where he'd set up his kit at the edge of the stage. Place was becoming like a circus. Scene of crime boys, lab guys, Faulds, Murray, photographer – and that was just the inside. Outside, the journalists and the press photographers were gathering. Knew something big was happening.

Faulds emerged from the gents buttoning up his fly. Looked round the room, found McCoy and came over. 'Done a bit of asking around,' he said.

'In the bogs?' asked McCoy.

'Very funny,' said Faulds. 'It's definitely Johnny Smart's pub. No matter how much the owner protests.'

'Can you bring him in?'

'Think so. All the stuff downstairs gives us an in, never mind Malcolm McCauley. He'll deny it, of course, but it gets us up and running. See what happens. What you doing?'

'Waiting for the doctor to come down to ask if I can see him. Want to do it here before they move him to the hospital, all be fresher.'

'Rather you than me,' said Faulds.

McCoy sat on the edge of the stage, watched everyone doing what they were supposed to be doing. Murray was sitting with Faulds in one of the booths, no doubt trying to work out how to approach Smart and his big Edinburgh lawyer. McCoy knew exactly what the lawyer would do. First, he would deny any relationship between Smart and the Royston. Then, if Faulds and Murray got the owner to break, he would say it was one of his many assets, one of the many properties he owned across the city, and how on earth could he be held responsible for what happened or didn't happen in each one. And so the dance would go on.

Could hear the jukebox from next door. Somebody playing 'Spirit In The Sky.' He took out his fags and lit up. Even when they'd got Malcolm McCauley out the cellar, he hadn't seemed to realise he was with the police and he was safe. McCoy had done his good deed for the day and called the boy's father. He'd started crying on the phone, thanking him, telling him he owed him everything. No doubt he was on his way here now.

'Can I bother you for one?' Doctor Purdie had come over, nodded at McCoy's cigarette.

McCoy handed them over. 'How is he?'

'Not good,' said Purdie, sitting down beside him. McCoy noticed the cuff of his shirt was fraying beneath his pinstripe suit. Must be spending too much money on the gee-gees again. More money in Stevie Cooper's pockets.

'Physically he's been knocked about a bit, has a few cuts

and bruises. He's dehydrated, needs a good meal. All of which is fixable. It's his mind that's the problem.'

'What do you mean?'

'I don't know what happened to him, but whatever it was it's had a profound effect. Sometimes he's here, sometimes he's not. I've never seen it personally, but I've read about it. Dissociative disorder, it's called these days. If reality is too much to cope with, the mind shifts, moves to another place so the person doesn't have to deal with what is going on. Trauma, shock, there's been lots of names for it. I can't be sure what's happened, that's your department, but it was enough to make him retreat from reality.'

'Christ. Is he going to be able to tell us what happened to him?'

Purdie shrugged. 'Maybe, maybe not. How's your pal, Mr Cooper, by the way? Couldn't put in a word, could you?'

'Got any painkillers and I might be persuaded,' said McCoy.

Purdie searched in his bag, came out with a small brown bottle, handed it over. 'Strong stuff. Watch yourself. How's the ulcer? Mr Murray told me it was bad.'

'Did he now? Hurts like fuck,' said McCoy.

'Yes, they tend to. No smoking or drinking helps, but I don't have to tell you that, because you'll just ignore me like you're obviously ignoring the doctors at the hospital.'

'What'll happen?'

'If you do nothing?' Purdie looked at him. 'It will probably get worse. Might take a wee while but it will. Then one day it will haemorrhage when you're not near enough a hospital and you'll bleed to death.'

McCoy didn't say anything.

'You did ask.'

'Didn't expect you to be quite so blunt.'

Purdie stood up. 'It's my job to be blunt in cases like these. I get to be the bearer of bad news. You'll speak to Mr Cooper?'

McCoy nodded. 'How much you in?'

'Almost two grand. And it's going up every day. Good luck with your interview. Think you're going to need it.'

McCoy watched him walk across the dancefloor and back through to the pub. Dropped his cigarette on the floor and ground it out. Time to speak to Malcolm McCauley.

FIFTY-FIVE

They'd put Malcolm McCauley in the wee dressing room for the comedians and singers the Royston had in on a Friday night. The medic had cleaned him up, put him in a hospital robe and blanket to wait for the ambulance to take him to the Royal. He was sitting on an orange plastic chair staring into the mirror above the counter. Face bright in what was left of the working bulbs surrounding the mirror. He had some cuts and bruises on his face, a gash across his nose, was holding the blanket tight around him, eyes flitting around the room.

'You all right, son?' asked McCoy.

He nodded into the mirror. 'Is my dad here? I want my dad.'

'He's on his way. Be here soon. Need to ask you a few questions.'

'They made us watch,' he said. 'Took our blindfolds off, left the gags in our mouths. I bit through mine.'

'Who did?' asked McCoy. 'Who?'

Malcolm shook his head. 'They smelt of beer and cigarettes and one of them stank of sweat like he hadn't changed his clothes in a long time.' Stopped. 'Where are my clothes?'

'Getting washed,' said McCoy.

Malcom turned round, looked McCoy in the eye. 'When they cut Danny's fingers off I shat myself. Do I need to tell them that?'

McCoy shook his head. 'Not if you don't want to.'

Malcolm sat back, starting fiddling with a frayed thread at the edge of the blanket around his shoulders.

'Maybe we can start at the beginning,' said McCoy. 'Who asked you to set the fire?'

Malcom shook his head. 'I don't know. Colin just said we'd get twenty quid each. Set fire to an empty shop. Told us in the pub. Me and Danny had been doing speed for a few days.' He smiled. 'Weren't thinking too straight.'

There it was. Finally. Confirmation that the boys had set fire to the salon.

'Why three of you?'

'The three musketeers,' he said. 'Did everything together. You seen the film? One for all, all for one.' His head cocked to the side. 'There's rats in here, you know. I heard them last night. Thought they were going to eat me. Can they do that? Rats?'

'Don't think so,' said McCoy. 'What happened after you set the fire?'

'We ran like the clappers. Went to the pub to spend our money. Got wasted. Fell asleep in someone's flat in Roystonhill. Next thing I know ten polis are in the flat shouting about arson and murder. One of them had a tattoo on his arm. Mum and Dad.'

'One of the polis?'

'No. The one that stamped on Colin's balls until they burst. Will my dad be here soon?'

McCoy nodded. Had the feeling this would be the last chance to get any sense out of Malcom, even if he was already starting to get scrambled.

'Anything else you remember about the men who took you?'

'We got chips. A bottle of Irn-Bru. The sweaty man came into the white box and told Danny that if he sucked him off he would let us go.' He stopped. Rubbed at his eyes. 'So Danny did. And he didn't. Do you think my dad will be angry?'

McCoy shook his head. 'No, he'll just be happy you're safe.'

'I'll have to die though. For what I've done. It's all I can do. For those women . . .'

McCoy gave it one last go. 'Do you remember anything about the man asking the questions? Did you see him?'

Malcom shook his head. 'He sat behind us. For a while I thought he might be God but I'm not sure. Was he? If he was, will you tell him I'm sorry?'

'Yes, I will.' Had had about as much as he could take. Stood up as the door opened and a uniform appeared. 'Ambulance is here.'

McCoy walked back into the function suite, watched the shiny curtains shimmer in the breeze. Wondered whether Malcom McCauley would be better off dead. Not his decision to make, but he had the feeling he would be soon, either by his own hand or by some shiv in Barlinnie. He stepped out into the car park, found the ambulance driver having a fag by the fence. Told him McCauley needed to be on suicide watch.

At least they had found one boy alive. Didn't help them much, couldn't tell them anything useful. Just had to hope Murray and Faulds got something out of Johnny Smart. He turned over the engine. Decided to go and see Wattie at the station, wanted to see a friendly face. Wanted not to think about what Malcolm McCauley had gone through. Wanted to sleep tonight. Maybe he'd stop drinking tomorrow.

FIFTY-SIX

Wattie wasn't there when McCoy got back to the station. 'Still up at the fruit market,' as Billy the desk sergeant told him through a mouthful of crisps. He sat down at his desk and decided it was an omen. If Wattie wasn't there, then he was going to go and get drunk. Fuck his ulcer and Dr Purdie. Today had been a tough one. Kept imagining what Malcom McCauley had seen. Wasn't surprised the poor bloke's mind had gone.

He wrote a list of things he had to do tomorrow in his red jotter.

Salon woman
Take key to locksmith, see if they can identify it.
Paul Cooper?
Landlord of the Royston – get him to talk.
Trisha O'Hara, trace parents, let them know.

Was just about to add *Buy more Pepto-Bismol* when his phone rang. Picked it up.

'Desk sergeant said you were in,' said Wattie. 'Just about to leave the fruit market and I'm starving. I'm going to stop at the White Tower. You want anything?'

Thought of fish and chips made McCoy's stomach turn over. No way could he eat that. 'I'm all right.'

'Fine. Just as long as you remember I asked and you're no getting any of mine,' said Wattie then hung up.

McCoy swore under his breath. Wattie had gone before he'd had a chance to tell him he wasn't going to be there. Now he'd have to wait for the stupid bugger to turn up. Rooted around in his drawers, eventually found what he was looking for, a half-bottle of Bell's left over from some Christmas party. Put it in his pocket and headed for the toilets.

He put the lid down, sat on the toilet and locked the door. Took a long drink from the whisky bottle. Smiled. Maybe he was more like his dad than he thought. Maybe he should go and find him. They could get pissed together. Talk over old times. Remember that time you locked me in a cupboard for two days? What a laugh that was. And how about that time you and your 'pal' Jamsie took turns knocking lumps out me because I poured two cans of beer down the sink to stop you drinking them? Happy days.

He took another slug. Stomach felt like he had eaten broken glass.

Wondered if there were any photos of his dad still floating about. Probably. Took another slug. And another. Decided he had to get going before Wattie came back. Couldn't face talking to him, to anyone. He was too deep in his memories, so deep into them he was going to have to drink himself out and fuck the consequences.

Too late. He walked back into the office and Wattie was sitting at his desk shovelling something into his mouth.

'Where you been?' he asked, after he managed to chew it down.

'Toilet,' said McCoy. 'What's that bloody smell?'

'Chicken chow mein and egg-fried rice,' said Wattie. 'Bloody White Tower shut down last year. It's a Chinese now. Couldn't be arsed going anywhere else so I thought I'd give it a try. It's no bad.'

McCoy sat down at his desk. Wondered what Wattie would say if he took out the half-bottle. Decided he didn't care.

'I was thinking,' said Wattie. 'Maybe you should come and stay at ours tonight, see the wee man.'

McCoy took the half-bottle out his pocket. 'I've got company,' he said.

Wattie shook his head. 'That's not going to help.'

'That right?' asked McCoy. Took a slug. 'Seems to be.'

'You'll hurt yourself.'

'Aye, well, guess what? I'm hurt already. Fucking destroyed, to be exact, so it's not going to make much difference, is it?'

'So what am I supposed to tell Murray when you don't come in tomorrow because your ulcer is bleeding again?'

McCoy stood up, looked over at Wattie. 'Tell him what you fucking like.'

He put his coat on, started heading for the door. Stopped, walked back to Wattie's desk. Pulled the carrier bag out from under the empty foil containers and held it up. Even through the stains from the chow mein you could still see what it said. Bright red letters.

'The Happiness Chinese Restaurant,' said McCoy. 'Fuck me.'

FIFTY-SEVEN

McCoy had a mug of black coffee from the station kitchen in between his knees. Kept taking sips, trying to avoid spilling it all over himself every time Wattie turned a corner.

'That working?'

'Think so,' said McCoy.

They were driving round George Square heading for the Gallowgate. The streetlights had come on, as had the rain, windscreen wipers thumping back and forwards.

'Chinese people? You think they're involved?' asked Wattie.

'God knows,' said McCoy. 'The place is probably nothing to do with the Happiness Hotel but it's worth checking out. And sorry.'

Wattie looked at him, then eyes back on the road in front of them.

'For asking me to yours. Thank you. I was being a dick.'

'No change there then,' said Wattie. 'I was thinking—'

'Oh God,' said McCoy.

Wattie ignored him, kept going. 'Idea is that the fire is a turf war thing gone wrong. Whoever did it didn't know the women were in there, just a horrible accident.'

McCoy nodded.

'Okay. But what if that ends there. And whoever took the boys is a vigilante, nothing to do with Dessie Caine or Johnny Smart. They don't know that's the case, nobody does. People still think it's some sort of terrible arson murder and those boys knew what they were doing. So what if the vigilantes are nothing to do with the turf war, have no connection to it? Probably didn't know the Royston had anything to do with Johnny Smart. There's no trail to the fire. So how the fuck are we supposed to find them?'

The car stopped and McCoy looked in the window of the cafe at the Tron, people at tables, waitress writing stuff in a wee pad. Turned to Wattie. 'I've no idea,' he said. Car started again. 'You're right. If it's not Johnny Smart we're still nowhere. Only hope is Faulds and Murray connect him tomorrow.' He finished the last of his coffee.

'And if they don't?'

McCoy didn't know what to say. Looked out the windscreen. 'There's a parking space there. Pull over.'

Wattie pulled over into Spoutmouth Street and parked the car opposite the Lough Erne pub. 'This is a long shot, you know.'

'Yep,' said McCoy. 'But it's the only one we've got.'

Last time McCoy had been here, it had still been the White Tower fish and chip restaurant. Now the ornate building on the Gallowgate was called the Happiness Restaurant. It had a yellow sign with red Chinese characters and a menu in a lit-up box in the window. He pushed the door open, a bell tinkled and a Chinese man emerged from behind a curtain of plastic streamers.

He smiled and pushed a menu towards them, got his notepad and pen out.

The Happiness looked just like every other Chinese takeaway McCoy had ever been in. Wallpaper with cranes and bridges, a calendar with red tassels pinned to it. A red vinyl bench seat to wait on and a pile of folded paper menus.

McCoy put down the keys on the Formica counter. The big metal one and the two with the Happiness Hotel fobs. The man looked up at McCoy. Shook his head.

'Happiness,' he said. 'This Happiness Chinese restaurant.'

'You recognise these?' asked McCoy.

The man looked at them uncertainly. Shouted something behind him and a ten-year-old boy in his school uniform appeared from behind the curtain.

'My da's English isnae great,' said the boy in a broad Glaswegian accent. 'Can I help you?'

'Do these keys have anything to do with this place?' asked McCoy.

The boy repeated the question in Cantonese, listened to his dad's reply.

'Naw,' he said. 'Says he's never seen them before. You polis?'

McCoy smiled.

The boy went into the kitchen, reappeared with a large paper bag of prawn crackers. Handed them to Wattie. 'My da says the polis are always welcome here.'

McCoy thanked them, put the keys back in his pocket. Walked out into the street, door tinkling as it closed behind them.

Wattie leant against the car, methodically feeding prawn crackers into his mouth.

'Well, that was a waste of time,' said McCoy.

'Don't know about that,' said Wattie. 'These prawn crackers are good.' He held out the bag. 'You want one?'

McCoy shook his head. Grease staining the bottom of the brown paper bag was enough to tell him his stomach wouldn't stand for it.

'This is the only bloody place in bloody Glasgow with Happiness in its name. Thought we were onto something.'

Wattie munched another cracker. 'It's a Chinese takeaway, no sign of a hotel.'

'C'mon, we'll have a look round the back,' said McCoy. 'Can't do any harm.' He nodded over at the Lough Erne. 'I'll buy you a pint afterwards.'

'Done,' said Wattie. 'These things are making me thirsty.'

The back of the restaurant was the same as any other. Overflowing bins. Big empty cans of cooking oil, back door ajar to reveal a tiny kitchen with an elderly man stirring woks on two gas burners.

'Stinks round here,' said Wattie.

McCoy kept walking along the back of the building, wasn't really sure what he was looking for, just didn't want to give up yet. The back was nowhere as ornate as the front of the building, just plain brick. He was just about to call it a day, turned to tell Wattie he'd given up, when he saw another bin.

This one was different: neat, shiny metal, lid firmly in place. He walked over and took the lid off, peered inside. It was full of bulging plastic carrier bags, handles tied in knots. He picked the top one up, put it on the ground and tried to untie the handles. Was no use, he'd no nails and his fat fingers couldn't get in between the knots. He gave up, cursed and pulled at the side of the bag. It stretched, then burst open, contents tumbling onto the wet ground.

McCoy looked at them. They had the right place after all.

FIFTY-EIGHT

'Yuck,' said Wattie, poking at the used condoms on the ground with the tip of his shoe. 'What else is in there?'

McCoy squatted down, really wished he had a pair of gloves, and started rooting about in the bag. He pulled out some balled-up paper hankies, dropped them on the floor. A porn mag with the cover ripped off and half the pages stuck together was next. He could feel something heavy in the bag, was dreading what it was, steeled himself, grabbed it and pulled out a half-empty tub of Vaseline. He put it on the ground and stood up, wiped his hands on his raincoat.

'You can do the next bag,' he said.

Wattie shook his head, lifted it out the bin, managed to undo the knots in the handles, and tipped the contents out.

'Not sure why you'd need that stuff in a Chinese restaurant,' said McCoy.

He was looking down at a wet towel, some more hankies, a crumpled picture of a man giving another man a blow job and a set of handcuffs with one of the locks broken.

He looked back up at the building behind them. Could just make out a row of windows on the first floor, dark blinds pulled down.

· 263 ·

'Has to be a way in,' he said. 'Come on.'

They walked back round to where the car was parked. McCoy hadn't seen any other way in. Decided it was time to go back and be a bit less polite to the man and the wee boy in the Chinese restaurant.

'Maybe that's not just for the pub,' said Wattie.

'What?'

'That door,' said Wattie, pointing.

There was a door between the pub and the restaurant. It was painted green like the main pub doors, had a sign on it: LOUGH ERNE DELIVERIES.

'It'll be the way round to the cellar,' said McCoy. 'Like the Royston.'

'Let's see,' said Wattie.

They crossed over and Wattie pushed the door open. They were in a long narrow alley. Couple of wooden crates with Bass Special on them near the entrance. They stepped over them and kept going. The alley ended and they stepped out into the pub's yard. Sure enough, the cellar was there. Double doors in the ground, empty metal kegs beside them. A back door with a glass panel, could see the flickering light of a TV in the pub through it.

McCoy looked round, realised they were looking at the back of the restaurant, could see the three windows up above them. He moved along, was hard to see, light from the pub door fading the further he got from it. Was sure he could see something in the gloom. Went to get his lighter out and Wattie beat him to it. A flicker and then he held it up.

There was a door in the wall of the yard.

McCoy looked at it. Was worth a try. He got the big key out his pocket. 'Hold the lighter near the lock.'

Wattie bent down, lighter in hand.

McCoy pushed the key into the lock, slipped in easily. Couldn't be, he thought, couldn't be.

He turned it.

Nothing.

Then the lock gave, and the door swung open.

FIFTY-NINE

'You're kidding me on,' said Wattie.

They were standing outside the door, looking at a hallway with a set of stairs at the end. The hallway and the stairs were swept, clean, faint smell of bleach. The walls were painted a pale blue colour, light coming from two white glass globes in the ceiling.

'You ready?' asked McCoy.

Wattie nodded and they started climbing. They reached the first-floor landing. A window on the right looked out onto the Gallowgate, cars passing, people waiting at the bus stop across the road. There were three doors leading off the landing, one was ajar. McCoy pushed it open, walked in. It was a large room, mostly empty, a long roll of white paper pinned to the back wall, various camera stands, and spotlights arranged to face it. There was a chair in front of the paper, a school desk in the corner and a pile of ropes neatly coiled on the floor.

McCoy's stomach rolled over. Knew exactly what he was looking at. Knew the door in the corner would lead to a darkroom. Knew there would be different kinds of costumes in the cupboard by the ropes. Knew the smell of talc and air freshener.

'A photo studio,' said Wattie. 'Is it for what I think it's for?'

McCoy didn't trust himself to speak.

'Jesus Christ,' said Wattie. 'This is where Ally took the pictures?'

McCoy nodded. Turned and walked out, stood in the hallway, looked out at the street below.

'You okay?' asked Wattie, following him out.

'Fine,' he said. 'Ulcer's just playing up a bit, shouldn't have drunk that whisky.' He dug in his pocket and took out the two other keys. 'May as well try these.'

He tried the first key in the nearest door, didn't fit. Tried the other key and the door opened. It was smaller than the other room, looked more like a hotel room. A bed, a dresser, a mirror, all illuminated by the streetlights shining through the window. At first McCoy thought there was a body on the bed, stepped back, bumped into Wattie. He switched the light on and realised it wasn't a body, just someone sleeping.

The person started moving. They sat up and Paul Cooper was looking at them. He rubbed his eyes. Scratched at himself under his vest.

'Fuck,' he said. 'Fuck.'

McCoy left Wattie and Paul in the bedroom, stepped back out into the hall. Didn't want to stand in there any longer.

Paul emerged a couple of minutes later dressed in jeans and sandshoes, Wattie behind him.

'No running this time,' said McCoy. 'I mean it.'

Paul nodded, led them through to the studio room.

'So,' said McCoy. 'Are you going to tell us what the fuck is going on?'

Paul had just woken up, hair was all over the place, still had the mark of the pillow on the side of his face. Looked his age suddenly. Just fifteen. 'What do you want to know?'

'Just start at the beginning,' said McCoy. 'What is this place?'

'Only place I could think of to hide,' said Paul. 'And believe me, it's the last fucking place I wanted to be, but I ran out of options.' He opened his arms, looked around. 'This place was Ally's big idea. How he made real money.'

'I get the photo studio,' said McCoy. 'That was his business. What are the bedrooms for?'

Paul looked like he was deciding whether to tell him or not. 'My dad,' he said. 'You need to promise me he doesn't hear about any of this. Promise?'

'I promise.' Tried not to think about how many times he'd said that and not meant it. 'Just tell us.'

'I've no really had a home these two years. The social wouldn't let me stay with my dad, was in Ireland for a while but that didn't work out.'

'You mean since your mum died?' asked McCoy.

'Aye. No way was I going into some fucking children's home. Not in a million years. No matter what the social said. So I ran. Ended up spending some time on the streets.' He smiled. 'Then I ran out of money, you always run out of money. You know a guy called Sister Jimmy?'

McCoy nodded.

'He told me to go and see Ally at Paddy's. Said it was easy money. And it was. Ally used to have a wee flat at the Saltmarket. You'd go up there and take your clothes off and he'd take some photos. Gave you two quid a go. Maybe some money for chips . . .'

He stopped.

'Then he got an idea. Says to me how about two or three guys get to take your photo and I pay you more? Didn't make any difference to me so I said yes. I turn up at the flat and there are two guys with cameras, schoolteacher types, middle-aged. So Ally tells me to strip down to my underwear and they start snapping away. Took hundreds of pictures yet they never put more film in their cameras. Funny that.'

'And then I see one of them talking to Ally, speccy guy in a tweed suit, whispering away, hard-on poking out his trousers, and Ally's like, "Oh, I don't know," and shaking his head. Then he comes over to me. Asks me if I'll take the pants off and I'm thinking he's running these guys, suckering them. So I say, no way. Then Ally persuades me and I take them off. Ally goes back to the guy, and the guy looks like he's died and gone to heaven, and he hands Ally a fiver. And that's how it all started.'

'Is this where you met Trisha?' asked McCoy.

Paul nodded, carried on. 'Ally had a pal, guy called Barrett, right wee creep. Used to get girls from some home he was working at in the West End. He persuaded her to come here and see Ally. Barrett got a commission for every girl he sent. Got any fags?'

McCoy handed him one and Paul lit up.

'So after that night with the camera guys Ally had bloody dollar signs in his eyes. Started pulling the same sketch every night. Sometimes me, sometimes Trisha, sometimes some other kid with no money. Always the same scenario. And then he gets big ideas. Leaves me in the room with one guy snapping away and this guy takes his dick out and says that Ally said I'd wank him off for another two quid.'

He took a drag.

'So I did. Half to me and half to Ally.'

'And then he got this place?' asked McCoy.

Paul nodded. 'You can see what happened. Can only charge two quid for a wank in a photo studio or a blow job from some girl on the run from Barrett's home. But a whole night in a nice comfy bed. He could charge pretty much what he wanted. So he set this place up, rented it off the people downstairs. Used to call it the Happiness Hotel, thought it was funny.'

McCoy turned to Wattie. 'Do us a favour? Have a good look around, see what you can see.'

Wattie got up and wandered off.

'Is that what Trisha was doing then?' asked McCoy.

'At first she was, but she got scared.'

'How about you?'

'No,' said Paul. 'I got too old-looking, too big.' He smiled grimly. 'I wasn't what they were looking for any more.'

'What was Trisha scared of?'

'She started seeing one of the punters out in the street.'

'She went out on her own?'

'No,' said Paul. 'I mean on the street, following her, turning up everywhere. She told Ally she didn't want to see him any more, and he was telling her he was a good customer and he'd get more money from him, but she wouldn't do it. Then one night she got a whisky from Ally before a punter arrived, Dutch courage he said, and next thing she remembered was waking up in Room 1 with a sore arse and the smell of the guy's aftershave all over her.'

'Ally drugged her?'

'Said she'd be better just keep doing what she was told where this guy was concerned.'

'Did she say who he was?' asked McCoy.

'No, never said his name, just said she was to call him Daddy. Was always very polite, well dressed, smelt of aftershave.'

'So why did you run the other night at the pub?' asked McCoy. 'You not want to stay with your dad?'

'It wasn't that. I just didn't want anyone to know where I was: you, him, anyone. Look at it. Ally's dead, that cunt Barrett's dead, Trisha's dead. Who's left?'

'You,' said McCoy.

Paul nodded. 'Someone is making sure nobody knows what happened here.'

'The man that was following Trisha?'

Paul shrugged. 'I don't know. But whoever it is, he isn't going to get me. Not if I can help it.'

'McCoy?'

Wattie was standing in the doorway, waving for McCoy to follow him into the first bedroom where Paul had been sleeping.

Wattie held up a tiny square microphone attached to a wire. 'A bug.'

'You sure?'

'No. I'm no expert but it looks like one.'

'Where was it?'

'Taped to the bottom of the headboard.'

'And where does the wire go?'

'Let's find out.'

He tugged the wire and it went taut, stretched under the bed. Wattie got down on his knees, looked under the bed. Came back out.

'It's taped to the join between the wall and floor.'

McCoy went to the end of the bed, spotted the wire. It had been painted over the same colour as the skirting board, was hard to see. He followed it along the wall and out into the hall where it disappeared into a cupboard.

Paul came into the hall, and the three of them stood staring at the cupboard.

'You know what this is?' McCoy asked Paul.

Paul shook his head. 'Never seen it before.'

'Open it,' said Wattie.

McCoy stepped forward, pulled at the door. It was locked. He stretched up, ran his hand along the top lip of the cupboard, fingers stopped on a small key. He brought it down, put it in the lock and turned it.

The door opened and they were looking at a large reel-to-reel tape recorder. Piles of unused tape spools behind it.

'Well, well,' said McCoy. 'Looks like Ally was operating a wee blackmail scam as well. No wonder he could afford the fancy flat.'

SIXTY

By the time they left the Happiness Hotel it was past eleven. All they had found in the cupboard were blank reels, no recordings. Ally must have hidden them somewhere. Paul was half asleep, sitting against the wall of the hallway. No way was McCoy letting him out his sight, not for a while anyway. Was still trying to process what he'd told them, work things out in his head, and when he did, he'd have more questions. Didn't want to have to track him down again.

Paul stood up. Yawned, stretched.

'How do you feel about staying at your dad's?'

'No way,' said Paul shaking his head. 'He'll batter me for running.'

'No, he won't,' said McCoy. 'I told him that I told you to run or I'd have to arrest you. He's fine about it. And I can't think of anywhere safer for you than your dad's.'

Paul didn't look convinced.

'Look, if we found you here, someone else might too. It's not safe.'

'He's right,' said Wattie. 'No way anyone's going to get to you if you're with your dad.'

'Aye, okay.'

'C'mon,' said McCoy. 'We'll drop you off.'

They got in the car and headed north towards Springburn. Paul was in the front seat talking to Wattie about football. Suited McCoy fine. He could sit in the back and have a think, try and work out what the hell was going on.

If whoever was following Trisha, her regular, had killed her, that made some sort of sense. Maybe it was unplanned, something happened and he lost control. Then he'd have to cover his tracks. Make sure the people who knew about him and Trisha weren't around any more to talk. Maybe he'd started threatening Ally, making sure he kept his mouth shut.

They turned off Parliamentary Road and drove into Springburn. McCoy was hoping Cooper was still at Memen Road. Soon find out.

Maybe the guy decided that frightening Ally wasn't enough, needed to make sure he never talked. After that, he was left with Barrett. Same thing. No way a wee creep like Barrett wouldn't try a bit of blackmail. He had to go too. That left Paul.

He realised Wattie was looking at him. That the car had stopped. 'We're here. You want me to come in with you?'

McCoy shook his head. 'We'll be fine.'

They made their way down the street, remnants of a fire glowing in one of the front gardens.

'What we doing here?' asked Paul. 'I thought my dad had a big house in the West End?'

'He does,' said McCoy. 'Doesn't seem to like it any more. Hasn't been there for a good few months.'

There was a boy McCoy vaguely recognised standing in the close entrance. Lad with a skinhead and hare lip.

'He in?' asked McCoy.

The boy nodded, let them pass.

They climbed the stairs, McCoy hoping Cooper wasn't entertaining some female company, and knocked on the door. Jumbo answered it, half-open *Commando* comic in his hand.

'Mr McCoy!' he said, smiling. 'And Paul! Come away in. He's in the kitchen.'

He was. Cooper was sitting at the table, vest on, braces pushed off, can of beer in one hand, fan of cards in the other. He looked up as they walked in. Saw Paul behind McCoy, jumped up and hugged him.

'Brought someone to stay,' said McCoy.

Paul was squashed into his dad's chest, managed to get 'let me go' out. Cooper did, then hugged him again. McCoy could tell he was drunk but he was happy drunk, full of good wishes for all men. He eventually let Paul go. Couldn't stop looking at him.

'Deke?' McCoy had just noticed who Cooper was playing cards with.

Deke got up, handed him and Paul a can each. 'Welcome back.'

'Deke, why don't you take Paul and find him somewhere to sleep,' said McCoy. 'I need to talk to his dad.'

Deke nodded, and he and Paul went off.

McCoy shut the kitchen door, sat down at the table. 'You got anything stronger?'

'One of those days, is it?' asked Cooper, grinning.

'You've no idea.'

Cooper got a bottle of whisky and a mug with Snoopy on it out one of the kitchen cupboards and put them down in front of McCoy. He poured a good measure, drank it over, poured another. Rubbed at his eyes. Between his dad and the photo studio he was having difficulty staying in the present – memories kept tugging at him, trying to draw him back.

'Where'd you find him?' asked Cooper.

Was easier to lie. 'Staying at some other squat in Garnethill, place is full of them. I need him to stay here for a while, stay inside.'

'Why?' asked Cooper.

'He thinks someone is after him. Could just be imagining it, but keep him here for a couple of days until I make sure, eh?'

'Who's after him?' asked Cooper, bristling.

'Just some ex of his girlfriend's. Paul stole her away, it seems. Another young lad, stupid wee boys' argument. Nothing to worry about.'

Cooper grinned again. 'Like father, like son,' he said. 'Dirty bugger.'

'Just keep him in,' said McCoy standing up. He took the bottle of whisky and put it in his coat pocket. 'Okay if I take this?'

'Aye. You okay?'

McCoy shook his head. 'No.'

McCoy walked down the stairs, nodded at the skinhead boy, and stepped out into the fresh air. He spun the top off the bottle and drank back. His stomach could fuck itself. Everything could fuck itself tonight. He needed the whisky to stop thinking about his dad. To stop thinking about being thirteen and stripping his clothes off for Dirty Ally. To forget the quid Ally had put in his hand after he'd taken the pictures.

He took another slug, started walking back to the car. Could see Wattie sitting in the front seat, shoving crisps into his mouth. Suddenly thought he was going to burst into tears, just sit down on the ground and give up. Wasn't sure he had it in him to fight off the past tonight. Took another slug and made himself keep walking. Decided to ask Wattie if the offer to stay at his was still on. Knew that the last thing he should be was by himself tonight.

26th May 1974

SIXTY-ONE

McCoy woke up with a hangover and a baby staring at him. He blinked, rubbed his eyes, but it was real.

'Wee Duggie wanted to say hello to his Uncle Harry,' said Wattie, dangling the baby over him.

McCoy sat up in bed and Wattie dropped Wee Duggie into his arms.

'Look after him for a minute,' he said. 'I need a pee.'

McCoy looked down at the baby. He didn't look very happy. He'd a rusk in his mouth and was chewing away.

'Your teeth sore?' asked McCoy. 'That what's up?'

Wee Duggie didn't answer, just stared at him with his big blue eyes.

'Where's monkey?' asked McCoy.

Duggie's face crumpled. McCoy realised he'd said the wrong thing. Duggie's face went red, he opened his mouth and the wailing started.

Mary appeared in a dressing gown, glowered at him. 'What did you do to him? And this room smells like a bloody brewery.'

'Nothing!' said McCoy as she picked the screaming baby out his arms. 'I just asked him where monkey was.'

Mary was rocking the baby back and forward to no great avail. 'Don't say that bloody word.' She spelled it out. 'M.O.N.K.E.Y. is lost. It's a fucking nightmare. I'm going into town to try and buy another one today. If I don't find one, I swear I'm going to make Wattie tell the polis to look out for a lost orange fluffy M.O.N.K.E.Y.'

She shooshed the baby and rocked him. McCoy lay back down on the bed. Listened to Wattie making breakfast in the kitchen, Mary talking nonsense to Wee Duggie, walking him up and down the hall. The sounds of normal lives. A sound he hadn't heard for a long time. Was a good sound. He let his mind drift back to Paul Cooper. Realised he'd been so distracted by his dad and the photo studio that he'd forgotten to ask him about Malcolm McCauley, why he was in the picture with him and Trisha, if he knew anything about the fire.

Could hear the kettle boiling in the kitchen. Needed to get up and face the day. If all had gone to plan, Murray and Faulds should be getting Johnny Smart in today for his interview, see if they could shake the tree. He should really go and see Lachy, see if he could give him a better description of the man who had been threatening Ally at the market. Could well be the same guy who had killed Trisha and Barrett.

Now Wee Duggie was laughing. Mary must have managed to distract him from the missing monkey. He should go and see Bert Cross at the Great Northern as well. See if he could remember any more about the man who'd given him the money to say Ally jumped.

McCoy got out of bed and realised he still had his trousers and socks on. Oh, well, at least it would save time. He got his shirt off the back of the chair, put it on and started buttoning it, found his shoes under the bed. Heard Wattie shouting him in for his breakfast. Put his shoes on and shouted he was coming.

SIXTY-TWO

It all started well. Murray had even reserved the nice interview room. Faulds had been called to the interviews of the fruit market workers. One of them had seen a van backing up to the storage unit the boys had been held in, might have seen the driver, and so McCoy had been drafted in. Been told in no uncertain terms to be on his best behaviour, to sit tight, only speak up if he noticed something.

Even the QC seemed amiable enough. Sir Roddy Ogilvy. Turned out he was a Hawick fan, remembered Murray lifting the trophy for them. Murray and him chatting away about the team's chances this year. Was all going well until Johnny Smart turned up and saw McCoy.

'Tell him to fuck off,' he said, standing there in his chalk-stripe suit and lavender tie. 'He's no interviewing me.'

'He's not,' said Murray. 'I am. That okay with you, is it, Mr Smart?'

Smart looked at Ogilvy, a slight nod. He pulled out the chair and sat down.

Ogilvy unscrewed the top of his fountain pen, wrote the date at the top of his yellow pad, sat back in the chair.

'So, Mr Murray,' he said in his posh Edinburgh accent, 'you wished to ask my client some questions?'

'That's right,' said Murray.

'I can't imagine why,' said Ogilvy, 'but be my guest.'

Murray shuffled his papers. Looked right at Smart. 'As I'm sure you are aware, the Royston pub is now a murder scene. Malcolm McCauley was also found there in the cellar, no doubt awaiting a similar fate. Do you have anything you want to tell us about that?'

Smart was about to speak but Ogilvy beat him to it. 'I'm lost, Inspector. What do these unfortunate events have to do with my client?'

'It's his pub,' said Murray.

Ogilvy reached into the inside pocket of his jacket, pulled out a small leather notebook, flicked through it until he found the page he was looking for. Smiled, looked at Murray. 'I'm afraid you are mistaken, Mr Murray. The pub belongs to a Mr Kenneth Shields. His name is on the title deeds, and he is listed as the licensee.'

McCoy had to hand it to him, Ogilvy was good.

'Are we done?' asked Ogilvy.

'No,' said Murray. 'I don't know how familiar you are with Smart's business interests, Mr Ogilvy, but he is the de facto owner of the pub. A fact we can get witnesses to testify to. Nothing goes on in that pub without Smart knowing about it. Just like the Waverley Arms, the Ring of Bells, Thatcher's and most of the pubs in Germiston.'

'I see,' said Ogilvy. 'And where are these witness statements?'

McCoy groaned inwardly. They didn't have any and they weren't likely to get any. No one was stupid enough to go on the record against Johnny Smart.

Murray didn't say anything.

'I see,' repeated Ogilvy. 'Non-existent witness statements

connecting my client to some pubs. Is that all you have?' He smiled. 'Or don't, as the case may be.'

'There was a large quantity of blood all over the floor of the function room in the Royston,' said Murray. 'How do you account for that?'

'We don't,' said Ogilvy. 'My client is not a clairvoyant. He has no relationship with the pub in question.'

Murray's hand was grasping the edge of the table. McCoy could tell he was close to blowing. Didn't blame him, he was getting the run-around from a consummate professional.

'Okay,' said Murray. 'Let's move on. What's your relationship with Dessie Caine, Mr Smart?'

Ogilvy nodded. Johnny Smart was allowed to answer that one.

'He's a fellow businessman in the north of Glasgow. We occasionally run into each other at charity events. Just like I occasionally run into you, Mr Murray. Why do you ask?'

Murray put his pen down. McCoy braced himself. 'I don't have time for this, Mr Smart, so I'll make it plain to you and Mr Ogilvy here. You are a crook, the Royston is your pub, and two boys were tortured and murdered there on your say-so. The boys set fire to Dolly's Salon on your say-so. Part of a turf war you are having with Dessie Caine. That five people died in the fire may have been an accident but it's still murder. Hard as you're trying to cover your tracks and make sure nothing leads back to you, it's not going to work. If you think this charade with Mr Ogilvy here is the end of it, you are very much mistaken—'

'Mr Murray, I think—'

Murray rolled right over Ogilvy. 'Because it's just the beginning. I am going to nail you to a fucking wall if it's the last thing I do. Three women and two little girls dead. Two teenage boys dead. And all because you want a bigger share of fucking Haghill. You're guilty as sin and I'm going to prove it. Now fuck off out my station.'

There was silence for a moment. McCoy could hear Murray's breathing, see his white knuckles. He looked at Ogilvy, who'd decided that discretion was the better part of valour. He picked up his notepad, stood up, affirmed to Johnny Smart to do the same. Smart looked like he'd seen a ghost, face pure white. They left, closed the door behind them.

Murray let go of the table. 'Give me a cigarette,' he said.

McCoy handed them over and Murray lit up. 'You okay?' Murray nodded.

'That get us anywhere?'

'I doubt it,' said Murray. 'But it made me feel better. Hawick man or not, I wasn't far away from punching Ogilvy right in the face.'

'Now that I would have liked to see. So what happens now?'

'Fuck knows,' said Murray. 'We've got nothing.'

McCoy thought for a minute. 'That's true. But they don't know that.'

Murray turned to him.

'They don't know Malcom McCauley is away with the fairies, do they? For all they know, he's singing away like a canary, naming Smart. Maybe we should get Mary to say as much in the paper, say he's helping the police with their inquiries, providing substantial information about what happened to him and where. That might flush something out.'

Murray dropped his cigarette on the floor, stamped it out. 'Those things are bloody horrible. But that's a good idea.'

SIXTY-THREE

'He was a bit of a wanker, to be honest.'

They were sitting round the table in Stevie Cooper's kitchen. McCoy had had to get them out of bed, seemed to have been celebrating the return of the prodigal son the night before. Stevie was chugging water out a pint glass with Tuborg written on it, Paul sipping a cup of tea. Deke and Jumbo were standing by the door.

'What do you mean?' asked McCoy.

'Malcom was a posh boy, so he always felt he had something to prove,' said Paul. 'Take more drugs, get into more fights, that sort of thing. Used to call his mum and dad for money, then be a real cunt to them when they turned up. Thought it was funny. Everyone else just wished they had a mum and dad to come and get them. Would have been grateful.'

'You know the other two who set the fire?'

Paul shook his head. 'Malcolm had started hanging about Royston, desperate to get in with one of the teams, suppose that's where he met them. Trying to be one of the boys.'

'You know him, Deke?' Cooper asked, stifling a yawn.

'Not really,' said Deke. 'Saw him hanging about a few times. Sitting up the back in the Big Glen trying to look tough.'

'So if someone asked him to set fire to the salon he'd have done it?' asked McCoy.

'Like a shot,' said Paul. 'Exactly what he was looking to do. Be a villain. Be accepted.'

McCoy nodded. 'What about the guy following Trisha? She said he was a grown man, well-dressed, professional sort?'

'Yeah,' said Paul. 'She thought he was married, was mid-thirties at least.'

'You ever see him? Could you describe him?'

Paul shook his head. 'All I know is what Trisha told me.'

'Okay. Being married would make sense, wouldn't want to be exposed. Still must have had an awful lot to lose to do what he did.'

'Must have,' said Paul.

McCoy stood up. 'I'll leave you to it. What's the plan?'

Cooper yawned again. 'I'm going back to my bed, not as young as I was. Deke and Jumbo will make sure Paul's all right.'

'No leaving the flat,' said McCoy. 'Remember what I said.'

Paul saluted. 'Yes, sir.'

Jumbo walked McCoy down the stairs. Could tell there was something on his mind. He looked troubled, kept fiddling with the cord on his anorak. They stood outside the close and McCoy lit up. Knew he was going to have to be the one to ask.

'Something you want to talk about?' asked McCoy, throwing his match into the garden.

'Do you remember a while ago you said you would help me fill out the forms for me to be a gardener for the Corporation?'

McCoy nodded.

'Can we do it? It was fine when we were at the place in the West End. I got to do the garden every day.' Jumbo looked at the line of burnt-out gardens piled with rubbish that comprised Memen Road. 'But there's nothing here.'

'You sure?'

'You said we could do it in the spring. That's now.'

'Certainly is,' said McCoy. 'Even though it's bloody miserable. I'll get the forms for you and we'll do it together, eh?'

Jumbo grinned. McCoy knew what was coming next. 'And you'll talk to Mr Cooper, won't you? You said.'

McCoy nodded. No idea what Cooper would say about his bodyguard leaving to plant flowers for Glasgow Corporation. Didn't think he'd be happy.

'What about Paul?' asked McCoy. 'You getting on with him?'

'He doesn't talk to me very much. I think he thinks I'm just a stupid idiot.'

'You're no idiot, Jumbo, so don't let him tell you that. How about Deke?'

The grin came back. 'Deke buys me *Commando* comics. He's a good guy. Said he'd take me to get some new clothes.'

McCoy looked at his dirty jeans, big jumper and quilted anorak. Pointed at his worn-out sandshoes. Reached into his pocket and found a fiver.

'Get yourself some of they fancy Adydad sandshoes on me.'

Jumbo took it. 'Thanks. I better get back. You won't forget, will you? The forms?'

'I'll get them,' said McCoy. 'Promise.'

Jumbo disappeared into the close and McCoy started walking back to the main road. Something about Paul Cooper was staring to niggle him and it wasn't just the fact that Jumbo didn't like him. His story about the mysterious man was a little bit too convenient, had come out too easy. Something else was bothering him about Paul Cooper too. Time to go and find out if his hunch was right or not.

SIXTY-FOUR

He tried the Great Northern first. Not there. Got out quick in case his dad turned up. Wasn't quite sure where to try next. Stood on the pavement outside trying to think. The pubs along Royston Road? Town? Maybe the grates behind the St Enoch Hotel? Realised he was staring right at the most likely place. The Charles Street flats across the road.

Bert Cross answered the door of the flat, Irn-Bru bottle full of God knows what in his hand. 'Ah, the very man,' he said, holding out the bottle. 'Arthritis. I cannae open the bloody thing. Break its neck for me, son, eh?'

McCoy took the bottle and followed Bert through into the living room. He looked around. 'Where is everyone?'

'She sent them all away,' he said. 'She's away into town for a few hours. I'm looking after old Walter next door.' He glanced at the bottle. 'That's my wages.'

McCoy sat down on a chair, opened the bottle, instant smell of what seemed like turps, and handed it over.

Bert grasped it in both hands, brought it up to his mouth and took a drink. 'What brings you up this way?' he asked, wiping his mouth.

'I need you to tell me the truth,' said McCoy. 'No nonsense, no not being able to remember. I've had enough. Unless you tell me what I want to know, I'm going to smash every bottle of this stuff. I don't care if you forget everything you tell me today if it ever comes to trial. You just need to tell me the truth right now.'

McCoy leant over, took the bottle out Bert's hands, put it down by his feet.

Bert looked at him with his bright blue eyes. Nodded.

'Okay. Tell me what really happened that morning.'

Bert looked at the bottle, looked at McCoy. Knew he didn't have a choice. 'He threw him off the roof. Dragged him to the edge, then threw him off. It was bloody horrible. Ally hit the ground and his head cracked, cracked right open. But he wasn't dead even after that. He started crawling, making this horrible wheezing noise. I looked up and the guy was standing there on the roof looking down, looking right at me. I don't mind telling you, son, I just about shat myself. I knew I couldn't run. I can hardly move at that time in the morning, everything's seized up.' He looked at the bottle again. 'Please, son, I need it.'

'You'll get it soon enough,' said McCoy. 'Keep going.'

'So I went over to Ally but he'd stopped moving by now. Just lying there, blood pouring out of him. Then the guy appeared in the yard.'

'What did he look like?'

'He was young, big lad though. Short hair.'

'What colour?' asked McCoy, knowing the answer already.

'Blond. He walked funny, like a sailor on deck. That enough?'

'Thanks.' McCoy handed the bottle back to Bert. He took it, poured half of it down his throat. McCoy watched him, could hear Walter next door singing 'Bye, Baby Bunting'.

Bert put the bottle down. 'He gave me a fiver, the boy. Told me Ally had jumped and that was all I had to tell them. And if I didn't, he'd be back and he'd kill me. The way he looked at me, son? I believed him.'

McCoy left him there, sitting on the couch shaking, trying to get the alcohol into his body as fast as he could. He pressed the button for the lift, looked out the window while he waited. Royston spread out below. Could see Dessie's house from here, the shell of Dolly's Salon, the park where they had discovered Ian Barrett. Could even see the proposed site of the new chapel pinned out on the grass opposite the old one.

The lift pinged, the doors opened, and he got in, pressed G. There was no doubt any more. Paul Cooper had killed Ally. Question was, what else had he done? Had he killed Trisha? Barrett? Maybe there was no mysterious man following Trisha, maybe it was him. Maybe that was the real reason he'd run from the pub the other day, was worried McCoy was onto him.

The doors opened and McCoy stepped out into the foyer, nodded a hello at the concierge in his glass-walled office, and left. Lit up. Didn't know what Stevie Cooper would do if he found out McCoy was going after his son. He and Cooper went back a long way, but it was like they said, blood was thicker than water. He sat down on a swing in the wee kids' playground, tried to think. Knew one thing: whatever he did, he was going to have to tread easy.

SIXTY-FIVE

McCoy decided to walk back into town. Rain was off and he needed time to think. He was getting mired in it all: the fire, Paul Cooper, Johnny Smart, the Happiness Hotel. All of it was connected somehow but he still couldn't see how. He was too close to it. Couldn't see the wood for the trees.

Paul Cooper looked exactly like his father, maybe he had his father's nature too. Maybe he'd killed his girlfriend in some sort of rage. Then killed the people that could connect them. Ally and Barrett. Was cold-blooded stuff, but he was Stevie Cooper's son after all, no matter if he was still a teenager.

He'd run after the photo had connected him to Trisha. Been evasive after McCoy had started asking too much about the mysterious man following her. Made sense. Bert Cross could connect him to Ally's murder, but how much was the word of an elderly alcoholic worth? If it ever came to trial and Bert knew what was good for him, he'd act confused, make himself as unreliable as possible.

McCoy turned onto Springburn Road, went into the newsagent and bought himself a packet of Regal, lit up and kept walking. There was nothing to connect Paul Cooper to Barrett or Trisha's deaths. No forensics, no witnesses, no nothing, and the trail was going cold.

Or maybe McCoy was making too big a leap. Maybe Paul had killed Ally and that was it. According to Lachy, the bloke who had been harassing Ally was young. Maybe Ally had something Paul wanted, and he wouldn't hand it over. Those pictures of Trisha they'd found at Barrett's. Pictures of himself?

If that was the case, who had killed Barrett and Trisha? And why? A client of the Happiness Hotel seemed the most likely, someone with a lot to lose if it all became public. He sighed, rubbed at his stomach under his coat, was starting to grumble again. Should have bought some milk and Rich Tea biscuits.

The problem was, if it was a guest of the Happiness Hotel, he was probably one of hundreds. Ally had to have had enough clients to pay for that posh flat. Maybe he should go back there, see if Ally had kept a record or account book. Maybe that's what the break-in had been about? Maybe that's what the intruders had been looking for?

McCoy realised he was coming up to Royston Road, decided to kill two birds with one stone. Turned in and headed towards the shops. Could see the salon from here. Wondered what would happen to it now. Not sure people would want to get their hair done again in a place where something so terrible had happened.

He hadn't really thought much about the fact that it was a hairdresser's that had been set on fire. Now that he did think about it, it seemed a bit weird. Arson attacks in territory disputes were invariably on pubs or bookies. Places that turned over a lot of money, where profits would be missed by whoever ran them. A hairdresser's in Royston could only make pin money, enough to turn over, so why target there? Dessie Caine had about twenty pubs in the area. Torching any one of them would have made much more sense.

He stopped in the street. Maybe that was the trouble. Maybe the reason the hairdresser's had been set on fire was nothing to do with a turf war and the fire had been set for another reason. What was it Una had said? That it was only Carole who was supposed to be there that night. Carole the cleaner, who they had all ignored, was she something to do with it? It was worth following up and he was here now anyway. May as well. Started walking again, dug some money out his pocket.

Una was working behind the counter at Galbraith's. Blue nylon tabard on. Faraway look on her face. Rang up his packet of Rich Tea biscuits and pint of milk before she realised it was him.

'Sorry, miles away. You back again?'

'Just passing through,' said McCoy.

'I saw you found that boy,' she said. 'May he rot in hell like the other two.'

Wasn't what McCoy was expecting. Maybe he should have known better.

'The girl Carole, that died in the fire? She lived with her mum you said?' he asked.

Una crossed herself. 'Her maw's dead, Mr McCoy. They think she had a heart attack from the strain of it all and fell down the stairs in her close.'

'When was this?'

'Two days ago,' said Una. 'God will never forgive me for saying this, but I'm half glad. She lived for that girl, looking after her was her whole life. When she found out she was dead, well, I've never heard anything like it, hope I never will again. Was the sound of someone dying inside, a terrible thing to hear. She's better where she is now, back with Carole.'

McCoy left Una at the counter, walked out the shop and crossed Royston Road. Sat on the wall by Glenconner Park. He pulled the foil lid off the pint of milk and drank half of it back, opened his biscuits and ate one after the other.

Thought about Carole, thought about her mum. Wondered what the fire was really for. Started to think they might have had the whole thing wrong from the start.

SIXTY-SIX

Phyllis was weighing something horrible when he got to the morgue. McCoy looked away quickly, asked her how long she would be.

'Twenty minutes,' she said. 'Away and sit on your steps.'

Suited him fine.

McCoy sat down on the steps of the High Court next door and lit up. He'd spent more time on these steps than he had in the morgue itself. Anything to avoid seeing stuff like whatever was on those scales Phyllis had been using.

She appeared at the morgue door just as McCoy was finishing his cigarette. She looked up into the sky, scowled and put her umbrella up. Rain was on again. She came over and stood under the court entranceway.

'If you think I'm sitting on wet stone in this coat, you are very much mistaken,' she said. 'You can buy me a drink or a cup of tea. Your choice.'

He plumped for the drink. The Whistling Kirk was across the road, but he hated the place, a coppers' pub. The Empire was only five minutes up Saltmarket. Much more his style. 'C'mon,' he said, getting up. 'I know a great place.'

'I rather think I would have been better sitting on the wet steps than these chairs,' said Phyllis, looking round.

'It's a great wee pub,' said McCoy. 'Full of character.'

Phyllis took in the collection of lowlife that made up the Empire Bar's afternoon clientele. Men with bookies' slips in front of them. An old woman in the corner having a conversation with someone who wasn't there.

'Full of something anyway,' she said. 'I'll have a gin and tonic.'

McCoy went to the bar, ordered a pint and Phyllis's drink. His pint came followed by a tumbler with half an inch of oily liquid in it and a wee bottle of tonic that wasn't Schweppes plonked on the counter. Knew he was on to a loser, but he had to try.

'Got any ice and lemon?'

The barman looked at him. Pot belly straining his dirty shirt. Smeary aviator glasses and a comb-over. 'Where you think you are, son? Rogano's?'

'Fair enough,' said McCoy, and scooped up the drinks.

Phyllis looked at hers with resignation, poured the tonic and took a sip, didn't look happy.

'So, Harry, what can I help you with?' she asked, putting her drink back down and pushing it away.

'Was that Moira Lownie's autopsy you were just doing?'

Phyllis looked surprised. 'It was. Why do you ask?'

'Did she have a heart attack?'

Phyllis shook her head. 'No. She broke her neck when she fell downstairs. Why do you ask?'

'Could she have been pushed?'

Phyllis didn't reply, just looked at him.

'What?'

'Until you tell me why we are sitting here discussing the unfortunate demise of Moira Lownie, I'm not answering any questions.'

'Moira Lownie was the mother of Carole Lownie who was killed in the salon fire.'

'Ah,' said Phyllis. 'And?'

'Could she have been pushed?' asked McCoy again.

Phyllis looked pained. 'Well, I suppose so. There's no evidence to suggest that, but short of someone seeing it happen, I'm not sure there would be. But she was a frail sixty-nine-year-old woman with emphysema who walked with a stick. It's not difficult to imagine she tripped, or became dizzy and fell. Besides, who would want to push her?'

'Not sure,' said McCoy.

'I know you, Harry, I can see the wheels turning behind your eyes. What's going on?'

A man holding a carrier bag came into the pub, started walking round the tables, showing the people what was in it. Arrived in front of Phyllis. He held the bag open to reveal five or six blocks of cheese, Ferguson's label and price sticker still on them.

'Cheese, hen?' he asked. 'Good stuff.'

Phyllis looked puzzled. 'I don't quite understand. What—'

'Move on, pal,' said McCoy.

The guy closed the bag and shuffled off.

'Was he selling that?' asked Phyllis. 'Stolen cheese?'

McCoy nodded.

Phyllis shook her head and McCoy carried on. 'I'm wondering if one of the women was the intended victim of the fire, that it wasn't all a horrible accident. Only Carole Lownie was supposed to be working that night. The others were there by coincidence. Maybe someone wanted to kill Carole Lownie.'

'Then killed her mother?' asked Phyllis. 'Why?'

McCoy shrugged. 'Haven't got that far yet. Anything weird in Carole's autopsy?'

'I don't know,' said Phyllis. 'I didn't do it. Gilchrist did it. We needed to get them all done as soon as possible so we split them between us.'

'Can you look at his report? Check it?'

Phyllis shook her head. 'Harry, Robert Gilchrist has been doing autopsies longer than I have. Carole died of smoke inhalation like the others.'

'Just have a wee look, eh?'

Phyllis sighed.

'Thanks,' said McCoy. 'I owe you.'

'You always owe me. How's Mr Murray?'

'Frustrated like the rest of us. How does he seem to you?'

'A bit distant, preoccupied. To be expected, I suppose. I'll be glad when this is all over and I can persuade him to take a holiday.'

'Good luck with that,' said McCoy, standing up.

'Where are you off to now?'

'Royston.'

'Royston. The Empire Bar. Stolen cheese. It's a glamorous life you lead,' said Phyllis.

McCoy grinned. 'Want to come?'

'Normally I would be delighted,' said Phyllis. 'But I have to go and check an autopsy report written by the senior medical examiner, apparently. Call me in the morning.'

SIXTY-SEVEN

McCoy opened the door of the Big Glen and walked through into the welcome dry of the lounge. The shop women were sitting at their usual table, deep in a cloud of cigarette smoke and hairspray. He bought himself a pint, walked over and sat at the table next to them.

'The polis are back,' said one of the women and they all turned to look at him.

'Was looking for Una,' he said. 'She around?'

There was a moment of silence. An atmosphere he didn't understand.

'Don't think we'll be seeing her in here for a while.' It was the woman with the perm from the butcher's.

'Why's that?' he asked.

Another moment of silence, some of the women started fiddling with their lighters, polishing their specs on their jumpers.

'Is something wrong?' asked McCoy.

Tom Jones was singing 'Delilah' in the background, pools man going round the tables collecting money.

Eventually one of the other women spoke. 'She's showing.'

It took McCoy a moment to realise what she meant. She'd been behind the counter when he'd seen her this afternoon.

'You hadn't noticed?'

McCoy shook his head.

'You're not the only one,' said a woman in a pink fluffy jumper. Was meant to be whisper but she made sure it was loud enough for everyone to hear. Something about the women had definitely changed. Whatever Una had done, she'd stepped over some line. She wasn't one of them any more.

The woman with the perm lit up a cigarette, waited for her audience's total attention. 'You no get it, son? She's single, hasn't got a pot to piss in. No sign of a wedding ring, or even an engagement ring.'

'Ah,' said McCoy, beginning to understand. 'That's not ideal.'

'You're telling me,' said the woman. 'Understatement of the century.'

'Okay, since Una isn't here maybe you ladies can help me.' Looked round the table, none of them appeared to be in a particularly helpful mood. Decided to just carry on. 'How did Carole get the job in the salon? From what I understand she was a bit . . .'

'Simple,' said one of the women. 'She wasn't quite right. Nice girl but not the full shilling.'

'So how did she get the job? Did Dolly feel sorry for her?'

'Wasn't Dolly,' said the one with the perm. 'Her maw was never out the bloody chapel. Father McKenna fixed it up for her. Went to see Dolly and said she'd be doing everyone a great favour if she gave Carole a job. So she did.'

'She have any pals I could talk to?'

The woman shook her head. 'She just had her maw.'

McCoy left them there, had the feeling he'd got as much as he was going to from them. The ranks had closed. Una was on her own. Wondered who the father was. Some guy she'd met at the dancing probably. Good Catholic like Una wouldn't be on the pill. Poor cow was paying for it now.

He started walking back into town. Not sure if he'd got any further. A mentally handicapped girl who lived with her mum, why would anyone want to kill her? Like just about everything else with this case, it didn't make any sense. Maybe he was barking up the wrong tree. Maybe nobody had wanted to kill Carole Lownie after all.

Realised he was back outside the Great Northern. The door opened and the man that had been with his dad stepped out.

'Thought that was you coming down the road,' he said. 'Was watching out the window.'

The man was dressed in a pair of skanky jeans and a donkey jacket, brutal crew cut revealing a couple of scars on the back of his head.

McCoy went to walk on.

'He knew it was you.'

McCoy stopped, looked at him, heart thumping. 'What do you mean?'

'Your da's no great, son. Got hit by a car a year or so ago. Hit his head on the road. Not really been the same since. Got a cig?'

McCoy dug in his pocket, handed the packet over, realised his hand was shaking. 'Is he okay?'

The man lit up, shrugged. 'Good days and bad days. Started telling me about his son, how he was high up in the polis. Said he was too ashamed to say who he was, wasn't happy you'd seen him begging. Telling me how proud he was of how you were getting on.'

McCoy's stomach felt like he'd been knifed, hand went to his pocket to get his Pepto-Bismol, realised he didn't have any with him. Felt dizzy. 'Where is he now?'

The man shrugged again. 'Your guess is as good as mine. Might turn up before they shut the doors, might not. Says this place is like hell's waiting room. Hates it.'

'Can I trust you?' asked McCoy.

The man nodded.

McCoy dug in his pocket, pulled out a tenner, handed it to him. 'Give him this, but get him to buy some food before he gets started on the drink, eh? Chips at least. And to get himself some new clothes.'

The man put the money in his pocket. 'Will do. You all right, son? You've gone pure white.'

'I'm fine.' McCoy saw a cab coming along Royston Road. Hailed it and got in. Told the driver to take him home to Gardner Street. Didn't answer when the driver asked him why he was crying.

27th May 1974

SIXTY-EIGHT

Tom McCauley had a large raw steak held up to his eye. He was standing over the brick fireplace in his front room, his wife fussing around him and a tubby Labrador sitting at his feet, staring at the steak.

'He punched me right in the bloody eye,' he said. 'Soon wished he hadn't, I'll tell you that.'

McCoy forgot and sat down on the orange leather immediately sank into it, struggled to stay upright. Wattie decided to stay standing.

'So what happened exactly?' asked McCoy.

'When you get to my age,' said McCauley, 'you get up to pee in the night. Just a fact. So I get up about half three and I'm standing there pissing—'

'Tom!' said his wife.

'Sorry. I'm in the toilet and I hear a noise coming from Malcom's room.'

His wife stood up. 'I can't hear this again, I'll away and make some tea.'

'So I open the door and some guy is standing there, window wide open behind him. He looks at me, and before I can say

· 305 ·

anything, the bastard punches me right in the eye. Hurt like fuck and it made me angry. So I hit him.'

McCoy looked at the builder's big hand holding the steak.

'You did more than hit him,' said McCoy. 'You knocked him unconscious.'

'Aye, well, I was a boxer when I was young, made some extra money when I was working on the sites. Never goes away.'

The man Tom McCauley had hit was still out, lying on Malcolm's bed being attended to by an ambulanceman.

'So I hit him and then I called the polis.'

'Maybe just as well you knocked him out,' said McCoy. 'Did you see what he had on him?'

McCauley nodded. 'The policeman showed me. Dirty big knife.'

'A dirty big knife and a cosh, to be precise,' said McCoy. 'Wattie, go and see if you recognise the bugger.'

Wattie headed for the bedroom.

McCauley took the steak off his eye, sat down on the leather armchair. 'If it wasn't for you, Malcolm would be dead. I don't know how to thank you.'

McCoy shrugged. 'We got lucky. How is he?'

McCauley shook his head. 'Not good. Doesn't seem to know where he is or what's going on most of the time. He's—'

'Boss?'

McCoy looked up and Wattie gestured him into the hall.

'Need you to have a look, I think it's Sandy Gilmour.'

McCoy stuck his head round the bedroom door. Seemed to have been untouched. Poster of a racing car, Scotland team picture, the inside bit from *The Dark Side Of The Moon*. On the bed was a large man being sick into a paper bowl being held by the ambulanceman. He looked up when McCoy came in. Was Sandy Gilmour right enough. Was about to say something when he threw up again, missed the bowl.

McCoy moved back into the hall. 'It's him all right. Big bastard that he is.'

'Sandy Gilmour doesn't do anything unless there's money involved,' said Wattie. 'What was he doing here?'

'Trying to find Malcolm McCauley, I think,' said McCoy. 'Hence the knife and the cosh.'

'Who's paid him?' asked Wattie.

'Not sure,' said McCoy. 'But he's never going to tell us. No doubt he'll say it was an innocent breaking and entering and he forgot the knife was in his pocket.'

'He work for Johnny Smart?'

McCoy nodded. 'Trouble is, he works for everyone else as well.'

Back in the living room, McCauley had given up and handed the steak over. The Labrador was now in the corner of the room chewing away.

'Where is Malcom?' asked McCoy.

McCauley looked at him. 'I'm not supposed to say. For his own safety.'

'Okay,' said McCoy.

'But since it's you, he's in the locked unit at Leverndale.'

Leverndale was a large mental hospital on the Southside. Things were starting to make sense now. Whoever had been after him hadn't been able to find him in the prison system. Thought he might be at home and if he wasn't? The big knife would help his parents tell him where he was.

'They're assessing him,' said McCauley. 'Seeing if he's fit to stand trial.'

'Doesn't sound like he is,' said McCoy.

McCauley shook his head. 'He's not right.' He looked up at McCoy. 'I don't know if this means anything, but I got to see him yesterday, half an hour.' He smiled. 'Took him twenty minutes to realise who I was. Anyway, when I was leaving, he said, "I'm sorry, Dad. If only she'd never given us the money."'

SIXTY-NINE

'She?' asked Wattie as they drove back into Glasgow.

'Probably just rambling,' said McCoy, watching a man trying to get a dog to stop jumping up on him. Lights changed and they moved off again. 'The boy's head is scrambled. Like his dad said, he doesn't know where he is half the time.' He yawned. 'Can you drop me off at Springburn?'

Didn't want Wattie there when he told Cooper his suspicions about Paul. Had no idea how he was going to react. Less likely to go nuts if it was just him. Or so he hoped.

'Where you off to?' asked Wattie.

'Need to see a man about a dog,' said McCoy.

'Top of Memen Road do you then?'

'Perfect,' said McCoy. 'Smartarse.'

Cooper was in the room McCoy never wanted to go into when he arrived. His work room. He sat down at the kitchen table and watched Deke put the tea on. Kitchen was tidy for once. Deke must be the one trying to keep things tidy. Wouldn't be Cooper or Jumbo.

'How's it going?' he asked. 'The new job.'

'No bad,' said Deke, filling the kettle. 'Just got to pick your moments with him. I'm learning to do that.'

'So am I,' said McCoy, 'and I've known him for twenty years. Dessie know about it?'

Deke nodded. 'Must do by now. If he wasn't happy, I'd have heard about it by now.'

There was a thump from the other room, a low moan.

'Who's in there?' asked McCoy, wincing.

'One of the debt collectors. Does Possil. Kevin somebody. Got sticky fingers apparently.' He smiled. 'So Stevie's breaking some of them for him. Sugar?'

McCoy had just finished his tea, was lighting up, when Cooper appeared in the doorway. His arms and the vest he was wearing were covered in splatters of blood, as was his chin. He looked at Deke.

'Get that prick out of here. He's done.'

Deke walked out the room.

Cooper pulled his bloody vest off, started washing himself in the kitchen sink. 'You not got a home to go to these days?' he asked, lathering up his bloody arms. 'Always bloody here.'

'Need to talk to you about Paul,' McCoy said, wishing he'd picked a better time. Cooper still looked wound up from the beating he'd just given.

Cooper turned round, started drying himself off with a dirty blue towel. 'What about him? Wee bugger fucked off again last night, no been back.'

Deke appeared again, handed Cooper a new vest in a packet.

'I think he killed someone.'

Cooper stopped rubbing at his chest with the towel, looked at him. 'What did you say?'

McCoy had said it now, had to keep going. 'I think he killed a man called Ally Drummond. A witness saw Paul push him off a building, then he gave him money to keep quiet about it. And a warning that he'd be back to kill him if he didn't.'

Cooper sat down at the table, started unwrapping the vest. 'And why would Paul do that?' he asked quietly.

'Think Ally had photos of his girlfriend – dirty photos – and he wouldn't give them back. Was printing them up and selling them.'

'You sure this guy didn't just fall?' asked Cooper.

'Don't think so.'

'And why wouldn't he give the photos back?'

'I don't know. Maybe there was someone else wanted the photos, someone Ally was more scared of than Paul.'

Cooper was fiddling with the new vest, unfolding it, then folding it up again. 'Seems to me he had a reason then, didn't he?'

'Had a reason to be angry,' said McCoy. 'Not sure he had a reason to kill him.'

'Maybe he just got carried away, didn't mean it. It happens.'

McCoy nodded. Didn't want to press any harder. Cooper was on a knife edge already. Didn't like it when he got quiet, was a worse signal than him shouting.

'Deke, away and get me a shirt.' Deke disappeared. 'And what are you planning to do with all this information about my son, Detective McCoy?' asked Cooper. 'Told anyone else what you think?'

McCoy looked at Cooper. Wasn't sure if he was trying to be funny or whether that's what he was now. Just another polis. Cooper had missed some of the blood when he'd washed himself. There was a splatter of it across his forehead. Dark red lines under some of his fingernails. Blood from someone that had wronged him.

'Not yet. I think we need to speak to him first,' McCoy said carefully. 'Find out exactly what happened.'

Deke put a dry cleaner's parcel on the table.

'Sounds like an idea,' said Cooper, pulling the vest on. 'Best not jump to any conclusions, eh?'

McCoy could feel sweat running down his back.

'Maybe this Ally killed his girlfriend and that's why Paul was after him. That would make sense.'

'Could be,' said McCoy. 'Need to ask him about that as well. But he said that she told him she was being followed by a well-dressed man, so not sure that description fits Ally.'

'Maybe it was Johnny Smart,' said Deke. 'That would fit.'

'Don't think he's that way inclined,' said Cooper.

'Is he a poof?' asked Deke.

Cooper shook his head. 'Been married twenty years, still worships the ground his wife walks on. Fuck knows why, she's a face like a skelped arse.'

He opened the parcel, pulled out a blue short-sleeved shirt from the pile of ten and put it on. Buttoned it up. Looked at McCoy. 'You need to find Paul. Take Deke with you, he can help. Okay?'

McCoy nodded. And report back, he thought. Still, wasn't in a position to say no. He stood up. 'We'll find him. Have a word, sort things out.'

Cooper looked up at him. For once McCoy couldn't read him at all. 'That's what we'll do,' he said. 'That's what we'll do.'

SEVENTY

Deke had the same idea as McCoy. Sister Jimmy.

McCoy pushed the door of Equi open. Was greeted by the smell of coffee and bacon frying. Stomach rumbled. Hadn't eaten anything that morning.

He nodded at Eddie behind the counter. 'Two coffees, two bacon rolls. All right with you, Deke?'

Deke pointed to the back of the cafe. 'Looks like we're in luck.'

Sister Jimmy was sitting in the booth, head against the wall, eyes closed. Paul Cooper was leaning on him, head down.

'What they been taking?' asked McCoy.

'Looks like mandies,' said Deke.

'Oh, well, at least they're not going anywhere. Be able to have our breakfast.'

By the time the breakfast had arrived, Sister Jimmy and Paul still hadn't moved. McCoy took a bite of his roll, waited. Stomach didn't seem too bad.

'How come you left Dessie?' asked McCoy. 'I never asked.'

Deke shrugged, took a sip of his coffee. 'Dessie's okay but he's got too many lads. Didn't want to still be collecting from the pubs in five years. Needed to do something to get on.'

McCoy nodded. Made sense.

'You think Paul will join the team?'

McCoy tried the coffee. Okay so far. 'Don't know. Makes sense in some way. The family business and all that, but from what I've seen, Paul's not one to do what he's told and Stevie will have a problem with that. And if Paul's a bit wild, he's an easy target for people wanting to get at Stevie. I'm guessing you'd rather he didn't.'

Deke smiled. 'Didn't think it was that obvious. Don't want to be babysitting him for the next few years, and I've a feeling that's what I'd end up doing.'

McCoy finished the last of his roll. Had managed half his coffee. 'C'mon,' he said. 'Let's wake the babes in the wood.'

McCoy prodded Sister Jimmy's shoulder and his eyes slowly opened, took a wee while to focus. Two untouched cold coffees on the table.

'Hoped I was dreaming,' he said.

'No such luck,' said McCoy. 'Mandies?'

'Your pal, Spider. Think we were the fucking guinea pigs, told us to take two.'

He sat up, pushed the coffees out the way, and lowered Paul Cooper onto the table. 'You looking for him?'

McCoy nodded.

'Thought you might be. Make sure and tell his dad I never touched him, because I didn't, okay?'

'Will do,' said McCoy. 'Where were you anyway?'

Sister Jimmy rubbed at his eyes. 'Where weren't we? The Arms, Vintners, some flat in the West End. Christ knows. He was determined to have a big night. I could hardly keep up.'

'What was the occasion?' asked McCoy.

'Today's his sixteenth birthday. Wanted to celebrate.'

'I didn't know that,' said McCoy.

'Not many people do. Don't think his dad did either. That's what set him off. Wouldnae go home last night.'

Deke leant forward and used his thumb to raise Paul's eyelid. Eye didn't move, just kept staring straight ahead.

'He's out for the count,' he said. 'Why don't I stay here, give him another couple of hours to sleep it off, and then I'll take him up to his dad's? We'll never move him like this.'

'You sure?' asked McCoy.

'It's fine. I'll sit here, drink a few coffees, listen to Sister Jimmy's tales of life in the fast lane.'

McCoy stood up. 'I'll see you back at Stevie's this afternoon.'

He left them there. Sister Jimmy back asleep against the wall, Paul passed out on the table, Deke watching over them. He stepped out the cafe back onto Sauchiehall Street and lit up. Trisha O'Hara dead at fifteen. Paul Cooper's sixteenth birthday spent in a drugged stupor. This town was getting harder and harder. Was glad he wasn't young now. Wasn't sure he'd survive.

SEVENTY-ONE

McCoy got out the car and stretched. Call had come in from a uniform, thought McCoy might be interested. Tosh Burns and a couple of Dessie Caine's other lads had been hanging about outside a lock-up at the other end of Forge Road. Had been there for a couple of hours.

Wattie pulled over and McCoy lit up, looked over at the lock-up. Tosh and the two other lads were standing there smoking. Tosh looked over, didn't look happy to see him.

'What's the plan?' asked Wattie.

'Fuck knows,' said McCoy. 'I'm not even sure why we're here. I've had enough of Dessie and his pals to last me a life-time. Maybe we should just bugger off.'

Just as he said that, the door of the lock-up burst open and a man staggered out, his hands up to his face, blood seeping through his fingers. He came over to Tosh, and Tosh handed him a towel from the sports bag at his feet. He held it up to his face, yellow towel red within seconds.

McCoy winced, looked away.

'Lovely,' said Wattie. 'Funny thing is, I saw the wife yesterday. Me and Mary were in Mothercare getting things for the wee man and she was loading up on baby clothes.'

'Chrissie Caine? Christ, I hope she's not pregnant. God help the wean if she is, it'll be at Mass twice a day.'

'Least of its troubles,' said Wattie.

'True. Suppose we better go and see what's going on,' said McCoy with little enthusiasm.

'You sure it's safe?' asked Wattie. 'Looks like he's handing out doings.'

'Soon find out,' said McCoy. Soon as he opened the car door, Tosh said something to the bleeding man and he started running. Disappeared round the back of the lock-up.

'Where's he going?' asked McCoy.

'Who?' asked Tosh.

McCoy shook his head. Was going to be like that. 'What's going on, Tosh? Who's in the lock-up? Dessie?'

'No idea,' said Tosh. 'Don't know what you're talking about.'

'I just saw a man come out of there who was obviously the victim of a serious assault. That gives me every right to go inside.'

'Be my guest,' said Tosh, stepping aside. 'Don't tell me I didn't warn you.' He reached into the sports bag and pulled out another two towels. 'Take these if you're going.'

McCoy took them, started walking towards the lock-up door.

'You sure about this?' asked Wattie.

'Nope,' said McCoy and pulled the door open.

The smell hit him first. Could smell alcohol and hairspray, and under that something else, something like the smell of an animal in a cage. It was dim, took his eyes a few seconds to adjust, only light was a dirty skylight.

Dessie was up the back. He was naked, standing with his hands against the wall, dripping with water, a couple of empty buckets on the floor beside him.

'You got the fucking towels?' he asked, not turning around.

McCoy walked over to him, held them out. Dessie turned, took one out his hand before he realised who it was. Stopped.

Started to laugh. 'I'll say something for you, McCoy. You've got balls all right.'

Took the towel, started to dry himself.

McCoy took a look around the place. There was a chair in the corner surrounded by bottles of beer and whisky, a suit and shirt hanging on a nail hammered into the wall, two patches of dried blood on another wall. McCoy moved back towards the light and his foot hit something. He looked down. Three cans were on the floor by half a dozen empty milk bottles.

'Christ, Dessie,' he said. 'You've no been drinking that, have you?'

Hadn't seen anyone drinking hairspray in milk for years. Not since his dad was in his darkest days. You sprayed the hairspray into the milk and the gluey plastic stuff that held your hair in place floated to the top. You took that off and drank the milk, now full of propellant or alcohol or whatever the fuck was in the can.

'What I drink is my business,' said Dessie.

He took the other towel from McCoy and wrapped it around his waist, sat down on the chair, and took a long slug from one of the whisky bottles beside it. McCoy realised then that he was still pissed or out of it from the hairspray. The makeshift shower hadn't been to sober him up. Just to wake him up enough so he could keep drinking. Dessie looked like he'd been drinking for days. Even with the shower, he could smell the sweat and alcohol off him. His eyes were red-rimmed, unfocused, a thick five o'clock shadow covered half his face.

McCoy picked up one of the beer cans, opened it and took a drink. Held it up. 'Cheers,' he said.

Dessie laughed again, held up his whisky bottle.

'What you doing in here, Dessie?' asked McCoy. 'You've got loads of pubs you could drink in.'

'Told Tosh and the boys to lock me in here for a day or so.' He smiled a drunken smile. 'Until the storm passes.'

He took another drink of the whisky. On his chair, towel round his waist, he looked like a fighter who'd gone too many rounds, back in his corner, bruised and battered.

McCoy went over to the suit, got the vest and underpants that were tucked in the pockets of the trousers and handed them to Dessie. He took them, then threw them against the wall.

'No finished drinking yet,' he said.

He took another slug and McCoy noticed his knuckles were bruised and bleeding, hand swollen up. McCoy nodded over at the dried blood on the wall. 'You been going a few rounds with the brickwork?'

Dessie didn't answer. Head was down, hands on his knees. He looked tired, like even he had had enough. He looked up, focused on McCoy. 'You ever been fucked over, Harry McCoy?'

'Oh, yes.'

'Then you know how I feel.' He leant over and held up his whisky bottle.

McCoy clanked his can against it. 'Who's fucked you over then?'

Dessie shook his head. Opened a can of beer, drank most of it back in one. Looked at McCoy. 'I shouldn't be talking to you, McCoy. What I should be doing is kicking your fucking head in.'

'Why's that, Dessie?'

Another slug of the beer, half of it spilling down onto his chest. Dessie's head went down again, almost talking to himself. 'Because you made him do it.'

'Made who do what? I don't know what—'

The door opened behind them. Light flooded in.

'Dessie Caine! You shut your fucking mouth.'

McCoy turned round to look, and Dessie's wife was standing there, Tosh and another heavy behind her. He turned back to Dessie but he was slumped over his can, head down, spit drooling onto the floor.

'Dessie?' he asked. 'What did I make who do? Dessie?'

Didn't have a chance to ask anything else before Tosh and the other heavy pushed him out the way and grabbed Dessie under his arms. They pulled him up, head still dangling down, and half walked, half dragged him towards the door, Dessie's wife staring at him, face rigid with anger, surely not a Christian thought left in her body.

The door banged behind them and the light went dim again. McCoy looked over and realised Dessie had left his fags and his lighter sitting on a folded-up newspaper on the floor. He lifted the packet of Embassy and put it in his pocket, noticed what was written on the page of that morning's *Daily Record*.

Plans for new Chapel 'On Hold', says Glasgow Diocese

He picked it up, held the paper under the skylight. Seemed the diocese was 'seeking alternative funding'. He put the paper down. What Dessie had said made sense now. They had fucked him over good and proper. After all he'd done and his dream of a new chapel, the church had pulled the rug out under his feet. Couldn't all be down to McCoy confronting Dessie and Father McKenna in the park, could it? Surely McKenna had to have heard the rumours about where Dessie's money really came from. Maybe he'd just never heard it from a policeman before. Maybe that was the last straw.

No wonder Dessie wanted to kick his head in. Everything he'd been working for all gone because of him. Whether it was true or not, it seemed like Dessie thought McCoy was to blame. Next time he saw Dessie, he would have to watch out, he wouldn't be as drunk next time. Wasn't going to let McCoy get away that easy.

Wattie appeared at the door, jangling the car keys in his hand. Peered in. 'Christ, it stinks in here. You ready to go?'

McCoy nodded.

When push came to shove, people like Dessie didn't stand a chance against the church. They were amateurs. The church was happy to dump them soon as they'd stopped being of use. Was damn sure they weren't going to give back any of the money Dessie had raised. They'd just get another frontman for their fundraising activities. One with a cleaner public image. One that wouldn't cause them embarrassment one day by appearing in court charged with something or other.

He started walking to the door. Found himself actually feeling sorry for Dessie Caine.

SEVENTY-TWO

'Can we go back via Sauchiehall Street? Just want to check on something.'

Wattie nodded, turned the car down towards town. They passed the cathedral, no crowds outside today, just a few nurses from the hospital queuing at a burger van.

'What was up with Dessie?' asked Wattie. 'Why was he on a bender?'

'Dessie's used to calling the shots, being in charge. Bit of a shock when he realised he wasn't. He's no daft though, he's not doing it in public. Has his reputation to uphold.'

'Who is then?' asked Wattie.

McCoy pointed upwards. 'The man upstairs and those who serve him.'

'I'm not even going to ask what that's supposed to mean,' said Wattie, pulling in at the kerb.

McCoy got out and started walking. He'd just passed Treron's when he noticed the spinning lights up ahead. Must be an accident, someone run over. Was only after he'd walked another block he could see the lights were coming from an ambulance and a panda car parked outside Equi. He started running.

First thing he saw was Sister Jimmy being helped to the ambulance, his jeans and yellow T-shirt soaked with blood. Face was pale, could hardly walk, two ambulancemen on either side of him taking his weight.

'Jimmy!'

Sister Jimmy looked up, saw McCoy. Tried to speak and his face creased in pain.

The ambulanceman told McCoy to give them a minute, let them get him settled in the back of the ambulance. McCoy left them trying to get a moaning Sister Jimmy up the step and headed inside Equi.

He showed his card to the uniform at the door and went in. The black-and-white tiled cafe floor was covered in bloody footprints, back booth was awash with it, had even splattered up onto the framed map of Sicily on the wall. McCoy looked away quickly, stepped back, and almost bumped into Tony, the owner. He was standing by the counter, apron and hands covered in drying blood.

'What happened?' asked McCoy. 'You okay?'

Tony looked anything but. 'I'm not sure. I was making coffee, I look up and the boys in the back are fighting. Next thing there is blood everywhere and one of them runs out.'

'Which one?' asked McCoy.

'Tall, red hair.'

Deke.

'What about the other boy, the one with short hair?' asked McCoy.

'He runs too.'

'Was he okay?' asked McCoy.

'I don't know,' said Tony. 'He had blood all on him, I don't know . . .'

Tony burst into tears. His wife came out the kitchen, put her arms around him, and the dam burst. Great racking sobs as his wife tried to comfort him.

McCoy walked back towards the entrance, found the uniform. 'What happened?'

'We're still trying to work it out,' he said. 'Was all over by the time we got here. Just one lad lying in the back, blood pouring out of him. Seems there were another two with him, but they'd scarpered. By the look of the one that got stabbed, probably some poofs' squabble that got out of hand.'

McCoy managed to resist the urge to punch him, headed for the ambulance.

Sister Jimmy was lying down on a stretcher, medic attending to him. Another medic was standing at the door.

McCoy pulled him aside. 'How is he?' he asked.

'He's a lucky bugger is what he is. Stabbed twice. First wound just missed the artery in his thigh, second one just missed his liver. Inch closer with either one and he'd be in real trouble. As it is, he's got two very nasty flesh wounds and he's lost a lot of blood, but he'll be okay.'

'Can I talk to him?'

'I'd hurry up if I was you, I'm about to give him a shot of morphine.'

McCoy stepped up into the ambulance, squatted down by Sister Jimmy.

'Christ,' said Jimmy, face contorted. 'Not you again.'

'What happened, Jimmy? You okay?

Sister Jimmy nodded. 'What happened is your pal tried to kill Paul.'

'What? Deke? You sure?'

'Course I'm bloody sure. I should know, I got in the way.'

He grimaced as the medic started wiping the blood away from the wound in his leg with what looked like a tablecloth.

'Just tell me what happened,' said McCoy. 'From the beginning.'

Sister Jimmy lay back on the stretcher, took a breath, winced.

'We're just sitting there, mandies wearing off. Starting to feel a bit more alive and your pal Deke's chatting away, friendly as can be. I get up to go to the toilets, come back, and he's got a bloody knife out and Paul's backed against the wall, blood pouring out his chest.'

The medic pulled Sister Jimmy's arm out from under the blanket, started wiping the inside of his elbow with a pad of cotton wool dipped in alcohol. 'Just a wee prick,' he said.

'Story of my life,' said Sister Jimmy, tried to smile. 'Anyway, your pal's about to go in with the knife again, and I pull him away, so the fucker stabs me in the leg, then he stabs me in the stomach. It was so fucking sore, McCoy, I swear I thought I was going to die. I fall on him and Paul takes his chance and runs. By the time Deke gets up and disentangles himself from me he's well gone.'

Sister Jimmy closed his eyes as the morphine went in his arm.

'Who'd have guessed it? You, a hero,' said McCoy.

'Me,' said Sister Jimmy, 'I'm more than just a pretty face.' And then his head slumped to the side.

'He'll be out for a good while,' said the medic. 'We're going to take him up to the Royal. You coming?'

McCoy shook his head, stepped down from the ambulance. He walked across the road, sat down in the bus stop by Tiffany's and lit up.

Was only one reason he could think of as to why Deke would try to kill Paul Cooper. Paul was the last one standing that knew about Trisha, Barrett and the Happiness Hotel. Someone wanted him silenced. Was starting to think Deke coming to work for Stevie Cooper might not have been as coincidental as it seemed. Maybe he'd been working for Dessie all along. Waiting for Cooper or himself to find Paul, biding his time. If that was true, McCoy had just served up Paul on a plate.

A bus stopped. Doors opened and the conductor looked at him.

'Sorry!' said McCoy. 'I'm just sitting here'

She shook her head, the doors closed, and the bus moved off.

Why did Dessie Caine want Paul Cooper dead? If he did, there had to be a chance he had killed or arranged for someone to kill Trisha and Barrett. But why? Dessie Caine was many things, but he wasn't a well-dressed man – the opposite, looked like an unmade bed most of the time. Stank of beer and fags, not aftershave. So if he wasn't the man who'd been sleeping with Trisha at the Happiness Hotel, who was? And why was Dessie doing their dirty work for them?

He stood up, started walking back towards the station. Realised he could only think of one well-dressed man that Dessie knew. Stopped and hailed a taxi. Got in and told the driver to take him to Royston. St Roch's Chapel.

SEVENTY-THREE

McCoy stood outside the chapel, realised he was kidding himself. What did he really have to confront McKenna with? The crime of being well-dressed? He was clutching at straws. Seemed to be all he was doing lately.

He was just about to go when the chapel doors opened and the congregation started coming out. McKenna appeared, stood in the doorway shaking hands as the people left. Shoes shined, hair slicked back, surplice over his neat grey suit.

Maybe what Wattie had said the other day was true. McCoy was as guilty of prejudice as the rest of the Glasgow cops. He was always first to believe the worst about priests, always suspected they were hiding something rotten behind the authority and ceremony.

He'd just got his Regal and lighter out when he heard the shout.

'McKenna! You dirty fucker!'

He looked around, tried to work out where it had come from. McKenna was doing the same thing, smile fixed on his face. Must have seen who it was before McCoy. His face fell, started trying to usher the crowd away from the chapel entrance. McCoy looked to where McKenna had.

Paul Cooper emerged from the crowd, staggered up the path to the chapel entrance. His clothes were drenched in blood, and his blond hair was red. The crowd backed away from him as he tried to make his way up the path towards McKenna.

He stopped, shouted again. 'I'm still here, you fucker! You didn't get me, did . . .'

Paul coughed and a stream of blood poured out his mouth, splattered onto the ground. He wobbled, fell against the railings and crumpled. McCoy ran forward, grabbed a terrified-looking man, told him to get in the chapel and call an ambulance. He knelt down beside Paul, tried to ignore the blood, held his hand. His eyes were rolling back in his head, face deathly white. His breathing was fast, too fast.

'You'll be okay, Paul, just hold on. Hold on!'

Paul's eyes settled, seemed to recognise McCoy. 'McKenna . . .'

'What about McKenna?' asked McCoy.

Paul coughed up some more blood. McCoy wiped it away from his mouth. Eyes were wild now, was struggling to get the words out.

'Room 1,' said Paul. 'That was his.'

His eyes rolled back and his mouth slumped open, blood still pumping from the wound in his shoulder. McCoy looked round, hoped the ambulance was coming. Eyes stopped on McKenna standing a couple of yards away. He looked back at McCoy, ran his fingers through his hair, walked towards the chapel.

SEVENTY-FOUR

'I really have no idea what you are talking about, Mr McCoy. I don't know anyone called Trisha O'Hara or Ian Barrett, and as for, what was it? The Happiness Hotel? I'm afraid you've completely lost me.'

They were sitting in the wee office at the back of St Roch's Chapel. A cosy room with rugs on the floor, leather armchairs and Father McKenna looking so scrupulously mystified at McCoy's questions he would have happily punched him in a heartbeat. Cultured half-Irish half-Scottish tones smoothing over any difficulties.

McCoy still had Paul's blood on his hands, had tried to wash it off in the chapel toilet, but hadn't got it all, could see it under his fingernails. Wondered if Paul was going to make it. He was still breathing when they got him in the ambulance, could only hope. He looked at McKenna. Had to give it to him, he was calm, unruffled by what had happened, or McCoy's questions. 'What about Ally Drummond?'

'Again, I have no idea who that is.'

'Paul Cooper said Room 1 was yours. What does that mean?'

McKenna looked thoughtful. 'Was that what he said? I'm afraid I couldn't make it out. He was probably delirious with the pain, not making any sense.'

McCoy kept going. 'You do know Trisha O'Hara. She was the girl in the photo I showed you.'

'Not this again,' said McKenna, looking exasperated. 'I thought I explained to you how that picture was taken. Do I need to do it again?'

'Paul Cooper called you a dirty fucker. You're a young man, what, early thirties? Same age as me. Can't be easy staying celibate.'

'Yes, but it is part of the calling. Now, is there some police aspect to these questions or are you just trying to provoke me?'

McCoy changed tack, hoped it would work. 'What happened to Dessie Caine's chapel fund?'

For the first time McKenna looked uncomfortable. 'You should know. You were the one who was so determined I hear your accusations that day in the park. After that, we here at the diocese reconsidered how closely we wanted to get involved with Mr Caine.'

'Wouldn't look good for you, would it? When it turned out the new Archbishop's best pal was a gangster. So you dumped him. That right?'

McKenna nodded. 'Crudely put, but yes.'

'I saw him this morning. He wasn't very happy about it.'

'I don't doubt it,' said McKenna. 'Desmond and his wife are devoted to the church and the people of Royston. It must be a great disappointment to them.'

'Yet you still dumped him. Saint Dessie cast adrift.'

McKenna purposely looked up at the clock on the wall. 'Is there anything else I can help you with, Mr McCoy? It seems to me that a dying boy attempted to get to the chapel for help, for succour. As to what he said or didn't before he passed out with the pain, I can't imagine it having much worth or credibility. All we can do now is pray that he recovers. Now . . .'

McCoy couldn't think of anything to say. Without any evidence McKenna would be able to bat him away until the cows came home. Fuck it, may as well leave him worried. 'The Happiness Hotel. We found a bug in the wall of Room 1, you know. Wire from it leading to a big reel-to-reel tape recorder in a cupboard in the hall. Big piles of recordings beside it.'

McKenna blinked, ran his tongue over his top lip.

McCoy stood up. 'I'll let you know if we hear your dulcet tones, eh? Way you speak, won't be difficult to identify them.'

He walked back through the chapel and out into the afternoon rain. Was a cheap shot but it was all he had.

SEVENTY-FIVE

'I get off in ten minutes,' said Una. 'I heard what happened at the chapel. Is the boy okay?'

'I hope so,' said McCoy. 'I'll meet you outside.'

He stepped out Galbraith's. The usual boys were standing at the off-licence up the street. Still stopping people and asking them to go in for them. Finally an old jakey stopped, struck a bargain. McCoy looked the other way down the street. There was a small crowd outside the Great Northern. Didn't look like his dad or his pal were amongst them.

He walked to the phone booth, ignored the smell of piss and called the station. Asked to be put through to Wattie. 'You talking to me?' he asked when the phone was picked up.

'Aye, I shouldn't be though,' said Wattie. 'You've been a right arse.'

'That's probably true. Point taken. Anything going on there?'

'Fuck all,' said Wattie. 'It's like everyone's just given up. Phyllis phoned though. She's looking for you. Where are you anyway?'

'Royston. Probably no be back in until tomorrow. You fancy a pint if I get finished here?'

'Babysitting,' said Wattie glumly. 'Mary's away to the pictures with her pal. But there's cans in the fridge if you want to come round.'

'Sounds good,' said McCoy. 'I'll see you later.'

McCoy put the phone down, felt in his pocket for more coins. The boys from the off-licence walked past, cans of beer in their hands. He dialled the morgue. Asked for Miss Gilroy. A few clicks later and Phyllis said hello.

'I heard you were looking for me,' said McCoy, trying to get his fags out his pocket.

'Indeed I am. As instructed by your good self I went over Carole Lownie's autopsy. Nothing there.'

McCoy swore under his breath, stuck a cigarette in his mouth.

'But . . .' said Phyllis. 'I also talked to Gilchrist.'

'And?' asked McCoy hopefully.

'And Carole Lownie may have been pregnant.'

'Pregnant? Wasn't she not right?'

'Mentally, yes, physically she was in fine condition,' said Phyllis.

'How sure was Gilchrist?' asked McCoy, finding his lighter.

'Not sure at all – that's why he didn't put it in the report. With deep organs like the uterus they can sometimes be left without too much damage even if the body is badly burned. In this case the heat was so intense it was badly affected. It seemed to have been slightly enlarged, which would indicate a pregnancy, but with no undamaged blood to sample he couldn't test for hormone levels. Being as he couldn't be certain, and the woman was unmarried, he decided to leave it out to spare the family.'

'Christ,' said McCoy, lighting up. 'I wasn't expecting that.'

'Yes, I can see how it might complicate things a bit.'

McCoy saw Una coming out Galbraith's through the phone-box window. 'Need to go, Phyllis. Thank you.' He hung up and hurried out the phone box.

'I thought you'd gone,' said Una.

'Just making a call,' said McCoy.

They started walking down Royston Road. McCoy wasn't quite sure where to start. Una didn't look pregnant to him, but maybe women could recognise these things earlier. Decided to just plunge in.

'I think Carole Lownie was pregnant.'

'She was,' said Una.

'How did you know?'

'Dessie told me.'

McCoy stopped walking. Looked at her. 'How did he know?'

'How do you think?' She bit her bottom lip, looked like she might cry. 'If I'm going to do this, I need a drink. Not the Big Glen, I don't want to see them all.'

A taxi was coming up the road. McCoy hailed it. Told the driver to take them to Shields.

SEVENTY-SIX

McCoy sat Una down in the lounge and went up to the bar. Got a pint for himself and a gin and orange for her. Walked back to the table and put the drinks down. There was music playing, sounded like Perry Como, someone like that. Drunk guy at the other side of the room singing along, performing like he was at Carnegie Hall.

'You don't have to tell me anything, Una,' said McCoy. 'It's up to you.'

She smiled. 'I've got to tell someone. Either that or I'm going to go mad.' She took a sip of her drink, composed herself and started. 'You know I'm pregnant?'

'Your pals at the Big Glen made it clear.'

'I bet they did,' she said. 'Turned out they weren't really pals after all.' She looked at him. 'Dessie's the father.'

'What?'

'Dessie Caine's the father.' She looked down at the table, picked up a beer mat and started ripping it. 'Wasn't supposed to happen but it did.'

'Were you seeing each other?'

She nodded. 'I know it sounds weird, but when it started

· 334 ·

off, we had some good times. What can I say? Dessie's the big man around here. I was flattered. Not that difficult to get your head turned when you work in a grocer for three bob an hour then go home every night to the telly. Dessie started talking to me one day after Mass, then he started coming in the shop more than he needed to.' She took another sip. 'Then he started taking me for drives in his car, out for dinner. Never in Glasgow, always somewhere else. Dunfermline, Callander, places like that. One night we finished dinner and he said he'd a room booked upstairs.' She smiled again. 'Not sure I could have said no even if I'd wanted to. Which I didn't.'

'How long did this go on for?' asked McCoy.

'Six months or so. Then I told him I was pregnant, and everything changed.'

'What did he say?'

'He didn't say much. Then his wife turned up at my door the next day. Have you met her?'

McCoy nodded.

'I can't read her. She's all Legion of Mary but she must know what Dessie does for a living.'

'Some people are good at not seeing what they don't want to see.'

'Anyway, I'm not ashamed to say I was terrified. She comes in and sits down, looks round the flat and says, "You are a gift from God." Not what I was expecting, I can tell you. She sits beside me on the couch, takes my hands, stares right into my eyes. Tells me she and Dessie have been trying for kids for years, can't have any. Says she's barren. Horrible word, that is . . .'

'Then?' asked McCoy.

Una took another sip of her drink. 'Then she tells me I'm a single woman living in a bedsit who works in a shop. There's no way I can bring up a baby. She and Dessie are going to bring it up.'

'Fuck,' said McCoy.

'She didn't ask me. She told me. She'd take me to Ireland to have the baby and I was to stay there for a year. She'll take the baby as soon as it's born and come back to Glasgow.'

'What did you say to that?'

Una shrugged, pulled a wee embroidered hanky out the sleeve of her jumper, wiped her eyes. 'I didn't know what to say. Half of me agreed with her. I wasn't sure I could look after a baby by myself. She made it sound like she was doing me a favour, the baby wouldn't want for anything.'

'But?'

'But the next week, Dessie takes me out again, some hotel near Loch Lomond. We have our dinner, and we go upstairs and . . .' She stopped talking, wiped at her eyes again.

'I meant it, Una,' said McCoy. 'You don't have to tell me all this.'

'I want to,' she said. 'I want someone to know. So after we've, you know, he sits up in bed, big grin on his face says, "I'm on a roll." I ask him what he means and he says he's got Carole pregnant too. I couldn't believe it. He's all proud of himself, thinks he's some sort of big daddy. I thought I was going to be sick. I says, but Carole's not right, she's like a child, and he says, "I know, that's why it was so easy."'

She stared up at the ceiling, tried to stop the tears coming, but she couldn't. Started crying, looked at McCoy. 'And he's going to be the father of my child. A man who could do something like that and boast about it.'

McCoy put his arm around her shoulder, let her cry it out for a bit. 'Look, the baby's yours. You don't have to give it to Dessie and his wife.'

Una tried to smile, didn't quite make it. 'Yes, I do,' she said. 'The last thing his wife said to me before she left was that if

I didn't hand the baby over, she was going to find me and she was going to set Dessie's boys on me. That they were going to rape me over and over, then they were going to cut me and then they were going to kill me.'

SEVENTY-SEVEN

McCoy sat back on the kitchen chair, took a sip from the McEwan's can. Wattie had finally got Wee Duggie off to sleep after a long battle.

'His bloody teeth better turn up soon,' he said, opening a can. 'This is murder.'

'They will do,' said McCoy. 'What happened to Paul Cooper? Did you hear?'

Wattie nodded. 'He's in the Royal. Police guard on him. Your pal Stevie went up to see him, wasn't happy about it. Shouting and bawling at every bugger.'

'I'll bet,' said McCoy. 'He going to be okay?'

Wattie shook his head. 'They don't think he's going to make it through the night. He's lost so much blood.'

'Christ. Does Stevie know what happened at Equi? With Deke?'

'Don't know,' said Wattie. 'He saw Paul, but I don't know if Paul was able to speak. He'll find out though. He's your pal, you know there's no way he'll let what happened lie.' He reached behind himself and got another two cans off the counter. 'Not sure I understand the whole story myself.'

'Paul Cooper was the last one standing. Whoever killed Trisha O'Hara and Barrett wanted him dead.'

'And who's that?'

'Not sure, maybe McKenna.'

'What? Father McKenna? Are you sure?'

'Nope. And he wouldn't soil his lily-white hands. Think he might have got Dessie to organise it all for him.'

Wattie screwed his face up. 'Don't know about that.'

'Me neither, still trying to stick the whole thing together.'

'So that guy Deke was working for Dessie all along?' asked Wattie.

'Looks like it, a spy in the camp. Just waiting for the right time to get to Paul. If I was Deke, you wouldn't see me for dust.'

'You really think Dessie killed Trisha and Barrett just because McKenna asked him to?'

'Maybe,' said McCoy. 'Works for both of them. McKenna gets to be archbishop with no worries at getting exposed. Dessie has an archbishop in his pocket.'

'And what about the fire? Who did that? And who killed the boys?'

'Might be able to tell you tomorrow,' said McCoy. 'Have to go and see someone first.'

'Who?'

McCoy tapped the side of his nose. 'That would be telling.'

Wattie shook his head. 'You really can be a dick, McCoy. You know that, don't you?'

'You're not the first to let me know, doubt you'll be the last.'

They both turned as a wail came from the bedroom.

'Penance,' said Wattie. 'Away and see to your godson while I tan the rest of these cans. Least you can do.'

28th May 1974

SEVENTY-EIGHT

Leverndale Hospital was on the south side of Glasgow. A grim Victorian building surrounded by huge grounds. McCoy yawned as he drove up the road to the front entrance. Wee Duggie had gone back to sleep eventually and the cans had got tanned, along with half a bottle of whisky.

He parked the car beside a Rover and got out. Stretched, took a swig of Pepto-Bismol and walked into the entrance. There was a reception desk just beyond the front door. He flashed his police card, looked as serious as possible, and told her he was here to see Malcom McCauley.

The lady behind the desk picked up the phone and called. Two minutes later a big lad with a set of keys the size of his fist appeared. Held his hand out. 'Zebedee,' he said.

'You're kidding, right?' said McCoy.

'No. My mum and dad are Plymouth Brethren and I've heard all the jokes, believe me. This way.'

After what seemed like half a mile of corridors they arrived at the locked unit. Zebedee started opening the three doors it took them to get inside.

'How is he?' asked McCoy. 'Malcolm.'

'He's what I call a radio,' said Zebedee. 'Sometimes he's tuned into our world, sometimes he's tuned into a world of his own. You just have to get lucky when you speak to him.'

Malcolm McCauley was sitting on an armchair in the day room, blanket over his legs, half-eaten slice of toast on a plate on the arm of the chair. He was looking out at the grounds, seemed to be talking to himself.

'Malcolm,' said Zebedee. 'Man here to see you. Wants to have a wee chat, okay?'

Malcolm didn't respond.

Zebedee picked up the plate, shrugged. 'I'll leave you to it.'

McCoy sat down next to Malcolm. Waited for a bit, wasn't quite sure what to do. Realised Malcom had turned and was looking at him.

'Do you remember me?' he asked.

'I think so,' said Malcolm. 'But I don't know where from. Were you in my class at school?'

McCoy shook his head. 'I'm a detective. I found you at the pub. Do you remember?'

Malcolm's face clouded. 'There were rats in that pub,' he said. 'I could hear them. In the walls.'

'So you said.' McCoy wasn't sure this was his best idea but decided to keep going. 'Your dad told me you said, "I wish she'd never given us the money." Do you remember saying that?'

Malcom nodded, reached his hand up to rub his eye, and McCoy saw the bandage on his wrists emerge from the sleeve of his pyjamas. Suicide watch couldn't have been working too well.

'Why did you say that, Malcolm? Did you mean a woman gave you money to start the fire?'

Malcolm looked out onto the grounds again. A gardener with shears was walking towards a clump of rose bushes. 'That's what they used to cut Danny's fingers off.' Turned to McCoy. 'Do you think they fed them to the rats?'

McCoy shook his head.

'I thought I was set,' he said. 'Do something like that and I was in.'

'In?' asked McCoy.

'In with the bad boys.' He smiled. 'That's what I wanted to be. A bad boy.'

'Why would you be in with the bad boys?'

Malcolm looked at him like he was stupid. 'She was Dessie Caine's wife. We were set.'

McCoy walked back to the car, lit up on the way. Tried not to think about the bandages on Malcolm's wrists and whether he'd ever get out of there. He got in the car, turned the key. Took the key out again. The engine died and he sat there for a while. Watched the gardener. Tried to ignore the pain in his stomach. Tried to think.

SEVENTY-NINE

No lads at the front gate this time. McCoy walked up the path and knocked on the front door. Stood for a minute, waited. Was just about to turn and go when the door opened.

Chrissie Caine was standing there.

She saw him. Went to close the door.

McCoy stuck his foot in the gap and pushed his way in.

The big living room was empty. No one in Dessie's seat, no Tosh sitting at the table, no heavies hovering in the background, no dog. He looked around, couldn't believe it. All the pictures of Jesus had been turned to the wall. Every one of them. Statues of the Virgin Mary on the mantelpiece were facing the wall too.

Chrissie stood by the fireplace. Was only then McCoy realised she was swaying. Drunk.

'What's happened here?' he asked.

She looked round at the walls. McCoy noticed the crucifix around her neck had gone too.

'Maybe I don't want to look at Jesus any more.' She laughed. 'Or maybe he doesn't want to look at me.'

'Where's Dessie?'

'You tell me. You saw the state he was in yesterday. Probably back in the garage.'

'Been shopping, have you, Chrissie? Mate of mine saw you in Mothercare.'

The colour drained from her face. She pulled a chair out from the dining table and sat down. Leant over to the sideboard, opened a drawer and took out a bottle of vodka. Splashed a good measure into her glass.

'No shortbread and tea on a tray this time?'

Chrissie didn't say anything, just sat staring into space.

McCoy went to move towards the table. Stepped back in fright. The dog that had growled at him last time was lying by the couch, half-eaten bowl of food by its head, dead eyes staring up at him.

'What's happened there?'

'Rat poison,' said Chrissie, not looking at him.

McCoy pulled out a chair, sat down at the table. 'I know about Una. And the baby.'

'You don't know a fucking thing,' said Chrissie. She grabbed the bottle, almost knocked it over, splashed more vodka into her glass. Drank it back.

'What don't I know?' asked McCoy.

Was like she was talking to herself, just above a whisper. 'What it feels like to live in hell.' She took another glass off the sideboard, poured a good measure, handed it to McCoy. Was the last thing he wanted but he took it. She sat back on the chair.

'Why are you in hell?' asked McCoy.

She shook her head.

McCoy suddenly realised she was even drunker than he thought she was. She looked at him. She was having difficulty focusing, kept blinking, shaking her head.

'You don't know what it feels like every time you go to the shops you walk past babies in prams, wee toddlers holding their mum's hand. Sixteen-year-olds with weans they don't even want. And each time that pain gets worse and worse. So don't you fucking dare tell me you know anything about me. You know fuck all about me.'

Chrissie took another swig, some of the vodka dribbling down her chin. Didn't seem to care.

'I put up with it all. With Dessie coming home covered in blood, with him pawing all over me stinking of beer and sweat. With him fucking everything that moved. Telling me I couldn't give him what he wanted. I put up with this house, my house, being a fucking zoo, full of his boys drinking and talking filth and that fucking dog barking all day.' She looked at McCoy. 'I put up with it all because I wanted a baby. That's all I ever wanted.' She sniffed, wiped at her nose with her sleeve. 'That baby's Dessie's, and we're going to raise it, give it the home it deserves.' She held up her glass. 'Lucky me, all my dreams have finally come true.'

'You don't seem that happy about it.'

'Don't I? What the fuck do you care?'

'I don't,' said McCoy. 'I care about Carole Lownie though.'

Was like an electric current had gone through Chrissie's body. Suddenly she was alert. Eyes focused.

'Must have been a shock,' he said. 'To find out—'

'That your husband had been fucking someone else?' said Chrissie. 'He's been doing that for years, I told you—'

'About the baby.'

Chrissie's glass stopped halfway to her mouth.

'How much did you pay the boys again?' asked McCoy. 'Twenty quid? That's not much. All to get rid of one poor simple woman that your Dessie got pregnant. How's that feel, Chrissie? That why you're in hell?'

Chrissie's head was down. She mumbled something under her breath.

'What?' asked McCoy. 'Can't hear you.'

She looked up at him, venom on her face. 'It was sorted! It was all fixed, and then he got that stupid fucking girl pregnant. There's no way Dessie's having some halfwit kid trailing about after him. How do you think that looks? People laughing in the street. Dessie Caine fucked a retard and look what he got.'

Chrissie was shouting now, spittle flying out her mouth. She stood up, weaved her way to the sideboard, tried to get a cigarette out of an onyx box sitting on top of it. Couldn't manage it. Turned, started to walk towards McCoy's cigarettes on the table, stumbled, fell to her knees.

'Get out my fucking house,' she said. Tried to get herself up, couldn't.

'Five people died in that fire,' said McCoy. 'Two more boys to cover it up. Seven fucking people, Chrissie. All to keep Dessie's reputation as a big man and so you could play happy families. Was it worth it?'

Chrissie looked up at him. 'I don't know what you're talking about,' she said. 'Now get the fuck out my house.'

EIGHTY

Murray stopped making notes in the pad on his desk. Put his pen down. Sighed.

'Let me get this straight. Malcolm McCauley, a boy whose mind has completely gone, tells you that Colin Turnbull, who's now dead, told him it was Dessie Caine's wife who paid them to set fire to Dolly's Salon.'

McCoy didn't like where this was going.

Murray continued. 'And then, added to that, we have the drunken ramblings of Chrissie Caine, all relayed to you with no witnesses present. Correct?'

McCoy nodded.

Murray sat back in his chair. Looked tired, worn out by it all. 'That's not even enough to get her in for a formal interview, never mind charge her with anything. Have you got any evidence of Dessie kidnapping and killing the boys? Anything concrete at all?'

McCoy shook his head.

'So what you are really telling me is that we've got nothing,' said Murray.

'Come on,' said McCoy. 'We've got to be able to—'

'To what?' Suddenly Murray was shouting. 'You think I've

decided not to proceed to annoy you? That it's all about Harry bloody McCoy!'

'No, it's just that—'

Murray slammed his fist down on the table. Leant forward. 'It's just that we have no fucking evidence. We've failed to do our jobs. You may know what happened, but it means fuck all unless we can prove it. And we can't. Do you understand that? Is that going in?'

McCoy nodded.

'You want to put these people in jail? Then get me provable facts. Stop pouting and sulking because you think you're so fucking clever and we're letting you down. You hear me?'

McCoy could feel his neck going red. Murray wasn't wrong. He'd been too quick to act the big man, tell him he'd solved the whole thing.

'I'm sorry,' he said.

'Aye, well, so you should be.' Murray started fumbling for his pipe. Looked like the storm might have blown over.

'So what happens now?'

Murray sighed. Sat back. 'Three bad boys set fire to a hair salon for a lark. It should have been empty but unfortunately there were people in there. The boys get taken by vigilantes who kill two of them. We can't find the vigilantes, but you know what? Most people think they deserved it so they don't really care. No one has any appetite to charge the third one, so he stays in Leverndale all his days or until he manages to finally kill himself. Case closed. Everyone moves on and looks forward to the next grisly story to fill up the newspaper. That's what happens.'

Murray finally found his pipe, lit up and disappeared into a cloud of smoke, waved it out the way. Continued. 'It's happened before, and it'll happen again. So we bide our time and we get Dessie Caine for something else and we make sure the judge goes for the longest possible sentence and we have a quiet drink in the pub that night and kid ourselves that that makes it all okay.'

'What if that's not enough?' asked McCoy.

'It has to be,' said Murray. 'We're polis. We obey the law. End of story. When you've been doing this as long as I have, you realise you can't win every time. No matter how much you want to. You move on, hope you get another chance to nail someone like Dessie Caine to the wall.'

McCoy left Murray's office, sat back down at his desk. Hurt him to admit it but Murray was right. They had failed. Failed to do their jobs, failed to get a conviction. Let the women and the kids down. Even let the two boys down. He picked the bottle of Pepto-Bismol up off his desk and swallowed some over. He might have been smart or lucky enough to figure out what had happened, but it wasn't going to do any good.

He thought about Chrissie lying drunk on the floor of her living room, Jesus with his back turned to her. No matter how much she drunk, she'd never be able to forget what she'd done. Seemed like she was in hell already. No Jesus any more, no Mass, no hope for the afterlife. Maybe that was all McCoy and Murray were going to get. That her life would never be happy, that she'd drink herself to death in a cycle of guilt and self-loathing, thinking about the fire every day.

'Penny for them.' Wattie was standing next to his desk, carrier bag in his hand. 'How did it go with Murray?'

'Not enough evidence,' said McCoy.

'Christ,' said Wattie. 'So what happens now?'

McCoy shrugged. Couldn't bring himself to tell Wattie it was already done. That the fire was becoming the past, something they'd shake their head about and move on from.

'What about the relatives? What are they supposed to think?'

'Same as us all,' said McCoy. 'Three bad boys and a horrible accident.'

Wattie sat down. Put the bag on the desk, an orange furry head sticking out of it. 'Billy on the desk told me to give you a message. Some bloke called Lachy phoned, said he had something for you.'

McCoy stood up. He needed a drink and going to see Lachy was the perfect excuse.

'Want me to come with you?' asked Wattie.

McCoy shook his head. 'You're all right. Away home and give Wee Duggie his new monkey.'

EIGHTY-ONE

Paddy's Market was packing up for the day by the time McCoy got there. Stallholders already starting to clear away everything they were selling. He walked towards the back of the market, past the cafe and its smell of stale grease and towards Lachy's pitch. He sold just about anything connected with electrics. Stall was piled high with a jumble of wire, batteries, soldering irons, toasters he'd fixed, radios he was working on.

'You looking for me, Lachy?'

Lachy looked up from some electronics magazine he was reading. Looked completely blank.

'It's me, McCoy. Polis man.'

Memory kicked in. 'So it is, son. You got my message then? I phoned the station, didn't know what else to do.'

McCoy nodded. 'Got it all right. That's why I'm here.'

Lachy carefully folded the top corner of the page of the magazine he was reading, closed it. 'How have you been?'

'I've been better, Lachy. How about you?'

'Bit the same. Funny thing is, I miss him. Ally. He was a crotchety old bugger, but he was a pal and I don't have many left. Getting old, I suppose.'

'You ever want to go back home?'

'To Lewis?' Lachy shook his head. 'I'd like to see it again before I die but I don't think that's going to happen.' He smiled. 'Can hardly walk from here to the bloody Empire Bar any more, never mind make it all the way up there.'

'So what have you got for me?' asked McCoy.

'Well, the owners want to rent out Ally's stall, asked me to clear anything that was left in it. Did that, then remembered he had a box, kept it under the floorboards underneath his stall. It's where he kept the bad stuff.'

Lachy looked a bit uncertain, rooted around in the carrier bags at his feet. Came out with a slim envelope file. Handed it over. McCoy took it.

'On the top,' said Lachy. 'The first one.'

McCoy felt queasy, didn't want to look, but he had to. He opened the file, took out the envelope on the top. Had a look. A couple of words in faded blue ballpoint pen that sent his stomach turning.

Harry 3/7/55. Full set.

'I'm sorry, son,' said Lachy. 'I had to have a look, make sure it was you.'

McCoy felt dizzy, like he was looking at blood. 'Ally told you?'

Lachy nodded. 'You okay?'

McCoy shrugged. 'Going to get a drink. Come along to the Empire when you're packed up. On me.'

'Thanks, son.'

McCoy folded the file over, managed to stuff it into his jacket pocket, turned to go. Stopped. Looked back at Lachy's mess of a stall. 'Where did that come from?' he asked.

'That?' said Lachy. 'It was under Ally's stall as well. You can record over them, you know, use them more than once, I think. Someone'll buy it.'

'Can I have it?' asked McCoy.

'Sure, son,' said Lachy. 'I'll get a plastic bag for you.'

Lachy disappeared behind the stall and McCoy picked up the big round reel-to-reel tape. There was a label on it. Same writing that was on the envelopes in his pocket.

Room 1

EIGHTY-TWO

McCoy sat at a table in the back of the Empire, pint and a whisky in front of him. He downed the whisky in one, took a slug of the pint, and pulled the file out his pocket with shaking hands.

Remembered now why Ian Barrett had seemed familiar when he'd seen him lying in Glenconner Park. He had met him before. A long time ago.

July, 1955. He'd been thirteen. Him and his dad were living in a single end in Shettleston. Damp on the walls, an outside toilet that was always broken. Two cushions his dad had got out the midden as a bed. Rats that came out the cracks in the wall as soon as it got dark. His dad had gone out on the Friday night for 'a wee drink', still hadn't come home by Monday afternoon. McCoy had had no idea where he was. Could have been in hospital, jail, in some flat still drinking. He'd had two slices of bread on the Friday night for his tea. Since then, nothing. He was starving and he was scared.

He'd left the flat, wandered into town. Found himself in Hope Street looking in the window of a cafe. Was so hungry his stomach hurt. Noticed a man sitting in the window was looking at him, waving him inside. He went in, smell of the hamburgers and chips more than he could stand.

'You look hungry, son,' said the man.

McCoy nodded, could feel the saliva filling up his mouth.

'Why don't you sit down and we'll get you something to eat,' he said. 'Have a wee chat . . .'

McCoy took another drink of his pint and slid his finger under the flap of the envelope. He reached inside, pulled out a set of negatives in a glassine bag. He took a strip out, held it up to the light in the ceiling. Looked at himself. Wiped his eyes, forced himself to look at all the photos. The ones Ian Barrett had taken that day to sell to Ally. Couldn't look at them for long. Put them back in the envelope.

There were seven other envelopes in the file.

Elaine 12/2/60
Robert 15/7/59
Bobby 24/9/64
Jimmy 4/5/61
Samantha 20/10/68
Neil 23/8/70
Angela 8/7/70

And him. Harry 3/7/55. Just another victim. Just like the other names on the envelopes. Just like Carole Lownie and the girls in the salon and poor dead Trisha O'Hara lying dead in Sighthill Cemetery. He was sick of it, so sick of it. All the damaged people he'd seen, all the dead ones, or the ones lost to drink, desperately trying to obliterate their lives.

He wasn't sure he could look at any more of them. Maybe he'd done it, reached his limit. Seen as much as he could stand. Time to stand aside and let someone else fight the good fight. Trouble was, there didn't seem to be anyone else. He put the envelopes back, got up, ordered another pint and a whisky. Sat back down.

Maybe that's what Chrissie Caine was now. Just another victim. He was sure she hadn't meant to kill all those women. Just the one Dessie had got pregnant. All that damage for fucking Dessie Caine. The Dessie Caine that had tortured and killed those boys, tried to blame it on Johnny Smart. That wasn't some accident. Dessie knew exactly what he was doing and where he was doing it. Killing them in a pub Johnny Smart probably didn't even know he owned. Owner too terrified to say anything in case he got another razor across his face.

Dessie Caine knew exactly how much cutting off a finger would hurt. Exactly how much force it would take to squeeze the life out of Trisha O'Hara. Exactly how little people would care when someone like Ian Barrett was found dead. Exactly how thankful Father McKenna would be. Exactly how much he would be in his debt.

He drained his whisky.

And he was going to get away with it.

Drank half the pint.

Looked down at the plastic carrier bag by his feet.

Or maybe he wasn't.

Lachy was walking towards him. 'Took longer to pack up than I thought. You been watching the telly?' Nodded over at the silent black-and-white set bolted to the wall in the corner.

'Aye, something like that,' said McCoy. 'Sit down and I'll get you a drink.'

McCoy sat there for the next couple of hours getting quietly drunk with Lachy. Content to just listen to his tales of his dad's fishing boat, about coming to Glasgow in the thirties, about his son killed in the war. Was happy just to have the company.

He got the last round, proposed a toast. He held up his glass, as did Lachy.

'To all the people that fell through the cracks,' he said. 'Gone but not forgotten.'

And by the time he and Lachy rolled out of there at closing time and McCoy put him in a taxi, he had a plan.

'For all the people who fell through the cracks,' he said to himself.

McCoy walked down towards the Clyde, to the back of Paddy's. Didn't take him long to find what he was looking for. Three men and a woman passing a bottle, sitting round a metal barrel with a fire blazing in it.

He smiled at them, took a drink from the bottle when it was offered. Got the file out his pocket and fed the envelopes into the fire one by one. Last one was his. He watched the envelope catch, then a blue flame as the negatives caught fire. Watched it burn.

'For all the ones who fell through the cracks,' he said to himself, took another slug from the bottle. 'For them.'

29th May 1974

EIGHTY-THREE

'Five hundred quid,' said McCoy.

Dessie Caine sat back in his chair and looked at him. They were sitting in the back of the Big Glen, Dessie's heavy boys up at the bar keeping an eye on proceedings. Dessie had a couple of empty pint glasses on the table on front of him. Hadn't started the real drinking yet. This wasn't the Dessie he'd seen in the garage. This was the Dessie that ran Royston. In control.

'Not much for what it is,' said McCoy. 'It's what you've been looking for, isn't it? That's why you broke into Ally's flat.'

'Might be,' said Dessie.

'Don't give us it, Dessie. I don't have time for you trying to play it cool. Thanks to your clean-up operation, that tape is the only thing left connecting McKenna to Trisha O'Hara. You have that, and McKenna's right back in your pocket. New chapel gets built, you're Saint Dessie again.'

Jukebox whirled and 'The Old Rugged Cross' started up.

'Where did you get it?' asked Dessie, nodding over to his lads to bring him another pint.

'Doesn't matter,' said McCoy. 'Point is, I've got it. One-time offer. Five hundred quid. You in?'

Dessie lit up, cigarette held in tobacco-stained fingers. 'Didn't take you for the type, McCoy.'

McCoy shrugged. 'Let's just say I came to my senses. Not getting any younger. Need to look after number one these days.'

A man built like a wrestler delicately placed a pint down in front of Dessie, picked the empties off the table, took them back to the bar.

'Tomorrow. Just you and me. No heavy lads like that clown. Right?'

'Where?' asked Dessie.

'How about where it all happened? The Happiness Hotel. Room 1. Midday.'

Dessie took a slug of his pint, looked at McCoy over the glass. 'Where's that?'

'Just ask your pal, McKenna,' said McCoy. 'He knows where it is.' He stood up. 'Remember, five hundred cash. Just you and me.'

Dessie nodded.

McCoy walked past the two heavies and out the pub. Leant against the wall, took his Pepto-Bismol out and drank half the bottle down. If Dessie Caine didn't kill him, his stomach would. He put the lid back on the bottle, started walking down the road. Turned his collar up against the rain. Shoe was still leaking.

He'd done it. Put his plan in action. If Dessie turned up at the hotel tomorrow, it was all the proof he needed. Meant McKenna had told him where it was. Meant McKenna had definitely been the man in Room 1, the one who'd been following Trisha O'Hara, the one who got Dessie to kill her. Only twenty-four hours to find out.

30th May 1974

EIGHTY-FOUR

McCoy sat on the edge of the bed, chewed at his thumbnail. Had been up since six, couldn't sleep. He'd called in sick, said his stomach was playing up and he was going to spend the day in bed. He looked round Room 1. Didn't want to be here any longer than he needed to be.

'For all the people that fell through the cracks,' he said to himself. Had been saying it to himself over and over all day. Making himself believe it. He was just getting his fags out his pocket when there was a knock on the front door. Felt his stomach turn over, stood up, went down the stairs and opened the door.

Dessie Caine was standing there, suit and tie, still reeking of last night's beer, fag in hand.

'You by yourself?' asked McCoy.

Dessie nodded and McCoy held the door open. 'Come in.'

Dessie followed McCoy up the stairs to the hallway, looked about.

'McKenna tell you where it was then?'

'Aye.'

'Chapel back on?'

Dessie smiled. 'Let's just say things are looking that way. Where is it then?'

'In there,' said McCoy, pointing to Room 1. Held his hand out and Dessie stepped by him and into the room. As soon as he did, McCoy pulled the door shut, turned the key in the lock. Breathed out. Could hear Dessie shouting, asking what was going on. He stepped away from the door as Dessie started pounding it. Tried to keep calm.

He knocked on the door of Room 2. It opened, and Stevie Cooper stepped out. He was down to his vest and trousers, covered in blood from head to toe. He'd a bloody bayonet in one hand, a bloody hammer in the other. He wiped at the blood on his face with his arm and left clean space around his eyes.

McCoy could hardly bear to look at him. 'You done?'

'One down, one to go, isn't that what they say?'

McCoy looked round his shoulder into the room. Could see Deke on the floor, or, rather, what was left of Deke. He was lying in a pool of blood, so much of it McCoy could smell it. Was splashed up the walls too. He looked away.

'He in there?' asked Cooper.

McCoy nodded.

Cooper moved into McCoy. Looked him in the eye. 'Want you to remember something, McCoy. No matter what wee game of setting the world to rights you're playing, I'm here for one reason.' He looked at Room 1. 'That cunt in there sent the cunt I've just done to kill my son. And for that he's going to die. Got me?'

McCoy nodded.

'Now get the fuck out of here. I've got work to do.'

McCoy turned to go as Cooper opened the door. Heard Dessie say 'what the fuck' before the door shut again. He was halfway down the stairs when he heard the screams. Started to run.

Three months later

EIGHTY-FIVE

McCoy stood under the trees in Glenconner Park, trying to stay out the sunshine. There was a crowd of a couple of hundred gathered round the building site. Little platform in front of it. Bunting, photographer from the local paper.

'You're never going to tell me, are you?' asked Wattie.

'Tell you what?' asked McCoy. 'I don't know anything about it. I was in bed sick that day.'

'Aye, and I could flap my arms and fly to the moon.'

Something was happening over at the platform. The crowd parted and Archbishop McKenna climbed up the stairs and stood there in the sunshine. Waited for the noise to die down.

'Ladies and gentlemen, welcome to the ground-breaking ceremony of the new St Roch's Chapel. As you know, the road here has been a difficult one, but today, finally, we can start building our new chapel.' He smiled, waited for the clapping to subside. 'There is one person I really need to thank for that, and that is Chrissie Caine.'

He clapped, and Chrissie climbed up onto the platform, baby in her arms. She was wearing a black coat and a black hat. Baby dressed in pale blue, fast asleep on her hip.

'Without her incredibly generous donation from her late husband's estate we wouldn't be standing here. The diocese, and most particularly myself, wish to thank her for her remarkable generosity.' More applause. An altar boy handed a wee silver spade up to Archbishop McKenna. 'And now it's my great pleasure to turn the first sod. To the new St Roch's!'

Archbishop McKenna helped Chrissie down from the platform and they made their way over to the building site.

'We don't have to stay for all this shite, do we?' asked Wattie.

'Just another ten minutes,' said McCoy. 'Away and buy us some ice lollies. I'm boiling.'

Wattie nodded, wandered off towards the shops on Royston Road. McCoy stood under the tree and waited for the crowd to disperse. Didn't take long. He started walking towards the building site.

McKenna was handing the spade back to the altar boy when he got there. He recognised McCoy, turned to walk away.

'Need to talk to you,' said McCoy.

McKenna stopped, turned back. Looked pained. 'What can I do for you, Mr McCoy?'

'Just wanted to introduce you to someone,' said McCoy. 'When poor Dessie passed away, there was no one to run Royston. Luckily someone stepped forward.'

He motioned over the road to where Stevie Cooper was standing outside the old chapel, his son Paul at his side. Cooper raised a hand.

'That's him. Stevie Cooper is his name.'

'I'm not sure how this concerns me,' said McKenna.

'Really? Well, let me explain. When Dessie passed away, Mr Cooper there inherited some of his fittings and fixtures – including a certain reel-to-reel tape recording.'

McKenna froze.

'We had a wee listen to it, me and Mr Cooper. Filthy stuff.

I didn't think a man of the cloth would even know those words. Mind you, suppose everything's in the Bible one way or another. Sodom and Gomorrah and all that, eh?'

McKenna tried to say something. Mouth was moving but nothing was coming out.

'Can recognise your voice anywhere. Mind you, I wasn't expecting it to be saying the kind of things you did, but there you are.'

McKenna's face drained of colour.

'So, if me or Mr Cooper there ever hear so much as a whisper that you're up to your old tricks again, you're finished. No Dessie Caine to clear things up this time. No nothing. You got me, you fucking disgusting waste of space?'

McKenna nodded.

'Say it, you prick.'

'I've got it.'

McCoy turned and walked away. Could see Wattie coming out the newsagent with two ice lollies in his hand. McKenna didn't need to know that the tape was useless. All that was on it was garbled murmurs, sound of bedsprings squeaking. He crossed the road and took an ice lolly from Wattie. Peeled the paper wrapper off, grimaced.

'I don't like strawberry,' he said.

'Hard luck,' said Wattie. 'It was all they had. Did I just see your pal, Cooper?'

McCoy shook his head. 'Don't think so.'

'That right? Must have been some other bugger that looks exactly like him then.'

'Must have been,' said McCoy, trying to eat his ice lolly before it melted all down his hand. 'Lot of six-foot buggers with blond quiffs about these days.'

'You really are a dick, McCoy,' said Wattie, shaking his head.

'So you keep telling me.' He dug in his pocket, got the car keys out. 'You want to drive or will I?'